A DIRTY ASSIGNMENT

Both men were charging the swinging door. Handsome-face was in the lead, gun in hand. Carpenter stepped to one side and back. They burst through the swinging door. Carpenter smashed his heavy Colt revolver into the face of the handsome one. He dropped like a pole-axed steer, spraying blood.

Ferret-face had great reflexes. He slid to a stop and went down on one knee. He was clawing at the automatic in his back pocket, pulling it free. Carpenter's Colt blasted, lighting up the dark kitchen. The round slammed into Ferret-face's chest, throwing him back into the swinging door. His automatic went off, into the floor. He was fighting to bring the heavy gun back up. Carpenter's second round slapped him in the face, below the right eye, chasing brains and blood out the back of his head all over the door. The acrid odor of gunpowder hung heavy in the dark room.

We will send you a free catalog on request. Any titles not in your local book store can be purchased by mail. Send the price of the book plus 50¢ shipping charge to Leisure Books, P.O. Box 270, Norwalk, Connecticut 06852.

Titles currently in print are available for industrial and sales promotion at reduced rates. Address inquiries to Nordon Publications, Inc., Two Park Avenue, New York, New York 10016, Attention: Premium Sales Department.

THE BLUE BROTHERHOOD

Ernest O. Zimmerman

LEISURE BOOKS NEW YORK CITY

A LEISURE BOOK

Published by

Nordon Publications, Inc.
Two Park Avenue
New York, N.Y. 10016

Copyright © 1981 by Ernest O. Zimmerman

All rights reserved
Printed in the United States

1

THE BLACK 1954 CHEVROLET POLICE CRUISER MOVED slowly along Loch Raven Drive through the darkness. Officer Frederick Carpenter was behind the wheel with Officer Sean McGee riding shotgun. The headlights were turned off, for it was important that their quarry be taken by surprise.

McGee looked intently through the pines, planted twenty years ago by the CCC, in lines as straight as soldiers' ranks. The long-needled pine trees diffused the pale moonlight between their branches. The moonlight glinted off the Gunpowder River. The river dammed up a mile to the south, forming the vast watershed that provides the Baltimore metropolitan area with its drinking water.

"Slow enough, McGee?" Carpenter glanced at his partner's profile in the dim light. The old break in McGee's nose kept him from being labeled handsome, but his neatly clipped auburn hair and clear complexion attracted women of all ages. His emerald green eyes did nothing to repel them. Women were drawn to him with no conscious effort on his part.

"Ease off a hair more, Fritz. If I spot anything, I want to pinpoint it so we can find it when we get out to walk back to it. Too bad we had rain today, or we could get off this damn blacktop and down among the trees, near the water, with the car."

Carpenter slowed down slightly. "Yeah, no use hanging up the car in that slop. The Sergeant would piss all over us if we'd call a tow truck to get us out of the mud again."

"Never fear, Sean is here. Have I ever got you into any serious shit? Besides, this is all part of your training. You want to be an all-around cop, you gotta listen to us senior officers. That's the system. You young gung-ho types need the guidance of the salty ones. Why, what would you do with your time between calls?"

"I've got a feeling you're going to tell me . . . so go ahead, tell me what I'd do between calls."

"Okay, Fritz, just settle back and drive this bucket of bolts, and I'll lay it on you while I scan the pines for our friends. Police work is mostly a waste of time. What do we average, one, maybe two or three calls a shifts, right?"

"Wrong, last night we had about nine calls."

"Quiet, my son. I'm talking about average days. Okay, with an average of three calls a day that leaves you about five hours a day to use up for other things, like chasing speeders, directing a little traffic, and cruising your post to bullshit the taxpayers into feeling a little more safe or protected by seeing the police. Holy Mother, if you didn't find a little something to do to keep your mind occupied, what would happen?"

Carpenter shoved his hat back on his head. "We could always grab a little more sleep, McGee."

He nodded. "Good, now you got it. Don't let the time drag by. Boredom would send you up the wall. You'd get mean and frustrated from riding around with your finger up your ass all day. You'd become a headhunter and go around writing tickets all day on some poor slob who probably doesn't deserve it and can't afford it. You'd go home from work grouchy and kick your dog, beat your kid, pick a fight with your bride if supper wasn't ready. If your supper was ready, you wouldn't eat it. In short, you would suffer from the Bored Police Syndrome and be one more miserable bastard who took his frustration out on his family. Boredom leads to frustration, which leads to ulcers, heart attacks, strokes, and limber peters."

Carpenter exploded with laughter. He was a tall, dark man. His wide chest and shoulders suggested power. His narrow waist and hips made it difficult for him to buy suits off the rack. The wedge shape of his body was emphasized by tailored shirts, but his extreme neatness was always marred by an unbuttoned collar.

"Don't laugh Fritz, I'm not bullshitting. You've got to waste your time in a way that makes your day go by nicely, in your own way. You can do what you want as long as you don't get your ass in a sling and don't rat out another cop."

"The code of silence, huh, McGee?"

"Right. You can't trust the public, kid. They don't know how fucked-up the whole system is and don't want to know. The average guy on the street wants laws enforced, as long as they apply to someone else. Look at how bent out of shape people get when you write them a summons. Shit, some of them will beat lumps on your head for a lousy two-dollar parking ticket."

"Tell me about it," Carpenter said.

McGee rambled on as though he didn't hear. "When they have something stolen, they want you to be their personal Gestapo men. Break heads, lock up the Pope, just get the thief, unless it gets personal. If it's a case of friends or relatives, you better not deprive them of their rights, whatever they are. They want you to be invisible most of the time, visible all the time, a doctor when they're hurt, a lawyer when they think they need legal advice, a comforter of the old and poor, a servant to the rich, a protector of the young, a guardian of their rights, fearless and completely honest, except when they personally want the fix to go in and last, but not least, we must be pure . . . no, we must be eunuchs."

"Hey, McGee, those ass-holes want a lot for thirty-four hundred dollars a year, don't they?" He turned the steering wheel toward the center of the road to avoid a pothole. Tree branches overhead cast dark shadows over the road and gave an aura of isolation to the scene. There was no traffic in sight.

"You said it, Fritz." He sat up straighter. "Hey, look, we got one! See it, down by the point, almost in the water! Get your fuckin' foot off that brake!" He shoved the young officer's foot off the pedal. "You want the bastards to see the brake lights? Go ahead, I got 'em zeroed in. Drive down past the bend in the road." Eyes still squinting into the darkness, he said, "Good, this is far enough." He pulled the mike from its cradle on the dashboard and depressed the button. "Car 22, 10-7, Loch Raven, investigation. Ease the door open Fritz, don't slam it, the s.o.b.'s will hear you." Outside, the night air was cool and damp, and sharp with the odor of pine. The cry of a loon from across the lake shattered the silence.

"Kind of makes the hair stand up on the back of your neck," Carpenter said in a low voice. "Every time I hear one, it makes me shiver. Wonder what they make all that noise about?"

McGee laughed softly. "He probably wants to get laid and is calling his favorite piece of loon pussy. C'mon, Fritz, let's get the show on the road."

Both men double-timed back around the curve in the road and stopped, uncertain as to where McGee had made his sighting.

"I'm looking for a dead, broken off tree . . . ah, here it is," McGee whispered. "See, down there, right between this row of trees near the water."

"I see something glinting, are you sure it's—"

"Damned right I'm sure. Didn't you know the Irish can see in the dark? Come on, follow me, no talking now."

They walked through the darkness into the woods on a foot-thick rug of pine needles. Carpenter stayed close behind his partner, who gave the appearance of a large, dark, nocturnal creature plodding through the dark woods as if it were his home. Abruptly, McGee stopped short, causing Carpenter to bump into him.

"Looks like some type of laurel in the way, pal. I'll just feel my way forward and around and just . . . oop, Christ!"

McGee disappeared before Carpenter's eyes. There was a great crashing of brush and loud curses.

Carpenter slid his feet forward, feeling gingerly for the hole. It was there, all right, about five or six feet deep, judging from the sounds of whispered curses coming from the bottom.

"Hey, you okay?"

"Sure, I'm okay," McGee snapped. "I can see you against the sky. Give me a hand out of this fucking trap, will you? That's it, over this way a little . . . look out, the side's caving in!"

Both men were now on the bottom of the hole where they sat and surveyed the situation.

"You black-hearted Irish bastard! I thought you could see in the dark."

"Glad you could join me. Never mind the insults. I'll give you a boost out of here. Hope you didn't scare our friends off down by the water."

After helping each other out of the hole, the men returned to the business at hand. Stealthily they moved another 150 feet over the pine needles and around the bushes to the edge of the pine trees. No more than ten feet away was a new 1954 Buick sedan parked on the gravel of the beach. The windows were down and the radio played a popular tune, barely audible. "Sha-boom, sha-boom, life could be a dream." The door on the passenger's side was open and the interior of the car was illuminated by the dome light.

They were not a minute too soon—they had arrived just in time. McGee approached the big sedan on the driver's side. Carpenter moved quietly up on the opposite side. Both participants were oblivious to anything but each other. The woman lay flat on her back with her buttocks on the edge of the front seat. One leg was pushed through the open window. Her other leg was draped over her partner's shoulder. The man, a short fellow, had both bare feet on the stoney ground. He was bent over the woman on the seat, pouring it home, grunting like a pig over a slop dinner. It was obvious that the rate of his stroke would bring it to an end very soon.

McGee shoved his head in the window, no more than a foot from the lovers' heads. "Hold it!" he screamed. "Stop! Police! You are under arrest!"

The man jerked up, hit his head once, twice, hard on the roof of the car, and collapsed back on the woman, who was screaming hysterically. She went limp, apparently fainting away. The man was not moving after his collapse from the head blows to the roof.

Carpenter rolled the man off the woman and out of the car onto the gravel.

"For a second there I thought this cat had gone 10-7," he said, bending over the man. "He's breathing, though . . . just dazed from banging his head."

McGee came around the car to Carpenter's side.

"God, that gave me a scare for a second. Thought for a minute that I went too far. Let's take a look at this guy and—Jesus Christ!" His face fell. "It's Father

Nelligan! No, yes, no, it is, it's Father Nelligan. Father, what the hell are you—I mean, did you—are you, are you all right? Here, let me help you up." He stared at the young priest. "I'm sorry, I didn't—he didn't—aw, shit, you shouldn't have done it! Don't you know you shouldn't have—aw, goddamn it!"

Lying there, blinking like an owl, Nelligan recovered his composure quickly. The two policemen could almost hear his mind working like a computer.

"Hand me my pants, McGee. What are you so flustered for? I'm only a man, after all." He stood and hurriedly pulled on a pair of dirt-smeared trousers. "What do you propose to do now?"

The woman in the car sat up and looked out at them briefly, then covered her face and started to cry. She was a large-breasted, big, good-looking woman, and very upset. She made no attempt to dress, just sat, crying softly into her hands.

Father Nelligan shrugged helplessly. "Well, McGee, it's up to you. My future in the church is in your hands. This is a married woman. You can ruin her life, too, if you wish." He looked at McGee evenly. "What are you going to do?"

"Do? Nothing. Not a damned thing. I'm not your keeper, Father. You're the priest. You figure out how to live with yourself. Go to confession. Go to hell. I don't care what you do. Let's go, Fritz."

They moved away, into the gloom of the trees, back toward the patrol car. Each man was silent now, lost in his own thoughts. Not a word passed between them. The loon's cry mocked them from across the dark lake.

Back at the car, the headlights were switched on, for the first time since they entered the pines. Each man stood in the road in the harsh glare to inspect his uniform. Both were smeared with clay from their fall into the hole.

McGee sighed. "Head back to the station, Fritz. It's

almost half an hour to roll call. By the time we get back and clean up, it'll be time to knock off. If the Sergeant gives us any who-struck-John about the mud on us, tell him we helped an old lady get her car out of a sloppy driveway."

Carpenter started the engine. "Okay, Sean, but I doubt if he cares."

McGee slammed the car door. "No? Well fuck him, what he doesn't know won't hurt him. I wouldn't want that snake to know about the priest. He hates Catholics, anyway, the bigoted prick. He'd rat Father Nelligan out to the Monsignor and force him to take disciplinary action." He lit a cigar and inhaled deeply. "He'd make an anonymous call to that gal's husband if he found out who she was, and maybe cause a homicide. Every time he wanted to jam it up a Catholic's ass, he'd tell the story of the priest balling the married woman at Loch Raven. You know what a bastard he is, Fritz. Will you keep your mouth shut?"

"Don't worry, Sean, I won't let Snake or anyone else know."

Satisfied that his young partner would remain silent, the usually talkative senior officer returned to his silent shell, thinking over the evening's stalk.

Carpenter didn't push the subject. He had never seen Sean McGee as rattled before, but it must have been a shock for McGee to catch his priest fucking like any other man. A cop needs somebody he can look up to, Carpenter mused, as he drove the police car through the deserted streets. Ah, well, that's just one more example of human nature. People are made to break the faith, to betray their trust. They seem to be here just to steal, lie, cheat, and fuck up all good things. He'd talk to his wife, Mary, about it when he got home tonight. But on second thought, he'd . . . it would destroy her faith in human nature. No, he'd keep his mouth shut.

His thoughts drifted back to the day he was sworn in, thirteen month ago. . . .

2

THE WRITTEN EXAMINATION WAS EASY FOR HIM. THE physical, performed by a doctor who didn't look very hard for any defects, lasted about five minutes.

Carpenter stood waiting for the officer to recognize him. Captain Thomas Hoffman was a large man. As he lumbered to his feet from behind the small metal desk, he resembled a grizzly bear. He had close-cut, reddish-brown wiry hair, a large nose, ruddy complexion, and a huge frame. He weighed close to 280 pounds. His uniform was too small. They probably didn't have a bolt of material large enough to make the coat, Carpenter thought. His hairy wrists hung out at least three inches from his navy-blue gabardine. He extended his hand to Carpenter in greeting, his fingers as thick as knockwurst sausages. Both his size and the slow, deliberate movements as he stepped from behind the desk suggested restrained force, a man capable of great violence.

"Carpenter, is it? Glad to know you. Have a chair. Welcome to the Brotherhood," he continued when Carpenter had sat down. "As you know, we are between training classes here. That means you start on the street without any training. Don't let that bother you. Most of that classroom bullshit will just put you to sleep anyhow."

He leaned back in his swivel chair, and it gave a complaining squeak. "Police are made on the street, not sticking their noses in some goddamn law book. We probably won't get enough men together for nine or ten months to start a class. The county commissioners are going to let us fill some existing vacancies here in Towson as soon as we can find the men. I'm starting you on Sergeant Samuel Harper's shift. He's working eleven to seven A.M., and he's had several resignations in the last few months. Here's your service revolver and fifty rounds." He pushed the gun across the desk. "Here's your cuffs and blackjack. And you'll need these," he added, indicating a nightstick and badge.

Carpenter reached over the desk and took the equipment without comment.

"Go over to the clerk of the courts office in the Court House and get sworn in. Go up to the range and get them to show you how to shoot that thing. Our tailor is in the four hundred block of York Road. Guy by the name of Albrecht. Get measured for a uniform. I'll call and tell him to rush a couple pairs of summer pants through for you. Buy your own black shoes. Report to work on May fifteenth. That'll give him about a week to make your pants.

He stood and Carpenter followed suit. "I'm only going to give you one piece of advice. Don't fuck with your Sergeant. Listen to him, or you'll find out why they call him Snake. Keep your eyes open and your mouth shut about what you see. Repeat, keep your mouth shut about what you see. Repeat, keep your mouth to yourself. Good luck. Get out of here now; I've got things to do."

It was starting to rain as Carpenter walked out of the old station house. A typical spring day in Maryland, he thought.

Hoffman must give that little talk to all the new men. Christ, he didn't even say hello. Snake Harper. Sounds like a character in a Western movie. Keep my mouth shut, he mused, stepping around a broad puddle. I can do that, I guess. That fierce-looking old bastard made a point of that. Keep my mouth shut. Jesus, you'd think that I was being considered for employment by a gang of outlaws.

He waited for a truck to pass by, then continued walking. He had an idea that these people were different from anyone else he'd ever worked around. Hell, he was just wasting time anyway. That layoff from the shipyard wouldn't last forever. When they called him back he'd kiss this outfit goodbye and get back to pipefitting, where he belonged.

It was 10:15 P.M. when Carpenter reported to work. His mind was racing with anticipation. He took one last drag from a Camel and flipped it behind a huge yew planted near the front door. It landed in a pile of its kind along with other debris. Beer, whiskey, and wine bottles, assorted trash paper, an old umbrella, an old shoe, and a faded, moldy army field jacket mulched the ancient evergreen. A sign over the door read *Towson Station*.

Carpenter glanced up at the dark sky. The air smelled like a fresh spring shower. It was a good night to start. He was not prepared for the blast of warm air that assailed his nostrils and grabbed his throat. He was to become very familiar with this odor and in time ignore it, or perhaps learn to live with it, but his first breath was almost too much. He gulped and fought the bile back down in his throat and tried to identify the source of this new foulness. Pine oil disinfectant fought a lost battle with old vomit, urine, stale tobacco smoke, dirty ashtrays, unwashed feet, sweat, and wet wool, cheap perfume, and boiling coffee.

An old desk sergeant glanced up from a battered *Life* magazine. He was old for a policeman, perhaps sixty, and he showed his age. His face was ravaged by harsh weather and whiskey. "Help you, mack? You're the new guy, ain't you? Say, is anything wrong? You're as pale as a ghost."

"Ah, I ah—no, it's just the odor in here."

"Oh, the odor! Saints be praised, my boy, that's the smell of people, of police work. Pay no attention to it," he said, grinning broadly. "You won't even notice it ten years from now. It's in the very heart of this old place, you know. Scrubbing and painting can make it go away for a few days, but it's always there, it always comes back. It's the same in every old station house I've worked in or been in. It gets to you. You know, I kind of miss it when I go away on vacation." He pointed to the coffee bar. "Have a cup of coffee. Roll call ain't for a half hour yet."

The strong, bitter brew helped settle Carpenter's stomach. He lit another Camel and absently glanced at wanted posters of convicted or suspected felons.

"Improving your mind, Carpenter?"

Carpenter wasn't aware anyone was in the station besides the old desk sergeant. He turned to face the newcomer, vaguely angry that anyone could approach him without being heard.

"I'm Sergeant Harper. Samuel Harper. Welcome."

He extended a cold, damp hand to Carpenter. As Carpenter was shaking his hand he was struck by the eyes of the tall, thin man. His eyes were completely devoid of expression—lifeless—no, reptilian. Carpenter suppressed an involuntary shudder.

"Glad to know you, Sergeant Harper."

"Follow me, Carpenter. We've got time before roll call. I want to get some information from you for my personal file I'll keep on you."

As he led the new man through the dingy hallways,

Carpenter noticed the crepe-soled shoes the sergeant wore. No wonder he hadn't heard him.

"Here we are," Harper said, swinging open a battered wooden door. "This is the Captain's office. I keep my personal files here, locked up."

He settled behind the captain's desk and retrieved a new manila folder and a form from a desk drawer.

"Let's see . . . Frederick E. Carpenter. What's the E for?"

"Edgar."

He scribbled the name on the page, then glanced up. "This the correct address on your personnel form?"

"Yes, sir."

"Who do you want notified in case of an accident or serious illness?"

"Mary, my wife."

"Shirt size?"

"16-5."

"Weight?"

"180."

"Height?"

"6-1."

He closed the manila folder. "Okay. That's all I need. I see that you're a pipe fitter. How come you're here?"

"I was laid off, lack of work."

"Well, if they don't call you back in a few months, you'll be hooked."

"What do you mean, Sergeant?"

"I mean that police work gets into your blood." The Sergeant spoke in a monotone. His face was completely devoid of expression. "Once you get a taste of it, you won't leave. It kind of ruins you for any other kind of work."

His eyes seemed to drill holes through Carpenter's head. His tone and look created an aura that seemed almost mesmerizing.

A large moth flew into the room, through the open window, evidently attracted by the glare of the desk lamp. The large-bodied, small-winged creature beat itself against the light briefly and suddenly, erratically flew about the room, crashing into walls, filing cabinets, and the desk.

Harper was sitting in the swivel chair behind the desk, leaning back, staring remotely at the younger man, as if his mind was a hundred miles away.

Suddenly, faster than the human eye could follow, his right arm shot out and grabbed the moth in flight. He held his arm straight out for a second or two, then slowly moved his closed hand to the desk top. Without taking his eyes from the middle of Carpenter's forehead, he opened his closed hand, a finger at a time. His left hand slowly came forth to the now partially free moth, who was now flapping one free wing furiously, seeking freedom from its trap. Harper casually plucked the wing from the small creature and tossed the remainder out the window.

Carpenter wondered if Harper had done that to impress him. He doubted it. It was a reflex. It had to be. That's it, he mused. That must be why they called him "Snake." He moved around without noise on his crepe soles and caught bugs in midair with his hands, Carpenter reasoned.

"Just a few words to get you headed in the right direction. I want you to know what I expect of you. You will walk the street in Towson as a regular assignment. You will be shown the boundaries of your post later tonight. You won't work in a patrol car until an opening occurs there. Figure on at least a year on foot. Your job is to maintain order, protect life and property. You represent the law out there," he said, his expressionless eyes flickering toward the window. "You are on your own. Get in the habit of carrying a few dimes with you. You might want to use a pay phone to call for assistance sometime. That does not mean that you are to call a car off its post to lock up every half-assed drunk you decide to. Walk them in if you can. Your main job is to keep the merchants happy. Go out of your way to lock thieves up. Keep the toughs and drunks moving. There are always a couple of ass-holes that want to try out the new foot cop. If and when they raise a hand to you, I want you to mess 'em up. That is to say, if a man offers violence to you, I want you to beat shitlumps on his head."

He turned and slammed the window shut. He belched behind his hand and reached into his pocket for a Tums. Crunching it between his teeth, he continued, "If you don't take these street fighters out, they never leave you walk your post in peace. Make sure that the first tough you bust stops at Union Memorial Hospital for stitches, right after you arrest him."

Sergeant Harper looked Carpenter up and down. "You look like you can take care of yourself. You're big enough. I can do without some of these little short cops they give me to work. They usually have to prove something to the street people, with their fists, every time they lock somebody up. A big cop commands respect. Your size won't always cut it for you, though. You'll have to learn to live with fear in your own way. Don't let it show, even to your sidepartner, when you get to work in a car. Sometimes it helps to use a little bravado. But sometimes that may get your ass in a sling. You may learn to be a cop. Those headquarters-type cops will show you the finer points and theories in the police academy. Those ass-holes forgot how to be cops years ago. This is the real training ground, out on some dark country road twenty-five miles from nowhere, where it's you and your partner against Christ knows what."

The Sergeant paused in his monologue. His face

contorted in pain as he leaned forward in the swivel chair. He broke wind enthusiastically, and smiled at Carpenter. "Sorry, this shift work tears my belly up. Now where was I?"

"Out on a dark road with my partner," Carpenter said.

"Right, another thing, you'll be offered a lot of things—money, pussy, booze, free food, free cigarettes, free movies, free dry cleaning, you name it. You won't be able to turn it all down. Remember one thing. It's not being offered for nothing. Every person you deal with has an axe to grind. Don't let them put you in the middle."

He placed his right thumbnail behind his front teeth and snapped his fist forward. The nail cracked obscenely. "Fuck them," he whispered. "Be selective in what you take. You won't like some of the things you see other cops do. There's not one damn thing you can do about it. You are the junior man in the department. We operate on seniority. That means you listen to your partner if he's got one day of service on you. Don't think about that too much, though, because you'll be solo for a good while, on the street. Feel free to bring any problems you have to me. Any problems, except problems that you may have with other police. Work that out between you. Any questions?"

"No sir."

"Okay. One more thing. If you ever go over my head for something, anything at all, I'll crucify you," he said, his eyes boring into Carpenter's. "Remember to control your mouth about what you see and do while you're working. There, that's enough training until those nervous headquarters cops get you in the classroom. Let's go listen to roll call."

Jesus, all of that speech in that emotionless, quiet voice. And those eyes! I wonder if anything can get to him. I wouldn't want to be the man to try him,

Carpenter thought.

The offgoing desk sergeant always conducts roll call. He is responsible for passing on orders from higher-ranking police, street conditions, items of general interest, tag numbers of stolen cars, and any other noteworthy information that police must exchange in order to insure the continuity of a twenty-four-hour operation. Some of this information is repetitive. It is difficult to maintain the interest of police in routine matters. The desk sergeants who care will do anything to keep the oncoming shift alert and receptive to their instructions. The offgoing and oncoming shifts always line up in ranks in the uniform of the day on opposite sides of the room, facing each other. The desk sergeant speaks from written material at a dais at the end of the room.

The old desk sergeant who provided the coffee earlier was arranging his notes. He pounded on the side of the dais with his open hand for attention.

"All right, you guys, knock off the shit. I want to go home and have a drink. Quiet! Quiet! Rather than read the roster tonight, I'm gonna introduce a new man to you on Sergeant Harper's shift. You can all file up here and introduce yourself. This here young feller standing next to me is Officer Fred Carpenter."

Harper's shift filed by first and was followed by the offgoing shift. Each man stated his name and shook hands, then resumed his place in ranks. Some of Harper's shift must have slept badly during the day as they appeared only half-awake and moved as if it were an effort to do so. Months later, Carpenter would realize that this was a general symptom of police working on the 11-to-7 shift. Apathy, a feeling of tiredness, heartburn, and constipation. The symptoms the body expresses at the outrage of being forced to stay awake when it wants to sleep.

The old desk sergeant knew how to deal with this

condition.

"Before we get down to business, I want to inform Officer Sean McGee that the defendent in case #172435 was dismissed in the Circus Court* today and was here demanding the return of the evidence you seized."

Officer McGee, a man of about 30, blinked his eyes. "Christ, what case was that? That case number doesn't ring a bell. I wasn't summoned in today. Must not amount to anything."

"Let me refresh your memory. Remember the guy you arrested up at Loch Raven for fucking a chicken? Well, he was dismissed at the request of the State Attorney. Lack of corroborating evidence. Your word against his."

"Oh, yeah, the chicken died on the way back to the station. What kind of evidence did he want returned? I don't remember taking anything off of that weirdo."

All officers were alert now, suppressing laughter, not wanting to miss a word from either man in their repartee.

"He wants you to replace the chicken."

The room exploded with laughter. The man standing next to McGee was pounding him on the back, laughing and screaming something into his ear. McGee could be heard laughing above the rest. For a time, the meeting was bedlam. Some of the police were clucking like pullets, others were crowing like roosters.

Carpenter looked at Sergeant Harper. Harper was smiling, but the humor of his mouth did not show in his eyes.

The desk sergeant was pounding on the dais again. He had them, they were awake now.

"Okay, you people, okay, let's listen up now. We had three stolen cars, all from the Loch Raven Boulevard area, all taken between approximately eleven P.M.

---

*Local police slang for Circuit Court

and seven-thirty A.M. A '50 Ford two-door, black in color, Maryland tag CF 1235; a '52 Chevrolet, light-green four-door, Maryland tag AA 7014; a '53 Buick, tan bottom, white-top four-door, Maryland tag BB 4440.

"We had a burglary over on Charles Street, the Jeffrey place, near Sheppard-Pratt. No list of goods yet, but it looks like a big haul in furs and silver."

"We had an indecent exposure at the Riderwood School, an unknown white male, in a dark car, no further description, tried to get little girls on the playground into his car. He shook his wang at them and chased 'em for a short distance on the playground. He was spotted by a teacher, who yelled at him and scared him away. Occurred about one P.M."

"Sam Rider, from the O.K. Bar and Grill, complained of colored males drinking in the alley and breaking bottles against the back of his building all night. He runs them, but they come right back. Says he never sees the foot man. Maybe the foot man can get in there tonight and roust some of those bastards out before Rider calls one of the nervous gentlemen from Headquarters. That's it, good night, gentlemen, sleep tight."

Sergeant Harper stepped behind the dais. "I don't have anything special for you, so hit the bricks. Joe, you met Officer Carpenter. Carpenter, you remember meeting Lehland," he said, nodding toward a large-framed man. Lehland was in his middle thirties. He was slightly overweight. The thin blond mustache he wore gave him a worldly appearance. "He's been our foot man. He'll show you the post tonight. I'll be putting him in the cars as relief man soon as you can learn what to do out there. It won't be a long indoctrination. I need a man for relief in the cars bad. Don't get the man fucked up on his first night, Lehland."

"I won't, Sergeant. You know me." He was unconsciously twirling his nightstick with great skill. He was a veteran cop.

"I know you, all right," the sergeant replied. "Don't forget that bunch of ass-holes down at the O.K. Bar. Take care of it. I don't want to hear any more noise from Sam Rider. You know he's connected with Headquarters. We don't need any of their attention, do we, Joe?"

"No sir."

"I'll be seeing you later on, maybe about two-thirty near Rider's place."

"Yes sir."

3

"LET'S GO, CARPENTER," LEHLAND SAID, OPENING THE station door. "I'll show the post from the southside up. We can start here on Susquehanna Avenue." The two men began to walk.

"The post goes from here, north to Washington Avenue, west to the Court House, and the east boundary is kind of undefined. You can walk east on Pennsylvania and Chesapeake or Joppa 'til you run out of business places to check. Not much over there, except the colored section. You know, some old houses, some pretty nice ones, too. Except for a few rotten young bucks, they're good people. They don't bother anybody. They kind of take care of their own problems. Harper likes us to go all the way through there and try to get a feel of what's going on, even if we don't do much about it." He turned to Carpenter. "What do they call you?"

"Everybody calls me Fritz, except my mother. She's got a thing about nicknames. She doesn't like to hear them, for some reason."

As the men walked, they tried the front doors of business places, then went through the alleys to check the rear entrances of the same places. No one had forgotten to lock their doors.

"Why do you check the doors of business places? Seems like if a man has a successful business, he'd have sense enough to lock his door."

"Because we've done it for eighty years. We do a lot of things that are a waste of time. When you find a door open, call the Desk Sergeant. He'll call the owner out of bed to check the place and lock the door. The Desk Sergeant notifies the District Sergeant, too. Sometimes he'll show up, sometimes he stays away. By the way, what do you think of our District Sergeant?"

"He's got a way with words, doesn't he? Has he ever shown any emotion about anything?"

"Not in my time around here. Wait 'til you see him in action. The man is deadly. The way he moves is uncanny. He moves his hands and feet like you wouldn't believe."

They turned into a dark alley. The smell of garbage was overpowering as they stepped around battered trash containers. A small cur glanced at them defiantly as he urinated on a bale of old newspapers. Lehland snapped the strap of his nightstick at the dog. The animal flinched and trotted into the darkness.

"Yeah, Harper's a hard case," Lehland said. "He was helping me check the street one night, me in the alley and him in front. You know that car dealer up on Washington and York?"

"Yeah, I remember it," Carpenter said.

"Well, since we checked the place, you know the back is lit up pretty good as a rule. That night it was as dark as Hades. I figured the nightlight was burned out in back. As I walked around the corner, I got clobbered over the head with something. It was a glancing blow and didn't put me out, and I guess I screamed. I went to my knees and tried to stand, but couldn't. There were three of them standing over me. One of them pulled my gun out and said, 'Let's blow his fucking head off.' I was too damned punchy to do anything. I figured that this was it. I'm not ashamed to tell you I pissed myself."

"I would have, too."

"Just as the bastard put my gun to my head, he made a funny noise, you know, like, huh! Next thing you know he dropped my gun and flopped over me. Everything was a blur then. More of the same, grunts and thuds, then not a sound. All three of them laying around me, out or making funny gurgling noises. I'm coming out of it fast. All of a sudden, there's a flashlight in my eyes and Snake leaning over me. Christ, I almost cried with relief. I thought I was going 10-7 and here I was able to get up. The only thing he said to me was, 'Come on, we got work to do. We got to make believers out of these bastards.' I held the flashlight on them and put the .38 where they could see it. Snake walked up to one guy, who was by now up on his knees and showing signs of life. He kicked him in the balls, once, twice, three times hard."

"Good grief! What did he do that for?" Carpenter asked.

"I guess he believes in swift justice, Fritz. When Snake was a patrolman his partner and him pulled a couple of suspects over up on Jarretsville Pike late one night. The car fit the description of one used in a holdup earlier. They recognized the two occupants as local farmers and put their guns away. The two farmers jumped them and stomped Snake pretty good. He lost one of his balls. They shot his partner with his own gun and crippled him for life. I guess it fucked Snake's mind up a little."

Carpenter whistled. "My God, no wonder."

Lehland laughed and spun his nightstick. "Anyway, I heard those funny sounds again. Huh! Huh! Huh! He turned to the other two and gave them the same treatment. Jesus, my balls hurt now just thinking about it. He told me to wait, that he'd be right back. In a few minutes he's back, driving a pickup truck with Pennsylvania tags. By now our friends are making a lot of noise crying, pleading, and holding what's left of their balls. When they finished puking he loaded them all in their pickup truck in back. He said, 'Come on, ride up front with me, those ass-holes aren't fit to run nowhere.' He drove us all to Union Memorial Hospital. They gave me about eight stitches behind the ear and let me go home."

"Thank God for small favors," Carpenter said.

The stench of rotten fish filled the alley. A drunk staggered toward them out of the darkness. Lehland shone his flashlight into the man's face. The derelict blinked into the light, tipped his battered hat, and bowed.

"Good evening, Officer Lehland. I'm just on my way ho-ho-ho-home."

"Hello, Harry," Lehland said, as he stepped aside. "Make sure you don't stop to rest on the way."

"Yes sir, thank you, sir," said Harry, as he lurched off into the darkness.

Lehland shook his head as he watched Harry fall over a garbage can and scramble back to his feet. "That could be me someday, Fritz."

"I doubt it. You've got too much class. Get on with the story of the ruptured burglars."

Lehland laughed, "Yeah, well anyway, those three yokels were all admitted to the hospital. They all got probated sentences in court. The judge figured they'd suffered enough. They let Snake off with a reprimand. I owe my life to him, I know. I'm grateful, but I'll never like the guy. He scares me. Funny thing, though, we didn't have one burglary on the street for six months after that. Those cats had the safe inside the dealer's office almost peeled. Detectives said it was a neat job, so they must have been pros."

"Did you ever hear any more from those burglars?"

"No, but you can bet they're all singing soprano now."

"Christ, that's terrible."

"Policing is a terrible, shitty business, Fritz," Lehland said. "You have countless little incidents like that every night all over the country. They don't usually turn out that way. The cop gets hurt most, as a rule, when he walks into something like that. I can only thank the man upstairs that Snake didn't stop to call for help when he heard me yell. They'd have wasted me for sure and probably blew Snake away with my gun on the way back to their truck."

They finished checking all the closed business places. It was 1:00 A.M.

"You hungry, Fritz? Let's go in here. The O.K. Bar makes the best crabcakes in Towson."

Lehland led the way into the tavern, a long, narrow place. There was a long bar on the right and booths against the wall on the left. The place was dark, even by local standards. Patrons were packed elbow to elbow at the bar. Teresa Brewer was belting out "Till I Waltz Again With You" on the juke box. It was a very noisy crowd, and she was being drowned out by the drinkers. Two women were tending bar, barely able to keep up with the thirsty crowd. They knew their trade well. There was an economy of movement in everything they did. They knew where all the bottles were. When they mixed a cocktail, they didn't measure. There wasn't a drop wasted when they poured a drink. They drew off draft beer as though they had been doing it all of their lives. Every man and woman seemed to be watching them. There was a lot of them to watch. Both were blondes in their early twenties. They were dressed identically in plain white cotton blouses and long black skirts. Neither woman was wearing a bra . . . it was very obvious. Both were firm, large-breasted, wholesome-looking girls. They smiled a lot, showing off their even white teeth. As they bent over into the cooler for ice or bottled beer, the drinkers watched intently, fondling them with their eyes.

"Sam, I want you to meet the new foot man, Fritz Carpenter. Fritz, this is Sam Rider, the owner of this fleshpot."

Sam Rider was a small, nervous, birdlike man. He stepped from behind the bar to acknowledge the introduction.

"Glad to know you, Officer Carpenter," he said, extending his hand. "I want to make you welcome. Stop in anytime. I like to see the police in my place."

He ushered them to the rear of the tavern into a deserted dining room. "Here, sit here, this is a private dining room. We only use it for big parties. Crabcakes okay?"

"That's good for me," Lehland replied.

Carpenter nodded.

"Fine. I'll make them up for you personally." Sam disappeared behind a stainless-steel door to the kitchen.

Sam Rider came in five minutes later. He carried two large, heavy platters. He put them down with a flourish.

"There you are, Officers, best fucking crabcakes in town. Hope you like Smithfield ham. Wait, I'll get you a couple of beers to drink with it."

Lehland picked up his fork. "He makes a good crabcake for the public, Fritz, but these are extra-big. Would you look at the size of them? They're as big as baseballs. Must be almost a pound of backfin in each one."

They were the largest crabcakes that Carpenter had ever seen. Each platter contained just one of the round delights, still sizzling from the deep fryer. Both platters were covered with paper thin slices of Smithfield ham. As Carpenter broke open the steaming cake with his fork, the fragrant steam assaulted his nostrils. Hunks of backfin crabmeat, as large as a man's thumb, a little parsley, just a touch of some spicy seasoning he couldn't identify, nothing more. Simple. Perfect. The men ate in silence, savoring their meal, washed down with several glasses each of National draft beer, served in frost-encrusted pilsner glasses.

"How about a piece of pecan pie to finish with?" Sam asked. "I believe there's about two pieces left."

Sam entered the kitchen only to return immediately. "Joe! Joe! They're out there again! They're breaking into the storeroom. I can hear glass breaking."

Lehland and Carpenter ran through the kitchen to the storeroom, piled high with cases of beer, liquor, and canned goods. No one was breaking in. Through the windowless bricked wall they heard the smashing of glass and muffled cursing and laughter. The rear door, a delivery door, was secured with a metal bar. Lehland carefully removed the bar and twisted the door handle, opening the door a crack. Ten feet away two young bucks were entertaining themselves by throwing empty beer bottles from the overflowing trash barrels against the wall.

"There, take that, you motherfucker! Here's another one, you honkey-fool! Ha, ha! Heh-heh! Here's one more, whitey! Come out here and we shove one up your white ass!"

Lehland turned to Carpenter. "Fritz, go out the front door, south on York Road, down Chesapeake until you get to this here alley. Keep out of sight. I'm going to bust out of here and grab one those bastards. The other one should flush right into your arms. Put the arm on him. Don't be too gentle. They're alley coons. You can't hurt them. I'll count to one hundred before I break out. Get going."

Carpenter ran through the bar, almost colliding with the cook and the tavern owner, who were heading for the back door. The crowd out front was dancing in the narrow area between booths and bar. Somebody had turned up the juke box. Eddie Fisher was blaring "I'm Walking Behind You." It seemed like everyone was dancing. Carpenter had to slow to a broken field canter. He collided with one couple. Cries of indignation were heard. He was almost to the door. A slick-looking cat with a greasy pompadour was swinging his partner, a buxom blonde, in a Fred Astaire-type twirl. She slammed into Carpenter, then fell in a heap onto a table filled with empty beer bottles. There was much cursing, crashing, and screaming. The man with the pompadour was standing there with his mouth open. Carpenter was through the door at last, out on the street.

Carpenter ran for all he was worth, slipped and scrambled around the corner at Chesapeake. He made it to the alley with his heart pounding, sucking in great gulps of air. He stuck his head around the corner. Both the bottlebreakers were visible. They were really enjoying themselves. Carpenter crouched on one knee. He peered from around the corner at the quarry. He felt a strange excitement that he had never experienced before. Exhilaration, anticipation . . . he had never felt so alive. His blood was coursing through his veins. He heard someone laughing. He glanced behind him. There was no one there. With a shock, he realized that the laughter had been his. He was laughing out loud.

He saw Lehland rush out the door and crash into one of the bottle throwers. Down they went. His companion was running down the alley toward Carpenter. He ran erect, his head held high, like a deer. He was almost on Carpenter. He was there. Carpenter struck him at the knees with a solid tackle.

The black boy was taken by surprise. He screamed like a wounded animal when he fell. He broke loose, scrambled a few feet on all fours, then he was up and running again. Carpenter was up in an instant, behind him, closing on him. The boy looked over his shoulder, screamed again . . . and the gap between them widened. The boy was very fast. He ran down the middle of Chesapeake Avenue, east through the black section. Carpenter was still in chase. The boy veered suddenly to the left, heading toward a five-foot solid-board fence. Carpenter instinctively slowed . . . nobody could clear that fence. The boy cleared the fence without slowing, or breaking stride.

My God, he must be another Jesse Owens, Carpenter thought. He slid to a stop at the fence, in time to see the boy clear the fence on the other side of the yard. All he saw then was a head bobbing in the darkness.

"Shit! He got away!" he said aloud.

Twang!

"What the hell was that?" Carpenter asked, again aloud.

Carpenter climbed over the fence and dropped to the other side. It was pitch dark. There were large shade trees in the yard. Dogs barked. Bedroom lights were being switched on.

"Who dat out dere? Get out of here now or I call de police. Get my shotgun, woman. Motherfucker prowlin' in my yard."

An outside spotlight was turned on. It was a blinding light. There, not five feet from Carpenter, was the runner, trying to get up. He clutched his throat with both hands. His chest was pumping, but he seemed to be strangling. Carpenter stepped forward to grab the boy. A wire clothesline, chest high, stopped him.

My God, he ran into the wire, he's strangling, Carpenter thought.

The boy managed a ragged wheezing breath, then another. He began to breathe normally again. Carpenter quickly handcuffed his prisoner's hands behind him. The boy responded to the pressure of Carpenter's hand. He was trembling, his head was held down.

"Let's go, young fellow, back to the O.K. Bar."

People were on their back porches, talking rapidly. Some hung out their bedroom windows, staring. Every dog in the neighborhood was barking, adding to the din.

"Whip his ass, Officer, mess him up. No-good trash prowling around people's yards. Damn boy, that's that Jennie's oldest. Can't do nothing with him. Ought to throw that trash in jail and keep him there."

The runner was walking normally now. Carpenter led him back to Chesapeake Avenue. Lehland was standing under a streetlight on York with his prisoner.

"Come on, Carpenter, I got things to do tonight. Let's hustle their asses back to the station." He looked the handcuffed boy up and down. "See you got Ezera and Jennie Jones' boy. He's a runner. How'd you ever get him? I've tried before and never even came close. He's a real rabbit."

"He ran into a wire clothesline in somebody's yard or I wouldn't have had a chance. Damn near cut his throat."

"Too bad it didn't," Lehland said. "Interrupting my dinner like that! We never got to eat our pie. Well, Sam Rider should be happy anyhow. You know, he came running back to the storeroom with a forty-five right after you left to get into position. He wanted to blow these guys away." Turning to the two youths, he tapped Jones lightly on the chest with his nightstick. "How come you birds are farting around the O.K. throwing bottles at the place?"

Jones shrugged. "No reason. Like to break bottles. Don't like Sam Rider. Him no good. Rich bastard ride around in big car, smoke dem big cigars."

Lehland pushed back his hat. "Fritz, you see before you two examples of what the social workers would call the socially deprived. They are clearly victims of their environment. Society is at fault for allowing conditions to exist that foster the growth of chaps such as these. They were merely expressing their distrust of the establishment and venting their rage at their lack of power and standing in the community."

"Where did you ever hear such bullshit?"

"My first wife was a social worker. She got her Master's at the University of Maryland. She was a great lay, but I got tired of listening to her shitty, superior, little pat answers of what's wrong with this country. She never liked cops, could not bear to be around my friends. She thought they were all crude and loud, and so very uneducated."

They walked their prisoners west on Chesapeake Avenue toward the station. The plate glass in the front windows of closed business places made cracking noises as it contracted in the cool of the night. Carpenter shook a Camel loose from his pack and offered one to Lehland. They lit up and continued their walk to the station house.

4

THEY WALKED INTO THE STATION WITH THEIR PRISoners, uncuffed them, and waited for their desk sergeant to finish a telephone conversation.

Sergeant Goulek had thinning brown hair and was in his middle forties. He could turn on charm or salty banter like a switch. He knew people and trusted only cops.

"Yes, Mrs. Smithers . . . Yes . . . Sure . . . You are right . . . I don't blame you . . . I would if I were you . . . Right. Look, I've got to go. I've got business here now . . . Right . . . Okay . . . Yes ma'am. You're welcome. Goodbye." He slammed the receiver in its cradle. "Gads, that old woman can really gab. She talked for an hour and a half tonight about her vegetable garden. What did these two hombres do, Joe?"

Lehland briefed the sergeant about the incident.

"That right, boys?" The sergeant turned to the two prisoners.

"Ya, Sa, Mr. Sergeant."

"How old are you guys?"

"Me, I sixteen. He seventeen," said Jones.

Both boys were perspiring freely. Their eyes were

huge in their ebony faces. Carpenter's prisoner was trembling. A raw spot on his throat was oozing blood.

"Shit, juveniles. No problem, I don't have to print them. Go on, men, hit the bricks. I'll notify their parents to come get 'em. Your report will be ready when you get in for roll call."

"Sergeant Goulek, did anyone ever tell you what a kind gentleman you are?"

"Don't you try to snow me with that 'gentleman' shit, Lehland," he said. "I've been accused of a lot, but nobody ever called me a gentleman. I'll cover for you, just give me the number."

"We'll call it in."

"Okay, now let me get this paperwork done. Get out, you're interfering with my rest."

"Hey." Lehland said, glancing at his watch, "I'm late for my appointment with my girl. Come on, Fritz, I'll show you where she lives."

"What did Goulek mean, cover for you?"

"Fritz, when everything is quiet around here, some of us grab a little sleep. Most everybody racks up when he gets tired. It's better than busting a car up when you get too pooped to drive. You got your radio to wake up with when they call you in the cars. Someday we'll have walkie-talkies to carry on the street, I guess."

Lehland dragged his nightstick over a barred grill covering a jewelry store front. The noise echoed through the deserted streets. A cat screamed its love call in a nearby alley.

"Listen to old Tom, the horny cat. Where was I, Fritz? Oh yeah, walkie-talkies. Then they'll give us a load of picayune calls on our post just to keep us hopping. Until then you let the desk sergeant know where you'll be. He calls you by phone if they start looking for you. We all have places to caddy up. We get keys from friendly merchants. They're glad to have a cop rest in their place. Gives them a sense of security."

"How do you wake up?"

Carpenter kicked an empty beer can off the sidewalk into the gutter. They crossed York Road into East Towson. Business places gave way to a shabby, old residential neighborhood.

"The desk sergeant gives you a ring on the phone if you want him to. I've got a built-in alarm clock in my head. Wakes me up when I want it to. Never failed me yet. It's from years of experience. Practice makes perfect. Don't worry so much. I won't let you get fucked up. I'm your teacher, remember?"

"I'll remember," Carpenter said.

"Here we are, Virginia Avenue. See that old white house across the street? My girl's got the basement apartment. Two fags live upstairs. A white gal lives in the top-floor apartment with a spade. Good setup. Nobody sees or cares what their neighbors do. You might say this is the liberal side of town. It's three A.M. I'll be out at exactly four. I never stay longer than an hour. See you on the corner of York and Shealy, then."

Carpenter watched his partner cross the street and let himself in with a key. They didn't turn any lights on. The streets were empty, silent now, save for the mute rumble of an occasional tractor-trailer passing through Towson on York Road.

He walked in the alleys behind rows of silent, dark business places. His feet were beginning to swell inside his new black calfskin shoes. The gunbelt seemed heavy on his waist. His feet crunched on broken glass. He was passing the O.K. Bar.

The crash of breaking glass behind him shocked him like an electric charge. As he whirled, hand clawing at his holster flap, a large rat leaped to the ground from the overflowing garbage drums, with a huge black cat bounding after him. He pounced on the rat six feet from Carpenter's shoes. The cat was an old hand. He had the rat by the back of the neck, lifting it clear from the ground. The unlucky rat was squeaking shrilly.

With a distasteful glance at Carpenter, the cat carried his prize 150 feet north and stopped under a bright nightlight. The alley was clear of garbage cans and debris. This was a good place to begin the age-old cat ritual of rough play, torture, and death. Carpenter moved on. He would not watch the rat suffer in the paws of his captor. He realized that he was shivering.

That scared me, that breaking glass. I must have walked right by that damned cat. Never saw him. I'll have to remember this alley. That fucking cat could have given me heart failure, he thought.

Elmer's place was open all night. The waitresses' names were embroidered on their blouses. Small hamburgers were ten cents, large hamburgers were twenty. Coffee was five cents. Conversation with Blanche was free.

Blanche did all the talking. Her assistant, Martha, was a shy young thing from Pipe Stem, West Virginia, according to Blanche. Martha's two front teeth were missing. She compensated for this by stretching her top lip down over the void when she smiled. It was a shame, as Martha's face at rest resembled a fine cameo. Her legs were long and beautiful.

Blanche was something else. She was very fat and her feet bothered her a lot. She was a compulsive talker and revealed all to Carpenter, as if she must purge herself in the next hour.

Martha was trying to reason with a drunk at the end of the counter. He refused to pay. His coffee was too cold, his hamburger was burned, and his soup tasted like piss. He was getting very nasty. He enjoyed the attention he was receiving from a truck driver who had just walked in. Martha was very soft-spoken and polite. She was new and couldn't cope with drunks. As she turned to walk away from him, he reached for her apron strings and pulled the bow out. Martha was trying to pull away.

"Goddamn hillbilly bitch, don't you walk away from me. I'll teach you." The drunk wouldn't release her apron.

Carpenter moved beside the drunk.

"Let her go."

The drunk whirled and jabbed his fingers into Carpenter's chest, hard, repeatedly.

"Who asked you to butt in?"

"Pay her and get out of here."

The drunk's fingers were punching Carpenter's chest like pistons.

"Fuck off, cop."

Carpenter grabbed the two offending fingers and twisted hard. He had the drunk on tiptoe, palm up, screaming in agony. All the fight was gone out of him. He danced around like a ballerina, anything to ease the pressure on the fingers.

"Get his wallet out of his pocket, Blanche."

Blanche moved quickly for a fat lady. She was as deft as a pickpocket. She had the wallet in her hand.

"Has he got any money?"

"He's loaded."

"Take ten bucks. Take out for the food and split the rest with Martha. That is, unless this chap objects."

"It's okay, it's okay! Please, my fingers, my God, my fingers."

"You want him locked up, Martha?"

"No, I—no. Just get him out of here, please."

Carpenter slacked off on the pressure a little, enough to let the man down off his toes. He led the man by the fingers outside, into the cool night air.

"Now you listen to me, you silly son-of-a-bitch. If I ever see you bothering those women again, I'm going to break your goddamn fingers off and shove them up your ass. Do you understand me?"

"Oh, Christ, please let me go. I was only kidding."

Carpenter released him.

The man spun on his heel and ran to a cab parked at the curb. He had to shake the driver to wake him. The cabbie rubbed his eyes, then pulled away from the curb.

Carpenter went back inside.

"What do I owe you for the coffee and donuts, Blanche?"

She stopped wiping the counter. "Are you kidding? Nothing. That nasty bastard has been coming in here about twice a week for the past month. This is the meanest he's ever been. We're all afraid to call the cops for drunks. Most of the time we can deal with them, but that guy was impossible."

Martha walked up to Carpenter.

"Thank you, Officer. I was scared of that man."

"Don't mention it. I'll be seeing you, ladies."

"Y'all come back now, ya hear?"

Carpenter grinned, and walked out onto the street.

Lehland was waiting for him at York and Shealy. "Hi, Fritz. Everything quiet?"

"Yeah, except for a drunk at Elmer's Place."

"What happened?"

Carpenter recounted his experience with the drunk.

"I couldn't have done better myself. That will make it easier for you. You made two friends at Elmer's. The word will get out and most of the local streetfighters will leave you alone now. You'll have to fight one or two. Remember, you don't go by the Marquis of Queensberry Rules in the street. Use your stick—shit, use anything you can get your hands on. You'll be okay. Were you in the Army?"

"Marine Corps. A mud Marine."

"Come on, Gyrene, let's walk over to Pennsylvania Avenue. It's time for my beauty rest."

They recrossed York Road to a mixed neighborhood of old, well-kept residential places and business offices. A baby was crying as they walked by a white-frame house. A light went on in an upstairs window and a young woman in a nightgown pulled the shade down. The baby stopped crying.

"I was in the Army for a year, just before the Second World War ended. Never left the U.S.A. Guess you were just a little too young for that one. You make Korea?"

"Inchon, Seoul, the frozen Chosen. I got to ride part way out. Shrapnel in the legs and back, frostbitten feet."

"Rough, huh?"

"No picnic, but I didn't really mind anything as much as I did the cold. That's all history now. We got the shit beat out of us there. I don't even like to think about it. How was your—ah—appointment?"

"Okay. She's a great lay, for a Goucher girl." Lehland held his hands to the small of his back and started to limp.

"Much cooze on the make around Towson?" asked Carpenter.

"You damn near have to beat it off with a stick, even an old guy of thirty-six, like me. Hell, there's Goucher College right down the hill—all girl, as you know; Towson State about eighty-five percent pussy, the County Court House girls, all the chicks that work in the offices around town, and Sheppard-Pratt."

"Sheppard-Pratt, the mental hospital?"

"Yeah, student nurses get their psychiatric training there. They all come from North Carolina, Florida, South Carolina, and Georgia. No local girls train there. They're just young, lonesome, bored Southern girls looking for a little diversion. Our duty, as good, clean, public servants is to provide an outlet for them. We have to give them relief, so to speak. Our aim is to satisfy. Oh, I'm not trying to lead you to a life of sin, young man. It gets to be one big bore out on the street sometimes. It helps to pass the time. It all depends on how you want to waste your time. A little cooze never hurt no man, unless you make a hog of yourself. Remember, if you mess around, not to spend all your time with one broad. Meet them while you work. Wham, bam, thank you ma'am, and back to work. You checked everything, all the doors still on?"

"Yeah."

"Let's get some rest."

They stopped in front of an old frame building on east Pennsylvania Avenue. "Smith, Smart, Sadler, and Associates, Attorneys at Law," the sign declared. A mockingbird was running through his repertoire of purloined songs in a dogwood tree in the side yard.

"Listen to that, Fritz. Silly bird doesn't know when to sleep."

Lehland produced a key from among fifty or so on a large ring on his gun belt. They entered in the dark.

"Take that leather couch. It sleeps pretty good. I'll take the big overstuffed mother here behind the desk."

The metallic sound of telephone clicking came from the desk. Carpenter stretched out on the couch.

"Hello, Sarge? Lehland here. Everything's quiet in Towsontown. Nobody on the road except damn fool truckdrivers and a couple of dumb cops. Snake around? He did? Good. We'll be at 823-0006. Give us a buzz about six-thirty, will you? Thanks."

He put down the phone. "Snake went home early. Goodnight. See you at six-thirty. Hope you don't snore."

Carpenter was already dozing off.

5

CARPENTER'S INFORMAL TRAINING PERIOD AS A FOOT patrolman lasted three days.

Sergeant Harper was discussing Carpenter's fitness for solo foot duty with Lehland after roll call.

"So, you think he's ready, Lehland?"

"As ready as he'll ever be. He's got balls. He'll do."

"That's good enough for me. Think you can handle it on your own, Carpenter?"

"I think so."

"Okay, Lehland, that makes you the relief man. Work 22 car with Trotta tonight. Don't forget your detail at the Rustic Inn. Remind Trotta. Sometimes he forgets. He knows the time."

Harper and Carpenter were alone now in the courtroom.

"Carpenter, I want you to remember your details out there on the street. You have two of them on this shift. I'm sure Lehland has told you. Whenever you can, be there when the O.K. Bar closes. He's afraid he's going to get held up again. About six weeks ago, two drapes came in about closing time and ordered a beer. They stalled around 'til the other customers left. The only ones left in the joint were those two blond bartenders and Sam, the owner. The women were restocking the beer cooler and Sam was doing his book work. When he looked up and saw them still at the bar at 2:00 A.M., he told them to hit the road. One guy pulled a .45 automatic and let go a shot in the ceiling. The other ass-hole pulled a knife and grabbed one of those beauties by the hair. He held her with the knife at her throat while the other forced Sam to open the safe."

"Jesus, how much did they take?" Carpenter asked.

"They got five thousand dollars out of that job—easy pickin's. Sam makes a little book, remember he's connected at the courthouse or some place. Let vice worry about that. You just worry about the stickup men. If Rider don't see you around there, he's going to call headquarters. They are a very frightened group of cops. They create a lot of details for the field men, just to protect their own asses. They call it CYA. Cover your ass. Remember that. If that place gets held up at closing time again, you and me are going to have to explain why you weren't there to shoot about six holes into those creeps. You savvy?"

"Right, Sarge," Carpenter replied.

"The other detail is something I want done. Keep an eye out from two A.M. 'til about three A.M. at Elmer's. That place is a magnet for drunks. Keep them moving. You'll find that if you keep the drunks on the move, you'll have less headaches on your post. By the way, I approve of your friendly persuasion of that shitty drunk there the other night. Don't look so surprised. Blanche told me. She tells everybody everything. Questions? No? Hit the bricks. See you in the morning."

The nights on the street passed quickly, especially from 11 to 3. The night people are out then. Carpenter was meeting a lot of them. He was beginning to recognize more of them each night. The tavern owners and barmaids were all friendly people. The foot man was always welcome. Food and drink was offered in every tavern. A few of the younger waitresses were very friendly. They offered Carpenter more than the establishment's food or liquor. He always explained to them that he was married. Several made it plain that they were willing to play on a part-time basis, on his terms. He laughed it away, but was tempted to follow through more than once.

The last scheduled night of 11 to 7 was a quiet one. The tavern owners all complained about the lack of business, except the O.K. Bar. Carpenter walked into the place at 1:20 A.M. The lovely young blondes were drawing draft beer as if there were no tomorrow. It was standing-room-only at the bar. Sam Rider himself was behind the bar, rushing to appease the thirst of the frantic crowd. It was a happy, noisy crowd. A local politician's daughter had been married the day before. These were the diehard, last stand drinkers who didn't get enough free booze at a six-hour reception at the local American Legion Hall. The politician, the only man in the place wearing a summer tuxedo, was very drunk. He gave a blank check to Sam Rider to pay for this orgy of boozing, along with an offer to pick up the tab for any casual patron not in his crowd who remained with them at closing time.

Sam Rider was out to break all records dispensing liquor. He spied Carpenter through the smoke and waved him to the end of the bar where there was a little space. He explained the situation quickly to Carpenter.

"I'm gonna run this guy's bill up out of sight, Carpenter. He's been coming in here for years squeezing me for contributions for this or that political bullshit. He's a cheap bastard. Never tips my beauties and wants everybody to buy him drinks. His family lives over in the Valley. They're worth at least ten or fifteen million bucks. I'm gonna try to get back what this chiseling prick has taken from me for the last ten years."

"I've never seen you look so happy, Sam."

Sam smiled and showed his tobacco-stained teeth. He slipped a couple of miniatures to Carpenter behind his bar rag. "To your good health, Officer. I haven't felt this good since my mother-in-law died. We're out of crabmeat. I'm sorry, this crowd's as hungry as cannibals. I've been trying to fill them up. I've got an extra waitress working tables. Charlie, my Chink cook, is threatening to quit as I'm working him overtime. How about feeding yourself back in the kitchen tonight?"

Carpenter was eating hot shrimp in the kitchen when someone began pounding on the back door. The door was jumping on its hinges. Charlie, the Chinese cook, grabbed a meat cleaver. Carpenter pulled out his blackjack, ran to the door, and lifted the bar off. He opened the door. The bottle breaker was there again. The Jones boy made no attempt to run. He was very excited, breathing hard. He was rolling his eyes around in his head.

"Dey hol'in' gun on Mr. Ruark! Dey got de white lady, oh, my Gawd, Officer, please come quick!"

Charlie was jabbering in Chinese singsong behind Carpenter.

"What the hell are you talking about?" Carpenter grabbed Jones by the shoulders. "Slow down. Say that again."

The Jones boy bit his lip and took a deep breath. "I workin' in Ruark's kitchen at night now, cleanin' up aftah de cook. He closin' up early. Last two men in de place hol'in' Mr. Ruark and Miss Alice up. I already turn de light off in de kitchen, gettin' ready to go home. I saw de men. Ran out de back, came here cause I knowed you allus here."

Ruark's Tavern was seven doors south of the O.K. Bar and Grill.

"Come on!" Carpenter pulled his gun and sprinted down the alley with the boy. The delivery door to Ruark's place was wide open. The boy was more sure of himself now.

"Come with me, I show you. Watch de floor. She greasy."

They tiptoed over the greasy floor to the swinging door. They looked through the glass in the door. The bar lights were still on. Jack Ruark and Alice, the barmaid, were sitting alongside each other at the bar. Two well-dressed young men were standing behind them, holding automatics to their heads. The blond one was snarling, with his lips pulled back from his teeth.

"Come on you cocksucker, where's the rest of it?" he screamed at Ruark.

"I told you. You've got it all. What more do you want? Don't hurt us. Just go."

"You cocksucker, I'm gonna waste you."

He started to pistol whip Ruark around the head with the heavy gun barrel. Ruark tried to stand. He got to his feet. Handsome-face brought the barrel down hard on the top of his head. Ruark fell to the floor, moaning. Alice began to scream. The black boy's eyes were as big as saucers.

"Go out front and throw something through the window," Carpenter whispered.

"Who, me?" The boy looked shocked.

"Goddamn it, yes, you! Have you got balls enough to do it?"

"I got balls."

"Hurry up."

The boy ran out of the kitchen door.

The blond man was behind the bar, sweeping bottles off onto the floor with his arm. He smashed a gallon jar of pickled onions with his gun barrel. He picked up a glass container of Planter's peanuts, and smashed it into the mirror behind the bar.

His partner was not idle. He put his automatic into his back pocket and pressed himself against Alice's back. He tore her blouse off her back and squeezed her breasts with both hands, hurting her. He was enjoying himself. His ferret face was a picture of rapture.

Carpenter's initial shock turned to fear. His mouth was dry and his hands were shaking. His fear changed to fury. He wanted to get at them, to smash them. Jesus Christ, I can't stand this anymore, he thought. That fucking nigger ran away. Wait till I get my hands on him. My God, I've got to stop them. I'll never make it across the room. Fuck it, I'm going in there now!

Carpenter set himself to burst through the door. A garbage can crashed through the front window.

"Cops! Oh, shit! Quick! The kitchen door!" one of the men screamed.

Both men were charging the swinging door. Handsome-face was in the lead, gun in hand. Carpenter stepped to one side and back. They burst through the swinging door. Carpenter smashed his heavy Colt revolver into the face of the handsome one. He dropped like a pole-axed steer, spraying blood.

Ferret-face had great reflexes. He slid to a stop and went down on one knee. He was clawing at the automatic in his back pocket, pulling it free. Carpenter's Colt blasted, lighting up the dark kitchen. The round slammed into Ferret-face's chest, throwing him back into the swinging door. His automatic went off, into the floor. He was fighting to bring the heavy gun back up. Carpenter's second round slapped him in the face, below the right eye, chasing brains and blood out the back of his head all over the door. The acrid odor of gunpowder hung heavy in the dark room.

Carpenter turned on the lights. The room was very quiet now, except for the bubbling noises coming from the handsome bandit. He didn't look so good, lying face up. With each breath, he was blowing bloody bubbles through his ruined nose. Carpenter stepped over the man and went into the bar. Alice was kneeling on the dirty barroom floor, cradling Jack Ruark's bloody head on her ample breasts. She was still crying. Sirens were approaching, out front he heard squealing brakes. Police were stepping through the broken plate glass window, guns in hand.

Sergeant Harper was beside Carpenter who stood with his back braced against the bar, Colt still in hand, muzzle to the floor. He was very tired. His teeth were chattering.

Harper looked at him closely. "You okay, Carpenter? Here, put your gun away. It's over now. You look like you've been shot at and missed, shit at and hit. Sit down here on this stool before you fall down."

One of the young policeman yelled from the kitchen. "Sarge, come back here, it's like a fucking slaughterhouse."

Harper returned in a few minutes. He had what could pass for a smile on his face.

"Nice work. You made garbage out of the bucktoothed one. That blond dude was strangling on his own blood, 'til we turned him over. You laid him open from cheekbone to cheekbone. His nose is punched in flat. Hard to stand up back there, with all that blood and kitchen grease on the floor."

Another policeman came inside. "Sarge, the ambulance is here for these people. The medical examiner is on the way for the stiff. Trotta's in the kitchen watching that ass-hole with the fucked-up face."

Ruark was conscious now and trying to stand. He was being restrained by the ambulance men and a young policeman. An egg-size lump was on top of his head. He was cursing fluently. It was a pleasure to hear him. Ruark cursed continually as they loaded him on the stretcher and carried him to the red Cadillac ambulance at the front door. He really had a vocabulary and didn't repeat himself much.

Alice was wiping the blood off her bare breasts with a bar rag. Her composure returned rapidly. She had retrieved a bottle of Old Fitzgerald from the mess behind the bar. She stopped dabbing her breasts for a healthy slug of bourbon.

"Look what that animal did to me! Look at my tits! Look at this, Carpenter! That dirty bastard."

She displayed herself to Carpenter as though he was her gynecologist. She was bruised badly.

Sergeant Harper jerked a red-and-white tablecloth from one of the tables and handed it to the woman.

"Here, Alice, cover yourself up. These are all young men. You'll make them all so horny they won't be able to keep their minds on their work here."

Carpenter started to laugh. He couldn't stop. It was the funniest thing he'd ever heard. The tears were flowing down his cheeks. He was shaking all over. His teeth were chattering.

"Give me that bottle, Alice." Harper poured four full ounces into an empty glass. He forced it on Carpenter.

"Here, Carpenter, drink it. Goddamn it, drink it, before you throw a fucking acey-duecey on me."

Carpenter gulped, choked, gulped, and gagged. The booze burned its way down to his belly.

"There, you're okay now. Hang on to yourself. We got a lot to do here. Don't drink anymore 'til you get home. Better talk to the detectives now and get it over with."

Harper turned to another officer across the room. "You there, Pope, call the B of I.* Let them take some pictures, maybe make a drawing of this dump. Let those forty-fives lay right where they are. Don't touch a

---
*Bureau of Identification

fucking thing or some son-of-a-bitch up at Headquarters is going to try to make us look bad."

He took his hat off and held it over his badge, retrieved the whiskey bottle from Alice, belted down about four fingers, and put the bottle on the bar. Putting his hat back on, he winked at Carpenter. "Don't ever booze in uniform, Fritz."

Harper turned and grabbed a passing policeman. "Lehland, take Alice home, or to the hospital, wherever she wants to go."

"Pope, you are in charge of the scene here. Don't let anybody come in but the cops. The rest of you guys, hit the bricks. Pope, you make sure those guns are dusted off by the B of I man. I want the prints of those two assholes run through the wanted file. He may as well print the stiff right here. It'll save him a trip to the morgue. You all straight, Pope?"

"Yes sir."

"Let's go, Carpenter."

The night air was clean and fresh. Carpenter breathed deeply. He was almost asleep on his feet. The Jones boy swaggered up to Carpenter. Carpenter looked at him and the boy returned the stare.

"Did I do okay, Mr. Carpenter?"

"You did just fine. You're quite a man. Thanks."

A big grin broke up the boy's black face. "Sure enough. Goddamn, I did good, didn't I? I'll see ya, Mister Carpenter."

The boy walked away, head held high.

They got in the sergeant's car. Harper started the engine and pulled into the southbound lane of York Road. He braked hard to avoid a drunk that stepped from the sidewalk into his path, cursed under his breath, and shifted to first. The drunk jumped back out of the way and sat down hard on the sidewalk. The cruiser peeled rubber when Harper pulled away.

"Looks like we had you detailed in the wrong bar.

How'd you learn about the holdup?" Sergeant Harper asked.

Carpenter told the story to Sergeant Harper, without embellishment.

"Did either of those ass-holes get any shots off?"

"The second guy through the door let one go, just as I shot him the first time."

Harper looked relieved. "Good. That'll show you weren't dealing with boys pulling a little prank. When you shoot somebody, you got to have as many things going for you as you can. I don't see any problems on this one. We had you watching out for this pair, but in a different bar. I'll lay you ten to one that a test slug from one of their guns will put them in the O.K. Bar in that last holdup."

"How come?"

"Ballistics. The B of I got a slug out of the ceiling at the O.K. that one of those birds fired during the last holdup. It wasn't bent up much. It's got enough to put the dude with the damaged snot locker away on that job, if we can get an identification from Sam Rider. I think he'll put him in. That's all work for the detectives and B of I. They can take statements from Ruark, Alice, and the colored boy. I'm going to take a statement from you when we get back to the station. Don't add any more to it than you just told me. The Lieutenant and Captain will want to come in and talk to you. Don't worry about them. Just lay it on them the same way you told me."

The car stopped in front of the Towson Station. Sergeant Harper made no move to get out. "One more thing. Let me see your gun."

Carpenter removed his Colt and handed it butt-first to the older man.

Harper flipped open the cylinder.

"Two empties. Buck-teeth has two holes in him. Where did you learn to shoot?"

"The Marine Corps. I was a coach at the Camp Matthews range when Korea started."

"I'll hold on to this until they let you come back to work. I imagine the State Attorney will take the case to the Grand Jury in a few days. You should have about a week off. Paid, of course. Let's go in. We've got a long night ahead of us."

Two seasoned detectives were the first to interview Carpenter. The entire tone of their interrogation was low-key and sympathetic. They were very thorough when Carpenter returned to the scene to re-enact the shooting for them. One of them turned the lights off in the kitchen and lit the lights in the bar. Bullet angles were checked and an exact drawing of the bar was made. After a long, time-consuming search, they recovered two slugs. Carpenter's second round, the head shot, was recovered in a corner. The ferret's round was found in a sinkful of dirty dishes. Carpenter's first shot never made it through the body of the holdup man. An autopsy later that day produced the slug.

The bright red blood had turned dark by now, almost black. Someone had tracked it around the kitchen. Small pieces of skull, brain, and other matter were dried on the swinging door. A great many flies found these remnants irresistible. They made a droning sound when disturbed. The smell and taste of death hung heavy in the kitchen.

Lieutenant Hollis was Carpenter's second interrogator.

"Hello, there, Officer Carpenter, nice to meet you. Sergeant Harper here has filled me in on the—ah, um—the—ah—shooting in Ruark's Bar. I don't come out much at night, I trust my sergeants. I'm only here to—ah—get enough—ah—information to make—ah, aah—a report to the Captain."

He stood at the desk sergeant's dais in the roll-call

room, fumbling with a report form and looking like a sick man, with the white stubble of beard on his sallow cheeks. The shirt he'd slipped on when the desk sergeant called him at home had a dirty collar and yesterday's gravy stains below the pocket. He had the sweet, sour smell of a dirty old man. When he spoke to Carpenter his upper plate slipped up and down, clicking against his lowers.

"Got to protect myself on this, you understand. I've got Sergeant Harper's report here, and your statement. I—ah—got the detective's report also. I'm going back to the, ah—scene and—ah—look around. Want to be sure I understand what the situation is. Don't want to make any mistakes on this one. Do you want to—ah—add anything to your statement?"

"No sir."

"Well all right then. I'd better get busy on my report. Got to have all my ducks in a row." He laughed humorlessly. "I'll probably be here all night as it is. I'm not complaining, mind you. That's my job, ha, ha. I'll see you—ah—later."

Lieutenant Hollis entered the office assigned to men of his rank. The clatter of his typewriter could be heard faintly through the thick walls. Harper raised his eyebrows and glanced at Carpenter.

"I was expecting a going-over from him, Sarge."

"Him? Shit. He wouldn't know how to give an old lady a hard time. That old fool has got enough reports now to build himself a volume. He's good now for seven or eight hours in front of that typewriter. It'll take about five pages to explain how much he agrees with the detective's report and five more to explain why he agrees with me. He'll have enough bullshit there to make the Captain cross-eyed."

"How does the Captain know what's going on?"

Sergeant Harper was seated behind a beat-up desk in the corner of the room. He picked at the blistered paint on the wall with his nightstick and watched the paint chip away and fall to the desk top. Tossing the nightstick on the blotter, he pulled several Tums out of his shirt pocket and chewed them. He burped behind his hand and laughed.

"I called him direct as soon as we came in, before I called that ass-hole Lieutenant. That's the way it is. When the Captain wants to find something out, he deals with us. Most of these lieutenants run around from station house to station house to get away from what's going on, when they do happen to be working, which ain't much. On call, they say they are. Balls. Who needs one of those mealy-mouthed sons of bitches for advice? Who could you call up for advice there in Ruark's kitchen?" He stood up. "We're all finished here, Carpenter. There won't be any legal problems here. I'll call you in two or three days, maybe a week, when to come back. Remember, we'll be working three-to-eleven turn then. I'll let you know as soon as the Grand Jury throws it out. Go home to bed. You get off a whole hour early. Remember, your pay goes on."

"Thanks."

"You got anything to drink at home?"

"Yes sir."

"Sometimes it helps."

"Yeah. See you, Sergeant Harper."

"Good night, kid."

6

CARPENTER COULD HEAR MARY SINGING IN THE shower when he unlocked the apartment door. He stripped off his tie, hat, and gunbelt, and tossed them on the sofa. As he was pouring himself a drink of Cutty Sark, the shower stopped. He dropped a couple of cubes into his glass and walked into the bedroom. Mary was giving "Kiss of Fire" a real workout. She could really sing. Georgia Gibbs couldn't sing it any better. She opened the bathroom door and walked into the bedroom, still singing. Her voice was muffled by a large bath towel she was using to dry her hair. Her face was covered as she leaned forward, rubbing her long, dark hair furiously. Carpenter looked at her lithe body absently. Mary had beads of water clinging to her breasts like tiny jewels. She was unaware that he was home and was toweling her hair, still leaning forward, when she noticed his legs and feet, near the door. She gasped and jerked upright.

"My God, Fritz! I didn't hear you come in!"

She instinctively covered her breasts with her towel.

"I'm sorry, I didn't mean to scare you. Why are you covering your boobs? The rest of you is showing."

He was erect at once. The fever was in him. He

wanted her right away. He pulled the towel out of her hands. She looked at the swelling in his trousers and laughed.

"Looks like you got a problem, here, Fritz. Can I relieve you of it?"

They pulled and tore at his shoes and clothing to get him free. He was naked, throbbing.

"Oh, my, look at that gentleman, he's so hard and big."

They were on the floor together. She guided him into her with three expert fingers. She had caught the urgency, the fever.

"Oh, fuck me fast, hard, hard, as hard as you can go. Come, hurry up and come."

They were bucking and lunging against each other. Mary was gurgling into his ear. It was over very quickly. She held him prisoner between her legs for a long time afterward, both of them savoring the time of peace and complete relaxation that always followed their lovemaking.

"You know, there's nothing like a quicky to start the day right. Now I can go to work with a smile on my face. I love you when you get that excited. Oh my, raping me on the floor like that! It's almost as good as when you take your time in bed. Come on."

She shoved him off her still-damp body. She jumped up and pulled him with her. They showered together, washing each other, laughing and splashing like children.

Later, drinking coffee together at the kitchen table, Mary looked him in the eye and shook her head slowly.

"Okay, Fritz, what's the matter?"

"I—ah, nothing. Why?"

"Please, don't bullshit me. We've been married four years and I know you. You're home early and you had a drink in the morning before breakfast. You've never done that before. When I put your gunbelt away, I noticed your gun was gone. Did you get fired?"

"I got suspended. I shot a man."

"Shot? What do you mean? Is he hurt bad?"

"He's dead."

The blood drained from her face as her jaw dropped. Her brown eyes opened wide.

"Oh, my God, Fritz! Why? Was he trying to hurt you?"

The words poured from Carpenter like a flood.

"He was sticking up Ruark's Bar . . . he tore the clothes off a waitress, like an animal. His friend beat Ruark around the head with a forty-five. I think they were going to kill both of them. I saw it all from the kitchen. They got scared and ran right over me. I didn't have any choice. I knocked one out. The weasel-faced guy pulled his gun. It happened so fast. I had to. I had to."

The tears came then. The dammed-up emotions gave way. Carpenter bent over the table, crying like a lost soul. Mary was beside him with her arms around him.

"Go ahead, Fritz. Let it out. Go ahead. Oh, goddamn that job! Goddamn it, anyway. Quit, you've got to quit! One week, one lousy week and this happens. It's too much. Suppose you'd have been killed? What about your mother and father? What would I do? Quit. I want you to quit. Oh, thank God you're all right."

Both were crying in each other's arms. They slowly regained control. Mary was the first to speak.

"Hey, my face is a mess. My boss will think you whipped me. Look at that clock. I've got to get dressed for work."

Carpenter sat at the table. The coffee was cold. His stomach burned like a blast furnace.

"I've got to run, Fritz. My carpool is outside. Give me a kiss. We'll talk when I get home. Go to bed. You look terrible."

60

Carpenter found some antacid tablets in the medicine cabinet. He was drained and exhausted. Sleep was a long time coming.

7

THE NIGHTMARE RETURNED AS SLEEP CLAIMED HIM. He had been free of it for months. It had been waiting to reclaim him when his spirits were at low ebb. He was in Korea, at the Chosin Reservoir. His sergeant was shaking him.

"Get up, Carpenter, it's time to go on watch. You can get Garcia up. He's two holes to your right. Keep awake. Have the radio operator call to let them know you're coming, or you're liable to get your ass plugged."

Carpenter crawled to his friend's foxhole and tapped the sleeping Marine on the foot. He was in his sleeping bag, and, against orders, the bag was zipped up tight. The Mexican-American youth was awake in an instant. He rolled out, ready to go.

"If we get hit at night, you're going to get cut up before you can get out of that bag."

"Fuck it. I'd just as soon get cut up as freeze to death. You know it never snows in Laredo. I can't stand this white shit. I haven't been warm since I left Texas."

They had the radio operator depress the transmitter button on the radio three times, pause and depress the button three more times. Out in the listening post, the squelch noise broke the silence—blip-blip-blip. They were awake. They duplicated the signal—blip-blip-blip. They would not shoot the Marines sent to relieve them.

Carpenter and his companion gathered their rifles and ammunition bandoliers and followed the radio wire down the long rocky slope. The wire was easy to follow, a long black line in the snow. The snow was eighteen inches thick and frozen solid. It easily supported their weight. It was five below zero. It was a fast trip downhill, two hundred yards forward of the Marine main line of resistance. The listening post was a round hole, six feet around and four feet deep. It contained the field radio, a few extra bandoliers of ammunition for the M-1 rifles, one dozen grenades, and two very frightened Marines.

"Get in here, get in! We heard something just a minute ago."

"What was it?"

"I thought it sounded like a horse whinny."

"Did you call it in?"

"Yeah, the Lieutenant got on and told us to stay out here for another fifteen minutes after you got here. I don't think he believes us, that son-of-a-bitch. He says he ain't worried about some animal; he's interested in Gooks."

Both pairs of men faced outward, rifles ready, eyes straining into the gloom. The fifteen minutes crawled by. Nothing broke the frigid silence.

"Good luck to you guys. I know I heard a fucking horse. Maybe it was just a stray farm animal."

Carpenter and Garcia were left alone in the hole. One half hour passed. They were starting to relax. Garcia began to nod.

"Go on, Manuel, don't fight it. Grab a few winks. I'm not that sleepy yet. I'll wake you in an hour."

"Okay, Amigo, you talked me into it."

Garcia sat down against the back of the hole and in

seconds was sound asleep.

Carpenter jolted awake. Jesus, I must have dozed off, he thought. The luminous hands of his watch told him that he had been asleep for ten minutes.

Crunch. Crunch. What the hell was that? Something on the right, it's moving, he thought.

He frantically pressed the transmitter button. Two blips answered him, meaning, go ahead with transmission. He spoke low into the mike.

"Charlie four, Charlie four. We've got movement on our right flank."

"Stand by, I'll wake the man."

The Lieutenant was on the radio immediately.

"Outpost One, what's happening?"

There was a crashing, breaking noise to the left. A horse screamed in fright. It had broken through the snow. More noise to the rear. A horseman passed their hole slowly, not ten yards away, to the right. Two more horsemen passed by to the left, jabbering together in their foreign tongue. The sound of the horse soldier's jangling equipment was loud and close by in the bitter cold air.

"Cavalry, cavalry, they're coming right for you! Jesus Christ, can't you hear them?"

"Get your asses back here on the double."

"I can't!"

"That's a fucking order, get in here!"

"It's too late, they're all around us."

Carpenter dropped the microphone and shook his friend awake. "Manuel, Manuel! Wake up! The Gooks are here!"

The boy's dark eyes were enormous. He grabbed his rifle and lunged to the front of the hole.

Chinese horse soldiers were everywhere on the hill, passing by slowly. They were all heading for the main line of the Marines. It was incredible that the listening post had not been discovered.

Carpenter stood by his friend's shoulder. "Don't shoot unless they fall in with us. We haven't got a chance if they spot us. Get down, for Christ's sake."

A single white flare lit up the hillside. A machine gun opened up on the right flank, followed by one on the left. All the Chinese were past them. They were almost to the Marine lines. Grenades were bursting up and down the line. The sound of rifle fire increased in volume until it was a steady roar. Flares were popping everywhere. It was bright enough to read a newspaper. Chinese bugles were turning blood to ice water. The cries of frightened men and horses filled the air. A few horseman made it inside the Marine lines, with burp guns hammering. The charge faltered, then broke and began to flow raggedly down the hillside. The Marine volume of fire slowed, then stopped.

A group of horsemen was heading in the direction of the listening post. Both Marines were on their feet now, enjoying the rout of the horse soldiers. Their elation turned to terror when they realized their post was in the path of retreat. There was no place to go. The horses were almost on them. They stood side by side in the hole and opened up with their rifles at point-blank range. The horses were going down, carrying their Oriental riders into the snow. Their rifles empty now, they pitched grenades out into the mass of wildly thrashing, wounded horses and men. Explosions showered snow, dirt, rock, and pieces of men and horses into the hole. They reloaded their rifles as two remaining horses regained their footing. Both animals ran riderless toward the hole. The heavy slugs tore into the breasts of the horses. One animal fell head-first into the hole. The other sank to his knees on the edge, great gouts of blood pouring from his flaring nostrils. The Marines were crushed under the weight of the dying horse. Garcia was dead, his neck broken. Carpenter was suffocating from the sheer weight of a thousand pounds of horseflesh across his face and chest. He regained consciousness when four husky Marines lifted the bloody horse from his body. He came to with perspiration freezing on his face in the cold.

Carpenter was sitting up in bed screaming, "Don't shoot, Manuel! Don't shoot! They don't see us!"

He realized that it was the old recurring nightmare. His hands were shaking as he lit a Camel.

"Fritz, wake up. Come on, get up. It's five-thirty. You want to sleep your life away?"

Carpenter woke up laying on his back. Mary was bent over him, rubbing his head. Her dark hair brushed his cheek. He had been sleeping in his shorts. The bedclothes were pulled out from the bottom of the bed. He was clutching Mary's pillow to his chest with both hands. His empty stomach was growling.

"I'm starving. What have we got to eat?"

"Your favorite things—stuffed rockfish, saffron rice, asparagus with butter sauce, and pumpernickel rolls. You must have slept pretty good. Look at that bed. Are you sure you didn't have a woman in here while I was gone?"

"No chance. You took all my juices before you ran off to work. I might be able to muster up a little more, though, if you play your cards right."

"You're so good to me. Thanks, but no thanks. Come on, get up. Dinner will be on the table in twenty minutes. You're all sweaty . . . yuck. Why don't you take a quick, cold shower? I'll make you a martini."

By the time Carpenter was finished showering, he was ravenous. He pulled on an old, soft set of khakis and beat-up slippers. He padded out to the kitchen. Mary had the oven door open. She was basting the fish with butter. The smell of baking striped bass was rich in the air.

"My God, that smells good. Where's my martini?"

"In the freezer. Get mine out for me, too, please."

The pair of martinis were straight up and very cold. The icy gin burned its way down to his belly.

"Ah, just what the doctor ordered. Five to one?"

"Who measures? Get out of here and let me set the table. About fifteen minutes more. The paper is outside the door. I couldn't bring it in . . . my hands were full."

Carpenter sprawled out in an easy chair with his drink and the paper. He pulled the rubber band off and slapped the front page open. Two-inch headlines shrieked to his face: Rookie Cop Kills One, Captures One in Towson Tavern Holdup.

Baltimore County Police today reported that two holdup men were surprised in the act by 26-year-old Officer Frederick Carpenter. Carpenter, a policeman for only one week, walked into the tavern at 2:00 A.M. this morning as the alleged holdup men attempted to flee. In the ensuing gun battle, 28-year-old Lee Packs, address unknown, was shot and killed. His companion, 22-year-old Robert Banks, address unknown, is under police guard at Union Memorial Hospital. Banks suffered severe facial injuries in his desperate attempt to avoid arrest. Police spokesmen said that Banks probably ran into a door in the kitchen of Ruark's Bar, injuring himself. Jack Ruark, the tavern owner, was treated and released for lacerations of the head and face. Carpenter was suspended, with full pay, pending further investigation and action of the State Attorney's office."

"Son-of-a-bitch."

"What did you say, Fritz? Come on, it's almost ready. Here, have a little more booze." She filled his glass from a small pitcher. "It makes your tummy feel good."

"They got the whole damned thing in the paper. Here, look at it."

"No, take it away. I've made my mind up. I don't want to talk about it or read about it. You told me all I need to know. The paper probably has it wrong, anyway. If you want to quit, that's okay. If you want to stay, that's fine, too. I've made my mind up. You could get killed down at the shipyard. Some dummy might drop a load of pipe off of his crane on your head. You could get run over crossing the street. You could have a heart attack when we're making love."

"Ah, what a way to go!"

"Let's eat, Fritz. I'm hungry. How does it look?"

Mary had her best on the table. She'd used her good linen tablecloth and napkins, her Stieff silver, and Havilland china. A single, tall white candle flickered in the center of the table. A four-pound striped bass rested on its side on a red glass platter. Creamy, succulent backfin crabmeat spilled from its stomach cavity. The crabmeat and fish were a light golden brown. Yellow saffron rice was heaped around the edge. A large boat of steamed fresh asparagus, swimming in a thick, rich butter sauce was beside each plate. A wicker basket near the fish was heaped with tiny, dark-brown pumpernickel rolls from Stone's Bakery.

"My God, it's beautiful, Mary. Sit down, I'll crack open a couple of cold Nationals."

Much later, their eyes met across the table. There were only scraps left. They were laughing, full, content, and happy.

"How do you manage to keep from putting on weight, little girl? You eat like a stevedore."

"You bang it all off me, that's how. Oh, I'm so full. I shouldn't have taken that last piece of fish. It was so good, though. I got it down at the fish market during lunch hour today. That and the crabmeat. You could taste the freshness, couldn't you? I kept it in the 'fridge at work."

"You said it. Lord, it was delicious. You know you

couldn't get that outside of this area. No kidding, I mean it. There's good seafood all over the place, but the great stuff is cooked right here in the Baltimore area. They don't even know how to cook it over on the eastern shore. Strange, isn't it?"

"Not so strange. Mama showed me how to use salt and pepper shakers, lots of butter, a touch of Old Bay seasoning, and a little mustard. There's nothing to it. Any beautiful, talented Baltimore girl with big boobs can do it."

"What do big boobs have to do with it?"

"They give the joint atmosphere. When a man can look up from the meal across the table and see big tits, it adds to the cuisine."

"Mary, did I ever tell you that you're a real character?"

"Many times, Fritz, many times."

"I mean that. This is a shitty time for me, and you are helping me through it. Please don't ever stop. Don't change."

"You shut up now, you hear. I get all damp down there when you get romantic and give me all that sweet-talk bullshit. If I weren't so full now I'd take you in the bedroom and make you forget what your name is."

"Promises, promises."

"Okay. You'll see. I'll get you later."

The dream returned to Carpenter once more. It was on the sixth and final night of his suspension. He was suffocating. The smell of sweaty horseflesh was strong in his nostrils. The weight was crushing him.

"Fritz, it's okay. It's okay. I'm here. Wake up."

Carpenter jerked awake. The familiar hand of terror left him. Mary was there, comforting him. He put his hand on her soft, warm hip. He felt an immense surge of relief from her presence.

"Are you all right, honey?"

"Yeah, it's all gone now."

"Same dream?"

"Yeah, it's always the same. It's just like I was back in that frozen hole with Garcia. It wasn't as bad this time. The only thing that really scared me was the smell. I could smell the horse on my face. I couldn't breathe. God, I wonder how long it's going to stay with me?"

"The Navy Doctor said it would gradually stop. After an experience like that it takes time to forget. It's only been two years. You aren't as nervous as you were when you first came home. I was almost afraid to sleep with you then, remember? Relax, sweetheart. See you in the morning. We'll go to Mama's, then maybe take a ride down to Annapolis. We can go to that joint you like down on the South River and eat some soft crabs and drink draft beer."

8

THE PHONE WOKE THEM AT 9:30 A.M.

"Hello, Carpenter? Sergeant Hyse here at the desk. Sergeant Harper asked me to call you. The Grand Jury threw your case out. Justifiable homicide. Report to work this afternoon at three, okay?"

"I'll be there." Carpenter scratched his head and rubbed the sleep from his eyes. He grinned at his wife and kicked the covers down.

"Who was that?" Mary asked, stretching her arms and yawning.

"The desk sergeant on the day shift. I go back to work this afternoon at three."

"Damn it. I wanted to spend the day with you down at the shore." She pulled his hair playfully and jumped out of bed. Her breasts strained the fabric of her short nightgown as she began stretching exercises by the bed.

The old sergeant was pounding on the battered wooden dais. "All right, gentlemen, all right. Quiet! I haven't got time to fuck around here all afternoon. I got to go home and cut the stupid grass. I got an announcement that pertains only to the lover boys and super studs around here. I got a call from old Doc Wolf, the medical examiner, today. Seems like a certain young cop who works here in Towson went to Doc Wolf for peter trouble. It burned when he made wee-wee. Now this certain cop had a smear taken by the Doc and you know what?" He glared at the assembled group. "Right, you perceptive young gentlemen, you guessed it. Our young stud with the burning wang has a case of old Joe, sometimes called the clap. Doc Wolf has been very gracious about this. He will not make a health department report on this gentleman, our errant friend. He is going to treat him and his wife free. Now, you may wonder how this concerns the rest of you. Allow me to enlighten some of you. It seems that our fellow officer, the one with the ailing wang, has been very friendly with a certain little dark-haired waitress by the name of Ida who works at the Golden Waffle."

His whiskey-red complexion darkened as he loosened his tie and sucked in a breath of air. The buttons on his shirt strained to the limit as his massive chest and stomach expanded. "A little bird told me that Ida just loves police," he continued. "In fact, this same little bird told me that Ida would like to screw every patrolman in Baltimore County, before she starts on the city force. Now, you young lovers don't have to worry about going to jail. I've already checked her out with her boss. She's not jail bait. She's twenty, going on forty-five."

A few of the police looked relieved. Five or six married men had their heads together whispering furtively. One man on the other shift vowed vengeance. Some looked guilty. McGee and Trotta were laughing. The desk sergeant was disgusted.

"Now, some of you guys are laughing. Some of you look like a little boy who shit himself. I could almost tell the men here who have got a little problem, just by your expressions. For the ones who are interested, the Doc will check you out anytime during his regular office hours for free. For the poor unlucky slobs that have infected their wives, he will treat your ladies free also. Everything will be held confidential."

"What's her name and address, Sarge? I don't think I know the little darling," McGee said.

The old sergeant chose to ignore him. "We had an attempted burglary last night at 6 BellonaAvenue. At about 0530 hours, an unknown white male attempted to crawl through the unlocked bedroom window of a twelve-year-old girl. He was scared off by the family dog barking at him. He fled south on Bellona Avenue."

"Lucky for the kid they had the dog," said Sergeant Goulek.

"You're right, Sarge. We got a teletype from Baltimore City Police reporting a rape on Bellona Avenue near the city line. An unknown white male entered a house at 0600 hours and raped a fourteen-year-old girl in her bed, while her parents slept in the bedroom next to the victim."

There was a lot of commotion in the booking room next door. Detectives were booking a man. Feet were scuffling and chairs were being knocked over. "You got no right to search me!" the prisoner screamed. One of the detectives slammed into the door to the roll-call room, putting his elbow through the glass. The sounds of slaps on flesh and cries of pain drowned out the desk sergeant. He paused, walked to the booking room, jerked the door open and glared inside.

"If you guys don't mind, we're trying to conduct a fucking roll call in here. Can't you beat that ass-hole up in your own office?" He returned to the dais. "Fucking soft-clothes cops go no finesse," he said. "Now to continue, we got a white paper hanger taking local businessmen up and down York Road. She's passed ten checks so far, for a total of two hundred, eighty dollars. She makes purchases of women's or children's clothing and other merchandise and writes her checks on the Greater Metropolitan Bank of Towson. Detectives made a composite picture for the merchants. The Captain wants every business place in the District to get one. That's all for today. Goodnight, gentlemen. I got to go cut the fucking grass."

Sergeant Harper stepped to the dais. "Okay, you guys hit the bricks, except Abe and Carpenter. I've got a job for you two. Carpenter, I want you to ride with Abe 'til about six P.M. Knock out as many of these Baltimore City traffic warrants as you can. When you finish up, work out the rest of the night on the street. Some nervous clown let these warrants lay around headquarters 'til they piled up, now they're screaming for us to dispose of them as soon as possible. Here's thirty of them. That ought to keep you busy. Abe, I made arrangements with radio to take your calls myself 'til about six, so you won't be bothered with anything but warrants. Carpenter, you got a school detail at three-thirty at Allegheny and Central. Help the little kiddies across the street. Better get rolling, it's almost three-fifteen now."

Officer Abraham Jacobson slid his bulk behind the wheel, after pushing the seat all the way back. He was a tall, thin, intense-looking young man. Several fresh razor nicks on his chin attested to the toughness of his dark beard. He fought a losing battle with his whiskers. He never looked clean-shaven. Spikelike black hairs peeked out of his nose and ears. Thick hair covered the backs of his hands and fingers. His head was completely bald. His face was creased in a perpetual frown. He was a compulsive worrier.

"I'll head right up to the school," Abe said. "The principal calls and raises Cain if the foot man is late. The Sergeant has been off my ass lately. I want to keep it that way."

It was a three-block ride from the station to the elementary school at Allegheny and Central.

"We're early, but you'd better stand outside the car on the corner. When the bell rings, they come charging out. You got to be there to stop them. I'd hate to see one of them get hurt," Abe said.

It was a twelve-minute wait before the children crossed the road. Carpenter was reading over the ten-signal radio code, attempting to familiarize himself with it and pass the time. He was on the corner only three or four minutes when he noticed a pretty young woman rush out the school door and run to a red MG convertible, parked about fifty feet from the intersection.

"Hey, Officer!"

"You calling me, ma'am?"

"Yes, could you help me here a minute, please?"

The woman, a stunning blonde, was attempting to lower the convertible top. She was struggling with a snap.

"I can't get this damned thing. Could you help me?"

Carpenter pulled the snap. It opened easily—too easily.

"There you go."

"Oh, thank you, Officer." She put her hand on his arm and blinked her eyes at him.

"You're welcome." He turned to go.

"Oh, don't go. The children won't be out for a few minutes yet. You're the new one, aren't you?"

"Yes, I guess so."

"I'm Sharon King. I teach here. Fred Carpenter, right? I'm so pleased to meet you."

Sharon King shook hands like a man. She didn't let go of Carpenter's hand. She looked him over from head to toe. She smiled and shook her head as though she had just made up her mind about something. Carpenter was getting embarrassed. She held on to his hand.

"I read about you in the paper. It must have been

awful. It took a lot of courage to stand up to those two. You're just the way I pictured you to be."

Carpenter pulled his hand away.

"What do you mean?"

"You look strong. You look like you'd stand up and spit in the Devil's face. You are a beautiful man." She looked at his crotch and smiled.

"Aw, bullshit, lady!" He could feel his face burning.

"I mean it. Are you married?"

"Very much so."

"It won't matter to me. So am I. I'd like to get a little bit of you." She ran her hand up his arm.

"Just like that, huh?"

"Just like that."

"Listen, Mrs. King, or whatever your name is. I like to make up my own mind about things like that, so go on back to school and beat your erasers, or whatever school teachers do after school."

"Why don't you stay after school with me and see?"

"You talk like some kind of nut. I've gotta go help the kids across the street."

"Okay, look, I'm sorry. Let's shake hands on it. I guess I was being awfully stupid and brash. I was only kidding. Don't get angry. Shake."

Carpenter took the extended hand. She grabbed his hand with both of hers and stepped forward, pressing her crotch against the back of his hand. She was strong for a woman. She released him almost immediately. He could feel the flush spreading over his face. She looked directly into his eyes. Not laughing, not mocking, but waiting, watching.

"My husband is thirty years older than me. He treats me like a daughter. He has a separate bedroom. He's a stockbroker. All he thinks about is making money. Think about me a little. I'll stop and see you some night when you're assigned to the street post."

"I've got to help the kids across the street." She put

her hand on his chest as he started to turn away.

"The bell hasn't rung yet. Don't you find me attractive at all? I've never made a fool of myself like this before. Look at me. Do you find me repulsive?"

"No, not at all. You know you're a pretty woman. You just come on like gangbusters. You're about as subtle as a kick in the crotch."

A white Lincoln was passing. The old lady driving braked and stared at them. She turned to watch them as the car slowed. She was so intent in her observation that the car's right front wheel hit the curb with a bang. Sharon King paid no attention. Carpenter could feel the perspiration break out on his back.

"Oh, I love it when you talk dirty to me. You make me so excited."

She was laughing at him. She was a very attractive woman.

The school bell rang.

Carpenter walked to the corner to see the children across the street. They stampeded like a herd of colts out into the Maryland sunshine. Their innocent, bubbling laughter filled the air. They spilled out of the school and waited obediently on the corner for Carpenter to stop traffic. There had been only one car passing since he arrived at the detail. He walked to the center of the street and had the children cross in a group. The last child, a freckle-faced redheaded boy of about nine, smiled up into Carpenter's face.

"Thank you, Officer."

The boy deliberately walked on Carpenter's left foot, then his right.

"Hey!"

"Can't catch me, copper! Yah, yah!"

The boy was off, running.

Jacobson was bent over the wheel laughing when Carpenter got back into the car.

"What's so funny?"

"You should have seen the look on your face when that little redhead walked on your feet. Your mouth fell open to your knees. Surprised you, didn't it?" He opened the glove compartment and tossed the pile of warrants in.

"This corner is full of surprises. Let's go get some coffee before we start on these warrants."

"I'm with you, pal."

Abe drove slowly through the quiet residential neighborhood. Fifty-year-old maple trees lined the streets. The car passed under the shade of the trees on Allegheny Avenue until they reached York Road, where the business district began. Abe parked the car in a restricted zone in front of Elmer's. They went inside and ordered pie and coffee.

"This is Fritz Carpenter, girls. Fritz, meet Hazel and Marge," Abe said.

Hazel put their pie and coffee on the counter and blinked her hot eyes at Carpenter. "Carpenter—you must be the one who—ah—I mean, ah—are you the guy that had the—um—trouble at Ruark's?"

"Yes."

Her starched uniform cracked and popped as she made a gesture with her arm. "Oh, gosh, Officer Carpenter, I didn't mean to be nosey and all, it's just that everybody in Towson is talking about you. You understand what I mean. All the merchants come in here in the morning and talk. They think you're just great. They say you're the best foot man that's come along in years. I guess it must have been unreal—I mean—oh, shit, there I go again. I talk too much."

Abe washed a mouthful of apple pie down with a gulp of hot coffee. "Looks like you're the rage of Towson, Fritz. That's the way it goes in police work. A hero one day, a bum the next. The trouble is, you never know for sure what the public is going to like. You can lock up some people and actually make friends with them. Bust some others and they have a vendetta against you for life. It seems like what we do is either excessively severe or too lenient. Everybody judges you differently, but they all judge you."

He shoveled the last of the pie into his mouth and wiped his chin with a paper napkin. The paper grated across his coarse whiskers. His eyes narrowed when he talked seriously. "I guess it's the American tradition. Most of them think police work is all writing tickets and shooting it out with bad guys. Hell, most guys do their twenty years and never run into a situation like you did at Ruark's. It will probably never happen again to a Towson cop for fifty years. Funny thing, though, some cops seem to attract action. They are always where it's happening. One thing's for sure though, it never goes down when you expect it. Here we are, sitting here now drinking coffee and bullshitting. Three minutes from now we could be facing anything. Sometimes it worries me. I've got a wife and three kids to take care of. At the same time, that chance of action, excitement, change or whatever, is what keeps me on the job. It can't be the pay, or the hours."

Carpenter poured some ice from his water glass into the strong, black brew as he considered this. He drained the cup and turned to Abe. "Maybe it's the men you work with."

"Yeah, that's part of it. It's a kind of brotherhood, I guess. No matter how you screw up, you don't have to worry too much about another cop ratting you out or talking. I hope that never changes, though I guess it will some day. If the pay would improve it would make the job attractive to more men and they'd tighten up. 'Til then you can do just about what you want as long as you listen to your Sergeant. We'd better start on these warrants. I wouldn't want Snake to think we were taking advantage of him."

They went to the cruiser and drove north on York

Road, in heavy traffic. The Greyhound bus in front of them poured diesel fumes into their lungs as the flow of traffic started and stopped. Abe got his chance to pass the lumbering bus when it stopped for a passenger at Sandy Bottom. He jammed it into second and shot around the bus into the clear.

9

"I LOOKED THESE OVER WHILE YOU HANDLED YOUR school detail. Here's the scoop on City traffic warrants. We get them sent out here in the mail by the hundreds. People don't pay their fines or show up for trial and the arresting officer down there gets his warrant for the arrest of the cat that ignored his summons. We take the warrant to the party named on the front here and notify them that we have a warrant in our possession and give them ten days to pay the fine. We go back and if they don't have the receipt showing payment in ten days, we lock them up and turn them over to the City Police." He swerved to the right to avoid a pothole in the road.

"I guess we have to do it for Baltimore city or they won't serve our warrants down there," Carpenter replied.

"Bullshit. The city won't serve our warrants. They claim they're too busy."

"Strange working relationship. I wonder why we serve theirs?"

"Who knows?" He shrugged and looked very Jewish. "I guess because we've been doing it for about fifty years. Maybe our Chief don't have balls enough to say no. He didn't make his rank by saying no to politicians."

He made a right on Seminary and slowed when the commercial buildings gave way to expensive new ranch-type houses.

"Here we are, that big house. We got two or three here, I forget which. They're all for the same guy. Hubert J. Bricker. Yeah, this is the place. I've been here before. They're all new, so it's just a notification. Walk up with me. I'll do the talking the first time, so you can get the hang of it."

A gray-haired, distinguished-looking gentleman of perhaps sixty was on his knees spreading peat moss among his juniper bushes. He looked up at the police and smiled pleasantly.

"Good afternoon, can I help you?"

"Hello, Mr. Bricker, nice to see you again. Sir, we have three warrants for your arrest. Baltimore City traffic warrants. We are not here to serve the warrants, but to notify you that you have ten days to satisfy them, or you are subject to arrest."

Bricker got to his feet and wiped his face on his sleeve. He took the warrants and looked at them briefly.

"Fine, fine. If you will just jot down the warrants numbers and place of offense I'll take care of them tomorrow. I've got to go downtown again. I get a lot of parking tickets in my line of work, you know. Hot day, isn't it? May I offer you some refreshment? Iced tea, a cold beer, perhaps?"

"No, thank you, sir. Here's the information you need." Abe handed Bricker the piece of scrap paper. "Nice talking to you. Goodbye for now."

"Nice seeing you again, Officer. Stop in whenever you see me outside working, for a chat. I'm always glad to see the police."

Back in the car, Carpenter turned to Abe. "He

certainly was a pleasant enough old man. His property must be worth a fortune. Must be a semi-retired professional man."

"He's a professional man, all right," Abe laughed. "He's an abortionist. He always works in the city. He lives out here with the snobs."

As Abe turned right on Charmuth, a four-year-old boy spotted the police car. He screamed in delight and ran along the sidewalk with his short legs pumping like pistons. He had a chocolate ice cream bar in his mouth. Abe slowed to a crawl. "Got a bite for my partner?" Abe shouted. The boy shook his head no and stopped running. Abe shifted to second and pulled away.

"Here we are, second house on the right. This gal has to be with us on this one. It's been twenty days since she was notified. See, the cop's notation on the back here. I don't know this woman, but be careful. They all get their feathers up when you have to lock them up."

They pulled into the driveway and got out. They approached a new, brick ranch-type house. The front door opened before they could knock. A brassy-looking blonde answered the door. She was dressed in very tight yellow toreador pants and a white silk blouse.

"Come in, I know what you're here for. I saw you pull up. I'm sorry, boys, but I didn't get a chance to pay that stupid old ticket. It just completely slipped my mind. I've been worried about my career. I'm an exotic dancer, you know, and my boyfriend and me had a fight. He walked out on me. I've had so much trouble. Couldn't you please, pretty please, just forget about little old me?" She stood in the open doorway and shoved her chest out for inspection.

"Not this time. You'll have to go along with us today," said Abe, grinning.

She ushered them into the living room and looked at them through half-closed eyes. Her false eyelashes were an inch long.

"Well, give me a chance to slip something else on. I wouldn't want anybody downtown to see me looking such a mess."

"Okay, but would you please hurry?" Abe said.

"Be right with you, boys."

She made quite a production of walking out of the room, rolling her fanny around and glancing over her shoulder to check the effect made on them.

Half a minute later she called softly. "Oh, Officers, would one of you please come here? I need your help."

"Come on, Fritz. She's going to try some kind of bullshit."

The men walked down the hall slowly. They passed a room used as a den. The radio was switched on low. The Ames Brothers were singing "Undecided." They passed an empty bedroom.

"I'm here, at the end of the hall."

The door was open a few inches. Abe knocked on the door.

"Come on in, don't be bashful. I can't figure out what to wear."

She was standing in front of an open closet, with her back to them, completely nude. She turned to face them. Most of her pubic hair had been shaved to accommodate the g-string she usually wore. She had large breasts and slender legs, and was moving her hips to the faint sounds of the Ames Brothers singing down the hall on the radio. With a wicked smile on her face, she ran over to Abe, put her arms around his neck and laughed into his face. She ground her pelvis into him, shoving him back against the door frame.

"Come on, I can take care of both of you big, bad police. Come on, you big hairy stud. Let's see what you got. You want a little head job first? Forget that old warrant, and I'll really turn you guys on."

"I—um, I—um, sorry, lady. I've got syphilis."

"What?! What did you say?"

"I have the syph. I appreciate your offer, but I've got syphilis. The doctor said 'no sex for two years.' Sorry."

"How about your partner? You look like a nice, clean boy." She had her arms around Carpenter, giving him a workout with her breasts and pelvis.

"Me, too. I got it too."

"What?"

"I've got syphilis, too. I got it from him."

"Are you guys putting me on? Just my fucking luck. I get busted by two syphed-up fag cops. Oh, Christ, this is too much. I can't stand it. Nothing goes right for me anymore. Wait a minute, I'll get dressed. No use wasting my time with a couple of sissy cops. I never heard of such a thing. Queers should not be cops."

She put on her yellow toreadors and white blouse in record time.

"Come on, you two creeps. The show's over. Let's get on the road. I've got a good mind to turn you two fruitcakes in for this. I'd bet they'd fire your asses in a minute if they knew you were queer."

She was still grumbling when they put her in the back seat of the police car. Abe started the engine and made a U-turn.

"Hey, this isn't the way to the station, you big faggot! I know where the Towson station is. What are you up to, anyway?"

Abe looked over his shoulder at her and smiled. "Take it easy, now, miss. I want to check and see if another client is at home. If she is, we can take her in, too."

"You got a warrant for another woman? Good. I'll have somebody to talk to besides you two pansies."

"Look at that next batch, Fritz. That's it. They got a paperclip on them. Ten of them, right? Rose Woodhouse's her name. She's a little strange. Watching the City Criminal Court in action is her passion. A couple of days a week she listens to every case on the docket. Parking her car is a game with her. According to Rose, parking on a public lot takes all the fun out of the trip.

"Her M.O. is to park five or six blocks away in a no-parking zone and put a sign on the dash, like 'Loading, back in a minute,' or 'Broke down, back soon.' Sometimes she uses a canvas bag she carries in her glove compartment to cover up parking meters. It's got 'Out of order' stamped on it."

Carpenter laughed.

"Don't laugh, there are times she gets away with it. Other times she gets a ticket. Usually there's no problem about arresting her, but she can be a real pain in the ass when she wants to be. All the cases she's seen makes her think she's Perry Mason."

Abe made a right turn on Timonium Road. Houses gradually became spaced further apart. Large estates behind tall wrought-iron fences sat complacently among the rolling green hills. Thoroughbred horses grazed in green pastures behind white fences.

Abe pulled into a private lane. Carpenter whistled. The house was a half mile from the road, nestled on a wooded hillside. It was white stucco and dazzling in the sunshine. Peacocks roamed the vast lawn and tame squirrels played tag on the cobblestone driveway as they drove slowly to the front entrance.

A butler answered the door, a tall, dignified old man. He was dressed formally, including gloves.

"Oh, dear. I suppose you have warrants again for Miss Woodhouse. Please wait here, Officers. I'll fetch her. She's in the library."

Rose Woodhouse came into the hall. She was dressed in a brown tweed suit. She peered at the police over the top of her old-fashioned glasses. She must have been at least seventy.

"Back again, Officers? Well, I suppose I could get a writ of habeas corpus from my attorney, but I don't have anything else to do this afternoon. I may as well get arrested. Don't worry, men, I won't fight you. I'm not armed."

"Thank you, ma'am," said Abe.

"Get my umbrella, Charles. It looks like rain. You may have Cook prepare dinner at the usual time. I'll be home early."

"Would you like Robert to pick you up at the Court House?" he asked as he opened the door.

"No, thank you, I'll manage. A cab will do nicely. Shall we go, gentlemen?"

"After you, Miss Woodhouse," said Abe.

Miss Woodhouse looked over her glasses at the passenger in the back seat. "Oh, how nice! A policewoman! I knew you all were after me again, but I had no idea you wanted me this badly," she gushed, as she slid in beside the stripper.

"You gotta be kidding, lady. I'm busted, the same as you are."

"Oh, how delightful. We can chat about our records. I have been busted eleven times. Traffic offenses, you know. How many times have you been in the slammer?"

"More than I want to think about," she shrugged. "What's the difference?"

"What were you busted for, my dear?"

"Lewd shows, prostitution, soliciting, drunk and disorderly, you know, shit like that. I'm an exotic dancer."

"A what?"

"A stripper. You know, I take my clothes off for money."

"Oh, that's wonderful. I wish my career had been as exciting as that. My father was in cotton mills. I was his secretary for thirty-eight years. If I had it to do over again, I'd have studied law. I just love criminal cases. I go downtown frequently to observe them. Judges in town are so much more decisive than our County

Circuit Court."

"I wouldn't know. They never tried me out here."

"Excuse me, ladies, but if you don't mind, I'd like to try to serve one more warrant on the way back to Towson. It's right on the way. Look at the top of the pile, Fritz. Schmidt, I think it is. What's the address?"

"Emil Schmidt, Crow's Trailer Park, York Road."

"We'll stop at the laundry or recreation room at the park. Somebody will know him. The guy that runs the place tips them off that we're coming if you get the lot number from him. They won't answer the door then," Abe said.

Abe started the engine and drove slowly down the cobblestone drive. Three peacocks were blocking the way. They ignored the car and stood in the driveway preening themselves under a pin oak tree. Spreading tree branches gave the bright sunshine a dappled effect as it played on the birds' brilliant plumage. Abe stopped in front of Crow's Trailer Park. The sign out majestically to the side of the drive and pecked at the grass.

Abe drove to the Timonium business district and stopped in front of Crow's Trailer Park. The sign out front was peeling paint. It read:

Crow's Trailer Park. No children or pets. Trailer for sale or rent. Office closed after 2:00 P.M.

"No help there, anyway. Here's the rec room and laundry room. Go get a fix on him, Fritz. I'll stay with the ladies."

The recreation room contained a beat-up Ping-Pong table, a Coke machine, and a pool table that had seen better days. An old man was shooting pool and didn't even look up when Carpenter entered the room.

"Good afternoon, sir."

"What's so good about it?"

"Well, I guess it's not so great, at that. It looks like rain. I wonder if you would help me, sir?"

"I doubt it. What do you want?"

"Could you direct me to Emil Schmidt's trailer?"

"What do you want with Emil?" he said, as he sunk the six ball in a side pocket.

"Oh, nothing serious. Just a police matter."

The old man looked up and sneered, "Bullshit!"

"Sir?"

"You heard me. Bullshit. You come to lock him up, didn't you?"

"Well, yes sir."

"Get the fuck away from me, cop. I ain't gonna tell you nothin'."

"Thanks."

"Don't mention it."

The laundry room was adjacent to the recreation room. Carpenter pulled the door open and entered. Ten washing machines and ten dryers were all working. The room was full of women. Most of them were middle-aged or older.

"Excuse me, ladies. Could anybody here tell me where Emil Schmidt lives?"

Carpenter's only response from the women was a few hostile or bored looks. Most of them continued to fold clothing as if he were not there. A plump young woman of about twenty was sitting by the soap machine reading *True Story* magazine. She looked up and smiled and started to speak, then apparently thought better of it. She dropped her eyes back to the magazine. Carpenter walked to her chair and squatted beside her.

"You know where he lives, don't you?"

"Trailer 64, last place on the left. Look out for his dog. He's a mean one. He bit me the other day."

Carpenter was aware of a person near him. A huge woman was standing beside him. She was dressed in brown slacks and a sweatshirt. Her arms and legs were as thick as a Russian woman discus thrower's. Her rear was as big as an Aberdeen Angus cow's.

"You told this cop." She glared at the girl and shook her fist in her face. "You should know better than to tell the cops anything. I got a good mind to smack the shit out of you. Emil's a good man. This son-of-a-bitch just wants to lock him up for some chicken-shit traffic warrant."

Carpenter stood up. She could look him level in the eyes without raising her chin. Sneering into his face, she shouldered him away and stepped close to the fat girl.

"I'm sorry, Mandy, don't hit me," the fat girl screamed as she ran out the door.

"My own sister, my own flesh and blood, talking to a stinking cop. Get out of here, you—you sneaky bastard. I hope you fall down and break your back, you lousy cop."

Carpenter strolled to the door and tipped his hat.

"I want to thank you ladies for your splendid cooperation."

He ducked out the door as the Amazon picked up a bottle of bleach to throw at him.

"Let's go, Abe!" He got in the car and slammed the door. "The natives are definitely not friendly here. Last place on the left, number 64."

"I saw the fat one run out crying. What did you do to her?"

"Her sister threatened to beat lumps on her head for telling me Schmidt's address. She must like Emil."

Abe coasted to a stop and lit a cigarette. "Here we are, Fritz. Go ahead. Show him the paper and bring him out. Watch that dog there. He don't look like he had his Purina today."

A large black German shepherd sat securely chained to a tree at the end of the trailer. "Thor" was painted over the door of a large, well-made white doghouse. Thor sat and watched Carpenter get out of the car. He made no overt move toward Carpenter. He merely sat and looked. He was a very alert, well-kept dog. When Carpenter knocked on his master's door, the dog rolled his lips back from his teeth and growled deep in his throat. Abe was enjoying it from inside the car.

"Look at him, Fritz, he likes you. He's smiling at you."

Carpenter could hear movement inside the trailer. He knocked again.

The shepherd stood and walked slowly to the end of his chain. He sat down. He was growling deep in his throat, looking at Carpenter intently. His chain was stretched as tight as a banjo string. No danger there. The shepherd stood, relaxing the pressure on the chain. The chain somehow fell from his collar. He was free. The dog turned his head, looked at the chain, and turned back to Carpenter.

"Look out, Fritz, he's loose," Abe shouted.

Carpenter was backing toward the car with the dog following, crouched down to spring. Carpenter flipped open his holster and pulled out his Colt.

A woman was screaming at Carpenter from the window of the trailer next door.

"Don't shoot that dog! Don't shoot! He won't hurt you. Don't shoot!"

Carpenter was near the rear of the car. The dog lunged at him. He turned and jumped onto the trunk of the car in one motion. The dog's teeth snapped shut on his pants leg near the ankle and tore away his new summer pants like a mouthful of tissue paper. Carpenter kicked at the dog to keep him off the trunk. The dog had his front feet on the trunk, snapping at Carpenter, feeling with his back legs for a climbing step on the bumper.

"Pull out, Abe, Jesus Christ, pull out. He's trying to

get up here with me."

"Hang on, Fritz, here we go."

Abe drove slowly away with Carpenter sitting on the roof of the police car, his legs over the rear window, feet on the trunk. The dog was following, frantic now, barking for the first time.

"Take it easy, Abe, there's nothing to hold on to up here."

Trailer residents, out tending their small lawns and gardens, stopped to stare in amazement at the spectacle. The dog was running in circles around the police car, biting at the wheels and barking enough to raise the dead, while the two women passengers were laughing and shouting with glee. Abe was blowing the horn and yelling at the dog. As they approached the recreation and laundry rooms, the grouchy old man and the women came outside. The women who had been so silent and busy with their laundry a few minutes ago were laughing, jumping up and down and cheering.

"Good boy, Thor. You put him on the roof," the Amazon shouted.

"Hey, Officer, how's the air up there?" an old woman wearing hair curlers yelled.

"Be careful you don't scratch the paint," another one yelled.

"Big, brave cop, look at him!" said a fat old woman with a mustache, pointing her finger at him.

"Good dog, Thor, good dog," said the grouchy old man.

"Why don't you come down and pet the nice puppy?" someone else yelled.

"Hey, cop, don't look now, but I think you pissed yourself," shouted the Amazon.

Abe stopped the car for traffic on York Road. The old man and women from the laundry room were following the car, on both sides.

The old man gave a shrill whistle with his fingers in his mouth. He yelled, "Here, Thor. Heel."

The dog sat down at the old man's side, looking up at him.

"Hey, cop, I'm Schmidt. How do you like my dog?"

Carpenter was boiling. He did not trust himself to speak.

Schmidt pulled his belt off his pants and slipped it through Thor's collar. He turned to the Amazon woman.

"Take him home for me, Mandy. I better go with these guys. Enough's enough. They're liable to kick the shit out of me."

"I'll be right down to bail you out, Emil, don't worry." She put her arm around him and kissed him on the cheek.

Schmidt looked up at Carpenter with a twinkle in his eye. "Come on down. He can't hurt you now. My girlfriend's got him."

Carpenter got down and held the door open for him.

In the back seat, Schmidt and the women laughed and talked like old friends.

"How do you feel, Fritz?" Abe asked.

"Great, just great."

"He didn't bite you, did he?"

"No, but look at my pants." He held the split seam apart and shook his head. "What a way to make a living."

Abe drove back to the station. Every block or so he glanced at Carpenter's torn pants and smiled.

They gave their prisoners over to the desk sergeant and turned to go.

Schmidt touched Carpenter on the shoulder and stopped him. He held out his hand.

"No hard feelings, son. You ain't mad at me for not tellin' on myself, are you?"

"No. I mean, hell, no, no hard feelings."

The stripper smiled and hugged them to her ample chest. "You guys are good sports. It's a damn shame about your—ah—condition. What a waste. If you ever decide to go straight, come and see me."

Rose Woodstock shook their hands. She pulled Carpenter's head down and whispered in his ear, "I left something on the back seat to take care of your trousers, young man. Humor an old lady. Take it and God bless you."

"Miss Woodhouse, you don't have to—"

"Fiddlesticks. I can't remember when I've enjoyed myself more. Thank you so much. Good luck to both of you."

"Come on, Fritz, I'll drop you off," said Abe. "We did enough of the warrants today."

A fifty-dollar bill was laying on the back seat.

"I don't think we should take it," said Carpenter.

"Don't be a sucker. Rose can afford it. You saw the way she lives. She probably spends that much in a week for parking tickets."

Abe picked the bill up, smelled it, and slipped it into his wallet. He took out a few bills and rolled them up.

"I don't know," said Carpenter. "It just doesn't seem right."

"Is this the first time somebody laid any bread on you?"

"Yes, it is."

"Well, relax. You got your cherry broken under nice conditions. This is good clean graft. Rose enjoyed her little trip down here. I thought she was going to pee in her pants when that mutt put you on the roof. You know, it was funny from inside the car," said Abe, laughing.

"It wasn't so great on top of the car. Thor damned near got a piece of my ass."

"Here's a twenty and a five." Abe slipped the tube of money into Carpenter's shirt pocket, and started the engine. A teenage girl in a red sweater and short shorts walked past as they pulled out into the street. She was working a hula-hoop on her trim hips with smooth jerks of her lower body. When she saw them admiring her performance, she turned and bumped her pelvis in their direction several times, and shot the finger to them. The hoop continued to swing as if it was a part of her body. The girl couldn't have been more than fifteen. Abe shook his head and grinned. He let the clutch fly out and sprayed gravel as he pulled into heavy traffic.

"That cash should help ease your hurt pride. By the way, we don't pay for torn or worn-out uniforms. Just get the desk sergeant to type up a requisition for a new pair. The tailor can make you up a new pair in a few days. Your wife may be able to fix that pair up. Good enough for night work, anyway."

Abe drove the car rapidly through heavy traffic and slammed on the brakes in front of Ruark's Bar.

"Here you are, Fritz, back on your post safe and sound. Nice riding with you. See you later."

10

THE OLD DESK SERGEANT BEAT THE SIDE OF THE DAIS.

"All right, gentlemen. I don't have to read the roster to see who is absent today. I see all your bright smiling faces. I should say, I see some of your bright smiling faces. The ones on this shift who required a shot from Doc Wolf don't look quite as happy as the others. Doc Wolf called a few minutes ago and told me that so far ten men in the station have turned up with the clap. Don't you guys think you're trying too hard in this public relations thing?"

The sound of a drunk vomiting in the booking room interrupted him. Rolling his eyes up, the old sergeant crossed himself, strode to the connecting door and jerked it open. Vomiting noises filled the roll-call room, as the odor came in the open door and settled around the officers in ranks. The old sergeant crossed his arms over his huge belly and smiled pleasantly to a motorcycle officer standing just inside the booking room.

"Tom, what the fuck you got against me?" the old sergeant said. Tom shrugged and said nothing.

The old sergeant looked at the prisoner with disgust. Another motorman was booking him. "I trust you gentlemen will have the janitor clean this fucking mess up," the old sergeant said. He slammed the booking-room door. The prisoner was having dry heaves and making a lot of noise. He returned to the dais, and continued as though nothing had happened.

"I ain't giving you people hell, you understand. It's hard to turn down all that free cooze when you're a young man. What's hard for me to grasp is how so many could be infected by one little split-tail. Some of you people had to go four miles off your post to tap this girl. Policing has changed. When I was out on the street, nobody came on another man's post unless it was to help out your fellow officer."

He paused, held his chest with both hands and belched. Tossing a couple of Tums into his mouth, he continued.

"The Captain got a call from the lady down at Windy Brae today. You know who I mean. The old gal that's in charge of the student nurses' quarters at Sheppard-Pratt Hospital. Seems like there's a regular parade of police cars dropping off the student nurses, or picking them up right at the dormitory. Now, she don't object to this. She likes the idea of you fine boys in blue giving the girls a ride in from town, especially after dark. We all know how dark the hospital grounds are. She just don't think it's right for uniformed cops to be hugging and kissing those hot little southern belles right at the front door of the place, in front of God and everybody. What the hell's the matter with you guys? Don't you know enough to pull off the road and get that bullshit over with before you get the girls home?"

"But Sarge, parting is such sweet sorrow," McGee said from the ranks.

"Bullshit, Sean, you know you're not out there to date girls all the time. Save a little time for police work, or that old gal is going to start taking tag numbers of the police cars and sending letters of complaint to the nervous folks at headquarters. I don't have to tell you what would happen if those chaps got a hold of this. They'd rather have a cop get caught stealing money than pussy any day. They'd transfer your Don Juan asses so far out in the boondocks your breath would smell like cordwood."

He paused, sniffed the foul air, and lit a cigar.

"Christ, sometimes I feel like an old man running a home for delinquent boys, what with all these complaints I've been getting about your love escapades."

He paused, puffed his cigar, and continued. "We had a rape reported at number 29 Bellona Avenue at 0430 hours. The suspect entered through the unlocked bedroom window of Marie Lucklow, the victim. Marie's a white female, age twelve. Her parents were asleep in a bedroom located in a different wing of the house. She woke up when he crawled in bed with her. Suspect held a nickel-plated handgun to her head and threatened to shoot her. He broke her nose with the gun barrel and pulled hands full of hair from her head. After forcing her to go down on him, he raped her, and bit her around the neck and shoulders. When he finished he shoved the gun barrel up inside of her. She passed out from the pain and came to as the rapist was leaving through the window. The family dog went after him as he stepped out on the lawn. He killed the dog, a cocker spaniel, with a blow to its head. Doctors at University Hospital were able to save Marie, but she lost a lot of blood from the cuts inside of her and her left nipple was bitten clean off her breast.

"Detectives talked to her at the hospital and could only get a poor description of the rapist. White male, late twenties, dressed in dark clothing. He was last seen running south on Bellona. Our plainclothes guys reported that Baltimore City Detectives handled a rape case just over the city line ten days ago that had an exact M.O. A fourteen-year-old girl raped in her bedroom in the wee hours and the rapist bit her nipple right off. We got a repeater here. This bastard needs gelding and hanging bad. That's it. Goodnight, gentlemen."

Sergeant Harper glared at his men with cold eyes.

"Any of you people got anything on your mind? No? Hit the bricks then. Don't forget your school details."

Carpenter got to his school detail at Allegheny and Central a few minutes early. A woman dressed in a blue turtleneck sweater and a blue skirt walked out of the door, smiled and waved to him. Sharon King had been waiting for him. He stepped off the sidewalk to let her pass. She ran to her convertible, put the top down, and jogged back to Carpenter. Her breasts were heaving from exertion as she stopped near him. He caught the scent of her perfume as she stood there looking at him.

"Hi, Fred. Have you been thinking about me a little?"

"Just a little bit."

"Good. That's encouraging. I wore a sweater today for you."

"For me?"

"Yes. I wanted you to see what nice breasts I have." She took a deep breath and turned to the side. "Are you a breast or a thigh man?"

"I always prefer the drumstick, then the wings."

She laughed and put her hand on his arm. "Oh, you have a sense of humor. I was beginning to wonder about that. Do you like dirty jokes?"

"I can never remember them."

"Neither can I. I love to talk dirty when I'm making love. It makes it so much more exciting. You'll see."

"I doubt it."

"Oh, don't say that. I've made my mind up already. I'd like you to give me a baby."

The back of her hand grazed his penis. It couldn't have been an accident.

"I'm sure your husband would appreciate that."

"He'd never know. It wouldn't matter. I told you that all he's interested in is money. He wants me to be happy. Don't be so tense. I don't want to have a long, sordid affair. I've got more brains than that. We both have too much to lose."

"Just a short, sordid affair would be okay, though."

"Of course. Look at it this way. When you are sixty years old, you can have fond memories of me. You can tell yourself that you made a lady happy. A brief fling or whatever you want to call it. You always regret missed opportunities, don't you, Fred? I'm sure that you have regretted not screwing some of the girls that were available to you. I'm available. I'll be around. Look for a blue Cadillac."

"Don't you drive that little red thing all the time?"

"Silly. How can you do it in a sportscar? I can just picture us. I suppose it can be done by very small people, but neither one of us is what you would call petite. Here." She handed him a scrap of paper. "This is my phone number. Call me when you get the urge. I'm always home."

"Won't the principal give you hell for being out here talking to me?"

"No. A teacher is always assigned to check the police on the corner. If you don't show up, it's my job to help the children to cross the street. It's also my job to inform the principal if you are late or don't come for your detail. I volunteered for the job. It gave me a chance to meet you."

"So you're the principal's spy."

"Yes, I suppose you could put it that way."

"I wonder what he'd say if he found out that his spy, Mrs. Sharon King, is trying to fuck the cop on the crossing detail?"

"Oh, I love to hear you talk like that. Say it again."

The bell rang. Seconds later, the flood of children

burst out of the door. They were all around Carpenter, laughing and jabbering as only small children can.

Carpenter looked the crowd of upturned faces over carefully.

"If you are looking for Jimmy Cox, the foot stomper, he's out with the measles."

"Oh, thank you, Mrs. King."

"Please rest assured that he will be reprimanded by the principal when he recovers, officer. We do not tolerate harassment of our police. If he ever acts up again, please inform the principal. I assure you he will be dealt with severely."

Carpenter shoved his hat back and laughed. "How quickly you slip on the righteous armor of the schoolmarm, Mrs. King."

Carpenter gave the children safe passage across the street. When he turned, Sharon King was opening the door to re-enter the school.

Carpenter was walking south on Washington, watching all the pretty girls go by. There were a lot of them, all shapes and sizes. He was admiring the legs of an exceptional blonde who ran past to catch the streetcar when a fat lady ran past him on the opposite side of the street. She shouted to the blonde.

"Hold that streetcar! Hold that streetcar!"

She shouldn't have bothered to yell. She beat the blonde to the car by three steps and ran alongside the moving vehicle, beating on the front door with her hand. The streetcar stopped and both women got on. The car turned the corner at Chesapeake Avenue, sparks crackling from the hot overhead wire that furnished its power.

"Hey! Stop that car, for Christ's sake! Stop that fucking streetcar!"

A fat man ran up behind Carpenter, winded.

"Oh, shit, she got away! That fat broad! She just hung a bad check on me for forty dollars. I recognized her when the checkout girl brought the check for me to okay. She fucked me for a bad check two weeks ago. You guys sent one of those composite pictures of her to the stores a few days ago. I'm Alan Brock, the manager at the Acme."

Carpenter ran out in front of a man in a pickup truck and threw up his arms. The pickup slid to a stop, inches short of striking him.

"What the hell's the matter with you, man? I could have killed you!" the driver screamed.

Carpenter opened the passenger's door and got in.

"We need your truck. Come on, Brock, get the lead out of your ass or we'll leave you. Take a left here on Chesapeake; we've got to stop that streetcar. There's a woman on it who just passed a forged check to this man."

The driver of the pickup sat and looked at Carpenter and Brock with his mouth open, as he toyed with his handlebar mustache. He was bald-headed and sun-tanned, wearing starched bib overalls and a red bandana around his neck. Brock became enraged.

"Goddamn it, you heard this cop! Get this fucking thing moving! That cunt just robbed me!"

"Why didn't you say so? I saw that streetcar just as he turned. Don't worry, I'll suck him up my exhaust pipe."

He let the clutch fly out. The truck lurched forward and stalled. He turned the key to start the engine. Click.

"I forgot. The battery's dead."

Brock was a wild man. "You son-of-a-bitch, you let her get away! I ought to beat the shit out of you!"

"You can't talk to me like that! I don't have to take that from you!" He glanced at Carpenter. "Do I, officer? Get out of my truck!"

"Take it easy, mister, he's a little upset. Come on, Brock, we'll give him a shove. We can still catch her."

They pushed the truck to the corner and down the hill at Chesapeake. The truck gained momentum. Halfway down the hill the driver threw it into second and slowed as the engine caught, backfired, and kicked over. They got in. The driver let the clutch out easy and they were on their way. The streetcar was out of sight. Picking up speed, they made a right turn on York Road just as the light changed to red. Two blocks south, the streetcar was stopped in heavy traffic. The driver took to the sidewalk, blowing his horn, scattering pedestrians. He was laughing with glee, bumping on and off the sidewalk, passing the stalled line of traffic on the right.

Two men carrying a piece of plate glass walked out of a store, intent on placing their precious burden in their truck, parked at the curb. The pickup was almost on them. The driver blasted his horn at them. The men looked up, dropped the glass, and jumped for their lives. The heavy glass crashed into a thousand pieces on the sidewalk. Carpenter looked back at them through the rear window. Both men were shaking their fists, cursing at the truck.

The traffic started to move as the driver bullied his way into the line. There were many protesting blasts of horns. They were in the clear. The streetcar was gaining speed, but the pickup pulled abreast of it near Towson State Teachers' College, as it stopped to pick up two old ladies. Carpenter jumped out of the truck and got on the streetcar. The fat woman was not in sight as he glanced around the car. Slowly he walked down the aisle, searching carefully. She was crouched on the floor between two seats on her knees, her fat rump jutting up into the air.

"You'd better get up from there, ma'am. You might tear your nylons," Carpenter said.

She looked up and batted her false eyelashes at him. "I'm looking for my earring. I dropped it on the floor.

Could you help me, please?" she said, in a strange, low-pitched voice.

"You've got both your earrings on, lady."

Brock was beside Carpenter. "That's her. Arrest that bitch. She's got me for two different bad checks."

"I'll have to ask you to come with me, ma'am," Carpenter said politely.

"I will do no such thing, young man," she said indignantly. "I haven't the vaguest idea what this—this—this fool is talking about."

"You don't understand, lady. You are under arrest. You've got to come with me," he said flatly.

The woman jumped to her feet and caught Carpenter with a straight left jab in the mouth, snapping his head back. He saw the knee moving at him just in time. The woman's knee caught him in the thigh as he turned to avoid it, with enough force to slam him back on an empty seat. She was on him in an instant, her hands around his throat, cutting off his wind. Kneeling on his chest, she shook him like a terrier shakes a rat.

"Let go of him, you bitch!" Brock said, as he grabbed her shoulder and tried to pull her off. She shook him free and stuck to Carpenter like a leech. Her face was twisted into a bestial snarl. Carpenter's ears were starting to buzz from lack of oxygen.

Brock got a handful of her hair and pulled. The wig came away in his hand. Carpenter looked into the face of a crew-cut man with false eyelashes.

"She's a man! She's a man! Look out, it's a man! She's killing this cop! Help us!" Brock screamed.

Carpenter reached for the transvestite's crotch, grabbed hard and twisted with all his strength. The man screamed like a wounded animal. He released Carpenter's throat and reached for the offending hand. Carpenter held on, as he gulped great breaths of air into his lungs and scrambled to his feet. Carpenter released him and ducked a roundhouse right aimed at his head. Rolling under the punch, Carpenter struck him in the Adam's apple with the back of his hand. Hands clutching his throat, he looked at Carpenter in horror, making hicking sounds, trying to suck air into his lungs. He fell to his knees.

Carpenter cuffed his prisoner's hands behind his back. Dragging him down the aisle by the ankles caused his dress to slide up, showing nylon stockings and black lace panties to shocked passengers. At the front door, Carpenter picked him up and slung him over his shoulder. He was a heavy load. Air whooshed out of his mouth when Carpenter dropped him on the grass beside the road. Muttering curses, he looked up at the two old ladies still waiting to get on the streetcar. The streetcar operator had not moved from his seat. Passsengers crowded at the windows cheered when Brock replaced the man's wig and adjusted it carefully.

Carpenter looked up at the operator. "It's okay, you can go now."

The streetcar operator just looked at Carpenter.

"Come on, mack, get moving. You've got traffic backed up clear to Towson."

The operator closed the door and the streetcar moved rapidly away. A motorcycle man snaked his way through the traffic.

"Hi, there, buddy. I wondered what was holding up things. Need a car to take your friend in?"

"Yeah, radio for help. I'm not going to walk all the way back to the station with this fruitcake."

A district car arrived in response to the traffic officer's call for assistance.

When Carpenter got back to the station with Brock and his prisoner Sergeant Goulek was reading a beat up *Readers' Digest* at his desk. He looked at the group that entered his office.

"Yes, ma'am, can I help you?" he said, as they approached.

"This is the prisoner that the traffic man radioed in about, Sarge," Carpenter said.

"Oh, I see. What's the cuffs for, Carpenter?"

"This is a man. He wrote a forged check and tried to cash it at the Acme store. Mr. Brock chased him out of the store and found me. We grabbed him hiding under the seat of a streetcar."

Goulek's eyes widened. "A man? No shit? You can't tell the girls from the boys anymore. Good work. He give you any trouble?"

"Some," Carpenter nodded. "He didn't want to come with us."

"Yeah, I see some bruises on your neck, kid. Did this punk do that to you?"

"Yeah, he grabbed me around the neck. He kind of took me by surprise." Carpenter shrugged. "I thought he was just a fat lady."

"Take the cuffs off this misguided son of a bitch," said Goulek. "I want to docket and print him." The prisoner gave him a hard look. "Don't you give me those mean looks, you weird bastard. I don't like touching you any more than you want to touch me. You are one lucky, fat faggot. I know some cops that would have shot your fat guts full of holes for trying to choke them."

The man began to cry. He was a pitiful, grotesque figure with mascara running down his face.

"Come on, now, stop all that shit," said Goulek. "We ain't going to hurt you, you poor bastard."

Goulek was frisking the prisoner. As his hands passed over the padded bra, he paused, dipped into the top of the dress and pulled out a small purse.

"Let's put the contents of your purse on the counter."

He emptied the purse on the counter in front of his desk. "Well, now, at least you ain't armed with nothing but eye makeup and lipstick. Let's see this driver's license. This your right address?" He handed the sobbing man a paper towel. Blowing his nose, the man nodded.

"There you go, that's all we need. I'm not going to print you here. Let the B of I do it. They got to take a picture of you anyhow. Listen, I'm going to put you in the cellblock back there. Only one other man's in there. He's drunk as a lord. You ain't going to try anything with him, are you?"

The man dabbed at his eyes with the paper towel and drew himself up. He squared his shoulders.

"I'll have you know that I am not a homosexual. I am a transvestite."

"Okay, okay, don't get your ass up in the air," Goulek said, reaching in his desk for a cell-block key. "We don't get one of you—ah—people every day, you know. When's the last time you had anything to eat?"

"This morning."

"I'll send out for some food for you and your drunk cellmate."

"Thank you, Sergeant. Have you got a cigarette, Officer?" He touched Carpenter on the elbow and blinked his swollen eyes. "I'm out and don't have any money of my own to get more."

Carpenter started to offer a cigarette, shrugged, and tossed him the whole pack. "Keep them. I've got a carton out in my car."

"Thanks. Look, I'm really sorry about your neck. I just wanted to get away."

"Don't worry about it. See you in court."

Brock walked out on the street with Carpenter.

"You got one hell of a tough job. I couldn't do it for one day."

"Oh, I don't know," said Carpenter. He grinned and cocked his hat to the side of his head. "It kind of grows on you."

"Well, to each his own. We can't all be grocery

clerks, can we? I haven't had that much excitement in the eight years I've worked in the grocery business. See you, Officer Carpenter. Take care of yourself."

"You take care, too," Carpenter said, smiling.

11

A POLICE CRUISER PULLED UP TO THE CURB AND stopped. Officer Sean McGee was working by himself.

"Hi, Fritz, get in. I'll drop you off down in the business district, if you want. I heard the motorcycle man call for a car for you down at Towson State. Amount to much?"

Carpenter got in and slammed the door. McGee started to pull away from the curb and jammed on the brakes. A well-built girl in a white knit dress was getting into a Hudson parked across the street. She flashed a lot of thigh as she slid behind the wheel and stuck her tongue out when she saw them looking. McGee sighed and pulled into the flow of traffic. Carpenter laughed and lit a Camel.

"I busted a fag for passing forged checks at the Acme. The manager and me took him off the streetcar."

"You got to watch those sweet guys. Some of them will fight."

"I know. I got a lesson today in streetfighting from a fat queen."

"Yeah, now that you mention it, you do have a fat lip. Are you cut inside your mouth?"

"Just a little bit," he said, touching his lip gingerly

with his tongue.

"Make out a special report on it later and get it in your record. You might have trouble later on and need a report to back you up. Hell, listen to me, I'm starting to sound like a lieutenant."

"I'm okay. If it bothers me in a few days I'll make out a report. Where's your partner?"

"Beau? The Sergeant gave him off three days to go home to Georgia for his sister's wedding. If the local speeders and drag racers find out he's out of town, they'll throw a party."

"Does he write a lot of tickets?"

"I'm not downing him, you understand, but he is really hung up on traffic," McGee said, flicking the ash from his Havana into the ashtray. "That's how he wastes his time between calls, unless I put my foot down. He's a real headhunter; wrote fifty tickets last month."

"How do waste your time, McGee?"

"I've got my own little quirk. I make a real effort to catch lovers humping. It makes my day when I can catch them in the saddle copulating, as they say it out in the Valley. They all react differently. Some of them want to fight, some cry, some run away. Some of them are even blasé about being caught in the act. I consider it sport, a challenge to find them and catch them in the act."

A priest in a Lincoln ran the red light a half block ahead. As the clergyman passed, McGee honked his horn and smiled.

"Probably on the way to give the last rites to some poor soul."

"Sure," Carpenter said. "You know, some people would consider your little quirk voyeurism, or even invasion of privacy."

"Could be. At any rate, don't knock it until you try it. It beats writing speeding tickets. You meet all kinds of people that way. You get a liberal education in the local sexual customs."

He pulled to the curb and parked in a prohibited zone. Flicking his Zippo, he relit his cold cigar, and grinned. "It's very enlightening to learn who is fucking who, or is it whom? Some of the local chaps have downright bizarre habits. It seems like most of the really pompous pillars of the community are very kinky. The ones that I catch are, anyway. Would you believe that one of the local politicians prefers little boys?"

"Nothing would surprise me about ying-yang," Carpenter said.

McGee turned the radio down and laughed. "Another of our elected officials enjoys being whipped. He carries his whip and rope in his car, likes to be tied naked to a tree out Loch Raven, and have a hustler whip his fat ass."

"You heard about the guy that wanted his lover, the chicken, back?" Carpenter nodded. "The desk sergeant was not putting you guys on about that," said McGee, blowing a perfect smoke ring. "It happened. I'm always catching the same two Goucher girls naked, bumping cunts in a parked car, parked in the same spot on Dulaney Valley Road. I asked them why they didn't try to find a more secluded spot. They laughed and said that half the thrill was the chance of being caught in the act.

"Just last night, I was checking out Lake Roland for parkers right after dark. I noticed about fifteen parked cars in the parking area, all locked up and nobody around. Most of the fishermen are gone by dark, so I cruised all over the park and playground. Nothing. I was just about ready to give up when I smelled woodsmoke. I got out and traced it to a large stand of pine trees. The wind had just shifted or I would never have noticed it. The trees are planted so close together you can't even walk between them."

"What did you do?" asked Carpenter.

"I circled around the other side of the trees, a good city block away, and found a freshly cut path. Somebody had taken an ax and trimmed off all the branches near the ground, so you could crawl through. I crawled about a hundred seventy-five or two hundred feet along this twisting little path and found them in a good-sized clearing in the center of the trees. There were about twenty couples laying around on blankets. Some of them were balls naked, humping in front of each other like farm animals."

"Holy mackerel, a circus," Carpenter said.

"Yeah, it was a wondrous sight to behold, Fritz. They had a good-sized fire built in the center. Three naked girls were roasting marshmallows and hot dogs on sticks. They had four tubs full of iced beer and pop wine. There were so many of them smoking pot that I got high just standing there smelling it. A portable was turned up just loud enough for all the party people to hear. Some of them were just laying around drinking beer, talking and laughing. The talking and laughing stopped like someone threw a switch. A little skinny guy walked up to me without a stitch on and offered me a beer and a piece of chicken. He said they were all students from Towson State. They called themselves the Nature and Pleasure Club. Initiation fees were fifty dollars to join and one hundred a year after that. They meet once a month with their girlfriends and booze it up and lay around grooving."

"The dues are a little high," Carpenter said.

"Yeah, but look what you get back: booze, food and congenial screwing companions. Anyhow, the skinny guy said they were into nudism a little and were trying some out in the open fucking. He said they didn't tolerate any hard drugs, but they all smoke pot and that pot was what had brought them together as a group in the first place, two years ago. Four of the girls had been knocked up and their boyfriends married them in the past year. What did he call it? Oh, yeah... a new experience in social interaction. He was afraid I was there to lock them up."

"What did you do?"

"I drank my beer, ate my chicken, and left. Man, I really wanted to stay. Makes me wonder if I dropped out of college too soon."

"What college?" Carpenter asked.

"University of Maryland. I wanted Towson State because so many of my friends decided on it. My father wouldn't hear of it. He said I'd get a better education at Maryland. He might have been right about that, I don't know. One thing is for sure though. They didn't have any neat social groups like my friends I found, out at Lake Roland."

The radio interrupted him. "Car 21, go to 8131 Loch Raven Boulevard. Boys stealing hub caps."

"10-4 Headquarters. See you, Fritz; got to go."

Carpenter got out and slammed the door. He stopped a tractor-trailer loaded with pigs to let McGee into the traffic flow. McGee burned rubber getting away. Carpenter resumed walking his beat.

A tall, husky youth with a greasy pompadour, black leather jacket, and boots was leaning against the wall of a shoestore on the corner of an alley. He was dangling an unlit cigarette from his bottom lip, trying hard to appear nonchalant. When Carpenter was about twelve feet from the alley, the boy turned toward the alley and placed his two little fingers in his mouth. After a single shrill whistle, he turned to face Carpenter with a smirk.

Carpenter got to the alley in time to see a group of men run around the corner at the other end of the alley. Without looking at the youth, he turned into the alley. About halfway down the alley, he noticed a single green die laying on the ground near the wall of the building. He continued walking. Another lookout was leaning against the wall at the opposite end of the alley and could have been the first lookout's twin. He had the same smirk and leather jacket. The crap shooters were out of sight when Carpenter reached him.

"You looking for somebody, cop?"

"Should I be?"

"I don't think you're going to find it, whatever it is."

Carpenter passed him without answering. He walked around the block, looking for a way to reach the roof of the row of buildings. He found what he was looking for near the corner, a telephone pole three feet from the building that was out of the sight of both lookouts. Using a convenient garbage can to step up on, he began his climb up the pole. It was easy to reach the first metal cleats. He was up the pole and on the roof in less than a minute. The places of business were separated by firewalls. Crossing the flat roof at a fast trot, he jumped the low walls dividing the roof into large rectangles.

Slowing to a walk, he dropped on hands and knees, and crawled the last ten feet to the edge of the roof at the alley. Looking cautiously over the side, he saw the craps players were already returning to play, thirty feet below him. Another telephone pole rose from the concrete alley twelve feet from the play area. Ten of them were huddled over an old army blanket. The green dice rolled across the threadbare blanket and rapped the concrete block wall.

"I'll bet twenty dollars," one of them yelled.

"Shoot, shitbird, you're covered," another one yelled.

Side bets fell in little green piles on the blanket.

"Six, the point is six," said a fat man with a beard.

"Come on, baby, two strings of rabbit shit! Be there! Do it!" pleaded the shooter.

Carpenter climbed quietly down the pole. He had his feet on the concrete. No one even looked up from the spinning cubes. He approached to within six feet of them. As far as they were concerned, he could have been a mile away. The shooter was still looking for a six. He was pleading with the dice.

"Come on, you sweet little green cubes, come on, motherfuckers, give me a six one time."

Carpenter blew his whistle into the nearest man's ear. There was panic in the alley. The players crashed into one another in the mad scramble to escape. The man in the lead stepped down on an old wine bottle and fell in a tangle of arms and legs. The nearest runners jumped over him like hunted deer. The last two fellows were not good high-hurdle runners. They both tripped and fell over their friend as he was scrambling to his feet. They were up in a second, looking over their shoulders in blind panic.

Carpenter ran toward them a few feet and stopped. They disappeared around the corner on to York Road. Carpenter walked back to the blanket and picked up eighty dollars in cash. He folded the blanket neatly and left it laying in the alley, put the green dice in the exact center of the blanket, and walked down the alley.

The talkative lookout was watching from his post. Carpenter made a show of counting the money and putting it in his pocket. He walked down the alley to the sullen youth.

"You were wrong. I found what I was looking for. Got any idea who it belongs to?" Carpenter said, grinning.

The talkative one didn't answer. He was cleaning his fingernails with a small pocket knife.

"Thanks for your help, young fellow. I couldn't have done it without you."

The street was full of people. Carpenter walked north on York Road and watched them hurrying by.

He walked into the outer lobby of the movie. An old lady with red hair was selling tickets to three teenage boys with acne.

"Go right in, Officer. Gilbert will be glad to see you."

A ruddy faced old man with a pot belly was sitting on a stool taking tickets. His face lit up when he saw Carpenter, and shook hands with him like an old friend.

"Good evening, Officer, it's a pleasure to see you. Gilbert Smithers is the name. I retired from the department twenty-five years ago. Never thought I'd wind up taking tickets in this old place. I used to come in here when I walked foot duty in Towson. We worked twelve-hour shifts then, sixteen on the change-over. Many's the night I'd steal a little shuteye in the manager's office. I had a key, you know. I didn't get your name, sir."

"Carpenter."

"Oh, yeah. You chopped down those two heist men awhile ago down at Ruark's place. Good riddance. Did that one in the hospital make it?"

"Yes sir."

"Too bad. Here son, take this key to the place," he said, removing one from a large key ring. "Be glad to have you use the office whenever we're out of here."

Carpenter took the key and thanked him. He watched the movie for about an hour. It was getting near the end of his shift when he walked outside.

Carpenter crossed the street and walked west on Pennsylvania Avenue. A blue Cadillac sedan was parked in violation by a fireplug. Sharon King was behind the wheel. The scent of her perfume drifted out the car window as he leaned over to greet her.

"Where have you been, Fred? I've been looking for you for an hour," she said, tapping her fingernails on the horn.

"I've been around."

"Come on, get in."

"It's late. It's ten-twenty," he said, looking at his watch.

"Do you want to wait 'til you get off to meet me, or would you like a quickie right now?"

"What do you prefer?" He grinned and shove his hat back.

Her dress buttoned all the way down the front. She looked at his face and began to unbutton her dress.

"Get in. You drive. Take me someplace close by."

Carpenter got in the car. Turning the powerful motor over, he pulled away from the curb, drove one half block and turned right into an alley. Driving one hundred feet he took a hard left and went perhaps one hundred fifty feet more. They were on a small private parking lot, behind an office building. The old mulberry trees around the lot had not been pruned for years. A wild tangle of trees around the border of the lot closed out most of the street lights. There were no other cars on the lot.

He turned the engine off and looked at Sharon. Her dress was completely open. She was naked under her dress as she climbed over into the back seat. Her pale blond hair looked like silver in the half light. She was on her back, one arm in back of her head, with her legs open. One hand caressed the pale blond bush between her legs.

"Come on, hurry up. I'm warming it up for you."

Carpenter climbed over the seat into the back. Sitting beside her on the edge of the seat, he put his hands on her breasts. Moaning deep in her throat, she fought the zipper to open his fly. He dropped his gunbelt to the floor. She was frantic to get his pants down.

"Oh, look at it! Just look! It's throbbing! Come on, hurry! Give it to me!"

He put his hands between her legs. She was wet and

ready. He knelt over her, between her raised legs, as she guided him in with a tilt of her hips and two expert fingers.

"Fuck me! Fuck me! Come. Don't hold back. That's it. Ah . . . ah!"

She was like liquid fire inside. The frenzy was on them both. He rode her like a wild horse. The Cadillac rocked on its supple springs. It was over quickly. She was kissing his jaw as she held him prisoner with her arms and legs.

"Oh, thank you, thank you. It's been so long."

She started to laugh in his ear. He sat up, angry.

"What's so funny?"

She was laughing out loud, her bare breasts jumping up and down.

"You—you—you forgot to take your hat off. I just noticed."

"There didn't seem to be enough time. You said you wanted a quickie." He smiled and pulled his hat lower over his face.

"I feel so good now," she said, stretching like a cat. "I didn't realize what I'd been missing. Thank you, Fred," she said, handing him a clean towel from under the front seat.

She slipped her dress on as he cleaned himself and adjusted his clothing. He got out and slammed the door as she climbed over the seat.

"It's ten thirty-five. I've got to get back to the station. I've got to leave a note for the day-shift desk sergeant. You know how to get out of here, don't you?"

"I should. This is my dentist's parking lot. You never kissed me, did you?"

"Sorry. I got hit in the mouth today. It's kind of sore."

"Next time. Good night, Officer. You do excellent work."

"We aim to please the public, ma'am."

He watched the big taillights disappear around the corner. A mockingbird was singing in the mulberry trees.

12

IT WAS A WEEK LATER. THE OLD DESK SERGEANT WAS beginning roll call.

"Okay, you guys, settle down. Let's keep it to a roar. Goddamn it, shut up! I ain't got all afternoon to be screwing around here. I got to get home and get my gear together. I'm going shad fishing tonight. The hickories are running in the Susquehanna and I feel lucky.

"We got a bad news teletype here from the City Police Department. A cop got shot and killed down there last night about ten-thirty. It happened near the old shot tower in sight of police headquarters. Officer Barney A. Smith was on foot patrol in the area and noticed this fruitcake walking around yelling at everybody that he wanted to take them down to the foot of Broadway and baptize them in the harbor. Witnesses saw the whole thing. Officer Smith walked up to this guy, who was dressed in sheets, like an Arab, and asked him who he was. The nut screamed that he was John the Baptist, and whipped out an old forty-five. The cop never had a chance. The son-of-a-bitch shot him down, then stood over him, and emptied the gun into him. Now, it just so happened that there were a lot of street people around, and they loved this young cop. A bunch of them rushed this freak and beat him to the ground. A couple of hustlers worked his head and face over with spike-heeled shoes and a newspaper boy stabbed him with a broken broom handle."

Every policeman in the room cheered.

"Yeah, I feel that way too, men. By the time the cops got there to help their buddy, he was dead. The fruitcake is in intensive care at City Hospital. He ain't expected to live. What a fucking waste. Makes you sorry you are a member of the human race."

A hissing noise came from the booking room. The coffee pot was boiling over. The desk sergeant ignored it.

"We started a collection for Officer Smith's family. He left a wife and three young kids. Funeral arrangements will be announced later. Guess they'll give him an inspector's funeral. You want to contribute to widow's fund, see the Captain before he goes home.

"I got some good news today from Doc Wolf. It seems like the epidemic of—ah—social disease that was sweeping the ranks here has been arrested. No new cases have turned up in the last few days. I was beginning to think that every man in the station had rapped this little floozie and had the clap."

"Ah, about that address of hers," McGee began.

"Fuck off, Sean. I got a lot of ground to cover yet."

The hissing noise in the booking room was becoming a steady roar. A crash of metal and loud curses, then silence. The old desk sergeant threw his notes down on the dais and stalked to the door. A cloud of steam and the odor of coffee drifted into the roll-call room. The janitor was inside mopping up the spilled coffee, muttering to himself.

"I burned my hand," he said lamely to the group of police looking in at him.

The old desk sergeant sighed, shut the door, and

returned to the dais.

"We had another rape reported last night. Same M.O. as that Bellona Avenue job. At 0320 hours today the Kaskaw residence on Lake Avenue was entered through an unlocked bedroom window. Pam Kaskaw, age fifteen, woke up with a man's hand over her mouth. He showed her a handgun, then raped her. He forced her to go down on him, then jammed the gun up inside her. Her mother came in the room to check on all the noise, and was shot twice in the chest by him. Both Pam and her mother are at Memorial Hospital in intensive care. Pam will make it, but her mother is in critical condition. No direction of escape known. Victim's father heard the shots. By the time he got to her bedroom, the rapist was long gone. Like the other rape, Pam had her left nipple bit off."

The old desk sergeant slammed the top of the dais with his fist. He closed his eyes and muttered something to himself.

"I got no description to give you. Detectives are standing by at the hospital waiting to talk to them. We need a break on this animal, men. I'm afraid he's here to stay until we take him down. Goodnight, gentlemen. I'm gonna have a big drink and go shad fishing."

Carpenter was five minutes early for his school detail at Allegheny and Central. Sharon King was putting the top down on her car. She looked up and saw him, waved, and smiled. She ran to him and looked him up and down with chicory-flower blue eyes. She blinked away tears in her eyes.

"What's the matter with you?" Carpenter said.

"Nothing."

"Bullshit. What are the tears for?"

"I'll tell you later on tonight."

"Tell me now."

"It will keep 'til later. I've got some good news and some bad news. I don't want to tell you now because I'll probably cry, and I have to go back inside. I wouldn't want the principal to get any ideas."

"Sure."

"Ye Gods, don't look so forlorn. It's nothing to concern you, Fred. Are you tired today?"

"No, should I be?"

"I don't know. I am. My legs are killing me. I'm all tender down there. That was quite a session last night. I've never had it like that before," she said, putting her hand on his arm. "You are some kind of great hunk of a screwing machine. Oh, I've got to stop talking about it. I could come, just thinking about it."

"You're a very sensuous lady, Sharon," he said, stepping away from her.

"I know. I've always been that way. Lately, when I'm sitting at my desk marking papers in the afternoon, my mind wanders to you. I get so excited I could scream. Then I cross my legs and kind of rub my thighs together and I come like mad. Does my fantasied lovemaking shock you?"

"Not as much as it excites me. Get away from me now, or I won't be in any condition to help the kids cross the street," he said, grinning.

Sharon King went back inside the building before the bell rang. The children came out in a group and crossed the street together. Carpenter was about to walk back to the business district when a young boy burst out of the door and ran toward the corner. Carpenter waited for the latecomer. It was the red-headed footstomper, Jimmy Cox.

He wouldn't look at Carpenter as he stood there, digging his toe into the mud next to the sidewalk.

"Mr. Policeman, Mrs. King said I was to tell you I'm sorry for stepping on your foot . . . so, I'm sorry."

"What did you do it for, Jimmy?"

"Aw, just for the hell of it. You ain't mad at me, are you? I won't do it again," he said, hanging his head.

Carpenter put his hand under the boy's chin and gently raised his face.

"No, I'm not mad. I know how it is. It's pretty tough sitting around a classroom all day when it's nice outside. I used to dip girls' braids in the inkwell."

"Hey! Neat! Why did you do that?"

"I don't know. Just for the hell of it, I guess."

"You know what? You're a pretty neat cop. I'd try that myself, but we don't use inkwells anymore. They did that in the old days, right?"

"Yeah, in the old days," he said, grinning at the boy.

"See you, Mr. Policeman." He smiled and waved his hand.

Carpenter was one block away from the school, when the red sportscar pulled over and stopped near him.

"Don't you have any papers to mark today, teacher?"

"Don't be vulgar, Officer. You know how marking papers gets to me. Get in, I want to talk to you."

He walked to the driver's side and leaned on the door. "Bullshit. If one of the old ladies on this street see me get in a car with a woman, they'd call and turn me in, for sure."

"Well, it's better this way, I guess. I can say this better with you a little distance away. First the good news. I'm pregnant."

Carpenter scowled. She looked at him, grinning. "Now get that look off your face. It's not you, it's my husband. I missed my second period about a week ago. I've always been irregular, but never two months in a row. I saw a gynecologist and he's sure. I want this baby, Fred. It's difficult for me to have a baby, for some reason. I've had two miscarriages in three years."

"I thought he treated you like a sister," he said. "Separate bedrooms and all that jazz, remember?"

"I remember. When the mood strikes him, he visits my room. It's not often. He's not a young man."

124

"What's the bad news?"

"The bad news is that I'm not going to see you anymore. The doctor forbids intercourse. He says it could cause me to abort."

A tear slid from her cheek, dropped down, and glistened like a jewel on the silky hair on her arm. He handed her his handkerchief. Laughing harshly, she dabbed at her eyes and clenched the handkerchief in her fist.

"I may have to go to bed for days at a time, but I'm determined to have this baby, and I'll do whatever I've got to do this time. You understand, don't you?"

"I understand, Sharon."

"I'll never forget you, Fred. It's been fun. Kiss me goodbye."

He kissed her awkwardly, leaning through the open car window. She was laughing and crying at the same time.

"You never were much of a kisser, Frederick, but you do have other redeeming qualities."

The car squealed wheels getting away. The resonator in its muffler purred in hollow harmony as she shifted expertly through the gears and was gone.

He was drinking a cup of coffee later in Elmer's place. Three truck drivers sat in a corner, drank their coffee, and enjoyed the free show provided by twenty Goucher girls, who were holding an impromptu jitterbug contest. They played the same tune over and over again on the jukebox, Bill Haley and the Comets' "Rock Around the Clock," and were encouraged by the three waitresses who cheered from behind the counter.

A fat, gray-haired man of about sixty waddled into the place. He saw Carpenter at the end of the counter, and kept patting great beads of sweat from his brow with a handkerchief. Rivers of sweat poured down his flabby cheeks, soaking the quarter-inch gray stubble, as he edged his way close to Carpenter and extended his hand in introduction.

"Name's John Hogg. Mind if I sit here next to you? You got to be Carpenter. I heard all about you from the night waitress here," he said, wheezing through his open mouth. "You got half the girls in Towson hot after you, from what I hear."

"I wouldn't know about that," Carpenter said, pulling his hand away.

"I bet you do. When I was your age I was ready to screw at the drop of a hat. Still go for a little bit of dark meat, if you know what I mean. Colored pussy. It's my weakness. I own just about every house in East Towson that ain't privately owned. Someday, I'll own them all, if this old heart don't give out on me," he croaked, tapping his chest with his thumb.

"I buy them up when they need to sell, cheap, and rent them right back to these coons. I like to deal with them. They treat me like I'm some kind of lord. They know I've got the power to put them out in the street on their black asses for back rent. People ask me if I'm afraid to walk around the colored section at night. Hell, look at this."

He pulled a large roll of cash from each pocket and waved it around Carpenter's face.

"See that. I always carry two, three, four thousand dollars in my pockets. Would I carry that if I was afraid? They know that if I kick the bucket, nobody else would carry their black asses when they fall behind. They'd wind up with no place to go. I'm good to them. Hell, I've carried one young widow over there for nine months now. She's got three little brats and I've never taken a cent for rent since her no-good husband died. All I ever ask from her is a little bit of her black cunt. Want to hear how I got started on black pussy?" he said, leaning close to Carpenter.

"Not really," said Carpenter, as he recoiled from the

odor of decayed teeth.

"Well, I'm going to tell you anyway. I was born in Mississippi on a big cotton farm my father had there. We had a bunch of coons living on the place that worked for us. One of them young, yellow-looking girls used to drive me half crazy with the hots, just walking by me. I was a young boy then, maybe fourteen. My older brothers used to laugh at me and tell me if I wanted her, to get her out behind the barn and take her," he said, coughing into his soiled handkerchief.

"I tried it out once, but she smacked the hell out of me and kicked me where it hurts. I went and got my older brothers, all four of them, and we went to her shack. Her folks were out in the fields working and she was home with the little ones."

Carpenter moved two seats away and ignored him. Hogg leaned over the space between them and with saliva running down his chin, continued. "We pulled the clothes off that wench and my brothers and me raped her right there in her mother's bed. She was a cherry, too, bled a lot, she did. I was last because I was the smallest. I never did forget that. All that smooth, dark flesh and her screaming and pleading. I get randy about it now even, when I think about it. I never got married. That ruined me for white women. Never could get it up for one, all that pale meat. I like it dark. I really like those people. Now don't get me wrong. I like to help them and want to stay friendly with the cops on the beat. Here. Here's fifty dollars," he said, pulling a bill from a roll and tossing it on the counter between them.

"Go on, take it. I got a few things going for me over there. A little moonshine . . . a little numbers. You name it."

"Put it back in your pocket," said Carpenter.

"Come on, I know you need it. You don't make no

real money as a cop. There's others that take it from me. Don't be a fool," he whispered, patting Carpenter on the back and sliding the bill over closer.

Carpenter stood up and grabbed him by the greasy lapels of his old suit.

"Now, you listen to me, Pig, Hog, or whatever the fuck your name is. I don't like your fucking looks, your goddamn story makes me sick, you smell like a pair of dirty socks, and I don't want your fifty dollars. Pick it up and get out of here or I'll beat lumps all over your fat face."

Hogg rolled his eyes in panic. His breath came in labored, wheezing gasps.

"Let me go. I've got a bad heart."

Carpenter released him. He picked up his money and went out the door, fast, without looking back.

Hazel, the waitress, was standing behind the counter near Carpenter.

"I heard the whole thing, Fritz. Somebody finally told that mean old bastard off. He's told that rape story to every waitress that works in here. In fact, he brags about it to everybody he talks to. What kind of man would brag about that?"

"A fat, dirty old man, I guess."

"Well, you made an enemy out of him today."

"A few enemies make life interesting, Hazel. I wouldn't have it any other way."

The Goucher girls were still going strong. One of them had turned the jukebox up. They were unaware of any exchange between Carpenter and Hogg.

Two hours later, Carpenter was walking through the black section. The front door of the old church was open. Inside, the folding chairs had been stacked up in rows along the sides of the single room. Boys were playing a rough game of basketball in the dim light. A middle-aged black man was refereeing the game. He saw Carpenter and gave his whistle to the biggest boy in the group.

"Here, Clarence, take over. Keep them from killing each other while I talk to the Officer. Sir, my name is Reverend William Brown," he said, extending his hand. "I'm the pastor here."

"Carpenter. Glad to meet you, Reverend. Got a pretty good game going, I see."

"Yes, it's good to give these kids a place to get off the street. They won't go to any of the county parks to play because the white boys always start trouble with them. This old building needs a new roof and some better lights, but we make out. I put up the backboards myself. Some of the older members of the congregation think they should play on the school grounds. That's okay, until it gets dark. There's no light out in back of that old school at all, so they started coming here after dark at first, just for someplace to go to other than to go home. Now they come here right after school and stay until about ten." He shrugged and grinned. "Someday we'll get some money to fix up this old place or even build a new church, and use this place as a recreation hall and meeting place."

"Good luck to you, Reverend."

Carpenter was walking along East Chesapeake, when he heard the woman scream. He couldn't locate the source. She screamed again and ran out of an old, rundown house, naked, directly across the street from him. Her three little girls ran beside her, clutching at her naked thighs. Carpenter grabbed her as she tried to run past him.

"What's the matter with you?"

"He's dead! He's dead!" she screamed, rolling her eyes. "Old John Hogg's dead. He were doing it to me and he just up and died. Oh, Lord, Officer, don't lock me up." She was trembling all over, her pear-shaped breasts bobbing around. Three black children were screaming incoherently, punching Carpenter in the thighs, as they formed a protective half circle around their mother.

"I didn't harm him. He's dead!" she screamed.

A crowd of black men and women, neighbors of the frightened woman, was gathering.

Carpenter shoved the hysterical woman toward a middle-aged woman standing nearby with extended arms.

"Here, take this woman and her kids off the street. I'm going inside."

He found Hogg upstairs in the front bedroom, laying on the bed face up. His face was purple, his lips black. He was not breathing. Carpenter pushed his finger into the flabby stubble at the back of the jawbone. There was no pulse. He laid there like a broken doll, staring blindly at the ceiling. His shrunken penis was almost hidden in the patch of gray pubic hair. He still wore his shoes and socks.

Carpenter picked up the man's dirty pants from the floor and checked the pockets. The two bankrolls were still there. He counted the money quickly. The largest roll amounted to $2,850. The smaller roll came to $1,675. Carpenter put the larger roll in his pocket and returned the smaller one to the dead man's pants pocket. He went to the window, raised it, and looked down at the sea of black faces looking up at him.

"Somebody call a radio car for me. Tell them I got a dead man at this address."

No one moved.

"Come, get a move on. This man is dead. We've got to get the coroner here. Call the station for me," he yelled.

"That you up there, Mr. Carpenter? I'll call for you."

Carpenter recognized the Jones boy as he left the crowd, and ran to the phone booth on the corner. He made the call, and came running back to the crowd.

"Come on in, Jones. I'll give you your dime."

"Not me. I ain't goin' in no house with no dead man. You can pay me later."

Sergeant Harper was the first policeman on the scene.

"What have you got?" he said, with reptilian eyes flicking around the living room.

"Fellow by the name of Hogg was banging some black woman and dropped dead. He's upstairs."

"Let's look at him."

They went upstairs to the bedroom. The smell of urine was strong in the room.

Sergeant Harper looked at Hogg's face and grunted.

"I know this guy. He liked to brag about raping colored girls down South," he said, placing a dip of snuff behind his lip. "He owns most of this part of town. He wasn't a very nice guy. You check his pockets yet?"

"No sir," Carpenter lied. He could feel the blood rush to his head as his throat dried.

"Let's see. Here it is," Harper said, pulling the cash out of Hogg's pants pocket.

"You can witness me counting this money, Carpenter. I'll turn it in to the property room today before they close. Let's see." He frowned and began counting the cash rapidly. "Sixteen hundred and seventy-five, right?"

"Right."

Two detectives walked into the room. Both of them were middle-aged, tired-looking men, wearing shabby suits and worn-looking shoes.

"Need any help, Sergeant?" one of them said.

"Yeah. There's a black gal around here somewhere, that lives here. This dude was banging her and went ten-seven on us. It looks like his heart. How about one of you guys finding her and taking a statement? One of you watch the scene here until the coroner gets here to make his fee. I got the money from the stiff's pocket and will be responsible for it. Carpenter and me will go to his rooming house and try to find out where his relatives live. We'll be responsible for the notification. Fair enough?"

"Has he got a wallet, Sarge?" asked the older detective, chewing on a toothpick.

"No wallet. I think I know where he rooms. See you all later. Let's go, Carpenter."

They went outside. The crowd had swollen to perhaps 100 black people. Several patrolmen were attempting to move them, with little success. Sergeant Harper turned over an old water barrel and climbed up on it. A hush fell over the crowd.

"We have a dead man inside and a lot of questions to answer. I thank you all for waiting out here. We'll take you all to the Towson station now for interviews. Please be patient. I'll have transportation here in five minutes. Carpenter, use my radio and call the wagon," he said, turning toward Carpenter.

Several people fell over each other in the mad rush to get away. The street was cleared in half a minute.

"How do you like my crowd dispersal method, Carpenter?" he asked, spitting a wad of tobacco juice at a stray cat.

"Great. They really evaporated."

"It never fails. Nobody wants to get involved with us. Sometimes it works to our advantage."

They were in the cruiser, driving slowly along Virginia Avenue. Harper pulled over to the curb in front of a gray asbestos-shingled house.

"He lives here. Let's see the landlady. Car twenty, ten-seven, nine hundred Virginia Avenue, investigation."

"Ten-four, car twenty."

A small, thin woman of perhaps sixty answered the door. She wore gold-rimmed pince-nez glasses and a black dress. She was very prim and proper.

"May I help you, Sergeant Harper?"

"Yes, you can, Mrs. Wilcox. We have some bad news for you. John Hogg just dropped dead over in the colored section. We were wondering if you knew where his next of kin may live?"

"Oh, my Lord," she said, clutching her throat. "I was just talking to him this morning when he paid his board. How did it happen?"

"His heart just gave out, I guess," Sergeant Harper said.

"I knew he had a bad heart, but he wouldn't go see his doctor after he found out. He wouldn't take medicine, and ate like a horse. Why, do you know he could eat four porkchops and all the vegetables that go with it and half a pan of cornbread? When he finished supper he would go up in his room and drink two sixpacks of National every night. My word, I never saw anyone eat like that one," she said, shaking her head.

"I was going to raise his board to eighteen dollars a week, just to make expenses feeding him. He was such a good man, though. Never bothered any of the other men boarders. He only had one bad habit, he never took a bath. The other men used to complain about his smell at the table. They used to be downright rude to him about it, but he never paid them any mind. He'd just sit there and laugh, belch, and keep on shoving food in his face. Poor soul. I guess no one will miss him much."

"Do you know where his folks live?" said Sergeant Harper, spitting discreetly over his shoulder.

"The only mail he ever got was the *Wall Street Journal* and a Christmas card from his old maid sister every Christmas. He told me that his brothers all died young and she was his only living relative. They lived in some town in Mississippi; can't remember the name. Come in and I'll take you up to his room," she said, throwing the door open wide. "I'll let you look around."

She showed them a ten by ten room on the third floor next to the bathroom. It was furnished with a bed, a straightback chair, and a chest of drawers. The furniture was old, beat-up odds and ends. There were no pictures on the wall. There was not a sign of a book or a piece of loose clothing or anything else to show that the room was occupied. Sergeant Harper pulled the closet door open. A three-foot pile of old *Wall Street Journals* was stacked on the floor in the back of the closet. A single pair of rundown brown shoes was beside the papers. A seedy old topcoat was hung on a wire hanger. The closet contained nothing else.

The chest of drawers held an old Gillette safety razor, four pairs of brown socks, one odd blue sock, two dirty handkerchiefs, three white shirts, two sets of underwear, three gray workshirts, one pair of gray workpants, and a heavy old tin fruitcake box.

"Lived kind of spare, huh, Carpenter?"

"He did that. What's in the old cake box?"

Sergeant Harper opened the box and dumped its contents on the bed. It was full of stocks and bonds. Eight bankbooks were on the bottom of the pile. Harper leafed through the bankbooks and whistled.

"Look at this, Carpenter. I make it at about seventy-eight thousand dollars in these bank accounts. He's got Coca-Cola, Texaco, AT&T, Noxzema, and other heavy stocks in that pile." He held up a brass key with a tag on it.

"This is a safety deposit box key. I'll bet that box is really loaded. Here's what we need," he said, separating an envelope from the pile of stocks. "The return address on this old envelope. Esther A. Hogg, R.F.D., Pine Hill, Mississippi. I'll send a teletype to the State Police down there to notify her." He turned to the landlady. "Mrs. Wilcox, if you will, just lock everything up here until you hear from his sister. If he owes you anything, you can settle up with her."

"He's paid up 'til next month, poor soul," she said, putting her bony hand on his arm. "Do you think he suffered much, Sergeant?"

"Why, no, ma'am," he said, smiling bleakly. "As a matter of fact, he had kind of a smile on his face."

"I'm so glad you told me that," she sighed. "Now my mind will be at ease."

"Thanks for your help, ma'am," Sergeant Harper said.

"Thank you, Officers."

They walked out on the street. Two robins were splashing in Mrs. Wilcox's birdbath.

"You don't have to come back to the station. I'll send the teletype and con Goulek into making the report for us. Want me to drop you off somewhere?"

"No, thanks," said Carpenter, lighting a cigarette with shaking hands.

"Anything wrong, Carpenter?"

"No, it's just kind of depressing. I just met John Hogg in a restaurant not long before he died. He tried to lay some money on me. I guess I was a little rough on him."

"Did he tell you his rape story?" Harper said, taking a fresh dip of Copenhagen.

"Yeah."

"He probably got himself all excited and went down there and jumped on that black gal. Don't blame yourself for anything. He's been around here for years and nobody could stand him. A few cops took his money, but he never had any action going for him. He just liked to impress people and lied about the numbers and the moonshine. I think the rape story was bullshit," he said, spitting a glob of juice at the birdbath.

"The poor ass-hole wanted attention. All he knew how to do was make money. Listen to me, kid. You can't bleed for every stiff case you handle. You're going to handle garbage like that as long as you're a cop. Try to think of them as ass-holes. There's too many losers in this world for you to sympathize with. Just do what you have to do, and don't take this shit too seriously. Police get a smell of life the way ordinary people don't. As a cop you'll learn that death has no dignity. When you die, you piss yourself and sometimes your bowels let go." He broke wind and chuckled.

"A lot of people die and nobody in the world gives a damn for them. I'll bet old Hogg's spinster sister don't shed a tear for him. If she does, the sight of all those stocks and bankbooks will ease her grief. See you later."

Carpenter walked two blocks to a stationery store and bought a large manila envelope and got twenty three-cent stamps from the machine. The newsboy on the corner gave him a free paper and an Esso station's men's room gave him the privacy he needed to handle his loot. Locking the door behind him, he addressed the envelope to the Reverend William Brown, Lennox Avenue, Towson, Maryland.

The money resisted when he tried to flatten the roll on newspaper spread on the floor, but after a few minutes the envelope was crammed full. Tearing a sheet from his notebook he wrote the following:

Reverend Brown,
    Please use this in your church-building fund. I'll be watching your progress.

                                      A friend

He read the note over and laughed to himself as he slid it between the bills. Unlocking the door, he walked outside. A truckdriver was waiting by the door outside, jumping up and down, holding his hand over his backside.

"Man, I'm glad to see that door open. I ate some bad chili in Glen Burnie. I've stopped to crap six times in the last twenty miles. I'll never get to York at this rate."

"Buy yourself a half-pint of blackberry brandy across the street at Ruark's. It never fails to stop the trots."

"Hey, thanks a lot, pal. I'm hauling a load of watermelon," he said, holding his stomach. "Grab off a couple for yourself."

"Next time, maybe. Thanks for the offer."

The man's eyes widened as he rushed into the restroom and slammed the door.

Carpenter walked twenty feet to a mailbox, dropped the envelope in, and walked away whistling. The dark mood had vanished and he was hungry.

The smell of sour beef and dumplings assaulted his nostrils when he opened the door of the O.K. Bar. Sam Rider was behind the cigar counter, working an adding machine. He waved at Carpenter and motioned him to go into the back room. The usual early evening crowd was there. The blondes were behind the bar trying to keep up with the demand for drinks, smiles, and conversation. He went through the deserted back room into the kitchen. Charlie, the cook, was boning a turkey with great finesse. He grinned at Carpenter and pointed to a pot of sour beef simmering on the back of the store.

"You likee?"

"Number one, Charlie. Don't stop what you're doing. I'll help myself." Standing up, he ate the glutinous, steaming mixture at the salad table and washed it down with a cold Lowenbrau.

13

IT WAS STARTING TO RAIN WHEN CARPENTER stepped out on the street. A streetcar rattled by, blue sparks dropping from the hot overhead wire. He walked fast through the fine, cold rain to pick up his raincoat at the station.

The rain was starting to soak through his shirt. Running to escape the rain, he passed the alley way at Read's drugstore and heard the low mumble of a man's voice and a woman crying. Carpenter continued for a few yards, torn by his desire to escape the cold rain and his impulse to investigate the trouble in the alley. He stopped, walked softly back to the alley, and looked into the dim space between the buildings. A woman was sprawled on her back, with her dress up to her waist. A man was standing over her, leaning down, slapping her face with his open hands, back and forth, slowly and deliberately. The woman was crying and pleading softly with him.

"No more, please, no more."

He stopped and leaned close to the woman and said something to her in low, savage tones.

"I won't! I won't! I—no, please!" she whined.

He resumed working her over with his hands, as if he

had all the time in the world.

Carpenter walked in within arm's length of them. The woman beater was intent on what he was doing. She was not pleading, but lay there trying to protect her face with her arms, accepting punishment like a dumb animal. Carpenter touched him lightly on the shoulder. Startled, he turned, tripped over the woman, and nearly fell. He recovered quickly and grabbed Carpenter in a bear hug, as he charged forward. Strong as an ox, he was shorter than Carpenter, but perhaps thirty pounds heavier and was in good shape with solid muscle. The strong odor of garlic was on his breath. He drove Carpenter backward and slammed him into a telephone pole.

Carpenter's hat went flying. He had his left hand free, but couldn't reach nightstick or blackjack. The tough was laughing now. He realized that he was much stronger than Carpenter. Shifting his arms slightly, he applied viselike pressure to clasped hands directly over Carpenter's backbone.

"How do you like that? You skinny little shit of a cop. I'm going to break your fucking back, a little bit at a time. You don't know who you're fucking with."

Carpenter could feel his captor's foot braced on the ground next to his. He brought his foot up and smashed down on the man's instep with his heel. Sucking in his breath sharply, the thug's grip eased slightly. Carpenter mustered all his strength and smashed down once, twice, three times. On the third blow he could feel the small bones break in the man's foot. He was hopping around on his good foot, holding the injured one, when Carpenter kicked him in the groin.

"Hah!" he grunted, as a look of horror came over his dark features. Holding his crotch, he went down to the ground. Carpenter squatted next to him and cuffed his hands. The handcuffs looked like toys on his thick, hairy wrists.

It was raining in sheets. Carpenter sat beside his prisoner in three inches of dirty water. His back seemed dislocated. There was no pain, just a ringing in his ears and the beat of the rain on his bare head. His hands were starting to shake. Too weak to stand, he sat in the wet alley, resting. The woman was standing in front of him, leaning over, talking to him.

"Are you all right? I thought he was going to break your back. We're both lucky. He's a champion weight lifter. How do you feel?"

Carpenter looked at the woman's face. Her eyes were already swollen shut. A trickle of blood ran down from the corner of her mouth. Her face was puffing up like a balloon. What was probably once an elaborate hairdo was a soggy ruin, hanging down in her face. She was missing one of her shoes.

"You look like hell, lady."

"You don't look so great to me either, sitting in that dirty mud puddle. Don't worry about me, I've been through it with him before."

"Who is he?" Carpenter said as he stood on rubbery legs.

Carpenter leaned against the wall and tilted his head back. The cold rain pounded his face and refreshed him, but he didn't trust his legs. He sat down in the mud puddle.

"His name is Buster Thorn. He works at the Action Beauty Shop. He's a hairdresser."

"A hairdresser? You've got to be kidding!"

"No, I'm not kidding. He was some kind of weight-lifting champion two years ago. I met him in Ruark's about eight months ago. I thought he was great at the time. Look, you might as well know. My name is Rose Murphy. I'm a hustler."

"A what?"

"You know, I turn tricks," she said, pulling up torn

nylons.

"What?"

"What kind of dumb jerk are you? I play for pay. You know, fucking, the old American pastime?"

"Oh, I see. What's he to you?"

"I lived with him for a while. I worked with four other girls in his stable."

"You mean he's a pimp?"

"Oh, you're starting to wake up. How long have you been a cop?"

"Not long." He put a wet cigarette into his mouth and thumbed his Zippo. The wick ignited, then sputtered out in the rain. He tossed the cigarette aside.

"It shows." She turned to Thorn and kicked him in the side. He didn't respond. He lay on the wet ground holding his injured groin.

"You should have come up behind this ugly gorilla and split his skull with your nightstick. You gave him a chance and he almost broke you in half."

"That's tough talk for a young girl. How old are you, anyway?"

"Nineteen. So what has that got to do with it? Is he dead?" she asked, leaning over Thorn. She touched him on the neck with her toe. "His eyes are closed. He don't look like he's breathing too good."

"He'll be okay. He has to go to the hospital, but he'll live. This son-of-a-bitch is going to jail for a while."

Three or four people were watching them from the street. The spectators stood in the rain, silently watching the cop in the mud puddle and the great hulk beside him, laying quietly, face down.

"Will one of you call a radio car for me?"

One of the group approached them slowly, ready to bolt at the first sign of danger.

"What's going on? I just want to see."

"Call a car for me, will you, mister? This man's hurt. He needs a ride to the hospital."

"He looks like he's dead."

"Will you for Christ's sake call?"

"Oh, yeah. Don't get sore. I just wanted to see."

A police car pulled into the alley before the man got ten feet. Officer Beauregard Barter was working by himself. He stopped a few feet from the miserable trio and got out. Barter was a short and thick man. He had mean eyes. Because he was short and a cop, he had something to prove to the world.

Carpenter got slowly to his feet. "Help me get this ass-hole in the car."

"What happened?" Barter rolled Thorn over on his back.

"He was beating the hell out of this lady. The son-of-a-bitch tried to break my back."

"This is Buster Thorn. Don't lock him up, Carpenter."

"What? This creep almost broke my back. Look at this lady's face."

"That's no lady. That's Rosie, a local pig. This guy works for me. He's my snitch. He turns a lot of good information for me."

Buster Thorn was showing signs of life. He sat up and groaned. "Help me up, Beau. This guy broke my foot and ruined my balls."

"Shut up, garbage. You're lucky he didn't put a bullet between your stupid eyes. Get in the car."

It took both of them to get Thorn in the back seat. Rose Murphy walked down the alley to Carpenter's hat, picked it up, returned to the car, and got in beside Beau Barter.

"Here's your hat, Officer," she said, turning to Carpenter in the back seat. "I never did thank you. I'm sorry."

Barter took the mike from the clip on the dashboard. "I'll head for Union Memorial and we can try to sort this mess out." He thumbed the button on the transmitter. "Car twenty-two, ten-seven en route to Union Memorial Hospital, I have an injured man and woman. The street man is with me, assisting."

"Ten-four, car twenty-two, time twenty-one hundred hours."

Barter drove Thorn to the hospital, where he was admitted for treatment. Rose Murphy was treated and released.

Sergeant Harper was walking out the door of the station when they returned. The rain had stopped and the sky was full of stars.

"Took you guys long enough down there. I thought you might be playing grab-ass with one of those horny nurses, Beau."

"Oh, no sir. You know me."

"I know you, all right. What happened?"

"Just a lovers' quarrel. A man slapped his girlfriend around in the alley next to the drugstore and Fritz walked up on them. He fell and broke his foot somehow, running away from Carpenter. You know him, Buster Thorn. He was fighting with Rose Murphy. She don't want him arrested."

"Broke his foot, huh? Good. That will keep that musclebound fruitcake off the streets for a while. He's one of your snitches, isn't he?"

"Oh, he's helped me out a couple of times, I guess."

"I'll bet he has. Carpenter, you look wet and tired. Get caught in the rain?"

"Yes sir."

"They say a good cop never gets cold, wet, horny, or hungry. That's bullshit, of course. I'm going home. I'll see you two tomorrow. Sleep fast. This is the short changeover."

Mary was sleeping on the couch when he opened the door of their apartment. The late movie was on. The cavalry was beating the Indians, as usual. His wife looked very young and vulnerable. She was lying on her side with her cheek on a large pillow that she embraced with both arms. She wore a short black nightgown. It was very sheer. The gown was up to her waist. The springy mound of dark pubic hair was a sharp contrast to her pale skin. She turned over on her back without waking. Carpenter looked at her smooth belly and cleavage between her breasts. She muttered something in her sleep. A trace of perspiration was on her upper lip. She was dreaming. Her breath became ragged, then slowed again.

He wanted her and felt desire flood down into his loins. Leaning over her without touching her, he smelled her secret places, under her arms, her belly, and the damp pubic area. Pulling his wet clothing from his body, he sat on the floor next to the couch. Putting his hand between her legs gently, he began to rub the clitoral area very lightly.

Her hips moved slowly in response to his searching fingers. He watched her face, as she slowly raised her chin and pressed the back of her head into the pillow. His hand was working fast now, her breathing was rapid. She was drooling slightly from the corner of her mouth. Her thighs squeezed together on his hand and her hips were moving faster in the age-old rhythm of sex. She was shuddering and coming when she opened her eyes and saw him.

"Fritz! What are you doing?" She sat up, confused. "Come on, get in me, don't stop! Hurry, hurry!"

She was growling deep in her throat. He entered her and rode her slowly, pacing himself for a long race. She was ahead of him. She ground her pelvis into him and clung to him with her arms and legs.

"Stop holding back. That's it. Oh! Oh!"

She was screaming in his ear as they went over the brink together.

"Wow, what a way to wake up!" She locked her legs around him. "No, you don't have to move yet. Soak it in me for a while. It was so good. I was dreaming some kind of mixed-up sex dream. That's the first time I ever woke up coming."

His penis was shrinking up, retreating from the hot moisture. She released him and handed him a towel from under her pillow.

"Here. Don't mess up my new sofa. I was determined to stay awake tonight, but the news and weather always put me to sleep. I was going to seduce you, darn it. It worked out, though. All's well, that ends well. I'm glad you did that. What made you so sexy? Is it just because I took a bath, washed my hair, had on my best nightgown, and had my pussy exposed when you walked in the door?"

"That could have had something to do with it. Come on, let's go to bed."

Carpenter stood and took Mary's hands. He pulled her to her feet and kissed her nose.

"What did you do today?" Mary yawned behind her fist.

"Handled a sudden death and stopped a guy from beating up a girl in an alley. It was kind of a tough day. I guess it keyed me up."

"And you took all that nervous energy out on my poor, helpless, sleeping body when you came in, right?"

"Right. Let's go to sleep. I've got to go back in at seven A.M. The short changeover, they call it."

They sat on opposite sides of the bed. Mary was winding the alarm clock.

"I'll set the alarm a few minutes early. You may wake up all stiff and ready, Fritz baby. I can't send you out there to lock up the bad guys with an erection bothering you."

14

SERGEANT HARPER'S SHIFT WAS ALL LINED UP FOR roll-call on time. There was not much horseplay or joking with the other shift. Changeover days are rough. Your body is used to working at certain hours. You have outraged your metabolism with the change. The men all suffer in different degrees. Rolaids, Tums, and other digestive antacids are much in evidence. Drug salesmen and pharmaceutical houses donate samples to the station houses by the gross. They are consumed eagerly by police. Anything to put out the fire in the belly. Too many cigarettes, rich food, irregular hours, and free booze, mixed with abrupt changes of boredom, fear, exhilaration, and excitement. The lack of routine is what attracts and holds men in police work, but the lack of routine wreaks havoc on their nerves and digestive systems.

Lieutenant Jarrel Hollis conducted roll call on the first day of the 7 to 3 shift. He called the men to order and went down the list of names. Each man answered to his name. Lieutenant Hollis went into a lot of detail. He read every report to the men that had happened in the past twenty-four hours. He spared them no details. He gave them all the trivial facts about when, where, who, how, and why on every case. It took a lot of time. There was no humor or sharp retort to grab the interest of the men. No one really listened to him. He finished at last. He removed his glasses and smiled. He was very proud of himself.

"There you are. I read everything. Nothing like being prepared when you go out on the street. Ha, ha. Any questions?"

Sean McGee raised his hand.

"What do you read all that bullshit for, Lieutenant? Nobody ever bothers us with all of that."

"Why, I've got to. I've got to read it. Got to protect myself, you know. Ha, ha. That's it, I got to protect myself."

"Protect yourself from what?"

"Don't get smart with me, McGee," he said, shaking his finger. "You know what I mean. Suppose somebody told the Captain that I read a bad roll call and held some information back. No sir. I'm going to read it all. I could get in trouble by not giving it all to you. How can you do your job if you don't know what's in every report?"

"I don't see what good it's going to do me to have you tell me at roll call that a dog pissed on an azalea bush on Providence Road at seventeen hundred hours and the weather was clear and there weren't any witnesses to the offense. Shit, Providence Road ain't even on my post."

Somebody laughed on Sergeant Harper's shift. The shift waiting to be relieved were suddenly alert and talking to each other.

"Don't be profane. The Sergeant might decide to put you in that car today."

"Bullshit. He works us in regular cars. I haven't worked that fucking car since I was relief man."

"I don't want to have to warn you again McGee, about that cursing at roll call. What am I supposed to do with these reports, if I don't read them?"

Sergeant Harper stepped up to the dais. He spoke low, but every man could hear him.

"If I told you what to do with those fucking reports, you would have me for insubordination. If you are all finished, I've got some announcements."

"I'm not finished," he said, shoving his chin out. "I got a complaint from the shift that relieves you. They said the trashcans were not emptied last night when you went home. I want you to see that it does not happen again."

Harper gave him a look that should have warned him. Lieutenant Hollis would not be put off in front of two entire shifts of men. He was plainly frightened of the younger man, but determined to carry it off. He shook his finger in Harper's face.

"I demand that you have those trashcans emptied each day before you go home."

Harper spoke softly, but his voice was pregnant with venom. "Drop it. Get out of this room while you can still walk."

Lieutenant Hollis began to shake like a man with palsy. "I want every man to stay in this room. I'm taking this to the Captain."

He ran from the room. You could have heard a pin drop. A man laughed. Another mumbled something. The tension was broken. The men were laughing and talking among themselves. The door opened. The captain walked in, followed by Lieutenant Hollis.

"What's the problem, Harper?"

"No problem, Captain, what do you mean?"

"Lieutenant Hollis said you defied him in front of two-thirds of the men assigned to the station."

"He's a liar."

Lieutenant Hollis was trembling. "Ask the men. Ask the men. They heard him."

The old Captain faced the double row of police. He

looked very tired. "Did anybody hear what Sergeant Harper said to Lieutenant Hollis?"

The silence was deafening. The Captain smiled sweetly and walked to the center of the room. Turning his back to Sergeant Harper's shift, he walked over to the offgoing shift. They snapped to attention, as he cleared his throat and squared his shoulders.

"You there, Al, how about it? Jerry, did you hear anything? Mac, come on, lay it on me."

Not a man spoke up. The Captain turned to Lieutenant Hollis and shook his head. "You don't have anything, Jarrel. Forget it. Why don't you take a ride over to Parkville and get yourself some breakfast at the Greek's?"

"I'm going to make a full report to you in writing, sir. I mean it. Every word goes on paper. I'm going to protect myself in this."

"You do that, Jarrel. I'll file it with the rest of them."

Lieutenant Hollis walked from the room, head held high. He went into his office. Almost immediately, the rap of a typewriter was heard through the heavy door.

Captain Thomas Hoffman turned to Sergeant Harper.

"You slipped through the net that time, Sarge. Lucky for you that cops are hard of hearing."

"Yes sir. Thanks, Captain."

"Don't thank me." He lowered his voice. "Why not see that those fucking trashcans are emptied, for the love of Pete?"

"I will. Thanks, boss."

"I'm going home. I've got enough of this place already today. I don't know why I don't take my pension. No guts, I guess."

He left the room. Harper stepped behind the dais.

"The offgoing shift can go. The rest of you guys hang around a while. I got some details to lay on you."

"Car 21, hang around the Riderwood School during

the lunch period. Some nut keeps exposing himself to little kids there. He shows up at noon. I guess he's on his lunchbreak then, too. The nut always hauls ass in a late model blue car, no tag number or other description."

A woman began to cry in the booking room. The door flew open with a crash. A young black woman wearing only a slip ran into the roll-call room with a woman detective in hot pursuit. The black woman was through the door to the hallway in a flash, as the woman detective slipped and fell to her knees, scrambled up, and ran out the door after her. McGee started for the door.

"Hold it!" Sergeant Harper snarled, "Let that pussy catch her own prisoner."

McGee shrugged and walked back to his place in ranks.

Sergeant Harper resumed his briefing. "Car 22, keep a look out up at Loch Raven for a large group of college kids skinny dipping around Pierce's Cove. Some preacher was up there crappie fishing yesterday along the bank and they pulled their clothes off right in front of him and jumped in. He tried to give them a little lecture about it, but six of the girls got out of the water and threatened to depants him and then ran away. He went to the headquarters people and complained. They got upset with us, as usual, for allowing it to happen and they wrote a threatening intradepartment order to us. If we don't stop that, they'll do such and such to us. The usual bullshit. Here it is on the bulletin board, if any of you want to read it.

"Carpenter, you are excused from Circus Court today. That fruit you locked up on the streetcar copped a plea. He got a year probation, with the condition he stay out of Baltimore County.

"Anybody got any idea where we can have our long changeover party this time? It's warm, so you might want a place with a swimming pool. Yeah, McGee?"

"I can get Berry's Quarry Club for us. The new manager is a friend of mine. He owes me. He got busted for operating under the influence two months ago, and I helped him out a little."

"Spare me the morbid details. That okay with the rest of you guys? Any opposed to it? No? Good. That's where we'll have it. This is the way we'll divide up the food-and-drink hustle. Carpenter, try to get a couple of hams. Trotta, some steaks; Pope, you get the beer; Barter, you get the charcoal, lighter fluid, and salt, pepper, vinegar, butter, and Old Bay seasoning. McGee, you get the crabs. Dhaw—get some good corn on the cob; the yellow will do. Jacobsen, get the pumpernickel rolls and a big slab of moonseed cake. I'll bring about twenty pounds of shrimp. Sergeant Goulek volunteered to bring a few bottles of booze. Did I forget anything?"

"Yes sir, the Polish sausage," Fancy said.

"Right. Fancy, think you can get us some good Polish sausage?"

"Can do."

"Good. Hit the bricks. I'll see you all later."

Carpenter walked outside with the rest of the men. Sean McGee opened the door of his car and shoved the front seat forward. He got into the back and pulled the seat loose. Checking carefully under the back seat, he replaced it. He took a penlight from his pocket and shone it under the front seat.

"What are you looking for, McGee? Tiny people screwing under the seats?"

"Funny, Fritz, very funny. For your information, I'm looking for guns, knives, razor blades, blackjacks, tire irons, and bricks. In short, I'm looking for anything that will do me in. A lot of cops lock people up without searching them. If the ass-hole doesn't use his weapon on the cop, he usually stashes it in the police car on the way to the station. He knows he'll get a deadly weapons charge hung on him if they find it on him. You might be surprised to know that I found a switchblade knife, a straight razor, a Colt snub-nose thirty-eight—fully loaded—a half-full whiskey bottle and a half-pound of grass under the back seat since I started working this car steady."

"I didn't know. What made you start looking for the stuff?"

"I'd been on about a year and was feeling pretty salty and competent. I got a call of drunken woman at the Kismet Café parking lot over on Falls Road about oh-three-hundred hours. My partner was visiting a nurse friend at her apartment for an hour or so and I didn't want to interrupt him, so I answered the call by myself."

He paused, took a Havana from his hat, and bit the end off. Holding it to his nose, he smelled, then licked the cigar all over. Lighting it with his Zippo, he inhaled deeply. Smoke poured from his nose as he resumed talking.

"I found the drunken broad, okay. She must have left the tavern and managed to get into her car, a big Lincoln Continental. When I got there the motor was running and her lights were on. She had passed out and was leaning forward over the steering wheel. Her head was pressing down on the horn and you could hear the blast all over the valley. I shut the engine off and tried to wake her up. It was no go. She was really juiced up. I looked in her purse. Her driver's license said Park Heights Avenue in Pimlico, so I decided to take her home. It was only about six blocks off my post. She was a little mite of a girl, and it wasn't difficult to pick her up and put her on the back seat of the police car."

They stood on the lot talking as the other police cars left, one by one. A traffic sergeant was sitting in a police car talking to a woman school guard in the corner of the lot. She stood by the car with her hands resting on the roof. Leaning inside the car, she kissed him, then stepped back. The sound of her laughter reached them, as she turned her head in their direction. McGee grinned at Carpenter and continued.

"I locked her car up and put the keys in her purse. I tossed the purse in the back seat and she sat up, looked around, and laid back down again. I got in the car and took off for her address. The next thing I knew this drunken little floozie was rapping me on the head with a nightstick."

"Ungrateful bitch," Carpenter said.

"You said it, pal."

They watched as the school guard got into a Ford convertible and drove off the lot, with the traffic sergeant following. McGee waved to the sergeant and winked at Carpenter.

"Anyway, I lost control and ran off the road into a cornfield. She hit me about three pretty good licks before I got stopped and grabbed that damn stick out of her hands. The bitch was like a wildcat. I managed to get her hands cuffed behind her back, and she gave up and started to cry. There I was in a fucking cornfield, in the wee hours of the morning, with a crying broad who had just put egg-sized lumps on my head with a nightstick. I turned the dome light on and looked at the stick. It belonged to the man I'd relieved in the car. He had his name burned into it. He'd left the thing in the back seat. Now you know why I look under the fucking seats. Perhaps you can learn something from my bad experience, you callow rookie."

"I think I have. What did you say to the guy who owned the stick?"

"Nothing. Not a bloody thing. I took the stick home. It was the start of my collection of back-seat things. I'm going to keep it all in a closet in the cellar and after I pension out in twenty, I'll open the closet and look my stuff over and reminisce. All except the grass, of course. I smoked that. Not bad stuff, really. From Morocco, I believe."

"How about the drunken broad? How much time did the judge give her?"

"Time? Who said I arrested her? I simply took her home and helped her to her front door. I was looking in her purse for a key when the butler answered the door in his bathrobe. She was from a very old family. Not much money, but an old Maryland name. The next day she called me and said she was glad I didn't take her to the hoosegow. She was very appreciative and insisted on taking me out to dinner on my day off. One thing led to another and we wound up in a motel out on Route 40 West. Between the sheets, she was very good, but I only saw her a few more times. I'm afraid she was a hopeless lush and got very aggressive when she drank. I read in the paper about a year later that she ran her car off a mountain road in western Maryland. She never regained consciousness and died about a month later. It's a shame. They say she was one hell of a good lawyer."

He sighed and knocked the ash from his cigar with his little finger.

"What are the long changeover parties like, Sean?"

"This shift has great parties. Snake makes us keep a good rapport with the merchants, even the shitty ones. It pays off. They donate every bit of food and booze we have at our parties. Snake and Goulek do all the cooking over charcoal. They'll like Berry's Quarry Club. It's a private swimming and tennis club up the county, in Cockeysville. They just put in a new kitchen, pavilion, and another pool, just for private parties."

"Do the married men bring their wives?"

"Not to long changeover parties. Some bring their girlfriends or anybody else, but no wives. It's kind of a marathon eating-and-drinking blast. You'll like it.

Bring your hams in the day of the long changeover. Goulek and Snake take off half a day early and have things all set up by the time we get off."

"I've got to go," said Carpenter. "There's a school detail at Allegheny and Central at eight-thirty. I want to grab a coffee and some donuts at Elmer's first."

"Come on, I'll drop you off. I'd join you, but I've got a breakfast date with this terrific Goucher girl at her apartment. She has boobs like melons and an ass like an Aberdeen Angus. Her first class is at ten. If I play my cards right, I can have her full of bacon and eggs by eight-thirty and full of Sean by nine."

He had coffee and donuts at Elmer's, then walked to Allegheny and Central. Carpenter was a few minutes early for the school detail. A severe-looking, middle-aged woman got out of her car, nodded her head to Carpenter, and walked into the school. The principal's spy, Sharon's replacement, could report that the cop was on time this morning. The children came in groups of three or four, pairs and singles. Jimmy Cox was one of the last to cross. Looking up into Carpenter's face, he grinned. Reaching into his lightweight zippered jacket, he just managed to pull a huge Golden Delicious apple from his pocket.

"Here," he said, smiling with missing teeth. "My mother gave me this for the teacher, but the hell with her. She's got false teeth and has to cut them all up with a knife when she eats them."

"Why don't you eat it yourself, Jimmy?"

"Nah, I got one in my lunchbox. Go on, take it."

"Thanks a lot."

"Ah, don't tell my mother, will ya? She'd whale the hell out of me if she knew."

"Mum's the word. I'll take it home and eat it tonight."

The boy ran at top speed to the school as the bell rang.

Carpenter was about to leave the corner to return to the Towson business district. A block away a little girl of perhaps nine was running toward the corner. Her thin legs pumped like pistons. A small dog, a black Boston terrier, was chasing her, closing the gap between them rapidly. He caught her and ran circles around her, barking and jumping up on her playfully. She stopped and spanked the little dog.

"Go home, Bingo! Mommy is going to be mad at you. Go on home, get!"

Bingo put his head down and trotted back the way he had come, glancing back over his shoulder at his idol in the red dress. The child ran to the corner, glanced back at the dog, and stopped. Bingo was sitting, looking at her.

"Go home, Bingo! You bad boy! Go on!" she yelled.

The dog started away slowly. She glanced at Carpenter in the center of the road.

"Okay, honey. It looks like he's going home now."

"He makes me so mad. He always tries to sneak away from Momma and follow me to school. I'm late now. I can't take him home."

"I guess he loves you."

"I guess he does, but he's a pest."

Carpenter watched her run toward the school. She was almost to the door when he heard the car's horn and the wheels screech as they peeled rubber off trying to stop. He turned in time see the big Buick's right front wheel roll over the dog, half a block away. The little girl saw it, too. She dropped her bookbag and lunchbox on the sidewalk and ran toward the intersection. The Buick was stopped and the driver was getting out. There was no other car in sight as the little girl ran through the crossing toward her dog, with Carpenter behind her, dreading what he knew he would find. The driver was an elderly man. He was pacing back and forth in front of the car, wringing his hands.

"My God, Officer, I wasn't going fast. The little pooch ran right out in front of me."

The child was on her hands and knees trying to crawl under the car after the dog. Carpenter picked the little girl up in his arms.

"Let me go! Let me go! Bingo's hurt. He's under the car, I got to get to him. Let me go!"

He carried her to the side of the road. She stopped struggling and wrapped her arms around his neck. She was sobbing and hiccupping into his chest. Sitting down on the curb with her in his arms, he held her. The driver of the car was bending over them saying something to the child.

"Here. Sit with her while I get her dog," Carpenter said.

Carpenter sat the child on the curb beside the old man and went to the car. The dog was lying on his side between the rear wheels. He was still breathing, in ragged short breaths. Sliding a finger under the dog's collar, he gently pulled him from under the car. Bright red arterial blood was pouring from his pug nose. Dark matter flowed from his rectum. The dog died in his arms as he carried it to the side of the road.

"Is he hurt bad? Is he going to get well? Let's take him to the vet's. He'll help him. Come on. Let's go."

Carpenter stood there holding the limp dog in his arms. He couldn't think of anything to say. A lump in his throat threatened to choke him, as he blinked back tears.

"Ah, he's hurt pretty bad, sis."

The child was calm. "He's dead, ain't he?"

"Yes, he is."

"Will you help me to take him home?"

"Sure."

The school principal was there with several teachers. The principal was a lean, middle-aged woman, wearing a black dress. She was out of breath and

157

perspiring.

"Thank God, it wasn't one of the children. We heard the horn and brakes and saw Jenny drop her books and run. That little dog was always following her. She won't be able to come to school today, I'm afraid."

"I'll take her and the dog home," said Carpenter.

"Here's her lunchbox and bookbag, Officer. Thank you so much for your interest in the child," said the principal.

The old man took the child's things from Carpenter.

"Please allow me to drive her home. I feel terrible about this. I was only going to play golf. I wish I'd stayed home today."

"Thanks. It wasn't your fault. He was trying to run across the road to his pal."

The man opened the trunk of the Buick. "Put the poor little fellow in here."

Carpenter placed the dog gently in the trunk and turned to the child. "Where do you live, Jenny?"

"I live on Woodbine Avenue. I'll show you."

They all got in the front seat of the car and left. It was only a four-block drive on maple-shaded streets to Jenny's house. She lived in a large new ranch-style house on an acre of ground.

Her mother answered the door and her eyes widened when she saw Carpenter's uniform. "What happened?"

"Bingo's dead, Momma. This man ran over him. I saw it. It was awful. I think I'm going to be sick."

They walked into the foyer. The living room was done in Early American and potted plants were everywhere.

"Poor little fellow. He got out on me today. He was a real escape artist and wanted to be with Jenny every minute. Go lie down in your room for awhile, honey."

Jenny ran and stopped near a large sofa. She turned to the old man and Carpenter. "I'm not mad at you, mister. You couldn't help it. He didn't suffer much, did he, Mr. Policeman?"

"No, he didn't suffer."

"Will you bury him for me in the back yard?" she said, looking at Carpenter.

"I'll be glad to," he said, smiling at her.

She tried to smile, but couldn't bring it off. She walked out of the room, her thin shoulders rounded and her chin on her chest.

"You don't have to bother with burying him." She brushed a wisp of blond hair back from her face. "My husband will do it."

"I don't mind. I told her I would. It won't take but a few minutes."

"I'll get the dog and meet you out back, Officer," said the old man.

Carpenter dug a hole eighteen inches wide and two feet long by three feet deep. The shovel slid easily into the red soil. The ground was soft and friable from the recent rain. Jenny's mother gave him a blue baby blanket to wrap the dog in.

"It's Bingo's blanket, Officer. He should rest easy with the blanket under his favorite hickory tree. On summer afternoons, this was his favorite spot."

The old man handed her a card. "Allow me to give you my card, ma'am. I'll be glad to pay you whatever you and your husband decide the dog was worth. I feel that I must do something. I'm afraid I'm disgustingly wealthy and can afford it. Call me when you have had a chance to estimate the value of the animal to your child. Please allow me to drop you off, Officer."

Carpenter tamped the last shovel full of sorrel loam on the grave and picked up his gunbelt and hat. He noticed Jenny watching from her bedroom window and waved to her. She waved back, her pale face framed by the window.

The old man dropped Carpenter off in the center of

Towson. He walked south on York Road, twirling his nightstick on its leather thong. A group of Goucher girls were waiting in front of the movie for the college bus to pick them up. They watched his performance with the nightstick as he approached. They were laughing and talking among themselves. As he was passing through the crowd, he missed a toss of his nightstick. The heavy rosewood stick struck him in the shin. The girls roared with laughter. He felt his face get hot with embarrassment. A pixie-faced girl stepped in front of him, blocking his way.

"Now I understand why they say policing is a dangerous job. Why, you could hurt yourself with your nightstick! Did you injure yourself, sweetie?" she said, with a smirk.

"Ah, thank you for your concern. It could have been worse."

"How so, my brave protector?"

She remained in his path, challenging him. He leaned over and whispered in her ear. "I could have hit myself in the balls."

Her eyes widened as her face turned scarlet. Angry sparks flew from her eyes. She regained her composure.

"I asked for that, I suppose. Am I blushing?"

"No, not at all."

She stepped to the side. He tipped his hat and walked away.

A man stumbled out of the O.K. Bar and walked into a mailman who was passing by. He brushed the mailman off, apologized, staggered to a new black Ford convertible parked at the curb and tried to unlock the door with clumsy, fumbling hands. The top was down on the car. Carpenter walked over and opened the unlocked door for the man.

"Say, why didn't I think of that?"

"Because you've got a load on."

The man crawled across the front seat and started to fumble the keys into the ignition. Carpenter leaned in and took the keys from him.

"Say, what the hell you doin'?"

"I'll take your keys to the Towson station," said Carpenter, pocketing the keys. "The desk sergeant will give them to you when you sober up. You can't drive like that, friend."

"Bullshit. I'm fine. Give me my fucking keys."

"No way. Wait here. I'll get you a cab."

He walked into the O.K. Bar and had the morning bartender call a cab for him. When he returned to the car, the drunk was crying.

"What's a matter? All I did was call you a cab."

"Ah, hell, it's everything. I found out this morning my Father's got terminal cancer. I'm having trouble with my wife. Now this. You're going to lock me up, aren't you?"

"No. I told you that I'd call a cab for you. You can go home. Where do you live?"

"West Seminary Avenue, 100507 to be exact. Over near Falls Road. Why?"

"The cab's here now. Come on, I'll help you out."

Carpenter walked to the driver's side and opened the door. The cab pulled in front of the convertible and blew his horn.

Carpenter beat his hand against the rear fender. The cab driver looked out the window at him and frowned.

"I called the cab. Take this man to West Seminary Avenue, 100507. Near Falls."

"Has he got any money? I don't like to haul drunks. the fare's two bucks over there."

The drunk lurched to the taxicab driver's window and stuck his head in. "I heard that. Sure I got money. I got plenty."

Reaching into his back pocket, he pulled out a fat wallet. The wallet was packed with credit cards and photographs, but no money.

"Hey, I been robbed! I had about a hundred and fifty dollars when I left the house. It's all gone. Look for yourself."

"Check your pockets," said Carpenter, holding the drunk by the arm to keep him on his feet.

The man fumbled in his pockets. He pulled out a money clip and a handful of loose cash. Carpenter took the clip and put it in the man's pocket and counted the money.

"A hundred and sixty-six. You have more than you thought you did."

Taking three of the singles, he gave them to the cabbie, folded the rest of the cash and put it into the man's wallet. He put the wallet in the man's back pocket and buttoned the flap over it. Carpenter helped the drunk into the back seat and shut the door.

"Take him home."

The drunk rolled down the window. "Wait a minute. Aren't you going to lock me up? I'm drunk. I admit it."

"You've got enough trouble, mister. You don't need to be arrested. Go home and get some sleep. You can pick your keys up at the desk when you get straightened out."

A passerby had stopped on the sidewalk to observe the entire incident. He was a picture of style and class in his gray flannel suit and carefully knotted maroon tie. He shook his neatly barbered gray head in disapproval. Carpenter walked over to the man.

"Can I help you, sir?"

"I've just witnessed a flagrant waste of the tax dollar here. Is it your habit to call cabs for disgusting drunks?"

"It was either call a cab or let him drive his car while he was drunk. I didn't want to assist him in killing himself, so I called him a cab. It's too bad it doesn't meet with your approval."

"I heard that drunk curse and abuse you. Did it ever occur to you that you could arrest him? I heard the whole conversation. Do you deny that he used profanity?"

"No, I don't deny it."

"Well, then, I demand to know why you didn't place that man under arrest. He can't be much of a man when he's totally drunk at eleven-thirty in the morning."

Carpenter shoved his hat back on his head and struggled to control himself.

"So you heard. Did you happen to hear him say that he just learned his father has terminal cancer? Did you hear him say his wife is screwing around on him?"

"I—I—why, no, I didn't. Did he really say that?"

"Listen to me, mister. I don't know who you are and don't give a damn. I happen to think that poor son-of-a-bitch had a right to get drunk at eleven-thirty in the morning, and I won't lock him up if I see him laying stupid drunk on the sidewalk this afternoon. I'll put him in a cab and send him home again. Now, another thing. I don't need anybody following me around second-guessing me about how I do my job, and if you don't like what I said you can stick it up your nose."

The man was very pale and shaking slightly. He strode to a chauffeur-driven Cadillac that blocked the northbound traffic lane and got in. The heavy car pulled away and stopped almost immediately. The man got out of the car and walked briskly back to Carpenter. He was smiling sheepishly. He held out his hand.

"I'm sorry. I was wrong, you know."

"I'm sorry, too. I was a little rough with you."

"Not at all, young man. I asked for it. You are a credit to the department. Goodbye."

He ran to the car and got in. The Cadillac purred away like a large cat.

Lombardo's Delicatessen was only two blocks off

Carpenter's post. He pushed the front door open and walked in. A hundred fragrant aromas filled his nostrils. It was early for the lunch crowd. Three Towson State girls were getting hard salami sandwiches with cream cheese on pumpernickel to go. Carpenter got one of the same. He ate his lunch at a table in the kitchen that the owner reserved for police. He thanked the owner for his lunch and walked north on York Road.

Carpenter was crossing the street at Pennsylvania Avenue when he heard the frantic beeping of a horn to his right. Lieutenant Jarrel Hollis was motioning for him to come to his car.

"Yes sir, what can I do for you, Lieutenant?"

"Ha, ha. Get in, Officer Carpenter. I've been looking for you. We always check the equipment in the patrol cars on the seven-to-three shift. We have to do it once a week or everything seems to disappear. Ha, ha, you know how it is with men. You got to keep after them about the cars."

Carpenter got in and slammed the door. "What do you want me to do?"

Lieutenant Hollis pulled the car away from the curb, and shifted gears delicately.

"You can help me check the equipment in the cars and replenish what is needed while the men wash their cars in the alley next to the station."

Carpenter spent the rest of the day assisting the lieutenant inspecting the cars.

He got home before Mary and found a note on the kitchen table, written in her beautiful, precise hand.

Dear Fritz,

You'll get home an hour before me on this shift, so I'm gonna put you to work. Please put the ham in the oven at 350° as soon as you get home. It's in the fridge in the pot you'll use. About 30 minutes later put the glaze on it. It's in the fridge on the bottom shelf. The string bean casserole and potatoes in foil go in when the ham goes in. You'll like the potatoes, those little red ones that you have a thing for. Have a martini. I'm putting that little pitcher full in the freezer right now. They should be icy cold by the time you get home. See you when I get home. I love you.

Love,
Mary.

With the oven set on 350, he opened the freezer compartment of the refrigerator and found the pitcher. Sipping cold gin straight from the frosty pitcher, he put the food in the oven as directed. The glaze of red wine, white and brown sugar, cloves and mustard clung to the spoon as he stirred it. The thought of tender ham basted in Mary's glaze started his stomach rumbling in anticipation. Another swallow of the martini eased his belly as he went into the bedroom, carrying the pitcher.

Carpenter hung his gunbelt in the closet and stripped. A long, hot shower eased his muscles. Toweling dry, he picked up the martini pitcher and walked to the kitchen. The aroma of the sizzling ham made the saliva pour into his mouth. He poured the glaze over the ham and left the cover off. The pitcher was half full when he returned it to the freezer. Returning to the bedroom, he pulled the covers down, collapsed across the bed and was asleep in seconds.

Dreams of flesh claimed him. Soft, sweet-scented breasts were in his face, probing his mouth, his nostrils. He woke to find Mary's warm, naked breasts brushing his face. She was leaning over him, naked, smiling. As he reached for her, she stepped back.

"No, wait. I want to do everything." She ran her hand down his stomach and caressed him. "Look, it's ready, Fritz. So am I."

Climbing over him, she brought her brown patch down to his body, easing her hips down on him slowly.

She was warm and wet as she guided him into her with three sure fingers. Still smiling, she eased her full weight down, down until she had it all. Her eyes were hot and wild. She no longer smiled as she started to ride his shaft slowly. Carpenter couldn't move. He was mesmerized by her hot eyes and held prisoner by her scalding loins. Mary was making that familiar growling noise deep in her throat when she lost control. Riding him fast, she arched her spine and tilted her head back as if she were fascinated with the ceiling. She was shuddering and coming as she caressed her full breasts with her hands.

Carpenter felt in control of himself as he pulled Mary over on her back and used her slowly. Screaming in his ear, she ground her pelvis into him, as he poured his juice into her body. They collapsed together and lay in each other's arms, soaked with perspiration, their wet bodies plastered together. He realized that the phone was ringing. Not moving from between her legs, he reached over and lifted the phone from its cradle.

"Hello."

"Hello, Mr. Carpenter. This is Mrs. Underwood, in the apartment next door. I heard screaming. Are you and your wife all right?"

"Ah, yes, we're . . . fine," he said, rolling over on his back.

"Oh, I'm glad. We've been having that awful burglar breaking in, and I didn't know what shift you were working. I thought something was wrong over there."

"No, it was the radio. I've turned it down. I'm sorry it disturbed you. Thanks for calling."

He hung up the phone and sat on the edge of the bed.

"Who was that, Fritz?"

"Mrs. Underwood, the old lady next door. She heard some screaming and thought a burglar was in here raping you."

"Ha! Little does she know. I wonder what she'd say

if she knew it was me, raping my husband."

She got to her knees and leaned against his back. Her nipples hardened as she rubbed her breasts on him. She flipped over on her back and opened her legs, laughing wildly.

"Oh, it was so good. You can hold off coming when I get on top of you. I'll have to remember that, when I want an extra special piece, but I couldn't stand it every time. It was so good I thought I was going to faint. My heart almost jumped out of my chest."

"That's quite a chest to jump out of. Your heart would be crazy to leave a nice place like that."

He stood and pulled her to her feet. "Come on, I'll wash your back for you."

"Wait a minute. I'll be right back."

She ran naked from the room and returned immediately.

"I had to turn the oven off. Come on, you can wash mine and I'll wash yours."

They took a shower together and dried each other with large, soft towels. They put their robes on, went to the kitchen, and had a leisurely dinner.

After dinner they smoked a Camel with their coffee and brandy, while they talked.

"Tell me about the seven-to-three shift."

"It's different. The Lieutenant and Captain are around on this shift. We did a lot of work on the cars and equipment."

"Is that all you did today?"

"No, I buried a little girl's dog for her. He got hit by a car, and I sent a drunk home in a cab."

"Ah, the poor little girl. How old is she?"

"I don't know. She's a little thing. She goes to the elementary school at Allegheny and Central. A man ran over the dog. It wasn't his fault. He said he'd pay for another one, and he looks like he can afford it."

"I hope he doesn't forget, Fritz. Dogs are like family.

When my old Lab died I almost went to pieces. Rex was fourteen. He'd go out in the goose blinds with Daddy all day and play with me when he came home, no matter how tired he was from retrieving. Rex would fall asleep with his head in my lap while I did my homework. Daddy let him sleep inside when he got old, on the cold nights, but he never felt comfortable in the house. He'd lick my face to wake me up and cry to go out and would sleep on top of a big doghouse. It had to be really wet and freezing cold for him to sleep inside his house. The cold and rain never seemed to bother him until he got old. Our vet said Rex had arthritis in his shoulders and hips." Mary sighed and blinked tears from her eyes. "Rex died of a heart attack retrieving a crippled Canadian goose that Daddy shot. Daddy said the old goose swam around in the freezing cold water for fifteen minutes before Rex caught him. He had a soft mouth and never put a tooth in a bird. He got that last goose by the wing and brought him back to Daddy. Daddy took that old goose and wrung his neck to put him out of his misery. Rex sat there and watched him. Daddy was putting an old Army blanket around Rex, when he licked Daddy's hand and just laid down and died."

A tear slid down Mary's cheek and dripped from her chin. She laughed softly and dabbed at her eyes with a napkin. Her voice was charged with emotion as she continued. "Daddy buried him and that old goose together under the apple tree in our back yard. That's the only time I ever saw him cry. He sat at the kitchen table and drank half a bottle of Old Granddad with the tears pouring down his face. Mama took the keys to his pickup and left. She was back in an hour with a black Labrador puppy. She smuggled the little fellow into the kitchen and put him in Daddy's lap. I guess we all cried and carried on. We are very emotional people, you know."

Carpenter looked at her gravely for a minute, then smiled. "I know, Mary. I wouldn't want it any other way."

15

THE OLD DESK SERGEANT RAPPED ON THE DAIS WITH his beefy hand. Rain beat on the windows in back of him and lightning flashed, lighting the gray sky. The post office building across the parking lot flared into view, then disappeared in the cover of the storm.

"Come on, you heroes. Shut up. It's getting so a day off don't help me out the way it used to. I need about three days off in a row to feel rested. This fucking eleven-to-seven shift is enough to kill a strong man. I don't know why I don't take my pension. I offered to trade Sergeant Goulek shifts for a couple of weeks, but he don't care for this eleven-to-seven crap any more than I do. I'll bet I drank a quart of Maalox last night and can't put out the fire in my belly."

Lifting his leg, he broke wind weakly.

"We had a busy night, with the storm. The weatherman says that we're going to have rain and strong winds all day. Maybe it will be over by the time I get back to work. You day men can see by the drowned-rat look on our shift that we had hell last night. We had about ten of those old maple trees around town blow down in the wind. It really screwed up traffic. We ain't had a chance to even grab a little fucking nap. Guess I shouldn't complain, at least I was dry. These poor devils have been wet to the skin from handling one accident after the other, all night."

The offgoing shift leaned against the wall in wet slickers, almost asleep on their feet, as the desk sergeant continued.

"It's enough to make a man wish he was a fireman. We had a drunk step on a hot wire and kill himself. Poor bastard smelled like roast pork, according to old Doc Wolf. The drunk was on the hot wire for half an hour before our men got there. They had to wait for the Gas and Electric fifteen minutes to get there and take care of the hot wires before our men could get the man clear of it. Those old hollow maple trees do it every time. They come down in a bad storm and break those hot wires loose from the poles. It's a wonder we don't have more people electrocuted. Be careful out there and stay dry. I'm going home to bed. Goodnight, gentlemen."

Carpenter was standing in the middle of Allegheny Avenue. The rain came down hard on the top of his hat and ran down the back of his neck. He was soaked under his raincoat. The wind was blowing at 25 mph and gusting to 45. At times, the wind would blow his raincoat up around his hips. His calf-high rubber boots were hot on his feet. He could feel the perspiration trickle down his backbone. The children were happy walking to school in the rain. The boys picked out the largest puddles to walk in. At last the bell rang. He looked around for latecomers. Sure enough, a small figure was running toward the intersection. A yellow slicker with a hood covered the tiny person from head to toe. There were no cars in sight. He motioned for the child to cross the street. The child stopped near him and looked up into his face. It was Jenny.

"Bend over, Mr. Policeman. I want to tell you something."

He squatted down to the little girl. She put her arms around his neck and kissed his wet cheek.

"I wanted to thank you for taking care of Bingo for me."

"That's okay, Jenny."

She gave him a big smile. Two of her front teeth were missing. "The man brought me a puppy dog just like Bingo last night. He's just a baby and slept in bed with me. He peed on my blanket."

"I'm really glad to hear that, Jenny. What do you call your new dog?"

"Boots. He's got four white feet. Do you think that's a nice name?"

"I think it's a fine name. Won't your teacher be mad at you for being late?"

"No, but sometimes she keeps me after school for ten minutes to punish me. Goodbye. See you tomorrow." She ran toward the school, swinging her bookbag.

The rain increased in volume. Water ran six inches deep in the streets as he walked back to the business district.

Elmer's Place was only half-filled with customers. Carpenter sat at the end of the counter. The storm was increasing in intensity outside. Lightning was crashing over Towson. He sat in his raincoat as water ran down and dripped on the floor around him. He was wet to the skin.

Millie put a steaming mug of coffee in front of him.

"Let me get you a big bowl of hot chili. I know it's a little early for that, but you look like you need something to warm you up."

"Sounds good."

He was putting the second spoonful of the fiery stuff into his mouth when the phone behind the counter rang.

"It's for you, Fritz. It's Sergeant Goulek, the desk man," said Millie. She stretched the long cord and handed him the phone.

"Hello," said Carpenter, swallowing chili.

"Hi, Fritz, I'm glad I caught you there. The Gas and Electric have a man working on hot wires in back of Rubin's Cut Rate Liquors in the alley. There are trees down, blocking both ends of the alley, so I couldn't get a car in there if I had one to send. They're all out of service on accidents. The gas man wants you to make sure that people keep out from under him as he cuts the wires loose. A lot of people use that alley for a shortcut on the way to work at the courthouse. You better cut through the liquor store from York Road, or you'll have to climb over those trees that are down."

"I'll get right over there."

"Be careful, kid. Don't get around any hot wires."

Carpenter shoved the bowl aside and smiled. "Put this on the side, someplace, Millie. I've got to go, but I'll be back."

He walked outside, into the teeth of the storm and leaned into the wind, making his way half a block south on York Road to the liquor store. Pulling the door open, he stepped inside. The Gas and Electric lineman was there, drinking a Coca-Cola. He was a bronzed giant of a man, perhaps thirty years old. He had on a short yellow slicker with a hood and heavy brown canvas workpants and high-topped leather boots, with spikes.

"Hi, Officer. We got a problem with people getting off the street cars out on York Road and cutting through one of the stores here to get through the alley. They're climbing over fences and going through people's yards to get to work at the courthouse. Pennsylvania and Chesapeake are closed off with trees down and car accidents."

"I noticed that traffic was blocked up southbound for about eight blocks," said Carpenter. He took his hat off and wiped his face with his handkerchief. "What do you want me to do, keep them away from where you're working?"

"Right. We made everything safe up there that's broken, but there are some loose ends up there I've got to cut down. This wind could whip them against the hot stuff and that would mean more trouble. The rest of my crew's working on the hot stuff we got down in the next two blocks, or I wouldn't bother you. Come on, I'll show you where to stand. It won't take more than a few minutes."

They went out into the storm. The winds had increased to near hurricane velocity. Visibility in the blinding rain was perhaps one hundred feet. It was necessary to shout into each other's faces to be heard.

"This is the first one. This pole here," he said, waving his arm at an area between the pole and the rear entrances of the business places. "I've got two short pieces of wire to cut down. The people keep running through here right where they fall." Four young office girls ran laughing through the rain, underneath the pole. "See what I mean?"

"Yeah," said Carpenter. "I'll stop everybody for you."

"Why don't you stand over there and control the rear exits of those four stores. I can't see too well up there because of that big maple in the back yard of the liquor store. It screws up my line of vision. Give me a chance to climb up to the top, and then blow your whistle to let me know it's clear of these young cunts passing through. I'll be done in a jiffy. I'll buy you a coffee when I finish."

"You're on. You know, I wouldn't climb that pole in this weather for a thousand dollars. You can keep your job; I don't want it."

The man laughed. His teeth were very white against his tan face. "Nothing to it. Here I go."

The lineman used his spikes to climb the wet pole and made it look easy. He climbed from Carpenter's line of vision as the maple tree between them obscured his view of the top of the pole. Carpenter stopped a large group of men and women as they emerged from the back door of a store.

"Hold it there, you people. There's a man working on wires up there. Stand clear and stop anybody that wants to pass through. It will only be a minute."

Carpenter blew a long blast on his whistle. In seconds, a heavy piece of wire about ten feet long hit the ground. The wind was gusting now, in fierce blasts. Another piece of wire fell into the water-filled alley. The tree fell into the pole and wires without warning. It came crashing down, brushing the lineman from the pole with its heavy branches. Carpenter caught a glimpse of him as he fell amid the limbs of the maple tree. The broken hot wires flashed and crackled with blue-white intensity as they hit the ground, trapping the lineman in the middle of a jungle of broken limbs and hot popping wires.

Carpenter started to run toward the pole, but someone grabbed the tails of his raincoat. He turned and jerked his coat free from the liquor store owner, whose eyes were wide with fear.

"For God's sake, man, you can't go near there. Those are high-tension wires. Wait, I'll call for help."

"You do that," Carpenter said. He turned and ran straight for the pole and almost stepped on a wire that was hidden under the smashed limbs. He jumped over the wire, then dove as hard as he could for the pole through the maze of broken branches and wires. He landed on his hands and knees and wiped blood away from his cheek where a broken branch had raked him. The lineman was lying on his back raising his head and dropping it, groaning in agony.

"Help me—for God's sake, somebody help me."

Carpenter got to his feet. The sour taste of bile was in his mouth and throat. Hot, crackling wires seemed to be everywhere. He set his teeth and dove for the lineman, landing on top of him. He was screaming in agony as Carpenter rolled off him. Carpenter forced himself to look at the injured man. His canvas pants were torn away from his legs and crotch. The slicker and the heavy shirt he wore under it were bunched up under his arms. His naked stomach and groin resembled a pincushion. Hundreds of splinters from the pole were impaled in his flesh. One large splinter was protruding from his abdomen, on an angle. His genital area and thighs were a mass of raw flesh and dark splinters. He had a compound fracture of the right leg. The fibula was protruding from the leg below the knee. There was very little blood.

"You got to help me with this pain," he shouted, his face gray with shock. "I can't stand it. Do something for me, for Christ's sake."

Carpenter took off his raincoat and tried to cover the man with it.

"Don't, please don't. Don't let anything get up against me. It hurts so bad, oh, sweet Mary, Mother of God, I can't stand it. Help me, for God's sake, help me. Shoot me. Shoot me! Please! Please!"

"Take it easy. Help is on the way."

"Bullshit, this fucking alley is blocked on both ends. Can't you give me something?"

"I'll go for something."

"No! No! Don't you move, you stupid bastard. Do you want to get roasted alive? There are wires all around us. Oh, Christ what am I going to do?"

Carpenter stood up. The liquor store owner was standing where he had left him. Carpenter cupped his hands to his mouth. He screamed, "Get me a bottle of whiskey!"

The owner pointed to his ear and shook his head. He couldn't hear. The lightning and thunder had drowned out Carpenter's shout.

"Get me some fucking whiskey, you son-of-a-bitch!"

He ran in the rear entrance of his store and came out in seconds with two fifths of whiskey in his hands. He came over to the edge of the wreckage and stopped. His first toss was short. The bottle was lost somewhere among the wire and branches. Taking his time on the second toss, he threw the bottle underhand, like a softball. Carpenter caught it and waved his thanks. He sat down beside the injured man and showed him the whiskey.

"Oh, my God. That looks so good. Help me up a little."

Carpenter balled up his raincoat and shoved it under the lineman's head and shoulders. As he raised him, the man screamed in agony. He opened the whiskey and held it to the lineman's lips. The man gulped four large mouthsful before he gagged. Carpenter waited for a few minutes to see if it was going to stay down and then helped him to drink again. The bottle was one-third empty when the lineman relaxed back against the raincoat. The raw bourbon was helping him. He looked up at the pole that hurt him.

"Oh, no. I'm ruined. Look for me. Are my balls gone?"

"No, they're still on. You got a few splinters in them, but they are definitely on. Why?"

The lineman pointed to an object hanging from the rough utility pole about seven feet from the ground. It was the crotch of his work pants. Carpenter pulled the scrap of material down and handed it to him.

"Oh, thank God. I thought that was my balls stuck up there. Oh, I hurt so bad. This is a new pole and it's still loaded with creosote. I didn't even hear the tree go. I had my safety belt unhooked. Give me another chance at that bottle, will you?"

Carpenter handed the lineman the whiskey bottle.

He realized that he was beginning to hear the injured man speak without shouting. The storm was easing off in intensity. Hearing someone call his name, he got to his feet. Sergeant Harper was standing just out of range of the sizzling wires.

"You okay?" he yelled.

"Yeah, we're both all right. He's hurt pretty bad."

"We got two Gas and Electric crews working on the damage at the ends of the alley. Don't move. We'll come for you when it's safe. Tell him we got an ambulance on the way from Fullerton. Towson ambulance is on the way to Union Memorial with some injured people."

"I heard that. I ain't hurt pretty bad, I'm hurt pretty good. Never cared for bourbon before today. Usually drink V.O."

There was about three inches of bourbon left in the fifth.

"I'm afraid you're going to have one hell of a hangover tomorrow. An ambulance is on the way here. Two crews of your friends are working on getting us out of here."

"Fuck it. I feel pretty good now. If only it wasn't a new pole. Old poles don't have as much creosote on them. It burns like a son-of-a-bitch. I feel sick. Help me sit up."

Carpenter raised his shoulders slightly. The lineman turned his head, belched violently, and fell back against the rolled-up raincoat.

"Thought I had to puke. You know you're crazy to come in here after me."

"I know."

"I'm glad you did. Where's that fucking ambulance?"

Carpenter stood and peered through the broken branches. The ambulance crew was waiting just outside the danger zone.

"Oh, my leg. Check my leg. I think it's broken."

"It is. Don't try to move it."

"Shit. I'll be out of work for a long time. Maybe I'm done climbing for good."

"Don't worry about that. You're going to be okay. You can always get a job as a cop."

"You kidding? Too dangerous."

The man passed out, either from his injuries or the bourbon.

Something was changed. Carpenter realized that the fallen wires had stopped spitting fire. The Gas and Electric Company linemen were running down the alley toward him. He sat beside the unconscious man. The deafening growl of chain saws nearby was music to his ears. In minutes the crew had cut a path through the branches.

A young bull of a lineman was the first to get to them. He shut his chain saw off and looked at his injured friend. His tanned face changed to a sick ashen shade.

"Jim, oh, my God, look at you. He's dead, ain't he?"

Carpenter shoved his finger into the unconscious man's throat in back of his jawbone. The pulse was strong and steady.

"He's okay. Come on, cut some of this shit out of the way for the ambulance men to get through. He's going to be fine."

The young lineman jerked the starting cord. The chain saw popped, then roared to life. He began sawing limbs for all he was worth. The ambulance men brought the stretcher to them. They were very professional. They immobilized the lineman's broken leg with a splint, cut the remains of his ragged pants from his body to examine him, and covered him with a sheet.

The oldest ambulance man took charge of moving him. He looked at the crowd milling around and whistled shrilly with his fingers in his mouth.

"O.K., listen up, you guys. He's not bleeding. Let's

get him on the stretcher. Don't bend his back. I need about four of you on each side."

The linemen took positions on both sides of their friend. Carpenter stood near his head.

"Okay, squat down and slide your hands under him. Get spread out even there. When I say the word, all of you lift him at once. Don't bend him. Keep him level. We don't want to twist his back. He may be broken up more than he looks. On the count of three, lift. Okay, now, one, two, three, lift. That's it. Easy now, keep that leg up, goddamn it! Easy . . . ease him down on the stretcher. Good. Thanks boys. We'll take him from here."

They carried him through the rear entrance of the liquor store. The wail of the siren rose above the steady hiss of the rain on the concrete. One of the linemen found the unopened bottle of bourbon in the mess of limbs. He gave it to the liquor store owner and the owner handed it to Carpenter.

"Take it back to the station with you, Officer. You deserve a few drinks."

One of the linemen handed Carpenter his raincoat. The weather-beaten old foreman shook his hand.

"Thanks for going in there to help our friend. You ever want a job climbing poles, call me. My name's Ezra Perkins."

"Thanks . . . but I'd be scared to death. I'll stick with the job I'm doing."

Sergeant Harper looked at him and shook his head. "Come on, Fritz. You look kinda wet. I'll give you a ride back to the station."

"Stop at Elmer's Place. I want to pick something up."

He went in and got six one-pint containers of chili. The storm had lost its gale force intensity. The rain continued at a moderate rate.

Sergeant Goulek hung up the phone as they entered

the office.

"It looks like the worst of it's over. The latest weather report said we've had six inches of rain since this storm started. That's a lot of fucking water. The only calls we are answering now are personal injury accidents and the like. We got about sixty calls backed up for us to pump water out of cellars."

He stood and kicked the swivel chair back. Walking over to the coffee bar, he poured three steaming cups of coffee and put them on the countertop in front of his desk.

"Did you ever hear of such bullshit? They want us to pump their cellars dry. I've been referring them all to the sewage pumping station down in Essex. One guy called back and threatened to get me fired if I didn't send a cop with a pump to his house right away. I told him to put on a pair of water wings and take a bucket down to his cellar and throw the water out the window. He said he changed his mind about getting me fired, that he was going to come right to the station and kick the shit out of me."

Goulek picked up his mug of coffee and took a swallow. "I can hardly wait for that simple son-of-a-bitch to get here. I'm gonna refer him to the Lieutenant. He's been sitting in his office typing one report after another. I believe he types up a report in triplicate when he goes to the bathroom to take a shit. How you making out, Fritz?"

"I'm fine, thanks," replied Carpenter.

"I got a couple of calls about you going to help that trapped lineman. The first call from the liquor store owner said you were probably electrocuted. He called back a few minutes later and said you were sitting under the pole drinking whiskey. One of these days some ass-hole is going to get the facts straight before they call in here. You don't look so good, kid," he said, tossing Carpenter a key ring loaded with keys. "Look in the supply closet there and get yourself a blanket to wrap up in. I got the heat turned on a couple of minutes ago. Those old radiators will be popping in a few minutes. Don't take those blankets in front, they're full of blood. Get one from the back, they just got back from the laundry."

"Thanks, Sarge."

"Come on back here and hug this radiator, you'll be fine in a while. Keep that blanket around your head and shoulders, like an Indian. I just gave my last drink of whiskey to McGee, or I'd give you a couple of shots. The damn fool waded out in a stream that was up over its banks to save a cat that was hanging on to an old stump, half-drowned. The cat scratched the hell out of his face and bit him on the finger for his trouble. That's the trouble with cats; they act like people. What's in the bag, Fritz?"

Carpenter pulled the bottle of whiskey out of the bag and put it on the desk. "Just happened to have a bottle of booze with me and some chili. Okay if we crack the seal, Sergeant Harper?"

"Hell, yes, I'll get some Cokes out of the machine and we'll have chili and bourbon for lunch. Watch out for the Lieutenant. If he catches us working on that bottle, he'll shit in his pants and have to report it to the Captain."

"Fuck him, Harper. If he gives me any of his bullshit I'll hide his typewriter. Come on, Fritz, don't be stingy. Give me one of those chilis."

Sergeant Harper came back with the Cokes. He pulled chairs up to the desk and handed each of them a Coke.

"Each of you guys drink about half down and I'll dose it up with booze for you. Damn, that chili smells good. Nothing like chili to get the system percolating again after you get wet."

They all sat down around the desk sergeant's

battered old desk to eat. The phone rang. Sergeant Goulek answered it and wrote down the information. He hung up, looked at Sergeant Harper, and shook his head in disgust.

"Sorry, Harper. You ain't gonna eat that chili. We got a signal 9 on York and Cedar. Kids trapped in their car. Nobody else is available."

"Son-of-a-bitch," said Sergeant Harper, chugging his Coke. He belched and put on his hat. "Let's go, Fritz."

The rain was now a fine drizzle. The air was noticeably warmer and a bright sun was trying to break through the thinning clouds. It was a short trip to York and Cedar. Harper pushed the car with reckless abandon, the siren screaming its blood-curdling song. They found the tractor trailer stopped in the southbound lane of traffic on York Road. The Chevrolet had crashed into the rear of the trailer. The car was half under the trailer, between the rear wheels. Its roof was peeled back to the rear seat by the brute force of the impact. The truckdriver had flares out and was directing traffic around the wreck. He walked up to the police car as they got out.

His legs were shaking and his jaw jerked up and down as he struggled to control himself.

"They ran into me at high speed. I was stopped in a long line of traffic. Their brakes must have failed. I don't hear or see any sign of life under there. What are you going to do?"

Just then, a tow truck arrived on the scene. Harper motioned the man to remain in the truck.

"Back up here and hook onto the car on the rear end. I'll get the tractor trailer to pull ahead. That might get it out."

The towman wheeled his big rig around in the road and expertly jockied it back to the wreck. He let out a few feet of cable and crawled under the wreck with the hook. He yelled to the police.

"Pull me back out by my legs. I'm jammed in here."

They pulled him out and half of the back of his shirt ripped away on a metal snag. Harper called the tractor trailer driver over.

"You all right to drive?"

"I'm okay. I'm shook up a little, but I can drive. Should I pull her ahead?"

"Yeah. Do it slow and easy. I'll be standing by your rear wheels. Watch me. Stop when I tell you."

The trucker got into his rig and started the big diesel. Harper motioned him forward. The giant rig expelled air from its brakes and inched forward. There was a grinding and terrible squealing of torn metal. The tow truck raised slowly in the front end from the strain. The big rig applied more pressure. The car popped out from under the trailer like a cork from a bottle of champagne. The tow truck dropped forward on its heavy springs. The driver and passenger in the front seat were decapitated. Their headless bodies sat upright on the front seat. The motor and dashboard were in their bloody laps. The front end of the car was folded into the back seat like an accordion. Sergeant Harper went to the police cruiser and returned with a blanket and the big handlight. He took Carpenter to one side, away from the morbidly curious crowd that was gathering.

"Those two in front never knew what hit them. I tried to look in the back seat to see if anybody was pinned in there. There's just a little bit of room. I can't see from out here with everything jammed together like it is. I'm not as wide as you. I think I can get through the rear window and feel around with my arm down between the seats. Just get these ass-holes away from here if you can. Keep them back. I smell gasoline. If somebody lights up a cigarette, we'll all go up in smoke. Okay? Move them."

Carpenter walked through the crowd to the car. One man was standing near the driver's window, taking picture after picture.

"Okay, mister, move out. Get back from here, you people. There's gas leaking. We could all burn up."

He turned to the morbid photographer. The man kept snapping pictures.

"Did you hear me tell you to move?"

The man did not even look up from his camera.

Carpenter reached through the front window and ran his hand down the dead driver's chest. His hand came away with gore clinging to it. The cameraman continued to snap pictures. He tried to shoulder Carpenter aside.

"Come on, mack, I got a right to take a few pictures. Give me a chance, will you?"

Carpenter put his bloody hand on the photographer's chest and wiped the mess on his white shirt. He looked away from his lens at last and looked down at his ruined shirt.

"Hey, what the hell? Ah! Ah! That's blood on me!"

"Come on, then, mister, give me a hand pulling these bodies out. Glad to get your help."

He put his bloody hand on the man's shoulder in a friendly manner. The photographer shook away the terrible hand and ran full force into the crowd, knocking a teenage boy down. Carpenter advanced on the crowd with his bloody hand extended. They shrank back.

"Come on, I need some help with the bodies. I'm looking for volunteers."

The crowd of curious citizens disappeared like magic. The sight of real blood was too much for them. He turned to the wreck and saw that Sergeant Harper was in the car, with only his feet visible in the broken rear window.

"Come here, Fritz. Nobody's in here. Hand me the

blanket."

Carpenter passed the blanket in through the shattered window. A few seconds later, Harper passed the blanket out to him. The heads were surprisingly heavy. Harper backed out the window, feet first.

"Looks like two young boys, Fritz. Put them in the trunk of our car. I see the coroner over across the street. He got here quick today. That's him right over there . . . that skinny old bastard in the baggy brown suit."

The scarecrow figure walked slowly past the tow truck to the wrecked car. He glanced in the window and turned to the police.

"I didn't even get a call on this one. I was on my way to a late lunch at the O.K. Bar. They're dead. See you later. Have the Desk Sergeant phone my secretary when you get their names and addresses."

"Right, Doc. Have a good lunch," Sergeant Harper said.

Carpenter put his grisly burden in the trunk and slammed the lid. They watched the emaciated old man walk to his Buick and drive away. The sun was shining and birds were singing in the ancient maple trees.

"He's a salty old bastard, Fritz, but he's got a heart of gold. Doc Wolf never charged one cop for treating them, and even makes house calls. He's kind of an anachronism, I guess."

A black hearse pulled up near the wreck. Two fat men in black suits got out and waved to the sergeant.

"Ah, here's the undertaker. Goulek must have called for him, even before we asked. Nothing like having a good man on the desk."

An accident investigation car arrived on the scene. They began taking photographs and measurements. It took them an hour and fifteen minutes with their special equipment to extricate the bodies from the wreckage.

The tow truck man used dollies to remove the wrecked car. Traffic officers took the driver of the rig to Traffic Headquarters for further investigation.

"Come on, let's go back and wash up a little and see if Goulek ate all that chili," Sergeant Harper said, dipping a pinch of snuff.

They arrived at the station and ate the cold chili and drank half the bourbon. One of the traffic men from the accident investigation division walked into the desk sergeant's office. Tall and barrel-chested, he wore a thin mustache.

"Hi, there, Andy, how'd it go?" said Carpenter.

"Bad, Fritz . . . bad."

"What's the matter?"

"I just went to Al's garage and tore the wreck apart. I can't find the heads."

"Oh, hell, I forgot. We have them in our trunk. They're wrapped up in a blanket. I'm glad you remembered them.

"So am I. Can you imagine the look on the three-to-eleven man's face when he checked the equipment in the trunk of your car this afternoon? I'll take them down to the undertaker. I guess he can sew them back on."

"Yeah, they weren't beat up too bad," said Carpenter, taking a big mouthful of bourbon-laced Coke. "Who were they?"

"Two local kids. Frank and Richard Wiloski. Sixteen and eighteen. I had Frank last month for exceeding seventy. His father's a big load. He got a lawyer and beat it in court."

"Who was driving?"

"Frank. At least the driver had Frank's wallet in his pocket."

"You notify the parents?"

"Jesse did. He said the father wanted the truckdriver charged with manslaughter. The big load wants to crucify him," said Andy, eyeing the food on the desk. "Say, is that chili you got there? Any left over?"

"Yeah, help yourself. It's cold," Sergeant Harper said.

"I don't give a damn. We haven't even stopped to piss all day. My stomach thinks my throat's cut. Can I take another one for Jesse?"

"Feel free," said Sergeant Goulek, as he picked his teeth with his thumbnail.

"Thanks, Sarge. That's one lunch I owe you. By the way, Sarge, how did the undertaker get there that fast?"

"I didn't call him. Doc Wolf and the undertaker have CB radios in their cars with a police monitor hookup. It makes for good business. They probably heard the police radio when you called out at the scene and headed right for you. They're getting like tow trucks. I reckon they found out they can make more money and save time by listening to us talk on the air."

"Yeah, it's getting bad," Andy mumbled, his mouth full of chili. He swallowed and wiped his mouth on the back of his hand. "Jesse and me got a call to a 9 I last week over on Pulaski Highway. Two tow trucks got there ahead of us. One had his hook on the back of the wreck and the other had the front hooked up. They were standing there in the middle of the road fistfighting over who had hooked up first when we got there."

Andy paused, scooped in two large spoonfuls of chili, took a swallow of Coke and continued. "We handcuffed them together with my cuffs and Jesse cuffed one of them to the car door with his. We called another tow truck to handle the wreck. The guy came all the way from Edgemere and it took a good while before we cleared up our investigation at the scene. Those two ass-holes were getting madder by the minute. By then they were mad at us, not each other. We were just going to let them cool off and release them. Anyway, when we took the cuffs off of them, the big ass-hole from Rick's Wrecking Service took a swing at Jesse."

Tilting his head back, Andy drained his Coke, belched, and lit a cigarette. "The ass-hole split Jesse's lip and knocked him on his ass. You should have seen Jesse bounce up off that concrete. Jesse's a small guy, but he did put some kind of shit lumps all over that big bastard's face and head. Used his fists, too. I kept telling him to use his tools, but he didn't need them. The other guy tried to interfere when Jesse knocked the big shit's teeth out and I cold-cocked him with my sap."

"Serves that prick right," Goulek said, tossing a couple of Tums into his mouth.

"Yeah, I kinda thought it was the thing to do at the time. Then we called two more tow trucks to haul in their tow trucks. We told the tow guys that came to sock it to them on the bill and took our friends to City Hospital to get sewed up. We charged them with interfering with an officer and assault. The judge over there let them go. He said the police have to learn how to be peacemakers without resorting to violence. Bullshit. He must think we don't know he smells ass-holes with every crooked ying-yang politician in the county, and would fix a murder case for a bottle of booze."

Andy gulped the last of his chili and wiped his mouth on the back of his hand. "Damn good chili," he said, smacking his lips. "When we get out on night work, we're going to lay for the judge around those stinking little beer joints he hangs in and get him for operating under the influence."

Sergeant Goulek gave the young traffic man a long look. He shook his head and smiled.

"Andy, my boy, you sound like I did twenty-five years ago. Don't fuck with the court system. You ain't no cherry recruit. You know what a common bunch of bastards appoint them. Don't take it personally."

"Sarge, I know what you mean. I don't care if they want to put a fix in, but I don't like a lecture in front of a court room full of people to go along with it. Fuck that bum. We're going to get him if it's the last thing we do. Thanks for the chili. Open the trunk for me, will you, Fritz? I don't want to forget my heads."

Sergeant Harper watched the young men walk out the door. Turning to the desk sergeant, he said, "You know, Al, those are two good young cops. They have a lot of shit to crawl through before they make twenty years. You think this job is going to make them cynical?"

"Hell, no," Sergeant Goulek replied, taking a belt of bourbon straight from the bottle. "It never made us that way, did it?"

16

THE OLD SERGEANT POUNDED THE DAIS FOR ATTENtion.

Okay, you people. I got everybody marked in here that's supposed to be in. Let's settle down. It's good to see everybody again. That was the worst storm in twenty years, according to the weatherman. People were still calling in here when I came to work last night complaining about flooded cellars. I would like to know what they expected us to do about it. They must think we have a thousand pumps and cops to man them. The fire department has a few men running around in jeeps pumping county buildings that were flooded. We're missing some equipment out of patrol cars. The usual stuff is missing after handling accidents and injured people like you men had to in this storm. The fire department has about three of our blankets and four rubber sheets. They'll drop them off this morning sometime, so if the daylight lieutenant gets upset over it, you know where it is."

The janitor stuck his head in through the booking room door and hissed at the old sergeant conducting roll call. The sergeant glared at him and dropped his notes on the dais.

"Yeah, Carl, what's the problem," he growled.

"Lieutenant Hollis wants me to wash the windows in here before I go home," Carl said meekly.

"Well, don't stand there with your finger up your ass, come in and wash the fucking windows for the Lieutenant."

Carl tiptoed in carrying a bucket of water and some rags. He glanced down the row of police and spotted McGee. He shook his fist at him, turned to the windows behind the sergeant conducting roll call and started to smear Bon Ami on the dirty glass.

"We had a homicide reported last night, Mr. A. B. Goodbody was checking his boat out after the storm last night about eight-thirty up at Loch Raven at the fishing center. He saw the body floating face down in shallow water about three feet from shore. An unknown white male, twenty-five to thirty, shot twice in the back of the head."

Carl stepped back from the window to admire his work. He made a face at the old sergeant behind his back. A few of the police snickered. The old sergeant turned to Carl, gave him a hard look, and prepared to read from his notes. Carl made a face at him and shook his fist at McGee. McGee made a circle of his thumb and forefinger, slid it over the end of his nightstick, and moved his hand back and forth rapidly. Carl began to jump up and down and jerked spastically.

"Ah! Ah! Ah!" he screamed. The old sergeant watched as Carl regained his footing. Carl pulled the bucket off his foot and started to wipe up the spilled water frantically. All the police in ranks were roaring with laughter. The old sergeant took Carl by the arm, led him to the booking-room door, and pushed him gently in the back.

"But I got to wash the windows," Carl said meekly.

"Out!" the old sergeant shouted. Carl shrugged and walked out. He slammed the door behind him. The old sergeant grinned, returned to the dais, and beat the side for order.

"Nothing like a goose-happy janitor to get your fucking attention. Where was I now?" he said, looking at his notes. "Let's see. The stiff. Nothing matches his description in the missing persons file. Detectives put out a teletype and are attempting to identify the body. The B of I man got a good set of prints off him. He figured that the body had been in the water only for a short time. Nobody opened up the fishing center concession yesterday because of the storm, so there's not much chance of developing any good witnesses."

"Don't worry, the homicide dicks will write it off as a suicide if they can't find any suspects," said McGee.

The desk sergeant eyed McGee with disgust and glanced down at his notes. "A prowler, possibly that Ruxton rapist, was seen attempting to enter a bedroom window at five-thirty A.M. this morning, at 109 Crabapple Lane. The next door neighbor spotted him and turned his German Shepherd loose on him. He called the radio room right away, and they notified the detectives that are staking out the neighborhood. Detective Jack Stable was three blocks away. Just as he pulled into Crabapple Lane, a black Chevrolet came hauling ass out of the driveway at 109. Jack pulled his car sideways across the lane and blocked it up. The prowler came at the car wide open and sideswiped it. He hit Jack a hard whack with his right front fender just as Jack let a round go. Jack is in Union Memorial with a compound fracture of his leg and a crushed pelvis."

"The getaway car was found abandoned, six blocks away, with the motor still running. It was a stolen car. Jack's round blew a hole through the center of the windshield, and probably missed that bastard. The German Shepherd was found dead in the yard with two bullet holes in his side. He had a bloody patch of black flannel in his mouth. I hope he tore the balls off that son-of-a-bitch. Goodnight, gentlemen, I'm gonna have a couple of shots and go home to bed."

Sergeant Harper stepped to the dais and cleared his throat. "There's a few details for us to take care of today. McGee, there's a wedding today at the Immaculate Heart of Mary Church. Be there at eleven A.M. to handle the traffic. Look sharp, because it's the Deputy Chief Inspector's daughter. You know he doesn't like uniformed cops because he's worked around detectives for fifteen years. He'll be looking for something to sore-ass about, so have your car washed and shine your brass up. Stop off at Mack's and get a shoeshine."

"Yes sir."

"Carpenter, we got a shitty note here from headquarters. It seems like kids are climbing around on the roof of the business places in the four and five hundred blocks of York Road on Friday and Saturday morning. They found a lot of beer bottles and used rubbers up there. It seems the good merchants don't want fucking on the weekends up there, so break it up. There's a few places to get up on the roof in the four hundred block by climbing telephone poles. I don't know how they do it in the five hundred block, but the kids must have found a way. The merchants know it's going on during the day because they can hear the kids running around up there and playing music and dancing. I wish we had time to read this masterpiece of sarcasm that the headquarters brass wrote to us about this little problem, but we ain't gonna play their little game. We'll just break up the parties on the roof, *sabe?*"

"Yes sir."

"Jacobson, the principal over at the Bear Hills School asked for a man to be on the playground of the school between ten and three today. They're having their annual spring festival today. Last year they had trouble with a bunch of tough teenage boys from Hamden. They went out there, and started fights and got food from the concession and refused to pay. They pulled the blouse off a thirteen-year-old girl, who happened to have tits, and felt her up in front of the whole crowd. We locked up about six of them, but about twenty or thirty got away from us last year. If they come back, call for help on the principal's office phone and we'll swoop down on those bastards and put a few lumps on their heads this time before we lock them up. Don't try to make a move on your own. This is a bad bunch of bastards."

"Right, Sarge."

"Any of you got something you want to say? No? Hit the bricks. I'll be taking calls for you guys when you're out of service on your details."

17

CARPENTER WAS CROSSING THE STREET AT YORK AND Pennsylvania when Sergeant Harper blew his horn and motioned him over. Robert Fancy was riding shotgun and was busy filling out a report attached to the clipboard.

"Any sign of the kids on the rooftop?"

"Yes sir. I found some college kids beer drinking and sunbathing up there. I gave them hell and sent them on their way. They won't be back. That was over the men's store in the four hundred block."

"Any activity in the five hundred block?"

"I heard music from up on the roof. It was the lady in the apartment over the barber shop playing her radio a little too loud. She said she'd keep it down."

"Good. Where you headed?"

"Back to the station. I thought I'd see if the men in the radio room wanted anything from Elmer's for lunch."

"Get in. We'll drop you off."

"Headquarters car 21, 22, and 23. Assist the officer on detail at the Bear Hills School on Falls Road. Fight in progress."

"Twenty-one's ten-four."

"Twenty-two's ten-four."

"Twenty-three's ten-four."

Harper dropped the car into low and tore away from the curb. The shrill scream of the siren was deafening between the buildings in the business area. He drove with reckless ease. The car raced at high speed through the heavy traffic. He approached an intersection that was blocked with cars turning in both directions. An accident seemed impossible to avoid. At the last possible instant the intersection opened up and the cars pulled out of the way. They missed a car on the right by inches, then hung a right, and slid around the corner. The Chevy shuddered like a winded horse and dug into the asphalt. They were through the traffic jam. They hung a left on Joppa and nearly hit a parked car west of the intersection.

Carpenter's throat was dry. The sphincter muscle in his rectum was clenched painfully. He sat on the edge of the back seat. His heart was pounding in his chest. Officer Fancy had his knees drawn up and his feet braced against the dashboard. Joppa Road was not a road to travel at high speed. It was originally an Indian trail in the 1600 and 1700s. Tobacco farmers rolled hogsheads of tobacco to market on it later. The road was full of small hills, dips, and dangerous curves. Sergeant Harper drove through this obstacle course as though he were on the salt flats of Utah.

Carpenter looked over the thin man's shoulder at the speedometer. They were traveling between 75 and 80 miles an hour. He closed his eyes and prayed for deliverance. It was better with his eyes closed. He was tossed around on the back seat like a rag doll. The screech and wail of the siren were grating on his nerve ends. The siren slowed and fell silent. The quiet was deafening. The car was slowing. They were stopped.

"Come on, you guys, wake up. We're here."

They bailed out of the car and raced for the back of

the school. Frightened children were running here and there away from the concession and ride area. The three policemen ran around the corner of the building, nightsticks in hand. A group of ten toughs had Officer Jacobson captive in the center of a loose circle. A big, raw-boned youth of about twenty was beating at Abe with a bicycle chain. Jacobson's shirt hung from his shoulders in shreds. He was trying hard to ward off the vicious blows with his nightstick. Abe was on his last legs, blood oozing from many cuts on his bald head and shoulders. The police were into the crowd of hooting, jeering punks, taking them by surprise.

Carpenter dug the heavy rosewood stick into the kidney of a fat youth who had his back to him. The fat one dropped to his knees and vomited on the blacktop. The tough next to Fats spun to face Carpenter in time to take the butt of the stick jammed into his mouth. Shattered teeth and blood flew over the front of Carpenter's shirt. The toothless one fell on his back and bounced up. Carpenter kicked his feet out from under him and brought the stick down on his skull. His scalp split open, like an overripe peach. He groaned and lay still, holding his head with bloody hands.

Carpenter looked to his right. Fancy had one of them laying at his feet out cold. He was swinging his stick at another of Abe's tormentors, who was trying to crawl away.

Harper was jumping around two who were kneeling, holding their damaged groin areas. Some of the toughs were running away. The last to face them was the chain wielder. Harper was moving around him slowly. He didn't even have his nightstick out. Fancy and Carpenter went to Harper's aid. Harper spoke to them in a quiet voice. He could have been giving them instructions at roll call.

"No, thanks. I'll take care of this one. Look after Abe."

Abe was leaning against a penny pitch stand. He was breathing hard, bleeding from many places. Incredibly, he was smiling.

"Get that son-of-a-bitch, Sarge," said Abe, with clenched teeth.

The chain man swung his weapon around like a bull whip. The chain took the sergeant's hat off and sent it flying. Stepping closer to Harper, he swung at his legs. Harper jumped over the chain like a child does a jump rope and grabbed the chain as it passed. He jerked it out of the punk's hands, casually tossed it aside, and moved in on the chain man. The toe of Harper's crepe-soled shoe caught him under the chin. Blood poured from the sneering mouth, as he bit off the end of his tongue. Putting his head down, he rushed Harper. Harper stepped aside quickly and hit him sharply on the ear as he went by. Harper followed and spun him around. Sharp jabs in the eyes split the tough's eyebrows open. He was helpless, blinded with blood.

Harper reached down and grabbed one of the hulk's hands. The wrist bone popped like a whip when Harper snapped it. He screamed in agony. Harper seized the other arm and broke the wrist like a straw. He was still screaming, standing upright, when Harper kicked him deliberately in the groin. The tough made a few hiccuplike noises and fell, unconscious. Sergeant Harper was not even breathing hard.

"There. We got a believer here. He's a good tough guy now. He won't cut up any more cops with a chain."

The rest of the shift ran to them from the front of the building, sticks in hand. Sean McGee led them.

"Looks like you're fine here," said McGee, laughing wildly. "We saw a few of them running south on Falls. We'll get the bastards."

They turned and ran toward their cars.

"Hold it," Harper barked. "Fuck them. Let them go. We got a few here to lock up."

"But they're getting away, Sarge."

"I said let them go," said Harper, giving McGee a hard look. "Take Abe to the hospital."

Sergeant Harper walked over to Abe Jacobson and looked at the cuts on his head and shoulders. He shook his head.

"How you feeling, Abe?"

"Like shit."

"Come on, McGee, take him to Union Memorial. The rest of you guys load these police fighters and take them to get sewed up. Take them to University Hospital. We don't want Abe to get shoved on the side for one of these ass-holes. Take your time getting there."

They loaded the lot of them into police cars and drove away. Patrons of the fair were returning. A group of women approached Sergeant Harper and Carpenter. The leader of the group, a nervous-looking, heavyset woman with gray hair spoke to Sergeant Harper.

"Thank goodness they're gone. They all came in about half an hour ago and went to the hot-dog stand. They ate a lot of hot dogs and refused to pay. We reported it to the officer and he called the radio room, then tried to hold several of them until you got here. One of them had a wire or something wrapped around his wrist. He started beating the officer with it. The children all ran in panic. I'm the principal here. I took all the ladies who were chaperoning and ran into my office. I'm afraid we lost our heads. Is the officer going to be all right?"

"He'll be okay. We sent him to the hospital," Harper said.

"Do you think it would be all right to resume our fair? Did you arrest any of those hoodlums?"

"Go ahead, you'll be fine now. We were lucky enough to grab a few of them, ma'am. I don't think they'll be back next year, but call us when you're planning your fair next year. We'll send somebody around to look out for you," said Harper, dusting his hat off.

"Thank you," she said, twisting a handkerchief in her hand. "It's terrible what the world's coming to. I'm sorry to put all of you to this trouble."

"No trouble, lady," said Harper, grinning coldly. "I wouldn't have missed it for anything."

Back in the car, Sergeant Harper put a pinch of Copenhagen in his cheek and reached for the radio mike.

"Car Twenty's ten-eight. Have the traffic division handle all calls until the district cars return to the district."

"Ten-four. Car Twenty. KGA340 testing 1300 hours."

Sergeant Harper dropped Carpenter off on the street in the business district.

Carpenter went into the men's room of a service station to wash the blood from his hands. Abe's blood and the blood of the police fighter turned the lather pink. He was very tired and his hands were shaking as he dried them. Walking half a block to the O.K. Bar, he shoved the door open. It was necessary to stand there in the gloom for a few seconds to allow his eyes time to adjust to the dim light. The lunch crowd was thinning out. The Four Aces were singing "Tell Me Why" softly. The juke box was turned down low. It seemed like a sanctuary inside the dark old bar. He waved to the daytime bartender, went into the back room, and sat at his special corner table.

Sam Rider burst through the kitchen door carrying a tray of food for the bar. He was followed by two waitresses bearing heavy trays. The trio disappeared into the front. Sam Rider returned and sat down at the table with Carpenter.

"Hi, amigo," Rider said, as he stretched and yawned.

"Christ, but I'm tired. I must be getting old. I've only been here for an hour and I'm ready to go back home to bed. How have you been, Fritz?"

"Busy, Sam."

"Say, you look a little shopworn, yourself. How 'bout if we both have a nice fucking drink and some lunch together?"

"The drink sounds good. I don't know about lunch. I had one hell of a heavy breakfast."

"I'll be back," said Sam, winking.

He returned with a bottle of Chivas Regal and two glasses of crushed ice. He broke the seal and poured.

"Say when, Fritz," he said, sloshing Scotch into the glass.

"That will do. Hold it! I don't want to get bombed."

"This stuff will never hurt you, kid. It's as mild as maiden pee. Here's to your good health."

Sam raised his glass and grinned. They tossed off the fine old Scotch. Sam poured himself another large one and slid the bottle over to Carpenter.

"Pour your own, pal. I got a heavy hand, and I don't want you yelling at me."

Carpenter poured a couple of ounces of the golden whiskey over the ice. He felt the Scotch working into his veins, relaxing him. Sam offered him a cigarette. Taking one, he lit up, pulling the smoke deep into his lungs.

"You look better already," said Sam, sipping his whiskey. "You got blood on your shirt. Handle an accident?"

"A fight. A bunch of ass-holes from the city came out to raise hell at the Bear Hills School Fair. Abe Jacobson grabbed one and got worked over with a bicycle chain. We went to help him and got a few of the bastards before they could get away."

"Son-of-a-bitch. Is Abe hurt bad? I like that guy. He can always make me laugh."

"He got his head, shoulders, and arms cut up. He'll be off for a while, but he should be okay. He did some bleeding."

"Those common bastards. Did you get the one that beat him?"

"Sergeant Harper did," said Carpenter, shivering.

"Say no more. I'll bet we got one less cop fighter to worry with."

"He won't be any trouble until he gets his arms out of the casts. I don't want to talk about it. I can still hear him screaming."

"That Snake is one hell of a cop. About five years ago, we had a big, nasty soldier in here drinking. The bartender cut his drinks off and tried to get him to leave, but the bum started breaking up the place. I was in the back room on the phone and missed some of it, but they told me about it. This soldier went about six feet four and weighed maybe two-twenty."

Sam picked up his glass and gulped his Scotch. He poured a little more into his glass and sipped it.

"When he started ripping the booths off the walls, the waitress called the cops. He slapped her alongside the head, knocked her cold, and ripped the phone off the wall. The bartender grabbed a billy club and came over the bar after him. He made a swipe at the soldier's head and rapped him a good one. The soldier didn't even blink. He took the billy club away from the bartender and broke the damn thing over his leg. The son-of-a-bitch was built like a gorilla. He was slapping the bartender silly when I heard the noise and went in."

Sam paused, took a drag on his cigarette, and gulped his Scotch. He put the glass down and grinned at Carpenter as he resumed the story.

"The soldier didn't let go of the bartender. He held him up with one hand around his throat, reached out and grabbed me by the wrist. One flip and he had me on my knees. He took both of us by our throats and was beating us together like rag dolls. Snake came in about that time and walked up to the guy, smiled at him, reached up with his foot like a ballerina and kicked him in the nose. The soldier dropped us and grabbed his fucked-up nose. I didn't even see it happen, but then Snake kicked him in the balls. The poor boob grunted and went down like a ton of bricks, holding his balls. Everybody says he always goes for the balls. Snake was looking for a phone to call an ambulance when he saw the waitress laying under the table crying. He mumbled something to her and went back to the soldier. The guy was out of it and didn't realize what was happening. Snake broke the thumb and forefinger on each of the soldier's hands."

"I'm starting to approve of his bonebreaking more every day," Carpenter said.

"Yeah, me too, Fritz, but the bartender gave him hell. He said he was a rotten bastard for hurting an unconscious man. Snake gave him a look that would have frozen antifreeze. He said real quietly, 'I don't tell you how to tend bar, do I? You got to break some bones to make believers out of the bad ones. If you don't like the way I handled this bastard, don't call us next time. Call the State boys.' I'll never forget the way those fingers sounded when he broke them. Like a nutcracker popping open an English walnut. I think about Snake every Christmas when I eat walnuts. As far as I'm concerned, he saved my life, or at least kept me from taking one hell of a beating. I send him a case of booze every year for Christmas."

"I don't feel like a heavy lunch, either," he interrupted himself, suddenly. "Wait a minute, I got something that Charley made last night on the back of the stove right now. It will fix you up."

He returned with two large bowls of wonton soup. A delicate broth covered the rich egg noodles. Each little noodle compartment was filled with either chopped beef or chicken. Crisp Chinese vegetables were packed in the bowl, peeking out from under the broth.

"Here, use a little white pepper with it," said Sam. "It adds a little something special to it."

The men ate the soup in silence. It was true. Wonton soup is soothing to the nerves and rests easy in a troubled stomach.

When Carpenter arrived home that day, Mary swung the door open when he put his key into the lock. Taking his hand, she pulled him into the room. Her arms clamped around his neck as she plastered herself against him and kissed him. Her tongue was a hot, sweet dart in his mouth. Clean and fresh from a shower, her damp hair brushed his face as she leaned back and shook her head like a playful colt. He slid his hand down her back. She had nothing on under her satin robe. As she stepped back, she glanced down and laughed at his fierce erection.

"My boss gave me two tickets to tonight's ballgame. The Orioles and Boston are playing. If you let me get on top, I'll take you with me," she said.

"Suppose I don't let you get on top?"

"Then I'll still take you, but I'll root for Ted Williams when he comes to bat. I'll act like a Boston fan and make everybody hate us."

"Well, I don't know," he said, brushing the back of his fingers over her erect nipples. "I wouldn't want you to overexert yourself. How about your heart?"

"You can take it easy when you put it in. Don't punch me in the heart with it. Come on . . . when we finish you can take me to Winterling's for dinner."

18

A WEEK LATER, THE OLD DESK SERGEANT WAS STANDing at the dais, conducting roll call.

"We had two indecent exposures yesterday at Goucher College. A group of girls in the drama club were practicing outside on the grass at four P.M. and a young white male, twenty to twenty-five, pulled up to them in a red Chevy convertible. He got out of his car and walked to within fifteen feet of them and opened his trenchcoat. He was naked from his waist to his knees. His pants were cut off above his knees and held up with pieces of string. He beat his meat for a few seconds in front of them and some of them started throwing their books at him. He jumped into his car and took off. About five minutes later this same fruitcake walked up to a classroom window of the chemistry lab and tapped on the glass. The teacher walked over and raised the window up a little and asked him what he wanted. He whipped open his coat and masturbated in front of the entire class. He ejaculated on the window and ran back to the red convertible and left. We didn't get a call on it for forty-five minutes, so the meat beater was long gone by the time we got there."

"Naturally, those hot Goucher girls made sure he

had a head start," McGee said.

"Very perceptive, clown." The old desk sergeant paused, took a Tum, chewed it, swallowed, belched, and continued with his report.

"We had three women clerks in the Courthouse get obscene phone calls between three-thirty and four P.M. yesterday. They all work in the tax assessor's office. This nut starts his pitch by saying he's a doctor taking a survey by phone for a statistical study sponsored by the American Medical Association. He asks them a lot of personal questions about their underwear and gradually gets to their sex lives. He wants to know in detail their likes and dislikes, how many times a month they get laid. The longer he talks, the bolder he gets. When they finally balk at his questioning he gets nasty with them and says he's not going to pay his taxes to a bunch of dirty whores. They weren't going to report it, but he told the third gal he talked to that he was going to get her when she got off work, beat her up, and suck her cunt 'til the top of her head caved in. She told the cop that took the report that she thought it was fun talking to him until he threatened to hurt her. We got a lot of strange bastards running around out there."

"Oh, I don't know, he sounds like a man after my own heart," McGee said.

"Quiet, you deviant, and be careful, because I got up to take a leak at three A.M. last night and the moon is full. That brings the jungle out in the citizens of Towson. No shit, any old cop will tell you to look out for that full moon, because it makes the natives restless. Goodnight, men. I'm going to my mother-in-law's for dinner tonight. If I'm not here tomorrow, it means that the moon got to her and she fed me poisoned meat loaf."

Sergeant Harper stepped to the dais. "Okay, quiet. The trial for the police fighters, as you know, was scheduled for tomorrow afternoon at three P.M. They are all represented by a city lawyer by the name of Smith. He asked the judge for an indefinite postponement. He wants to wait until Sabertino is out of the hospital. I was with the Captain when he went to see Abe today. Abe's a funny guy. The doctor down at Union Memorial gave him a bottle of painkillers to take, but he won't use them. He says he's afraid he'd become addicted to dope. He's not in too much pain now, though. We took him a case of his favorite bourbon and he was working on a bottle pretty good by the time we left him. Fritz, why don't you hustle him up a little gift basket of some fruit and stuff and tell him it's from all of us. Abe likes to eat and he's always scarfing up fruit."

"Yes sir."

"If you connect, you can deliver it if you want to. He lives over on Joppa Road near Bendix, number 1153 to be exact. Don't stay off your post for more than an hour or so."

"Right, I'll take care of it."

"Don't forget your church details, you guys in the cars. We don't want no preachers calling up Headquarters on us. Anybody got anything to say? No? Okay, hit the bricks."

Carpenter walked into the florist's shop and waited for the woman clerk to finish selling a floral wreath to an old man. She was a thin, severe-looking, middle-aged woman. Her lips were a thin slash in her face and her hair was pulled back in a bun.

"Can I help you?"

"Yes, ma'am, I'd like to price a basket of fruit for an officer who was hurt on the job."

"Do you mean Officer Jacobson?"

"Why, yes, ma'am. Do you know him?"

"I should say so. He caught some boys breaking windows of one of our hothouses last year. I read about those animals beating him with a chain in the paper this morning. Come on back to the refrigerator. I'll show you one that I just made up. It's our deluxe basket. We use only hand-picked, select fruit."

She got the basket out of the refrigerator. It was a work of art: Huge pears, yellow and red apples, and large navel oranges piled very high; a large pineapple was the centerpiece, surrounded with expensive imported cheeses and caviar in fancy red and brown pots. The whole works was covered with heavy yellow transparent plastic.

"How do you like it?"

"Ah . . . it's beautiful. Ah . . . how much is it?"

"For anybody else, twenty-five dollars. For you, nothing. We have come to love and respect Abe. He checks our business at night. It's a small thing. Why don't you let me give you a cup of coffee and you can watch me throw one together. It won't take long."

Ten minutes later he was lugging the heavy basket north on York Road. He hailed a cruising cab.

"Where to, Officer?"

"1153 Joppa Road. Near Bendix Radio."

"Hop in."

He put the huge gift basket on the back seat and got in front with the driver.

"I'm going over to Joppa and Loch Raven to breakfast, anyway," said the cabbie, waiting for traffic to pass. He pulled out behind a green Studebaker and blew his horn at a waitress, waiting on the opposite side of the road for a streetcar. She wiggled her fingers at him like a young child, although she must have been fifty.

"I go right by the 1100 block Joppa. Say, don't Abe Jacobson live there? I saw about him in the paper today."

"Yeah, the basket's for him."

The cabbie turned right on Joppa Road and slowed to let an old woman cross the street.

"I've known Abe for about six months now. He got me for driving my cab drunk late one night and just gave me hell and took my keys away from me. I don't usually drink, but my wife had just lost her job and my little boy was in the hospital with two broken legs. A car hit him on the way to school. I have never forgotten Abe. He seems almost too nice to be a cop. Excuse me, I didn't mean that the way it sounded."

"That's okay. I know what you mean."

"Is he going to be okay? I mean, is he hurt real bad?"

They were drifting down Black and Decker hill. The cabbie swerved to miss a hole in the blacktop.

"Bad enough," said Carpenter. "But he'll heal up in a few weeks."

"Thank God for that. Let's see, it's somewhere along here."

The cabbie slowed as they passed stone two-story houses that were built near the turn of the century. He hit the brakes and stopped in front of a house with a well-kept yard.

"This is it. I recognize that beat-up old Studebaker of his."

Carpenter opened the door and got out. He retrieved the gift basket and slammed the door. The cab driver got out and walked to Carpenter's side. He put something in his shirt pocket.

"Don't turn me down, now, Officer. It's a sawbuck. I want Abe to have it. Tell him to take his old lady out to dinner on me sometime when he feels better. Tell him it's from that drunk cabbie he gave a break to six months ago. Good luck to you, Officer. Take care of yourself."

Carpenter tapped on the door with his toe. He could barely see over the mound of fruit he held in his arms.

"Come on in, Gracie, it's not locked."

Carpenter braced the basket against the door frame and turned the knob. The door swung open. He stepped inside and closed the door with his foot. The living room was cluttered with children's toys. Abe was sitting on a brown leather sofa with his bare feet up on a hassock. All he had on was a pair of green pajama bottoms. He put the Sunday papers aside and stood up. The white bandage around his head and shoulders were in sharp contrast to his heavy black beard. He swayed on his feet and sat down quickly.

"Fritz, old pal. I've had too much Jack Daniel's. I thought it was Gracie coming home from church with the kids. Should have known. It's too early. She just left fifteen minutes ago. What you got there?"

"The men on the shift sent this fruit over," said Carpenter, putting the basket in front of the fireplace. "Somebody said you like it."

"I'm crazy about it. Can't seem to get enough of it. I scrounge a bag of apples every day at the Food Fair and eat maybe four or five while I'm working. Sometimes it makes me shit like a goose. Ha-ha! I'm a little bit drunk, Fritz. Don't mind me. I don't usually drink this early, but Snake and the Captain brought me a whole case of Jack Daniel's and I had a few drinks with them. I haven't felt this good since before that bastard introduced me to that bicycle chain. Doc Wolf stopped to see me last night. He said I could go back to work in a few days."

Abe shook a Lucky Strike from a pack he was holding and dropped a couple in his lap. He flipped his Zippo open and fired up the wick, but couldn't make the flame meet the end of his cigarette. Carpenter held Abe's wrist to steady the flame, but Abe leaned to close and singed the hairs protruding from his nose. He ground the unlit cigarette in an ashtray and grinned.

"Don't rush things," said Carpenter, sitting down on the sofa. "Stay home until you can get around without hurting. I guess it's bothering you a lot, Abe."

"Yeah. Don't tell the rest of the guys, but I cried like

a baby last night. I was sitting here trying to eat a sandwich that Gracie fixed for me. I don't know if it was the pain or my nerves or what. I just started to blubber like a kid, with my mouth full of good Kosher corned beef."

"Did the doctor give you something to take?"

"Yeah, but fuck that stuff," he said, waving his arms around. "I got wounded in Korea and spent two weeks in the hospital in Japan. I saw too many guys get hung up on the dope they gave them for pain. If it gets so bad I can't stand it, I'll take some. I'd rather drink a little booze. If I drink too much of that, I'll get sick and lay off for a few days."

"You're too much, Abe."

"Yeah, I guess so. All Jews are a little bit touched in the head. My father thinks I'm nuts to be a cop. He's in the catering business and he wanted to turn it over to me. He can't understand why I'm not interested. When I married a Catholic girl he gave up on me. He bought us this old house for a wedding present and hired himself a manager for his business."

Abe shifted his weight on the sofa and made a face when the pain cut into him. Beads of perspiration broke out on his face and neck. Carpenter looked at him and started to say something. Abe shook his head and grinned weakly. He started to talk rapidly.

"My father spends every winter in Miami Beach with my mother. They come back home in May and stay until July fifth, then they go to California to visit my mother's sister. They come back home in August and head back to Florida on October first. I guess some people like that kind of life. I don't feel like I'm living unless I'm working. Christ, I miss it already. Has police work got to you yet, Fritz?"

"I don't know. Sometimes I feel like I'm really doing something worthwhile. Other times, it's enough to make you want to resign from the human race. It really grows on you, though. There's a lot of good people out there that really depend on us."

Perspiration poured from Abe in streams. His bandages were getting wet.

"Face it, Fritz. You're hooked. You don't want to screw around with those greasy pipes anymore. You're a cop. Look at all the fun we have. Remember the day we were serving warrants and that dog put you up on the roof?"

"Yeah," said Carpenter, grinning. "How 'bout that stripper that wanted to divert us with a little bit of free pussy? Would you have taken just a small bit of that if you had been by yourself?"

"Sure. Why not? So would you. What's a little traffic warrant, anyway? How 'bout a drink, pal?"

"Just one and I've got to go. Where's your jug. I'll get it."

"Out on the kitchen," said Abe. "Straight back through that swinging door."

The aroma of cooking was fragrant in the warm old-fashioned kitchen. He got two clean glasses from a cabinet, filled them with ice from a bucket standing near the bottle of bourbon, and carried the bottle and glasses back to the living room.

"What's cooking out there? It smells good," said Carpenter.

"My favorite," said Abe, smacking his lips. "Roast guinea hen with sage dressing. Gracie is going to spoil me while I'm off. She said she's only going to fix what I like as long as I'm home. It's not going to be so bad around here. Just think, I won't have to shave. I'm going to let these son-of-a-bitch whiskers grow until I go back. I'll look like a Kosher Santa Claus. Come on, pour me a drink. Don't you have any pity on a poor, crippled cop?"

Carpenter poured their drinks and handed the smallest one to Abe. "Here's hoping you heal up quick,

Abe." He tossed the bourbon down and went to the door.

"Wait a minute, Fritz. Thank Rhoda Blumberg for me. You must have got the fruit at her place. She's the only fruit florist open on Sunday. Tell her I'll be back to work before we get on eleven to seven. She likes me to check her doors for her."

"Yeah, she thinks a lot of you. See you later, Abe." He reached into his shirt pocket. "Hey, I almost forgot. Here's a sawbuck. The cabbie that brought me here said you gave him a break one night. He wants you to take your wife out to dinner on him."

Carpenter handed the money to Abe and almost ran out the door to escape from the injured man's tear-filled eyes.

The second car to come along stopped and backed up to where he was standing. The man rolled his window down.

"Can I give you a lift to Towson?"

"Thanks. I'd appreciate it."

He got in and slammed the door. The big Hudson purred through the gears. The driver had the radio turned up. Teresa Brewer was singing, "Music! Music! Music!" The volume blasted his eardrums. It must have been turned up all the way. Carpenter fought an impulse to reach over and turn the radio down. The man was beating time to the music on the dashboard with his right hand. He held the powerful car on a steady sixty miles per hour, twice the legal speed limit. Carpenter discreetly put his fingers in his ears. Mercifully, it was a quick trip to Towson. Slamming his brakes on at York Road, he slid to a stop at the traffic light. He turned the radio down as Carpenter opened the door to get out.

"Hope you didn't mind the volume up like that. I can't hear too good."

"No, I didn't mind."

"What's that you say?" He leaned over the seat and cupped a hand behind his ear.

"No! It was okay!" screamed Carpenter.

"Good, good. Say, that Pearl Bailey is one great singer, isn't she?"

"Yeah, she's great."

"What did you say?"

"I said up your ass, you deaf son-of-a-bitch!"

"Oh, that's all right," he shouted, turning the volume up. "It's always a pleasure to help our firemen."

The big Hudson lurched forward and squealed wheels as the man shifted to second.

Carpenter had his hand on the front door of Elmer's when a car beeped at him from across the road.

"Hey, Fritz, come here. I want you to see what I've got in back," shouted McGee.

He walked across the street and looked into the back seat. A bushel of Red Delicious apples, two bushels of Golden Delicious apples, a tray of nectarines, two boxes of Bing cherries, and a bushel of huge grapefruit were stacked on the floor and seat. McGee burst into laughter when he saw Carpenter's look of astonishment.

"Nothing's too good for my partner. Abe always tells me he can't get enough fruit. I got my Kosher buddy enough fucking fruit here to founder a hippopotamus."

"Where in the name of hell did you get all that stuff?" asked Carpenter, scratching his head.

"Well, I've got a new produce stand on my post, over on Falls and Joppa. The old cunt that runs it has been doing good business. She's open every day of the week and brags that she makes two hundred dollars' profit on Sunday alone. Abe and me stopped in to see her a few times to get acquainted."

McGee grinned and took a Havana from the glove compartment. "You know how he likes fruit." He paused, licked the cigar all over and bit the end off. "We thought that she might come across with a few freebies once in a while. Abe took the old bag coffee and donuts every day for two weeks and she never even offered to pay him."

McGee put the big cigar in his mouth and lit it with his Zippo. He swallowed a lot of smoke and continued with smoke pouring from his nose and mouth. "One day when he thought he had her softened up with a big piece of moonseed cake, he picked up an apple—a big Winesap—and took a bite. She walked right up to him like he was robbing her and demanded ten cents for the apple. Abe paid her and we got in the car and left. He wasn't even mad. Hell, I've never seen that big Jew mad at anything. We have other sources of fruit, anyway. I think it was a challenge to him. He said that when he finally got her number and could eat free fruit from her it would taste sweeter than the rest. He's got her coffee and sweets once a week, at least, since then. He never even got a free tangerine. That tight-fisted old broad just brags about the money she's making. I decided to take a different tack with her today."

"What did you do, Sean?" asked Carpenter. "Grab her by her snatch?"

"Nothing quite so crude, my callow friend. She always gets to her stand early on Sunday morning to get set up because it's her best day. I went over to see her right after roll call. I was going to tell her she couldn't open on Sundays anymore because we got complaints about her violating the Blue Laws."

"Come on Sean, you know we don't worry about Blue Laws."

"That's right Fritz, but that old cunt ain't hip to that. I got there about seven-fifteen and didn't see her around. The stand was all set up with her fruit and produce and neither her nor her black helper was around. I noticed her pickup truck parked behind a huge pile of empty bushel baskets. I thought I detected movement inside it."

McGee paused dramatically and narrowed his eyes. "I sneaked up, and lo and behold, her black helper was packing peter into her like it was going out of style. I stood and watched them until he got himself off. No use spoiling his fun. My argument was with her. When that black ass stopped pumping, I opened the door of the truck. I thought they were going to die. The black helper pulled up his pants and pleaded with me not to arrest his boss. I told him not to worry about screwing, that I was there to lock up his boss for being open on Sunday." McGee laughed, puffed his cigar and coughed.

"Come on, finish telling me what you did," said Carpenter.

"Well, she pulled her slacks up and covered that grey-haired old snatch and asked me what I'd take to let her stay open on Sundays. It was all very business-like. I told her to start loading the police car with baskets of fruit. She put in the baskets of apples and grapefruit and stopped. She thought that was enough to allow Sunday sales. I politely pointed out that it is against the law to screw where you can be seen by the public and she put in the rest of the stuff. I made her promise never to charge me or my partner for a little fruit now and then. I've never seen a woman so mad before. She was still cursing me when I pulled off her lot. Can you imagine? After all that free coffee and donuts."

"Some people don't have any couth. Fuck her. Let's get some breakfast at Elmer's," said Carpenter.

"I just ate at Elmer's. I've got to help the people in my church get across the street. Do you think Abe will like his convalescent present?"

"He'll eat until he shits like a goose. See you later, McGee."

19

ELMER'S PLACE WAS EMPTY EXCEPT FOR A FIREMAN getting donuts to take back to the firehouse. He had a large brindle boxer dog with him. The dog was running through his repertoire of tricks for Millie and another waitress. He sat up, rolled over and played dead, gave either paw to his fireman friend, walked upright on his hind legs, and jumped through a hoop made of the stiff rawhide leash the fireman held in his hands. The girls encouraged him with many raw hamburgers and applause. The fireman saw Carpenter and winked at him.

"Hi, pal. This is Butch, our mascot. He's about to do his final act. He needs your assistance for this one. Pull your gun out and point it at him and say bang."

"What does he do then," said Carpenter, sliding onto a stool at the counter. "Rip my throat out?"

"Trust me. He won't bother you. Go ahead, take your gun out and pretend to shoot him."

Carpenter stood up, pulled out the heavy Colt, and pointed it at the alert dog. "Bang, bang."

The dog threw himself on his side and howled like a wolf. His body went limp and his tongue hung from his mouth. Everyone applauded. The dog remained on the floor, motionless.

"Give him another hamburger, Millie," said the fireman. "That's it. Toss it way up in the air over his head."

The girl tossed a large chunk of ground beef over the dog's head. He leaped to his feet and caught the meat in midair.

"Come on, you old bastard. Let's go back to the house."

The fireman handed the coiled-up leash to the dog. The dog carried the leash in his mouth beside the fireman. Carpenter held the door open for the fireman and his dog. The fireman said something to the dog. Butch stood on his hind legs and continued to walk beside the fireman in an upright position until they were lost from sight as they turned a corner.

Carpenter was halfway through his meal when the paperboy came into the restaurant.

"Hey, Officer, there's a little boy and girl around in back of the movie crying like hell. I asked them what's the matter and they said their dad was beating their mother up."

Carpenter dropped the fork on the counter and went to the door. "Come on. Show me."

The boy trotted ahead of him to Shealey Avenue and turned right. Carpenter was close behind him. They found the boy and girl sitting on an old orange crate in the alley. The little girl was perhaps five years old and her brother a couple of years older. They were dressed in clean, new clothing. The little girl was sobbing against her brother's shoulder. He had his arms around her, trying to comfort her, but was choking back sobs, himself. Carpenter knelt beside the children and spoke to the boy.

"What's wrong, fella?"

"My Mom and Dad are fighting again," he said, his jaws quivering. "We came home from Sunday School and he ran us out of the house. He said he was going to k-k-kill my Mom."

"Where do you live?"

"Two doors up on Shealey Avenue."

"You wait here, pal. Everything's going to be okay."

The paperboy followed him to the house. The fight was not difficult to locate. They could be heard a block away. The man's low voice was a threatening rumble. The woman was answering him in a shrill, piercing shriek. Carpenter opened the gate and walked into the well-kept front yard. A heavy electric iron came crashing through the screen and struck the concrete sidewalk. The plastic handle shattered into a thousand pieces. Carpenter turned to the paperboy.

"Have you got a dime?"

"Yeah. Why?"

"Run back to Elmer's place and use the pay phone. Call VA 3-2626. Tell the Desk Sergeant I need some help on Shealey Avenue, half a block east of York Road. Got it?"

"Sure."

"Get going."

The boy ran west on Shealey Avenue and disappeared from view. There was a lot of crashing and breaking of furniture in the front room of the house. Carpenter looked in the front window. They were standing in the center of the living room like prize fighters, swinging roundhouse punches at each other. The woman was broad through the hips and shoulders. She must have outweighed her husband by twenty-five or thirty pounds. As he watched them, she cocked her right fist back near her ear and threw the punch like a baseball. Her fist caught him square in the nose and sent him sprawling on the polished hardwood floor. She pressed her advantage and kicked him once or twice in the head with her saddleshoes. He reached up with his hands, grabbed her foot and twisted. She crashed over a coffee table and struck her forehead on the wrought-iron screen by the fireplace. She sat up, but was too dazed to move. There was a lot of blood flowing.

"I got you now, bitch. I'm going to choke your fat ass."

He grabbed her by the throat and started to squeeze. Carpenter tried the door. It was unlocked. Walking up behind the man, he struck him hard in the kidney with his fist. Retching, he fell to his knees beside his wife. He was a thin, small-boned man, but the muscles in his arms were like steel bands. Carpenter twisted the man's hands behind him. He snapped one cuff on, surprised at the strength in the whipcord arms. Carpenter had the free wrist in his hand and was applying pressure to bring it close enough to the other arm to snap the cuff dangling from the captured arm. The man's muscles loosened up.

"Okay, okay, you got me," he croaked. "Don't break my fucking arm."

Carpenter relaxed the pressure on the loose arm slightly. It was a mistake. The man brought his free arm back hard, the elbow tearing into Carpenter's stomach. The air went out of him with a whoosh. He was all over Carpenter like a bantam rooster. His small hands slid around Carpenter's thick neck, trying for a choke hold. Carpenter managed to suck some air into his balky lungs and chopped him in the nose with his elbow. The trickle of blood from one nostril became a torrent. He sat down hard on the blood-spattered oak floor, holding his crimson nose. The blood sprayed from between his fingers like a fountain. His wife crawled to his side and wrapped her thick arms around his head. The blood from her forehead mingled with her husband's. All three of them were panting like windblown race horses.

"Don't lock him up," she screamed, shoving Carpenter away. "I'm not hurt. I just fell down. We had a little too much to drink this morning. Oh, God, don't lock my little man up. I love him."

Carpenter stepped behind the man and pulled both of his arms behind him. He nearly had the dangling cuff snapped on the free wrist when the woman jumped on his back. He tried to shake her loose. She had her arms around his neck and her legs clamped around his hips. The little man scrambled to his feet.

"I got him!" she screamed, her mouth against Carpenter's ear. "I got him! Run! Run!"

"Hold on to that bastard!" the little man screamed.

He ran into the kitchen. Carpenter was trying to peel a finger loose from the woman's clenched hands to break her hold on his neck when her husband came back in the room. He had a butcher knife in his right hand.

"Hold him, Bessie! I'm going to denut me a cop."

Carpenter ran backward with the woman clamped to him. They crashed into a corner hutch. The air went out of her lungs in a rush into his ear. He was free. He clawed for his holster, keeping his eyes on the bantam-sized knife fighter. The woman was too fast for him. She ripped the revolver from his holster and threw it through the glass in the front door, as he brought his elbow back in desperation. It caught her in the solar plexus. She fell against the front door like a sack of grain. Somebody was trying to push the front door open. The knife-wielding man was closing on him. He was a wild-looking, bloody apparition as he moved in. Carpenter reached for his nightstick. It was gone, lost among the debris of the battle.

"I'm going cut you, cop," he shouted, tossing the knife back and forth from hand to hand.

A tall figure was closing on him from behind. The little man was moving the knife back to plunge it into Carpenter's stomach when a crepe-soled shoe caught him squarely in the balls. His knife arm was imprisoned by Sergeant Harper's hands. The knife clattered to the hardwood floor. His wrist bones broke with an audible pop, as he screamed into Carpenter's face. It was like sweet music in Carpenter's ears. Sergeant Harper broke every finger on the man's good hand as casually as if he were snapping twigs to start a bonfire. Dropping the unconscious man to the floor, he shoved him aside with his foot. The police outside mustered enough power to shove the woman aside and partially open the door. They came in with guns drawn.

"Put those things away, for Christ's sake," the sergeant growled. "It's just a little family quarrel. Take that fat sow and little runt here to Union Memorial. If either one of them opens his mouth or raises a hand to you, put a few more lumps on them. The department's tired of fucking around with this pair."

Sergeant Harper walked over to Carpenter and looked him over. "Are you hurt anyplace, Fritz?" he asked. "Maybe you better have the doctors look you over."

"No. I'm okay," said Carpenter. His hands trembled as he tried to light a Camel. "I might have pissed in my pants a little bit. I thought that knife was in my guts. Thanks."

"Don't thank me. Thank whoever you pray to that we got here when we did. When are you going to learn to wait for backup?"

"He was choking her. I couldn't wait any longer."

"Fuck her," Sergeant Harper said, shooting the finger toward the prisoners. "That's Bessie and Bob DeMonte. They've been beating hell out of each other on Sunday mornings for the last eight years. The neighbors don't even call up about them anymore. He gets paid on Saturday and they booze it up all night. They usually start in on each other about eight or nine o'clock Sunday morning. Bessie works over at the shoe factory on Pulaski Highway. Bob works as a stevedore down on the docks. Neither one of them ever miss a day's work."

Sergeant Harper paused and took a tin of Copenhagen out of his pocket. Opening the lid, he took a pinch and stuck it behind his lower lip. He grinned at Carpenter and continued.

"They used to drink in the local taverns, but they got barred in every joint from Waverly to the Maryland line, nine years ago. It seems like the police always got involved with them on the other shifts. I never had any personal dealings with them 'til now. There isn't a cop in this district that would answer a call here unless he had plenty of help with him. It looks like you're a kind of magnet for shit, Fritz. How did you get the word on them this morning?"

"The paperboy got me at Elmer's eating breakfast. He saw their kids crying in the alley down the street."

"Come on," said Harper. "We better check on them."

They walked down the street to the alley and found the children where Carpenter had left them.

"Go talk to them, Fritz. Bring them home. I'll try to get a neighbor to take them in. Look at 'em. Good-looking kids. I wonder what will become of them?"

Carpenter walked over to the children and sat down beside them on a garbage can. The boy raised a tear-streaked face to him. "Is it okay to go home now, Mr. Cop?"

"Everything's all right now, pal."

"Is Momma dead?" he asked, patting his little sister on the back.

"No, but she had to go to the hospital with your dad. He fell down and hurt his arms."

"Are you taking them to jail again?"

"Yeah. I'm sorry, son."

"That's all right. I'm glad he didn't kill her dead, like he said he'd do. Why don't the judge keep that mean little son-of-a-bitch locked up?"

"I don't know."

"That's what all of you cops always say."

He stood and pulled his sister to her feet. The little girl wouldn't look at Carpenter. She held her brother's hand with both of hers and looked at the ground.

"Come on, Cindy, let's go home. I'll take care of you. Don't worry. Momma will be home soon."

Carpenter sat on the garbage can and watched the two children walk out of the alley, hand in hand. He walked back to the house and found his service revolver in a purple azalea bed in full bloom. Picking up the Colt, he swung the cylinder open. The barrel was packed with peat moss. He cleared the bore with his pen and blew the excess debris from the frame.

The children were inside talking to Sergeant Harper and an old lady. Carpenter walked to the front door and looked through the broken glass. The room was a shambles. Blood marred the surface of the polished oak floor. The coffee table was split in half and the corner hutch was caved in. Broken glass and dishes littered the floor. The butcher knife was lying on the floor near the door, half hidden by a framed sign. He went inside, bent over, and picked up the sign. Embroidered on linen with great care, the sign read "God Bless Our Home." He put it in the ruined hutch and walked outside.

A feisty mockingbird was battling half a dozen starlings for possession of an old weeping willow tree. It was no contest. He disposed of his drab competitors in short order. The mockingbird flew to the top of the huge tree and sang a borrowed victory song to the vanquished starlings. They watched from a nearby telephone wire, made safe by their distance from his personal tree.

Sergeant Harper walked out of the house and stood beside Carpenter, looking at the well-kept lawn and the neat flower beds.

"They keep this old place looking good. The kids are taken care of. They both have jobs and send their kids to church on Sunday. What makes them want to kill each other on weekends?" asked Carpenter.

"You got me, Fritz," he said, tossing a couple of Tums in his mouth. "Why don't bird dogs fly? Fuck it. Let's go eat breakfast on Elmer. The old lady watches the little girl when the mother works. She'll take care of them and clean up the house. Don't think about things like this too much. You'll wind up out at Spring Grove. Let's go get some chili and donuts."

"I was almost finished eating when I got called away. You go ahead, I'll walk back to the station and start the paperwork on this thing."

"Suit yourself. Goulek will help you out if he's finished reading the Sunday funnies."

20

THE OLD DESK SERGEANT STOOD BEHIND THE DAIS. Two young patrolmen from opposite shifts were engaged in open-handed, not-so-gentle sparring at the opposite end of the room. A tall, slender cop was using his advantage of height and reach to keep his sparring partner away. The shorter man was taking sharp slaps on both cheeks. His face was red from the blows, but he continued to bore in on the taller man. The tall cop moved backward and tripped over a box of flares. The heavyset man dove on top of him and pinned his arms to his sides with his legs. He used his extra weight to his advantage. Sitting on the thin man's chest, he slapped his opponent on both sides of the face with stinging open-handed blows.

"Let me up, you fat ass-hole. I'll beat shit lumps all over your head."

"What's the matter, you skinny drip of piss? Can't you take as good as you give?"

The old desk sergeant smiled with genuine pleasure. "Would half a dozen or so of you spectators kindly separate the Pope brothers?"

Rough hands separated the brothers. They stopped struggling and assumed their positions with opposite shifts, facing each other. Both shifts applauded the brothers for their show.

"I'd have loved to watch you two chaps slap the dog shit out of each other all morning, but I didn't get a wink of sleep last night and I'm a little grouchy, so don't nobody fuck with me this morning. I'm tired, and when an old man's tired, it's dangerous to screw around with him. We will dispense with calling the roll. I see all the fresh faces of the seven-to-three shift here, so why fuck with that? Let me read you a special order from Headquarters. We got it in the morning mail. That means that the writer had to work Sunday to get it to us today. You all know that Headquarters is closed on Saturday and Sunday, so you can imagine how important they must have thought this matter is. Listen up, now. I wouldn't want you to miss a word of this.

"'It has come to my attention that in this unseasonal warm spell of the past week that certain officers throughout the county have been rolling up their sleeves to the elbow and loosening their neckties. Some officers have been removing their hats in the patrol cars. This conduct will not be tolerated. Any further deviation from uniform regulations will result in severe disciplinary action against the perpetrators. This order will be signed by every uniformed officer in the County, without exception. District Lieutenants will be held accountable for enforcing this order.'

"This order is signed by the Chief Inspector. Now, don't that order just make you tremble and shit in your pants in fear?"

One of the men on the offgoing shift broke wind. Everyone present laughed and applauded.

"Well said. That was my reaction to this terrifying order, too. They put the same order out every year at this time, word for word. I wonder what he means by severe disciplinary action? Christ, they sit up there in their air-conditioned ivory tower and take pot shots at street cops. How soon they forget what it's like out here. Did you ever notice that when they get promoted to one of those Headquarters jobs they start wearing soft clothes? In the summer they wear short-sleeved shirts and they never leave their air-conditioned offices except to play golf or to go eat lunch on one of their gambler friends. In the winter time, they can't play golf, so they sit around and rat each other out to the Chief and call about three staff meetings a week to harass the field captains. The field captains hate to see winter come. It brings the meanness out in that Headquarters bunch when they can't get out to the golf links, and they don't have nothing to do but fink each other out. It's too bad that nobody ever found any work for police bosses to do. I've seen some good cops ruined or brainwashed or something when they join that elite bunch up there in the nerve factory. So much for their silly bullshit. We got some police work here to talk about."

A middle-aged cop on the offgoing shift was asleep on his feet. Leaning against the man next to him, his head jerked up and down, as though his neck was rubber. His eyes snapped open when his nightstick hit the floor.

The old sergeant yawned behind his hand. "Me too, Andy."

Pulling a note from the clipboard the old sergeant started to read. "Officer Alvin Lackovitch, of the Pikesville District, stopped a car for speeding last night on Reisterstown Road at about midnight. He walked up to the driver and the ass-hole shot him three times with a twenty-two pistol. He never even got his Colt out of his holster. Lackovitch was wounded in both arms and took one in the jawbone, but reached into the open window and grabbed the punk's gun arm. His partner couldn't shoot for fear of hitting Lackovitch. He ran around the opposite side of the car and climbed in beside the shooter. The son of a bitch shot three holes in the windshield of his car in the struggle for the gun. They finally got the gun away from him and put a little shit on his head with their gun barrels."

Every man in the ranks cheered.

"Yeah, me too. I understand Lackovitch is going to be released from the hospital sometime today. He was lucky. The cop-shooter has not been identified as yet. He was in an unreported stolen Ford sedan when they stopped him. They are holding him at Pikesville station for assault with intent to murder. The desk man over there told me that the doctor put eighty-six stitches in the shooter's head and face."

The police cheered and stamped their feet.

The old desk sergeant smiled. "I thought that would grab you. I hope they used a dull needle on that son-of-a-bitch. He's lucky those boys of ours didn't make garbage out of him. We had a rape reported last night at 0300. The victim was Julia Spetzenbacher, white female, age forty-seven. Officer Brady found her walking along Loch Raven Drive at about 0330 this morning, naked as a jaybird. She wasn't beat up or anything, and Brady wrapped her in a blanket and called for assistance to search the area. She claims that six white men forced her into a car down on Pennsylvania Avenue in the city at ten o'clock last night and brought her out here to Loch Raven and gang-banged her. She claimed that they forced her to drink a pint of whiskey on the way out and all she remembers is them slipping the meat to her in a pine grove up near Pearce's Corner. We couldn't locate the scene or her clothes, much less any suspects. Brady brought her to the station and found her an old dress to put on."

The middle-aged cop was sleeping again. He leaned against the wall with knees stiff, snoring. The man next to him elbowed him awake. He jumped and dropped his nightstick.

The old desk sergeant frowned and continued. "She was taken to University Hospital for examination. The hospital called later and reported no signs of rape or recent sexual intercourse. Brady confronted her with this, and she cursed him out and said she just wanted to forget the whole thing. She refused to look at mug shots or cooperate in any way. Just for the hell of it, I ran a wanted check on her. Anybody want to guess who she is?"

"A sex-mad brain surgeon out slumming?" asked McGee, innocently.

"No, shitbird," said the old desk sergeant. "She's a fucking escapee from Spring Grove State Hospital. I called them to come get her and they asked if she had any clothing on when we nabbed her. I told them that she didn't. They said it's okay, because she always throws her clothing away when she gets away from them. Now you see why I'm tired and grouchy. That nut screwed me out of my nap. Goodnight, gentlemen. I'm going home to bed."

Sergeant Harper stepped to the dais. "Detectives are staking out all the Seven-Eleven stores in the district. One of their snitches got word that one of them is going down sometime today. Stay away from them unless we get sent there by the radio room. We don't want to fuck up their stakeout. They've been inside each and every store since they opened a few minutes ago. They'll be inside until closing tonight. Okay. Any questions? No? Good. Hit the bricks. Don't forget your school details."

Carpenter walked outside into the bright sunshine. Sean McGee was checking under the back seat of his opice car.

"Ah-ha! Hey, Look at this, Fritz. You never know what you'll find." He held a long hat pin, a cap pistol, and a half-eaten cold-cut submarine sandwich in his hands.

"Cold-cuts," said McGee, sticking his tongue out. "I can't stand cold-cuts. It reminds me of my college days. I lived on ham-and-cheese sandwiches and beer. Look at this hat pin. Can you imagine the chagrin of some poor cop if he had to go down to Union Memorial to get this thing extracted from his ass-hole? I wonder how long this bloody thing has been in here?"

McGee held up the pin and tested the point with his thumb.

"It was stuck into the seat, down into the upholstery near the back. I could have missed it a few times in my search."

McGee placed the stuff on the roof of the police car. Picking up the cap pistol, he twirled it on his finger like John Wayne.

"This damned cap pistol could pass for a thirty-eight in the dark. It was stuck down between the springs under the seat."

"Your collection grows," said Carpenter, poking the sandwich with his nightstick. "That submarine sandwich will be a real conversation piece twenty-five years from now."

"Smart ass," said McGee. Opening the sandwich, he pulled a few hairs from his head and slid them between the lunch meat. "I've got other plans for this sub. I'm going to cut off the chewed-up part. That will leave me with at least a half. I'll wrap it carefully and seal the paper with Scotch tape. Then I'll take it into the Lieutenant's office and leave it on the window sill. It's not too stale yet. He'll scarf it up like a hungry bear. I'm sure he'll figure that one of the other men in his golden circle left it for him. We may be lucky. Who knows what degenerate had this little treasure in their hot, dirty hands?" McGee rolled his eyes wildly and grinned. "Perhaps he will develop jaundice or severe heartburn. Maybe salmonella or even syphilis could take our trash-can-dumping Lieutenant."

"I would like to see him explain his syphilis in a written report to the Captain," said Carpenter, aiming the cap pistol at McGee's nose.

McGee took the cap pistol from Carpenter and put it with the rest of his find in his 1953 Mercury convertible, parked next to the police car. He lit a Havana and grinned at Carpenter. They leaned against the police car and watched the lot empty, as the other cars left, one by one. A motorcycle cop had been jumping on the kick starter of his big Harley for about five minutes. The motor refused to start. Conrad Klutz, the motor cop, was red-faced and swearing under his breath.

"Put a nickel in it, Conrad!" McGee shouted.

Klutz shot the finger at McGee and cursed.

"Turn the switch on, dummy!" McGee cackled.

Klutz checked the switch and jumped on the kick starter. The Harley thundered to life, blowing blue smoke at a group of Goucher girls passing on bicycles. Klutz tipped his hat to the girls and roared past them onto the street.

"Come on, I'll drop you off at Elmer's Place," said McGee.

They got in and McGee pulled off the parking lot into light traffic. He tapped the siren lightly as he passed the Goucher girls. They squealed and waved to McGee. He flipped a long ash off his cigar into the ashtray and glanced at his watch.

"I want to go over to Abe's before seven-thirty. His wife invited me for a breakfast of lox, bagels, and eggs. Abe's got me hooked on Kosher food. He trained his Catholic bride to cook his favorite dishes on their honeymoon."

"How did he like the ton of fruit?"

"I didn't see him yesterday. His wife had just put him to bed. She said he really had a snootful when she got home from church. Gracie told me it was the first time she was glad to see him loaded. He didn't sleep and was in a lot of pain the night before. He's got some kind of hangup about not taking medicine. He's afraid of becoming addicted or something."

"I guess we all have our little quirks."

"Here we are, Fritz," said McGee, pulling into a prohibited parking area in front of Elmer's. "Say hello to Millie for me. Tell her I'm saving myself for her."

Later that day, Carpenter was walking on Pennsylvania, near York, watching the crowds of pretty young girls hurry along York Road to lunch and shopping dates. Officer Beauregard Barter pulled his car to the curb near him and motioned for him to get in. Officer Barter's hands were shaking as he lit a cigarette.

Carpenter slid in beside him. He looked at Barter's shaking hands and grinned. "What's the matter Beau, you look kind of shook up."

"The Seven-Eleven store at York and Seminary just got hit by three men. The detectives were hid in back in the storeroom. They let them get the money and go outside. They made their move as soon as they hit the sidewalk. All three of 'em fired shots at the detectives and hit Dave Mackey in the knee with a shotgun blast. Our guys cut down two of them right in their tracks and feel sure they hit the third one in the leg. He ran limping into the woods behind the place. He's armed with an automatic. Dave Mackey's done on the street. Those motherfuckers blew the kneecap clean off his leg."

"How about the two men they shot?"

"They're garbage," he said flatly, taking a deep drag on the cigarette. "Dave fired from the sidewalk after they shot his leg out from under him and blew the top off of one bastard's head. It's something that a twelve-bore shotgun will do at fifteen feet. Mark Pollanski was his stakeout partner. Mark knocked the other one down with his first shot. The stick-up man still had a grip on his sawed-off shotgun. He got a shot off at Pollanski and blew out the front window of the store. Mark said he went a little apeshit then. He charged right up to those ass-holes and put two blasts into the wounded guy's chest and two more into the one that Mackey had wasted."

"I guess the Pollack blew his mind," said Carpenter.

"Yeah," said Barter, lips trembling. "Mackey said that Pollanski stood over them and kept clicking the hammer on his empty shotgun and pointing at them like he was still shooting. Christ, he made mincemeat out of those bastards. I was the first one there. He was shaking like a leaf. We had to pry his fingers off of that gun to get him to let go. We thought he was going to throw a seven on us. Sean McGee took him to his car and they got half a pint of hooch from the store across the street into him. He's okay now."

"That's good. I know how he feels," said Carpenter.

"I was helping the B of I man take pictures and puked all over the sidewalk next to those blasted bodies. Fresh shrimp salad. I'll never forget those hunks of shrimp mixed with all that blood," said Barter, gulping air in. "I'll never eat shrimp again."

"I don't think I would either, if I were you."

"The Sergeant has everybody looking for the one that got away. He sent me up here to tell you to get out of sight and watch York and Joppa for the rest of the day. It's no telling where that son-of-a-bitch will go. He's got to keep moving because he's hurt. If he hides in that woods he might bleed to death. Snake wants me to go all the way down York Road to the city line in case he slips through. He's a white male, dressed in a green sport shirt and tan pants, about thirty years old. He won't be hard to spot with that limp. See you, pal. Take care."

Carpenter got out and slammed the door. Barter swung the car into the heavy traffic and headed south on York Road.

Carpenter crossed the street to the cab stand. The dispatcher had his back to him when he opened the door and didn't hear him enter the small office. He was talking on the phone.

"I got it, twenty to win on Kit Cat in the first at Pimlico. What? Speak up, for gosh sake, you sound like you got a mouth full of shit. Ten to place on Rolling Home in the third at Pimlico. Right. Got you."

The dispatcher wrote the bets on a piece of paper, folded it, and put it in his shirt pocket. Carpenter cleared his throat. The dispatcher swung around in the swivel chair and jumped to his feet.

"Oh, shit! How long have you been standing there?"

"Long enough to cause you a fucking problem if I want to."

"Wait a minute, now. Give me a break. I don't handle much action here. How about twenty a week to lay off? I got a wife and kids. Don't lock me up, Officer."

"I don't want your money. You can take all the bets you want. I need one of your cabs for the rest of the day to use. I'm watching out for a man at York and Joppa and want to keep out of sight."

"Is that all? No problem. Take 501, it's parked out in back. Jimbo ain't due in until six P.M. anyway. It would just sit there all day. Here's the keys, Officer." He tossed a set of keys to Carpenter.

"Thanks," said Carpenter. "One more thing. What size hat do you wear?"

"Seven and a quarter, why?"

"I need it."

"Here, take it," the dispatcher said, pulling the hat from his head. "If you like it, keep it."

Carpenter carried the old windbreaker and the brown felt hat in his hand to the back of the cab stand. He got in and turned the engine over. He slipped the jacket on and replaced his uniform hat with the slouch hat. Driving to Joppa and York, he parked facing north and had a clear view in four directions. He settled back to wait. An uneventful hour passed. Two Goucher girls got into the cab and slammed the door. They leaned back in the seat, breathless from running.

"Goucher College," one of the girls said. "Take us to the ad building. Please hurry, we're late."

"Sorry, girls. I've got a dead battery. She won't start."

The girl in the blue blazer kicked at the back of the front seat. "You stupid jerk. Why don't you go across the street to get the gas station attendant to help you?"

"I don't like him, that's why. Besides, I use Crown gas, not Esso."

"You son-of-a-bitch, no wonder you're a cab driver. You don't have brains enough to take a shit on your own."

"My, my, such language and from college girls, too."

"Fuck off, you bastard!" she screamed. "I wouldn't ride in your cab if you paid me to. I don't have time to screw around with you. You're parked illegally, too. I hope a cop gives you a ticket."

They got out of the cab and slammed the door. He watched their trim backsides move as they ran across the street to hail a passing cab. He sighed and laughed to himself.

The suspect was limping along, two blocks away, headed directly for Carpenter. Taking his Colt from his holster, Carpenter slid it under his right leg. He took his gunbelt off and slid it and his uniform hat under the front seat. The suspect hobbled closer. He was a classic picture of a fugitive. He kept looking over his shoulder. A State police car came over the hill. The suspect saw the car and went into an ice cream store. The car passed him and continued south on York Road. The trooper stopped across the street from

Carpenter's cab.

"Hey, cabbie, you know better than that. Get your cab moving."

Carpenter pulled his badge from his shirt and held it out the window. "I'm a County police officer. Get the hell away from me."

"No need to get upset, friend. I'm just doing my job. You should know better than to park there."

"Will you please get the fuck away from here with that car? I'm staked out for a holdup man."

"Oh, why didn't you say so?"

The trooper proceeded south on York Road.

Five minutes crawled by.

"Jesus Christ, maybe he went out the back door. Maybe he shot the people in that store. I can't wait much longer. There's no telling what that bastard will do. I'll give him one more minute," he mumbled to himself.

He wanted to run into the store to get the man. His mouth was bone dry. His heart was pounding in his chest and sweat was pouring down his face from under the felt hat. His stomach was growling and he had an almost irresistible urge to urinate.

"Jesus Christ, what am I doing here? I'm a pipe fitter, not a cop. Fuck it. I'm going for help. Let him get away. I'm no hero," he thought.

Carpenter had the cab in first gear with the motor running when the holdup man limped out of the ice cream store. Looking up and down the road, he leaned against the building as though he had a problem standing. He started to walk again, toward Carpenter. His leg was bothering him badly. Holding on to the store fronts with one hand, he limped along. He was a block away. The afternoon shopping crowd hustled by him. No one gave him a second glance. He made his way, step by step, in Carpenter's direction. Limping to the intersection, he was a hundred feet from the cab.

Carpenter picked up the manifest from the seat beside him and pretended to study it. The suspect crossed the street, dragging his bad leg and hopping along like a lame horse. Carpenter saw the blood. It bubbled over the top of the suspect's shoe every time his foot hit the concrete. He made it to the cab and held on to the fender.

His eyes were wild with pain and fear. The bulge of the automatic was plain to see through his shirt, stuck under his belt. Sliding his hand along the cab, he barely made it to the door. Pulling the door open, he got in, leaned forward and put his head on his knees. Carpenter whipped his Colt from its hiding place and jammed the muzzle into the suspect's ear.

"Don't move, you son-of-a-bitch, or I'll blow your fucking brains out."

He was making snoring noises deep in his throat. Carpenter jabbed him in the ear with his revolver, hard. He gave with the force and fell forward against the dashboard, unconscious. Carpenter grabbed his hair and pulled him back. Ripping the open the suspect's shirt, he removed the .45 from under his belt. The hammer was back on the automatic. Carpenter popped the clip and joggled the rounds from the clip with his thumb. There were four loads left in the clip. He jacked the round out of the chamber and dropped the .45 on the back seat.

Carpenter's blood was pumped full of adrenaline. After his fear, he felt exultation. He backed the cab up a hundred feet to the old firehouse. Four firemen were sitting on a bench at the front door watching the girls go by. Getting out of the cab, he approached the firemen.

"Is the ambulance here or out on call?"

"It's here. I'm the driver. What's the matter?"

"I've got an unconscious man in the cab. He's been shot."

Three of the firemen ran to the cab and lifted the wounded man out. They laid him flat on the sidewalk and cut away his bloody pants leg. There were three holes in the man's thigh, two inches apart. He was very pale. Carpenter retrieved his gunbelt and hat. He tossed the old windbreaker and felt hat on the front seat of the cab. Recovering the .45 from the back seat where he had tossed it, he stuck it into his belt. The driver pulled the ambulance out of the engine house. They loaded the injured man onto a stretcher and put him in the ambulance. Carpenter got in back with the attendant. The driver pulled the powerful Cadillac into the southbound lane and hit the siren. The race with death was on.

The attendant pulled the suspect's eyelid back. "He's in shock. Help me to raise his feet. There. That will help him. He's lost a lot of blood."

The attendant was wrapping a tourniquet around the man's leg above his wounds. He tightened the strap. The blood slowed and stopped.

"Did you shoot this guy?"

"No. He held up the Seven-Eleven at York and Seminary. His friends and he shot it out with a couple of detectives. He stopped a few shotgun pellets."

"They look more like thirty-eight holes to me."

"Same thing. It's double-aught buck. They size up to about thirty-eight caliber."

"Where's his friends?"

"Dead."

"How 'bout the detectives?"

"One got hit in the leg. I guess they took him to the hospital in a police car to save time."

Carpenter tapped on the sliding window separating the driver from the back of the ambulance. The driver pulled the window open a few inches.

"Yeah."

"How about radioing your headquarters to call the

Towson station? Tell them Carpenter has the holdup man in custody en route to Union Memorial."

"Can do."

He slid the glass shut and reached for the radio microphone.

The attendant was holding the oxygen mask to the man's face. He felt the man's pulse. He dropped the limp wrist and shook his head.

"He's slipping away. I don't think we're going to make it. How long ago did he get shot?"

"About an hour ago. No, more than an hour ago. He's been trying to get away."

The attendant was giving the man closed heart massage. He continued the oxygen. The mask was strapped to the man's face.

"Take his pulse there by the jawbone, Officer."

Carpenter stuck his finger into the flesh at the base of the jawbone. He looked at the attendant and shook his head.

"I can't find it."

The attendant stopped the heart massage.

"Neither could I. Let me check again." The attendant probed one side of the jaw, then the other. "Nothing. Shit. He's gone."

He tapped on the window to his partner. The glass inched open.

"Take your time, Bob. No use killing us. He's a loser. He ran out of blood."

The ambulance was three blocks from Union Memorial. They continued to the hospital. The emergency room attendants met them at the door. They had been warned in advance by the fire department headquarters. Grabbing the man's stretcher, they ran into the emergency treatment room. They worked on him for ten minutes, fighting to ignite the spark of life.

The emergency room physician walked out into the hall and lit a cigarette. He shook his head and shrugged his shoulders.

"He bled to death. Too bad. If we would have gotten him a few minutes sooner he may have had a chance."

Carpenter dialed the number of the Towson station. The desk sergeant answered the phone.

"Carpenter, Sarge. He's dead. I'll come back with the ambulance."

"See if he's got identification on him, Fritz. Bring everything in his pockets back with you. Did he have the gun on him?"

"Yeah."

"He give you any trouble?"

"No. I was waiting in a cab at York and Joppa. He just walked up to the cab and got in. He passed out on the front seat as soon as he got in. He bled to death."

"Better him than you. Dave Mackey lost a lot of blood, but he's going to be okay. I just heard from the emergency room down there. They had Mackey and the stickup man laying side by side working on them. Did you run into Sal Trotta? He took Mackey to the hospital."

"No."

"He must have hauled ass back to continue the search for that bastard that just went ten-seven. I got to hang up, kid. The fucking newspapers are ringing the phones off the wall."

Carpenter walked into the emergency room. The wounded police officer and the dead holdup man were lying on tables five feet apart. A sheet covered the face of the corpse.

Dave Mackey was full of morphine. He waved his hand weakly to Carpenter.

"I'm Carpenter. How are you feeling, Dave?"

"No pain. As soon as they fill me up with blood and that other juice, they operate. They tell me I lost my kneecap. Son-of-a-bitch. I'll go nuts working one of those fucking light-duty desk jobs."

"Don't think about that now. Is there anybody you want me to call?"

"No."

"How about your family?"

"No family. I'm an orphan. They raised me in a Catholic orphanage in Philadelphia. I'm not married. The job's my wife and family, I guess. It works out better at a time like this. If I had a wife, she'd be going through hell now. Do me a favor, Carpenter?"

"Anything."

"Stay with me until they take me to the operating room."

Carpenter turned to the nurse hovering over the wounded man. She nodded her head.

"Sure. I'll stay until they throw me out."

"Thanks, pal. How's my Pollack partner doing?"

"He's fine. I heard they got a half pint into him and he straightened right up. He sounds like a good man to work with."

"I can close my eyes and see him charging right into the barrel of the sawed-off gun. He scared that bastard so much that he couldn't pump another round into the chamber. He's really an easy-going man. That Pollack never misses going to church and is always after me to get back to the Church. People surprise you. I always wondered what he would do when the metal was flying through the air."

"You never know what any man will do when he's facing death. I almost ran from this poor bastard laying here. He was almost dead on his feet. I was watching the intersection at York and Joppa, sitting in a cab, and could see him walking toward me from two blocks away. He staggered up to the cab and got in with me. I guess he thought he had it made. He passed out as soon as his ass hit the seat."

"You had too much time to think about it. It grates on your nerves that way. It's funny, when they rushed him in here, I actually felt sorry for him. I wanted him to live. Who was he?"

Carpenter walked across to the dead man's table. He pulled the sheet down and lifted the man's hips.

"Would you check his back pockets for me, nurse?"

She pulled a fat wallet from the man's left hip pocket and handed it to Carpenter. He turned the pants pockets inside out and found a worn Zippo lighter and sixteen cents in change. The wallet held two one-dollar bills and many pictures, a Pennsylvania driver's license listed to Alvin Hurst and a Maryland driver's license for Albert Hart. Both descriptions matched the dead man.

"He's either Alvin Hurst or Albert Hart or Joe Blow. It's a job for you detectives."

Dave Mackey didn't answer. The nurse checked his blood pressure and pulse.

"He's sleeping. You may as well go. He won't wake up now until he comes out of the operation. Don't worry. We'll take good care of him."

The ambulance crew was finishing up their report at the information desk. He walked out of the hospital and got in the back of the ambulance. The attendant rode in front with the driver. He lit a Camel absently with the dead man's lighter. Feeling engraving on the back of the lighter with his fingers, he turned it over. "Korea, 1951, First Marine Division. A.H." Carpenter was depressed when the ambulance dropped him off at the Towson station.

Detectives assigned to the case took the automatic, wallet, and lighter from Carpenter. Finishing his report, he walked into the desk sergeant's office and handed the forms to Sergeant Goulek.

"Sorry I couldn't take care of the paper for you this time, Fritz. The newspapers just eased up on me about ten minutes ago. I guess this one will make the paper all over. I'm glad we had two young cops at the store who can shoot. It's too bad about Dave Mackey's knee. Is he hurting bad?"

"No. They had him loaded up with stuff when I saw him. He fell asleep. I guess they have him on the cutting table right now."

"He's in a good hospital. I don't know how those bastards missed killing our detectives. Two of them had shotguns. I'm glad our men had the twelve-gauges with them. Shit, Fritz, you had to watch one of them die. That's not any fun. What say we have a little banger to wash the taste of this whole mess out of our mouths?"

"It sounds good to me, Sarge."

Sergeant Goulek reached into the lower left-hand drawer and produced a half-full bottle of Old Granddad.

"I thought you drank Canadian Club."

"I drink anything that the bail bondsmen bring into the station house. It's standard operating procedure for them to leave a bottle of hooch for station house use when they get a bond of one thousand dollars or over. It keeps a little something here for nerve medicine. Shit, look here. We got plenty."

He pulled the desk drawer open all the way. The drawer was packed with whiskey bottles. Filling two coffee cups half way, he slid one across the desk to Carpenter.

"At the rate arrests have been going in this station, we'll all be alcoholics," said Goulek, sipping the whiskey. "Course, the booze is extra. They pay ten or fifteen percent of their fee to the Desk Sergeant on every cash bond they go for. The desk man takes half and splits with the arresting officer. You ain't supposed to know about this until you get off probation, but it seems like you've been here a long time already. You've handled more than your share, kid."

"What the hell, its only what I blundered into," said

Carpenter.

"Yeah, kid, the shit kind of clings to you, don't it? I talked it over with Snake. We both think you're okay. Don't talk about it until after all of us old cops are dead. If it got out, the sob sisters and do-gooders would want all of us to rot in jail. It don't amount to much money for the average cop, but I don't think you are an average cop. Over the years you could save enough to buy yourself an acre of ground in Florida for when you retire. You interested?"

Carpenter swallowed a mouthful of bourbon and lit a Camel. "Sure, why not? I appreciate the trust. I'd never put you or anybody else in the middle."

"I know it, pal. I know it. Drink up, it puts hair on your feet."

They had just finished their drinks when a man walked into the desk sergeant's office and slammed the door. He walked to the elevated desk area and smiled pleasantly at them.

"Good afternoon, Sergeant Goulek. Hello, Officer. My name is Jim Monjer."

He was a big-shouldered, big-bellied man, about six feet tall and at least 245 pounds. His crewcut, dirty-blond hair was a contrast to his ruddy, beefy face. The striking thing about his face was his watery, pale blue eyes. They were too big for his face and seemed to pop out of his head as though there was pressure behind them. He handed Carpenter six or eight cards. Carpenter looked at the cards and laid them on the desk. The lawyer pumped Carpenter's hand as though he were a long-lost friend.

"Sergeant Goulek, I've been retained as Alvin Hart's attorney. I demand to see the property that the police took from his pockets at the hospital."

"I don't know anything about Alvin Hart. Who's he?"

"Don't get cute with me, Sergeant. If I can't get the

facts from you, I'll call the Captain."

Sergeant Goulek picked up the phone from his desk and handed it to Monjer.

"Help yourself. I hope you got the number. I can't give it out to civilians."

Monjer bit his lip and popped his eyes at Sergeant Goulek. He smiled and drummed his fingers on the telephone, then placed the phone carefully back on the desk.

"Ah, I may be mistaken about the name. The lad's mother called me a few minutes ago and asked me to represent him. I'm referring to the poor unfortunate that was shot by the County Police in front of the Seven-Eleven store. I understand he was shot by accident. A leg wound, I think."

"Sorry, I don't know anything about any accidental shooting or anybody by that name. I guess somebody has been pulling your leg, Monjer. Or, then maybe the nurse you got on your shitty little payroll gave you the wrong name."

"I give up," said Monjer, throwing up his hands. "I absolutely plead guilty. You can't fool an old policeman. I did get a call from the hospital from someone, I've forgotten who. No doubt someone who was interested in seeing that justice is served in this matter."

"Sure. Could it have been Alvin Hurst?"

"That's it. That's it. In my haste to get here, I must have copied it wrong."

"Sorry," said Goulek, putting his feet on the desk. "We don't have anybody locked up by that name, either."

Monjer's jowls quivered. He shook his finger in Goulek's face. "See here, Sergeant. Don't push me too far. I'm not without friends in this county, you know."

"Oh, yes sir. Sorry. Could the name have been Albert Hart?"

"Ah, yes. I believe we are on the right track. Will

you please show me the evidence that was seized illegally by the detectives from my client?"

"Sorry, sir. We don't have anybody locked up by that name, either."

The lawyer's face was scarlet. His eyes protruded from his head like carbuncles.

"I'm an officer of the court. I demand the respect that is due me, you ignorant fool."

Goulek stood up and looked the angry man in the eye.

"Listen to me, you silly ambulance-chasing son-of-a-bitch. We don't have anybody locked up on that Seven-Eleven job. You got bad information from your two-bit tipsters again. You struck out, you stupid asshole. They are all dead, wasted, garbage. Do you understand? We don't know who that cocksucker is in the hospital. He had a pocket full of identification. We won't know until we print his dead ass. There's no fee in this for you. No money. No publicity. Nothing. Now get out of here and leave us alone."

The anger faded fast in Monjer's eyes. He smiled like a mule eating briars.

"Ho-ho-ho. No bad feelings. A good attorney's got to get to the truth, no matter whose toes he steps on. Here you are, men. Have a cigar. Havanas. The real thing. I've got an appointment. Goodbye." He walked out briskly, slamming the door.

"So that's Jim Monjer. If I ever get in trouble, I wouldn't want him defending me," said Carpenter.

"He's a sweetheart, ain't he? Don't underestimate that fat slob. He's an expert fixer. He's not worth a shit in the courtroom standing up on his hind legs practicing law on his own, but he gets a lot of dismissals. He's got a few cops on his payroll that go over his cases with him and show him the weak spots of the state. They're on a salary. He'll give anybody that refers a case to him a kickback. He's built up a lot of volume in cases among the ten-cent thieves and drunken drivers. If they can try it in magistrate's court, he can fix it most of the time. He farms a lot of his work out to other lawyers when he has cases to go to Circus Court. I've seen a lot of lawyers come along like him. They ruin it for the honest attorney. He's everything a lawyer shouldn't be. Someday a bum like him will get in a position of power and trust and screw the whole state up."

"Why do honest lawyers put up with bastards like him?"

Goulek walked to the coffee bar and filled a cup half full. Returning to the desk, he jerked open the whiskey drawer and picked up the Old Granddad. He filled the cup to the brim and returned the whiskey to his desk drawer.

"Lawyers like to think of themselves as professional men, Fritz. No professional group likes to police itself and resists any outside group that tries to do it. It takes a scandal to get enough pressure to motivate lawyers to take action against their own. When one of them is convicted of a crime, then and only then do they take action. In the meantime, ass-holes like Monjer make a lot of coin. Be patient. He'll screw Uncle Sam out of a lot of taxes and someday the U.S. Attorney will nail his ass to the cross. Lawyers like Monjer bend and pervert the law every day. Eventually they get nailed for doing something stupid."

"He came on like he had an axe to grind with you as soon as he walked in the door, Sarge."

"Yeah," said Goulek, sipping from the cup. "Him and me go 'way back. I take money from some people, but not a bastard like him. I turned him down when he offered to pay me a percentage on all cases I called him on. He likes to get a couple of men on each shift working for him. That way he's got twenty-four-hour coverage. I wasn't too gentle with my refusal, I guess. I told him to stick his dirty money up his ass. He's been a little sharp with me ever since then. Fuck him. Life wouldn't be worth living without a few Monjers for enemies. Have another little banger. That hombre always leaves a bad taste in my mouth. You want that cigar?"

"No," said Carpenter, sliding the cigar across the desk to Goulek.

"I'll give it to Sean McGee. He's a cigar freak. A couple of Havanas will make him feel like a new man. He misses Abe. That Kosher cop kept Sean laughing all the time."

21

THE OLD DESK SERGEANT FINISHED CALLING THE roll at the dais. Two men on the off-going shift were laughing at some wisecrack another man had made on their shift.

"Cut the grab-ass men. We got serious business today. That Ruxton rapist hit again this morning at about 0400 hours. He got in the unlocked bathroom window at the Goldberg residence on Heather Road. Mr. Goldberg heard him when he bumped into a table in the hallway. Mr. Goldberg got out of bed and walked out into the hall. The intruder caved his head in with a blunt instrument. Mrs. Goldberg was grabbed in the hallway by the intruder when she went to see what all the noise was about. He slapped her in the nose with his handgun and decked her. When she came to she was gagged and tied to a chair in her daughter's bedroom. Her thirteen-year-old daughter was tied, wrists to ankles, and laying on the bed stripped naked. The rapist shoved his cock up the girl's ass right in front of her mother and forced the kid to go down on him after the anal sex. When he finished with her he bit her left nipple off and put it into his pocket."

In the shocked silence of the roll-call room the sound

of a child crying in the hallway filtered through the heavy door. A recruit cop on the offgoing shift laughed nervously and started to gag into his handkerchief.

The old desk sergeant's face was white and his hands trembled. He dropped his notes on the dais and held on to the sides of it.

"Then the bastard rammed his gun barrel up inside the girl's vagina. The kid passed out and he turned his attention to the mother. He kissed the woman on the cheek, stroked her hair with his bloody hands and left. It took about an hour for Mrs. Goldberg to work herself loose. She was calm and rational when our guys first got there, but flipped her mind in the ambulance on the way to Union Memorial. She got a broken nose, but will be okay, except for her mind. God knows if she'll ever be right in the head again. Her husband and daughter are dead. The girl bled to death on her bed and her husband died in surgery at Union Memorial."

"The only description we got is a white male in his late twenties, dressed in black slacks and sweater and armed with a long-barreled handgun. Detectives continue to stake out the neighborhood. The Chief assigned twenty extra uniformed men to detectives, to help out. The Captain asks that no extra patrol cars work the area of the rapes, unless the suspect is flushed out. We want to get this bastard, not run him away."

The old desk sergeant rubbed his eyes and sighed. "I got to sleep fast, as this is a short changeover, so I'll say goodnight, gentlemen."

Sergeant Harper stepped to the dais and looked at the men.

"I just want a word or two with you about the party today. It looks like all the stuff for the party's here." He waved to a pile of packages stacked in the corner. "I want you to carry it out and put it into Sergeant Goulek's pickup when you hit the bricks today after roll call. He's parked under that big mulberry tree down on the corner. The truck's in the shade, so that will help keep the stuff fresh. The only thing I've got to do is pick up the ice down at the icehouse when Sergeant Goulek and me leave to go up there with the food and stuff. McGee, they sure are fine crabs you got out there in the hall. Three bushels. We can eat 'em 'til they run out our ears. They're the biggest, fattest crabs I've seen this year. Where did they come from?"

"Down on the Wye River. I got this old girlfriend there. She went over twelve of her father's live boxes yesterday and handpicked them for us. All males and prime crabs. Not a paper shell in the bunch. Jumbos like that sell for at least eight dollars a bushel. Wait till I tell you what I had to do for that old gal to spring for these crabs. I—"

"We aren't interested in your sex life, Sean," Sergeant Harper said, taking a dip of Copenhagen. "We could probably write a short novel about what each of you bandits did or promised to do for all these goodies. Now, don't forget any of your details. We haven't had a beef out of Headquarters for missing one on this tour of day work. Keep it like that. Try not to get tied up with anything today. You don't want to work any overtime. We're going to have ham, beefsteak, and corn on the cob ready to eat at four-thirty this afternoon. That will give you all time to go home if you want to and change or get your bathing suits or whatever. We'll eat the shrimp and crabs later on when we get tired of playing cards." He paused and shoved his hat back. "Those of you that bring girlfriends, remember, this ain't no Sunday school picnic, so you better prepare them for some of the cussing you guys always do. If they can't take it, don't bring them. I don't want any fistfighting this time, either. You guys got any hostile feelings about each other, pick some other time to settle up. One more thing, bring all your loose cash you can spare. I'm going to take as much of it as I can away from you at the poker table. If we don't get busy, Sergeant Goulek and me are going to take off from here at around one o'clock to get things set up. Don't eat much lunch today. We got a lot of good food to eat. Questions? No? Hit the bricks."

Carpenter hesitated as the room cleared. "Sarge, I haven't picked up the hams yet. Could I borrow your car to run up to the Acme? Brock's got two big ones picked out. He usually gets in the store at seven to do paperwork. He should be there by now."

"Here's the keys. Take your time. In fact, use it all day. The Lieutenant's off today. If I need a car I can use his. You can work your post in a car today, as long as you get out and let the merchants see you. Don't bother to call in or out on the radio."

Carpenter drove to the Acme, picked up the hams from the manager, and returned to the station. He found the old pickup truck parked under the mulberry tree. It was a cool, breezy spot. A robin was gorging himself on the large ripe mulberries, and cocked his head to one side as Carpenter climbed up into the bed of the pickup. He put the hams in a corner in back of the crab baskets. The crabs were packed in crushed ice and seaweed to keep them alive. He pried the top back on one basket and reached under the wet seaweed. The baskets smelled of clean salt marsh. He found the back fin of a large crab and pulled it out of the basket. It was at least nine inches from point to point and heavy. The crab's claws hung limp from its body, but it could stay alive for a week or more in the comatose condition induced by the ice. It would not feel the searing heat that killed, nor would it struggle with other crabs and lose its claws. Carpenter replaced the crab in the sweet-smelling sea grass, wired the top shut, and got back in the police car. He drove slowly through the quiet residential streets wasting time, until his school detail. The police radio sqwaked intermittently about a drowning at Loch Raven and a holdup in Edgemere. Carpenter turned the radio down and half listened. He arrived at Allegheny and Central just as the school bell rang.

The sun warmed his back as he helped the children to cross the street. It was about 80 degrees at 8:30 in the morning. Another unseasonably warm day. Jimmy Cox was one of the last to cross the street. He handed Carpenter a large Winesap apple and winked.

"Don't tell my mother. She wants me to get in good with my new teacher. I don't like the teacher. She's got bad breath and her false teeth are always slipping. She lets the girls get away with anything, but sends us boys down to the principal's office all the time."

"Hang in there, pal," Carpenter said, hitting him lightly on the shoulder. "School will be over for the summer before you know it. Next year you'll get a new teacher. Maybe you'll get lucky and get a teacher who likes boys."

Jenny ran across the street just as the bell rang. She dropped her bookbag on the sidewalk. The bag flew open and papers scattered around on the grass. Carpenter walked over and helped the frantic child pick up her papers. Jenny sighed and shrugged her shoulders.

"I thought I was going to be on time today. I guess she will keep me after school again. Thanks, Mr. Policeman."

She walked slowly toward the front door as though she now had all the time in the world.

He drove back to York and Pennsylvania and went into Elmer's Place. The morning crowd was gone. The waitresses were cleaning away the dirty dishes and sweeping the debris from the floor. He was hungry. Selecting a large hamburger, a pint of chili, and coffee to go, he thanked the waitress and took his bag of food out into the bright sunshine. He went to the familiar alley in the four hundred block of York, and had climbed halfway up the pole to the roof, when he noticed legs sticking out the top of the trash dumpster in the alley. He stopped climbing and watched as the blue-denim legs thrashed around the open top of the huge garbage receptacle. The top half of the body attached to the blue-clad legs was rooting around head first in the garbage.

Climbing down from the pole, he put his bag of food down near the side of the metal dumpster. The scavenger was digging around inside the dumpster like an animal. Reaching up, he grabbed a blue leg and pulled. Carpenter caught the surprised boy before his thin body hit the concrete.

"Let me go! Let me go! For shit's sake! I'm not hurting nobody."

The boy's long, dirty hair was matted with debris from the dumpster and hanging in his eyes. He was incredibly filthy. A frayed old sweatshirt covered his bony shoulders. The blue denims were little more than greasy rags. The new white sneakers he wore were the only clean things about him. His eyes were bright with fear. He was about fourteen years old.

"What are you doing in the garbage can?"

"What's it to you? I'm not stealin' nothin'," he shouted. "Let me go."

"Bullshit. What are you, a runaway?"

"No, I live here in Towson," he said, looking defiantly at Carpenter.

"Oh, yeah? What's your address?"

"I forgot. I mean I don't know. Oh, shit, I don't live here. I'm traveling."

"Traveling where? Where do you live? Come on, you grubby little punk," growled Carpenter, twisting his fist in the ragged sweatshirt. "Tell me the truth."

The boy burst into tears. His thin body started to tremble. Tears washed clean streaks on his dirty face as they fell to the concrete.

"I'm going to my brother's house in Salisbury."

"Where do you live?"

"San Francisco. I've been hitchhiking for a month."

"You're going to have to come to the station with me."

"Oh, Jesus, mister, please don't make me go back there."

"Your mother and father will be worried about you. Maybe your brother can pick you up."

"I ain't got no mother and father." The boy wiped his eyes on a filthy sleeve. "I lived in a foster home and couldn't take no more from them."

"Did they treat you bad?"

"Bad? Look at this."

The boy pulled the old sweatshirt off. His back was a mass of freshly healed purple cuts and welts.

"They beat me every day with a piece of heavy copper wire."

"What for?"

"Bad school grades. Not keeping my room straight. Everything. Please, mister, don't take me back," he said, his jaw quivering. "My brother's nineteen. He said he was going to come out and get me as soon as he saved enough money. I'm almost there now."

"What's your name, pal?"

"Charles. Charles Hamilton. My mother's dead. My father left us when I was a baby."

"What were you after in that garbage can?"

The boy looked away from him. "Nothing."

"Come on, don't bullshit me, Charles."

"I was looking for something to eat," he murmured, looking at his feet. "I ain't had nothing to eat for two days."

Carpenter took the boy by the arm and led him to the sunny side of the alley. "Sit down and stop crying. I've got something for you."

He walked over and picked up the bag of food and carried it to the boy. "Here. You like chili?"

"It's your food, ain't it? I don't want to take your food away from you."

Carpenter opened the steaming container of chili, stuck a plastic spoon into the steaming hot, thick mixture, and handed it to the boy.

"Go on, Charlie. I'm too damned fat anyway. Besides, I'm going to a big party after work. I'll be eating and boozing all night."

The boy started shoveling the hot food into his mouth.

"Take it easy, kid. Don't burn yourself. Here." He handed the hamburger to the boy, and grinned. "I hope you like onions on your hamburgers. Let this coffee cool off before you have a go at it."

Charlie put the food away in record time. Taking the top off of the coffee, he held it in his thin, dirty hands like a prize. He slurped the dark brew and looked over the top of the cup at Carpenter. Carpenter handed the boy a Camel and lit it with the Zippo. Pulling the smoke deep into his lungs, Charlie smiled at Carpenter with bad teeth.

"You're the first cop I met coming across the country that didn't lock me up and give me a kick in the ass. I got picked up in a cow town in Nevada. I gave them a false name and address, and after trying to contact my people for a few days they gave up. They drove me to the city line and smacked the hell out of me and let me go. I got busted in Kansas City for swiping a bottle of milk off a woman's porch. They took me to the juvenile hall and held me for five days. The food was pretty good, but there was a bunch of older fag kids locked up with me. They were talking about gang raping me the last day I was there. I just walked away from there when they were taking us to the mess hall for supper. They didn't even try to stop me." Charlie took a long drag on his cigarette and sighed. "The Pennsylvania State cops picked me up for hitchhiking on the turnpike. I broke away from them when they were taking me into their barracks and hid in a big honeysuckle patch on the side of a mountain all day and half the night. A truckdriver hauling a load of pigs to Baltimore gave me a lift to Towson. He came to Towson to see his sister on the way. She fed me and give me these shoes a couple of days ago. I've been sleeping in back yards and eating junk out of garbage cans. I've been looking for a job, but I guess I look too dirty for anybody to take a chance on me. I wanted Jack, my brother, to see me with clean clothes on."

"What have you been living on?"

"Oh, out West there's a lot of vegetable fields," he said, taking the last drag on his cigarette and putting the butt out with his foot. "I'd grab a couple of carrots here and some potatoes there. Mostly truckdrivers would give me a ride. They usually bought me a coffee and donuts or a sandwich when they'd stop to eat. I think that truckdrivers are the best guys in the world. They talk tough, but I never met a mean one."

"Is that all the clothing you started with?" asked Carpenter, shaking his head. "It's a wonder you didn't freeze to death at night."

"I almost did that night on the mountain in Pennsylvania. In the country when it gets dark, I'd sleep in barns or hay piles. Dairy barns are the best. All the cows make it warm inside the barn. When I got put out in a town at night I'd sleep in laundromats or parked cars that I found open. It ain't been so bad. I tried to keep clean at first, but the only place I could wash in was the men's room at service stations. After a while I just gave up and learned to live with the dirt. What's your name, mister?"

"Just call me Fritz."

"What are you going to do with me?"

"Come on, Charlie, let's go see a friend of mine."

They walked to East Towson, to the site of the new church. The Reverend William Brown was stirring a gallon of white paint. He saw them watching him from the road and laid his paddle down, and walked out to see them.

"Hello, Officer. It's a beautiful day. I thought I might get the first coat of paint on this side of the building today. How does it look?"

"It's really fine-looking, Reverend. It looks like professional men built it. Reverend, this is Charles Hamilton. He's traveling through and needs a hot shower and some clean clothing. I thought maybe you could help him."

"Certainly." Shaking the boy's hand, he looked him up and down and smiled. "How do you do, Charles. Come with me."

They walked with the minister to his residence, next door to the church. He took the boy to the bathroom and gave him soap, a clean washcloth, and a towel.

"There you are, Charles. Close the door behind you, take off your clothing, and hand it out the door to me."

Charles closed the door. He handed the ragged sweatshirt and denim pants out to the minister.

"Where's the rest?"

"That's all."

"No underwear?"

"No sir."

"My, my," he said, pressing his lips together. "All right Charles, give yourself a good wash. I'll find you something clean to put on."

The preacher turned to Carpenter and motioned with his thumb. "Come on down the cellar with me, Officer. We should be able to fix him up with something better than this."

They walked into the dim cellar. The preacher switched on a bare electric light.

"Over here on my workbench is a box of used clothing that we got from the Goodwill people."

They looked through the box and found the boy a couple of shirts near his size and three pair of slacks, in almost new condition. Taking the clothing upstairs, they put it by the bathroom door and went to the kitchen.

"My wife's visiting her mother down in West Baltimore," said the preacher, taking a covered pan from the back of the stove. "She left me a pan of cornbread for lunch. Let's pack the lad a lunch."

The minister put half the pan of cornbread on the table and spread it with soft butter. He wrapped it in waxed paper and put it in a bag. Opening the old refrigerator, he peered in over his glasses.

"Nothing much here except some leftover pork chops from last night. They'll have to do."

He wrapped up the chops in waxed paper and put them into the bag with the cornbread. Charles came into the kitchen, wearing his new clothing. The pants were a good fit, but the sport shirt was a little large. His dark hair was clean and combed back, still wet from the shower.

"I feel like a new man," he said, holding out a neatly folded bundle. "Here's the other clothes. These fit pretty good. Ah, thank you, Reverend."

"No thanks are necessary, Charles. Give me the extra clothing and I'll put them into this big, old bag for you. We prepared a little food for you to take along on your trip. Have you come far?"

The boy looked at Carpenter and smiled.

"Yes, sir. A long way."

"Well I hope you get home soon, my boy," he said, patting Charles on the back.

"We've got to go, Reverend," said Carpenter. "I knew that I could get some help from you without a lot of hassle. It's appreciated. Come on, Charlie, let's get going."

Carpenter walked to the corner of Pennsylvania and York Road with the boy. He glanced at his watch.

"The Greyhound bus comes by here in just a minute," he said, taking a bill from his wallet. "Here's twenty bucks, kid. You can take the bus from here to the station in Baltimore. Buses leave to the Eastern shore from there just about every hour. It will take maybe three, four hours to get to Salisbury."

The boy's bottom lip was trembling. He was blinking back tears.

"Ah, hell, Mr. Fritz. Nobody's ever done nothing like this for me before."

The bus pulled up to the corner. The door swung open. Carpenter shook hands with the thin boy.

"So long, Charlie. I hope things work out for you. Listen to your brother."

The boy was sobbing openly as he got on the bus. He handed the twenty-dollar bill to the driver. Carpenter leaned inside the bus.

"Do me a favor, pal. Will you see that the boy gets a ticket to Salisbury when he gets downtown?"

"I'll be glad to, Officer."

The door closed and the bus moved away in the heavy traffic.

Carpenter walked across the road to the taxi stand and opened the door to the small office. The dispatcher was on the phone with his back to the door again. Hearing the door close, he turned in his swivel chair to face Carpenter. He finished taking the horse bet casually and hung up the phone.

"I just wanted to see if you got your cab back."

"Oh yeah, I sure did, Officer Carpenter," he said, chewing a cold cigar butt. "The fire department called and told me it was blocking their door. I walked up and got it myself. No trouble. They told me about that guy. I read about it in the papers, too. Good grief, three guys getting cut down by the cops for one holdup. At that rate the world will be running out of bad guys soon."

"I doubt it. There's a son-of-a-bitch born every minute, some place."

"Well, none of you cops got hurt too bad. That's the important thing. I don't know how you guys do it."

"I don't either."

"Look, I'm putting twenty bucks a week on the side for you," said the dispatcher, lowering his voice. "Think about it like money in the bank. If you change your mind it's here. You might run short."

"Thanks, I'll keep it in mind. What's your name anyway?"

"Horace. They all call me Hoss. I'm not pushing you on that cash. Just remember it's here for you in case you need it."

"I understand," said Carpenter, turning to go. "I'll see you, Hoss."

"Take care of yourself, Officer."

22

CARPENTER WENT HOME AFTER WORK, REMOVED HIS uniform, put his swimsuit on, then put on an old pair of Levi's, and pulled on an old sport shirt. It was four P.M. when he parked his car on the lot at Berry's Quarry Club. The man checking passes at the gate looked at his badge when he flashed it and nodded.

"Hello. You one of McGee's buddies?"

"Yes sir."

"They're up at the new pavilion," he said, jerking his thumb at a muddy road. "Go through that gate and walk up the hill. There's a thirty-acre pasture up there. You'll see the pavilion when you get up there. The ground slopes away from the hillcrest toward the Gunpowder River. I'd let you drive up, but the ground's pretty wet in spots. You'd probably get stuck in the mud. The contractor's going to blacktop the road and parking area up there if it ever dries out. Where's your girlfriend?"

"She couldn't make it."

"Too bad," he said, with a sly smile. "Quite a few girls here already. Enjoy yourself, Officer. Drink one for me."

Carpenter walked 100 yards up the steep hill. As he

got to the top, he looked out across the lush meadow. Purple clover was in full bloom and Queen Anne's lace splashed the green grass with white. The pavilion's new corrugated iron roof gleamed in the bright afternoon sunshine. Honeybees worked the blossoms everywhere. The swimming pool was near the woods at the far end of the pasture. A group of girls were laughing and splashing in the vast pool. The water was chicory-flower blue and very inviting. The smell of charcoal-broiled steak drifted on the breeze to him. Realizing that he had not eaten since the night before, he trotted the 200 yards to the pavilion.

Sergeant Harper and Sergeant Goulek were cooking steaks and Polish sausage over a charcoal fire in a new brick barbecue pit, built in the center of the pavilion in the kitchen area. The vast shedlike building was open on all sides with a concrete floor and filled with twelve-foot-long redwood picnic tables and benches.

The kitchen area was fully equipped with electric ranges and huge refrigerators, sinks, and beer coolers. Two of the tables were set with paper cups and platters. A third table nearby held their food. It was set with thin slices of ham, loaves of bread, pickles, a huge green salad, six large loaves of moonseed cake, a tub of country butter, coconut macaroons, pumpernickel sticks, and cheesecake from Stone's bakery.

The entire shift was at a table set up as a bar, drinking mixed drinks and draft beer. Sean McGee waved and motioned him over. He passed by the sergeants at the pit. Sergeant Harper was trimming fat from the edge of New York strip steaks on a table next to the pit. Looking up from his work at Carpenter, a thin trace of a smile worked at his lips. He picked up a cup of beer, gulped it down, and belched violently. "Good fucking draft," he said, wiping foam from his upper lip. He tested the edge of the butcher knife on his thumb and started to hone it on a carborundum stone.

"Glad you made it in time to eat," he said, his eyes flickering to Carpenter's face. "You like steak?"

"Number one, Sarge, I'm starving."

"Well, you'll like this beef. It had a quarter inch of mould on it from aging in the cellar over at Kismet Inn. Get yourself a drink. You're about three behind the rest of those bandits."

Carpenter walked over to the bar table. McGee frowned at him.

"Come on, Fritz," McGee said, taking him by the arm. "I'll mix the first one for you, then you can pour your own poison. What'll it be?"

"Scotch and water."

McGee mixed the drink, touched the cup to his broken nose, and handed it to Carpenter. "Drink fast, we're ahead of you."

The Scotch hit his stomach with a jolt. He felt the warm glow of the alcohol almost immediately in his veins.

"I've got to go slow, McGee. I haven't had anything to eat today. My stomach thinks my throat's cut."

Sergeant Goulek came over to the table and poured himself a drink of bourbon. He tossed it down, made a face, and poured a large Canadian Club for Sergeant Harper.

"Last call for booze before we eat, men. Drink up. We eat in about five minutes. Sean, run over to the pool and tell them pussies that if they want to eat with us to get their plump little asses dried off and come on."

McGee trotted off toward the pool. The girls were all out of the pool, lying on blankets in the sunshine. McGee knelt down and said something to them. He stood and raced up the slope to the pavilion, the girls running hard to keep up with him. They all got to the pavilion at about the same time, laughing and shoving McGee around like playful puppies. McGee climbed up on an empty table.

"Ahem. Ladies and gentlemen, may I have your attention, please? Dinner will be served in about three minutes, so this won't be a long speech. Welcome to our long changeover party. We expect everyone to eat all the food he or she can hold and drink enough booze to shut out the pain of the cruel, cruel world. There will be poker games after dinner, horseshoes, swimming, and touch football."

The crowd cheered.

"There will be no farting at the dinner tables."

The crowd booed.

"We will eat shrimp and corn on the cob and crabs for a snack later on."

The crowd cheered.

"Please use the restrooms for—ah—calls of nature. There will be absolutely no peeing on the grass."

The crowd booed.

"There will be two steaks for everyone here."

The crowd cheered.

"There will be no chasing of girls around the pool area."

The crowd booed.

"Everyone is expected to have a load on by nine P.M."

The crowd cheered.

"There will be no fistfights without clearing it with the sergeants."

The crowd booed.

"These lovely ladies have come in a group with Miss Rose Murphy. They are here to provide us with clean, healthy fun."

The crowd cheered.

"This is a day off for all of them. There will be absolutely no screwing before, during, or after the party today."

The men booed. The women cheered.

"This does not preclude you from making arrangements with the girls for a date in the near future."

The men cheered.

"The moonseed cakes for dessert come from Abe's secret source."

The crowd cheered.

"We've got three bushels of the fattest crabs this side of the bay."

The crowd cheered.

"There's not ten, but twenty pounds of shrimp to eat."

Everyone cheered.

"Can we meet the challenge? Can we eat it all?"

Everyone cheered louder.

"We have two halves of cold National beer on tap. We are duty bound to drink it all before we go home."

Everyone cheered.

"Now, gentlemen, allow me to introduce the ladies. I believe most of you know the lady responsible for bringing this bevy of beauties into our midst, Miss Rose Murphy."

The men cheered.

"Line up here, girls," he said, indicating a spot in front of him. "That's it. Now, I think I've got this right. Going from right to left, this is Ruth, Cindy, Betty, Pat, Cassie, Thelma, Wanda, Jean, Kitty, Lil, and last, but not least, Irma."

The men cheered and whistled loud and long.

"Come and get it," Sergeant Goulek yelled, "or I'll throw it in the Gunpowder. We got 'em rare, medium, and well done. We got the best fucking—er, excuse me, ladies—we got the very best Polish sausage in East Baltimore, made by our friend in Highlandtown, Jim Washolowski. Come on, McGee, you get in line first. I wish you could remember your school details as good as you remember the girls names."

"Have I ever let you down, Sarge?"

"No, and you better not. Come on, line up here by

the pit and get your meat. Everything else in on the other table. All we got to drink with it is draft beer or soft drinks. I'll make a big pot of coffee later, to help sober you heroes up. Take one steak at a time. Sam and me are going to keep cooking these beautiful little devils. We got at least two each, so don't be bashful. Eat until you think you got enough, then eat some more."

Carpenter was last in line. Rose Murphy got in line ahead of him.

"Hi, Fritz. How do I look now that I'm healed up?"

"I wouldn't have recognized you, Rose. You are really a pretty girl. I didn't expect . . . I mean, I didn't think . . . ah, I, ah . . ."

"You didn't think a hustler could look so innocent, right?"

"Right."

She laughed from deep in her throat. She could have been a college girl at a Sunday School picnic.

"I guess I don't fit your stereotype of a floozie," she said, looking into his eyes. "Thanks. I'm flattered. I really am. That's what a lot of the Johns tell me. Innocent, but sexy."

"Where did you meet all the—ah—girls?"

"We keep in close touch. We work a lot of conventions in Baltimore, New York, and Ocean City."

"I thought you were strictly local."

"I am, usually, but when a big convention is nearby, I go where the action is. You can make two or three grand a week at a swinging convention. Let's not talk about that. I'm starving. I'm glad McGee invited us. He's really a nice guy. If I was ready to quit the business, I'd try to con him into going South with me and my baby."

"He keeps you smiling. You'd never have a dull moment with him."

They moved closer to the hot barbecue pit. Goulek

wiped his face and head with a dishtowel, and flipped a few steaks over on the hot grill.

"What kind do you like, Fritz? Rare, medium, or well done?"

"Make mine medium, Sergeant Goulek."

Goulek speared a sizzling steak and slapped it on Carpenter's platter. He turned to Rose and bowed slightly.

"How about you, Miss Rose?"

"Well done. Burned, if you have one like that."

He selected a steak and slid it on to Rose's platter carefully. "Here you are. I was wondering what I was going to do with that one. It's going to be kind of dry."

"That's the way I like 'em."

Carpenter sat between Rose and Lil at the table. Lil was a plump, pixie-faced girl who talked little, but laughed at everything that was said. She had the appetite of a hungry coal miner. There was little conversation at the table at first. The steak was exceptionally tender and well-seasoned, with just a trace of garlic. The ham was succulent and sweet. The Polish sausage was a spicy combination of lean pork and spices, made as only the Polish people in Highlandtown make it by hand at home in their kitchens.

Both sergeants remained at the charcoal pit, eating steak with their fingers and tending the fresh batch of beef over the hot fire. Sergeant Goulek left the pit to draw two pitchers of beer and carried them to the table.

"Pass it around before it gets warm. Nothing like a cold draft to wash good beef down. Hey, miss," he growled, bending over Cassie. "You're out of steak. Let me get you another one. What's your favorite?"

"Medium, but I really shouldn't. I've got to watch my weight."

"Aw, bullshit, miss, you look fine to me. I'll get a platter of rares and mediums. The well-dones will be a while yet."

Most of them managed to eat two steaks. Sergeant Goulek went to his truck and got two bottles from the front seat. Looking around in the truck bed, he found a container of small paper cups and put a tube of cups and a bottle on each table.

"There you go, folks. A little sweet booze to take that bloated feeling away. Sip on a slug of this for a while and you'll be back asking for more steak in half an hour. Southern Comfort. Good for colds, moles, and sore ass-holes. Puts hair on your feet."

Sergeant Goulek returned to the grill and started to move steaks around. "We still got about six steaks here. I'm gonna take them away from the heat. I'll just stick them on the corner of the grate. Pull off a hunk with your fingers later on when you get hunger pains." He wiped his face and drained a cup of beer. "Kindly throw your dirty dishes in the can over by that pole when you finish. There's a set of horseshoes and pins with a hammer in the back of my truck for anybody that wants to throw a game or two. There's also a football and softball and bat for those of you who go in for organized grab-ass. I got a new deck of Bicycles in my pocket and a hundred bucks in my wallet, if anybody wants to show me how to play poker. Who's a good swimmer? Come on, one of you must know something about lifeguarding. We don't want anybody to get all smoked up and drown in the man's pool."

Carpenter spoke up. "I'll watch the pool for a couple hours. I'm too full to do anything but sit for a while."

After he poured Scotch into a large paper cup and added a few cubes, he walked down the gentle slope to the pool. He kicked off his old sneakers, slipped off his Levi's and shirt, climbed up into the lifeguard's big chair at the deep end of the pool, and relaxed in the warm sunshine. Sipping the Scotch, he watched barn swallows fly their intricate maneuvers above the pool. Occasionally one would glide down to the pool's surface and skim an insect from the calm water in midflight. Two policemen were choosing up sides near the pavilion for a touch football game. Sounds of laughter and hooting followed each selection. The girls were all chosen first. Five men and a woman were playing cards quietly at a table on the sunny side of the pavilion.

A buzzard was soaring in a thermal current, a thousand feet over the clearing. Carpenter heard the bark of a pair of hunting foxes in the woods beside the pool and the scream of the captured rabbit. Finishing the Scotch, he let the warm sunshine burn away the tension from his muscles. His eyelids were heavy and the buzz of honeybees in the wild clover soothed his ears. Carpenter's chin rested on his chest and he slept.

He jolted awake from the bang of the diving board. Sean McGee was bouncing up and down, checking the spring in the board. Ruth and Irma were on the concrete deck behind the board, waiting to dive. McGee executed a perfect jacknife and split the water cleanly with little splash. Ruth and Irma clapped their hands and cheered. Both girls were small-boned and big-breasted, with narrow waists and curving hips. Theywere dark-haired and very pretty. Neither could have been over twenty-two. Ruth wore a black tank suit and Irma wore a two-piece white suit.

They both dove from the board cleanly and swam side by side in a smooth crawl. They easily overtook and passed McGee. They were expert swimmers. McGee was more impressive diving than swimming. He chopped his way awkwardly to the end of the pool and turned to swim back. Switching to an easy breast stroke, he took his time swimming back. He swam to the lifeguard's chair, rested his elbows on the side of the pool, and panted from exertion.

"Ye gods, Fritz," said McGee, blowing water from his nose. "I asked these two cuties to walk down here to see an expert diver and swimmer. They asked me if I'd give them a free lesson. I should have known, you can't hustle a hustler." Turning his back to Carpenter, he watched them perform. "Look at them. They could give me lessons."

"You made the age-old error," said Carpenter, laughing. "You underestimated a woman. Two women, to be exact. What are you going to do with two of them?"

"Well, I don't know," said McGee, floating on his back. "They're easily the best-looking girls in the bunch. I can't make up my mind which one to lavish my charms on. Are you interested in one?"

"No, thanks. I'm gun-shy with hookers. I'd be afraid my cock would fall off."

"I guess it's true that they do more fucking than the average woman, but I'll bet the odds are less on catching a dose with them than with the average Towson lovely."

"Oh, yeah? Well, you can have my share, McGee. It would be kind of difficult explaining a case of Old Joe to my bride."

"True. I pity you married types," said McGee, spitting a stream of water on Carpenter's feet. "You lose your sense of adventure. Besides, I've been told you ain't a man until you've had three doses of clap."

"Have you made your quota yet?"

"No," said McGee, grabbing his crotch, "but I'm working on it."

The girls slowed their steady pace and stopped at the shallow end of the pool. Climbing out on the ladder, they squeezed the water from their hair. McGee climbed from the pool, trotted to the shallow end and said something to the girls. They laughed and each of them pressed against him. Irma pointed to the other end of the pool. McGee bowed to her and ran to the deep end of the pool. Retrieving their two large straw handbags from a poolside table, he trotted back to the girls.

McGee removed three cushions from the chaise lounges and put them together on the concrete deck. He sat down on the center one and the girls sat down beside him. Irma waved at Carpenter and smiled. Ruth took a cigarette from her purse and lit up, took a deep drag, and passed it to McGee. McGee pulled hard on it and passed it to Irma. Irma took her turn and passed it back to Ruth. The sharp odor of pot drifted back on the warm breeze to Carpenter. Ruth pulled a portable radio from her bag. Bill Haley and the Comets were singing "Rock Around The Clock." They lay back on the thick pads and smoked the rest of the joint together.

Afterward McGee was rubbing suntan lotion on Irma's back. Ruth bit him on the neck and demanded the same treatment. McGee poured lotion over the legs and arms of both girls and rubbed them simultaneously. Irma poured the rest of the bottle on McGee's chest and stomach and rubbed in the lotion. McGee grabbed both girls around the neck and pulled their heads close to him. He mumbled something to them. They burst into laughter and jumped up. Each of them grabbed a hand and pulled him to his feet. He picked up a pad and draped it over his shoulder. The girls put their arms around his waist, and they walked into the woods together.

Carpenter dove into the pool from his chair and started to swim laps. He swam for a long time before he heard someone dive into the pool. Lifting his head, he looked around. Joe Lehland was floating on his back and Abe Jacobson was sitting on the edge of the pool dangling his hairy legs in the pool. Carpenter stroked to Abe and held on to the side of the pool. He blew water from his nose and looked up at his friend.

"What happened to the touch football game?"

"Those dizzy broads kept grabbing me around the

neck. I was afraid they'd break the scabs off of these cuts. It's hot as hell running around in the tall grass anyway."

"What's your excuse, Joe? I never thought I'd see you walk away from a gang of pretty hookers in bathing suits."

Lehland paddled to the side of the pool and hung on to the side. He blew the water from his nose and laughed.

"Well, I'll tell you two old married codgers. I sat beside that gal Cassie when we ate. That's the one with the huge tits in the blue bathing suit. I thought I'd cop a little feel and I brushed my arm against her boobs when I reached for the butter. She leaned real close to me and whispered a sweet nothing in my ear."

"What do you mean, a sweet nothing?" asked Abe.

"She told me if I touched her tits again, she'd cut my balls off with her steak knife. Naturally, I apologized. She smiled and said it was okay. She said she'd go out with me after the party if I acted like a gentleman. I haven't laid a hand on her since then. It looks like they just want to relax and enjoy themselves. I noticed that Sal Trotta got smacked in the chops by that plump little blonde when he accidentally grabbed her halter and spilled her boobs out during the game."

Abe laughed and eased himself into the water. He held on to the side of the pool to keep his scabby shoulders and head dry.

"Ah, that feels good. These fucking scabs are itching like crazy. It feels like a bunch of ants walking around. Doc Wolf said not to get them wet for a few weeks." He let his mouth fill with water and fired a fine jet between his teeth at Lehland's ear. "Yeah, Joe, I think you're right. They must have got together and agreed on no hanky-panky before they came. No free samples to cops."

"I don't blame them," said Lehland. "We don't go

around policing on our time off. Why should they give their pussy away? Leave it to McGee. He said that he was going to bring a bunch of broads that liked a good time, but didn't go around giving their ass away."

Lehland climbed out of the pool and walked over to the edge of the concrete deck. Picking up a brown paper bag, he carried it to a table. He took out a bottle of Scotch and three paper cups full of ice.

"Let's drink this bottle of J and B. Come on, Fritz, we brought you a cup."

They sat at the poolside table drinking Scotch and watching the football game. The sun was low in the sky. The shadows from the trees in the woods close by lengthened until they covered the pool and their table. They watched a groundhog two hundred yards away slowly emerge from his hole and sit up on his haunches to watch the ballplayers. The groundhog watched the boisterous group for a long time before he moved into the sweet clover for his evening meal. At last the football game broke up. The players gathered around the beer keg under the pavilion. Two men were pitching horseshoes with two of the women. Someone turned on the lights in the pavilion over the card table. Floodlights came on beside the pavilion and illuminated the horseshoe pitchers' area.

"I guess we ought to turn the pool lights on," said Abe. "They won't be able to find us unless we do, Fritz."

"I know where it is," said Lehland, walking toward the side of the pool. "The box is right over here beside the lifeguard's chair. Here it is."

The submerged lights came on all around the deep end of the pool. There was a loud crashing in the underbrush of the woods beside the pool. Sean McGee and the girls walked into the dim light at poolside. He dropped the pad on a chaise lounge and fell back on it in feigned exhaustion. The girls sat beside him on the lounge with their knees together primly.

"Irma, my love, please hand me that bottle," he said softly, sliding his hand up her trim thigh. "I need something to revive me. Ruth, stay here beside me and hold your sweet-smelling hand on my fevered brow. I'm as close to death as I've ever been."

Lehland and Jacobson stared at him in amazement. Irma got the bottle from the table and wiggled back to McGee's prone form. He pulled the cork and drank deeply from the bottle. Ruth caressed his head and face. Irma fanned him with a bath towel. He took the bottle from his mouth and made a horrible face. He belched and raised the bottle to his lips again. One, two, three, more great swallows, and he fell back against the cushion like a weak old man, with his arms hanging limply to the sides of the lounge.

"Where in the hell have you been, McGee?" Lehland asked.

"Joe, Abe, Fritz," he said dramatically, extending his arms to them. "You must forgive me, my friends. I've violated the very rules that I dictated to you at the start of this party. I've been debauching in the woods with these two beauties. I've been practicing intemperance and sensuality with these wanton creatures. You might say we have performed certain sensual excesses and unspeakable sweet perversions together. My God, I came three times in the last three hours. We'd still have been there, but, alas, darkness fell on our sweet bed of ferns and the girls were afraid we wouldn't be able to find our way back to civilization. The girls have some of the finest pot that ever came out of Tampico. They have the smoothest bosoms and most velvetlike asses I've ever encountered. Their mouths taste of wild honey and they smell like new-mown hay."

Ruth looked at Irma and laughed.

"Quit that old police job, you wild-talking Irishman, and come live with us," she said, playing with the hair on his chest. "You won't have to do anything, except smoke grass and play with us between tricks. We'll make a rich man of you."

"Ah, my little beauties," he said, smiling and squeezing each girl's backside. "You've made me a rich man already. I'll never forget this wondrous afternoon with you two. You've introduced me to delights that I didn't know existed before. No, I'm afraid I can't live with you. I'd tear the heart out of any man that looked at you. I couldn't bear the thought of another man touching your lovely bodies. We must be content with an occasional meeting, whenever you have a—er, ah, free afternoon."

"You've got our number," said Ruth, pouting. "Promise you'll call us."

"I promise," he said, kissing each girl in the navel. "Run along now, girls. There's a shower house at the other end of the pool."

They walked away together, each holding the other around the waist, toward the shower.

"Ah, I hope you guys won't mention this to the rest of the shift," said McGee, scratching his crotch. "I'm afraid they'd feel cheated and really get pissed off at me. I didn't intend to do that, you know. The opportunity presented itself and I couldn't very well refuse them. I didn't want them to feel rejected."

"Sean, you are a bona-fide sex fiend," said Abe.

"Yes, I know. It's a great way to go. My God, I'm starving. Those little kittens drained all the juices out of me. Look, here comes the rest of the mob down the hill. Remember, mum is the word."

The card game was still in progress up in the pavilion. The remainder of the crowd ran down the slope to the pool area, carrying bottles of whiskey, ice, and setups. They put their liquor on poolside tables and jumped into the pool, laughing and screaming like lunatics. Carpenter climbed up to the lifeguard's chair, drink in hand. Tom Dhaw organized a game of follow the leader. He started the game with a comic dive from the board and hit the water with a great splash. They followed him, one by one, into the water. He swam the length of the pool in a spastic crawl, with his imitators following him. Climbing from the pool at the shallow end, he hopped on one foot halfway back to the deep end. He poured a paper cup full of whiskey, tossed it down, hopped on one leg to the edge of the pool and fell into the water backward.

The men had no difficulty duplicating the leader. Some of the women had a problem with the whiskey. Carpenter's plump dinner companion protested that she didn't drink whiskey. Everybody booed her. She held her nose and gulped the whiskey down without removing the cup from her mouth. Her eyes popped and she fanned her open mouth with her hands. She dropped out of the game and walked to the lifeguard's chair. She sat down on the edge of the pool with her legs in the water.

"Are you okay, Lil?" asked Carpenter, looking down at her full breasts.

"I don't feel too good. I shouldn't have drunk that stuff."

He climbed down and sat beside her. She was very pale and her face was perspiring, as she gulped great breaths of air into her lungs.

"Oh, I think I'm going to be sick. Please help me up."

He took her arm, pulled her to her feet, and half carried her beyond the glow of the lights into the tall grass between the pool and the woods. She sank to her knees and vomited violently onto the lush pasture grass. Carpenter held her by the shoulders as she leaned forward. She retched and heaved for a long time. At last she was quiet.

"All that good steak. It's a shame. I feel better now. Please help me up. Everything's spinning."

He walked her away from the soiled grass. She was heavy-footed and very weak. Her legs were like rubber. She sat down heavily in the clover and started to cry.

"Oh, shit, I'm drunk. I hate to feel like this. My face is all messed up. I got upchuck down the front of me. I wish I was dead."

"Wait a minute, Lil. I'll be right back. Don't go away."

"Don't worry," she said, pressing her hands on her stomach.

Carpenter ran to poolside, grabbed a large towel and dipped it into the water. She was stretched out on her back when he returned.

"Hey. You awake?" he asked softly, shaking her gently.

"Yeah, I just thought I'd lay down to stop the spinning."

"I got a wet towel to clean you up."

He wiped her face and arms off with the wet towel. She sat up and looked at him.

"I feel better."

She untied the top of her bathing suit and handed it to him. She laughed softly in the darkness and covered her breasts with her hands.

"Be a nice guy and rinse my halter out in the pool for me."

He rinsed the halter out in the pool and squeezed the water from the dark jersey. Returning to the girl, he handed it to her. She slipped the wet top on and tied it. Standing, she held on to his arm.

"There. I'm going to make it."

She started to laugh again.

"What's funny?"

"My Momma told me to stay away from whiskey and don't trust cops. She was right about the whiskey and wrong about cops. Thanks for helping me, Fritz. You and that big hairy guy are the only two that didn't make any passes today. I bet you're both married."

"I am. He is, too."

"You been married long?"

"Yes."

"Do you ever mess around with other women?"

"Not yet."

"Just my luck. I meet a nice guy, somebody I like, and he's married. He don't mess around, and to top it all, he's a cop."

"You can't win 'em all, Lil. If I ever did fool around, it would be with somebody just like you."

"Ah, you sweet bullshitter," she said, stroking his chin. "Don't you think I'm a little too—ah—plump?"

"No, not at all. I like my women with some meat on them."

"I'm solid. I'm about five-feet-four and weigh one-thirty. Here. Feel my boobs and fanny."

Lil put his hands on her ample breast and backside. She was solid and smooth. Carpenter pulled his hands away, thankful for the darkness. He was blushing like a schoolboy.

"That's a fact, Lil," he said, fighting a surge of lust. "You are really solid. We'd better get back to the others."

"Yeah," she said, trying to eye the front of his trunks. "I'd hate to take advantage. If you ever decide to bust loose, call me. Rose always knows where to reach me. No money involved. I'd love to take care of you, Fritz."

"Thank you, Lil. I'll remember you."

They walked back to poolside. The game was still in progress. Tom Dhaw was still leading. Robert Fancy and Beau Barter were the only ones left on their feet. They were very drunk. The rest of the crowd were lying around on chaise lounges, sleeping. Sal Trotta was lying face down in the tall grass beside the pool, heaving dry, gut-tearing heaves. Nothing was coming up. Sean McGee was lying on top of a picnic table, covered with a towel, snoring like a buzzsaw. Carpenter looked up the slope at the pavilion. There were only two men and a woman playing cards. The hookers were lying together on two blankets, sleeping the peaceful sleep of the righteous. Their blankets were spread on the concrete apron at the shallow end of the pool. Lil pulled Carpenter's head down and kissed his cheek.

"Thanks again. I'm gonna lay down for a while, too. Don't let us sleep all night. Tomorrow's a work day for us."

"I won't," said Carpenter.

He walked with her to the group of sleeping girls. She lay down with them. He picked up a couple of spare blankets and covered them all. He walked back to Abe and Joe Lehland. The bottle of J and B was almost empty. Abe and Joe were sitting where he had left them, staring at the pool lights, drinks in hand. Robert Fancy and Beau Barter were crawling on hands and knees. They made it into the damp grass and lay still. Tom Dhaw staggered up to their table and sat down.

"Bunch-a party poo-poo-poopers," he said. Leaning forward, he rested his head on the table and passed out.

Carpenter looked at Joe Lehland and Abe.

"I guess that leaves us. Some party. Let's go eat some crabs and shrimp."

Abe shook his head. "I'll be along later. Somebody should stay here and keep an eye open. One of 'em could wake up and fall in the fucking pool and fucking well drown. I'll call you if I have any trouble."

Carpenter picked up the Scotch bottle, drained it, and turned to Joe. "Come on, Joe, somebody's got to eat those crabs."

They walked up to the pavilion. Rose Murphy was playing head to head with Sergeant Harper. Sergeant

Goulek was sitting there watching them, chewing on a piece of Polish sausage. He saw Carpenter and Lehland sit down at a table spread with newspapers and stood up.

"Where's the rest of them?"

"Sleeping down at the pool. They had a little whiskey-drinking contest and they all crapped out," Carpenter said.

"Son-of-a-bitch," growled Goulek, licking his fingers. "Who's going to eat all those crabs and shrimp? I got 'em all ready, steamed the Goulek way."

"What way is that?" asked Carpenter.

"Well, I just boil the shrimp and crabs in beer. Separately, of course, but I season them the same. No salt, no spices, nothing goes in the pot. Cook them until they're done and take them out and put a layer of crabs in a double grocery bag. Sprinkle rock salt and Old Bay seasoning on that layer, add another layer of hot crabs, sprinkle them with salt and Old Bay, and so on until the bag's full. Put a piece of newspaper in the top of the full bag and twist it shut to keep the heat in and let 'em sit for an hour or so. I do the shrimp the same way." Sergeant Goulek blew his nose in a paper towel. "The thing you got to remember is no spices go in the cooking pot. Keep the salt and spices away from them until you lay it on 'em layer by layer in the bag. You have your seasoning covering each crab and shrimp that way. None of it gets blanched out by the steaming beer and it improves the flavor. Wait a minute. I'll get you a few pounds of shrimp and a bag of crabs. If you don't like 'em, I'll turn in my tin and go home to Georgia."

Reaching under a pile of burlap bags beside the charcoal pit, he got out two bags. He dumped about three pounds of shrimp in the center of the table and returned the almost-full bag of shrimp to the burlap-covered pile. Carpenter ripped open a full bag of the heavy red jumbo crabs on the table between them.

"Here's a couple of steak knives to eat your crabs with," said Goulek. "I'll get us a pitcher of cold beer and we can turn on to these beauties."

Returning with the beer and paper cups, he waited anxiously while they each peeled a jumbo shrimp and began to eat. Neither of them said anything. They finished chewing and swallowed. They attacked the tender, still-warm shrimp with gusto. He laughed and broke open a big crab.

"You don't have to say anything about liking them. You guys are eating like a couple of starving plowhorses. A man would never know that you both polished off two pounds of steak a few hours ago. People should eat more seafood. It puts lead in your pencil. This good seafood is what keeps me around here year after year freezing my ass off in the winter. If they knew how to cook it in Georgia, I'd have been long gone from here years ago."

"Won't your wife cook it for you?" asked Lehland, taking a swallow of beer.

"Hell, no. She hates anything out of the water. When she tries to cook anything that swims she cooks it to a frazzle."

"Why not cook your own?" asked Carpenter, licking seasoning from his fingers.

"Bullshit," said Goulek, licking a mouthful of yellow crab fat from his fingers. "I hate to cook. The only reason I cook at these parties is to keep you young heroes from ruining a lot of good food."

Picking the crab, Sergeant Goulek paused and held up a piece of crabmeat. "Ah, look at this hunk of backfin. These crabs are tasty motherfuckers, even if I did cook them myself. Look at that hard yellow fat in the corner of the shells. Must be a teaspoon in each point. These are the fattest, nicest crabs I've had in years. If the Lord made anything better, He saved it for

Himself. Three of these monsters would fill up a hungry man. I'll just eat seven or eight or so and quit. I don't want you guys talking about me."

They sat for hours, eating the delicious crabs and shrimp. The pile of empty shells grew on the table in front of them until it was difficult to see over the top. Rose Murphy and Sergeant Harper quit the card game and joined them. Joe Lehland got another bag of crabs and some shrimp for the newcomers. Carpenter kept drawing pitchers of beer to go with the spicy crustaceans. They opened yet another bag of crabs. Sergeant Goulek opened his belt and loosened his pants. He drained his draft beer and wiped his mouth and hands on a paper towel, burped and sighed.

"I gotta stop or I'll founder myself. I figure we ate about a bushel of crabs and maybe five pounds of shrimp. Not bad for a handful of amateurs. I guess we can't depend on the super-boozers down at the pool to eat anything. What time is it, Sarge?"

"Three A.M.," said Harper, draining his beer cup. "I've had it. I'm going to hit the road. If I eat another crab, I'll start swimming sideways. Listen, Al, I'm going to take Rose home. She came up with that plump chicken, Lil, and she don't have wheels. From what Fritz says, that bunch will be out of it until daylight anyway. Will you see that this mess gets cleaned up?" He waved his hands at the pile of shells.

"Hell, yes, go on. Joe and Fritz can help me out a little. We don't have that much to do. We can split up the leftover crabs and shrimp with the rest of the troops."

"Don't let anybody drive away from here drunk," said Harper, wiping his hands on a paper towel. "Those ass-hole State Troopers would love to lock up a County cop."

"Don't worry. I got water on now for coffee. We'll make them all drink some before we get going. See you at work."

Rose and Sergeant Harper walked to his car, parked beside the pavilion. He opened the door of the old Packard and she slid in. Turning the powerful engine over, he switched on the lights. The sudden light surprised a red fox two hundred feet away, down the slope. He ran into the laurel beside the road, looking back at the blinding light over his shoulder.

Sergeant Goulek poured a pound of coffee into the boiling two-gallon pot and removed it from the fire. He placed it on the side of the grill.

"There," said Goulek, making a face. "We'll let that sit there and stew for a couple of hours. It will be strong enough to take the balls off a brass monkey by the time they drink it. The fire will keep it warm. Come on, you two. Let's get this mess cleaned up. You can roll up that crab mess in the newspaper. I'll get rid of these empty bottles and the rest of this shit. Can you both stick around? I might need help getting that bunch sobered up at daylight. As near as I can figure, they drank twelve bottles of booze and that half-keg is floating in the ice water. I'll bet it ain't got two gallons left in it. That's a lot of booze in any league."

Both men agreed to stay. They cleaned up the mess quickly and put the leftover crabs and shrimp in paper bags. Sergeant Goulek went to his truck and returned with two old Army blankets.

"Here," he said, tossing the blankets at them. "It's getting a little damp. Grab a table each and get some shut-eye. I'll wake you up at sunrise. I always get up to piss then anyway. Goodnight, boys. See you in the morning."

Sergeant Goulek was shaking him by the shoulder. He sat up on the hard table and shivered. The older man shoved a cup of coffee in his hand.

"Wake up, Fritz. It's six-thirty already. You want a

banger to get your eyes open?"

"No," Carpenter groaned and rubbed his eyes.

"How 'bout you, Joe?"

"Yeah," said Lehland, stretching.

"Here you go, kid. Hair of the dog."

Lehland took the bottle and swallowed. He put his hand over his mouth and gagged.

"Damn, that one went up and down like a yo-yo for a minute. Sure settles your gut the morning after. Come on, it's freezing. Let's get the drunks up."

"Let's take my truck down. I don't feel like walking through that fucking wet grass," said Goulek.

The old pickup bounced down the pasture in the damp grass. Goulek pulled the truck up close to the pool.

"Where in the name of hell are they?" Goulek asked, peering into the mist. "I see some bodies under that blanket."

They got out of the truck, walked over to the blankets and pulled them gently aside. The girls were huddled together like sleeping puppies. Sean McGee was lying in the center on his back. His two playmates from the night before were each snuggled up to him, one on either side, resting their heads on his shoulders.

"Go get the coffee out of the truck, Joe," said Goulek. "It's in back. There's a tube of hot cups in one of those paper bags."

The girls slept on.

"Did you ever see so much nooky together in one pile before, Fritz? Look at that McGee there wallowing in all that flesh, that lucky bastard. Come on, ladies, rise and shine! Time to get up and pee! Get up, McGee! Time to go to work!"

McGee opened his red eyes and groaned. "Come on, Sarge. Give me a break. I'm sick. Ten minutes more."

"Bullshit," said Goulek, kicking McGee lightly on the soles of his feet. "Get up. We got to get our mess cleaned up before the owner gets stirring around. Ah, that's it, ladies. I'm glad to see those pretty eyes popping open."

"Ah, go fuck yourself, you old bastard. Let us sleep. Can't you see we're sick?" asked Cassie, whining.

"My, such language, from a lady." Goulek laughed and handed her a steaming cup of coffee. "Here's a cup of coffee, sweetie. Don't get your shit hot. It's time to go home. Come on, get up, or I'll throw your dainty asses in that pool. McGee, my boy, I'm glad to see you on your feet. Here, have a drink, lad."

McGee took a drink and dribbled whiskey down his bare chest.

"You look like death this morning," said Goulek. "Wash it down with some of this fresh coffee."

McGee took a swallow of the scalding brew and belched.

"That's it. McGee, where are the men?" asked Goulek, looking around.

"Huh?"

"Goddamn it, the men are gone. Where are they?"

"Don't know. I got cold and crawled in with the girls."

They found the rest of the shift on the floor in the men's shower. They'd moved inside during the night. Somehow, they had managed to line the floor with the canvas chaise lounge covers. Shivering in the cold of morning in their bathing trunks, they slept side by side.

"This is going to be easy," said Goulek, with a sly smile. "Each of you take two showers. When I say the word, turn on just the cold water and run like hell. They ain't going to be pleasant when they wake up. Okay. Get ready. All set? Let her go."

They turned on six shower heads and ran from the room. Outside, the girls were sitting up combing their hair, drinking coffee. There was much screaming and cursing from the shower room. The men came out rubbing the cold water from their eyes, shaking from cold, mumbling threats to McGee and Lehland. Sergeant Goulek walked up to the furious men.

"Don't give them hell, it was my idea. I ain't got time to screw around all day with a bunch of drunks. Now get back inside there and take a fucking hot shower and wake up sociable-like. You wouldn't hit an old desk man, would you? Come on, goddamn it. I got hot coffee here for you and a drink, if you want to ease your pain. Hurry up, or I'll throw it in the woods. The fucking party's over. You don't have to go home, but you got to get the hell out of here. I'm gonna wait ten minutes. If you're not in my truck by then, you can walk up the hill and down the other side to your cars. If you ain't ready, I'll leave your sad asses." He slapped Trotta on the back and laughed. "Shit, Sal, old man, your eyes look like two piss-holes in the snow."

The old pickup was packed with shivering men and women in bathing suits as it climbed the slope to the pavilion. It lurched to a stop near the dressing rooms.

"Okay. You all have five minutes to get yourselves dressed. Everybody off."

"Have a heart, Sarge. I got to take a crap. All of the girls have to pee," said McGee.

"Okay, McGee. Just hurry up. I'll wait ten minutes. Pee fast, girls, unless you want to walk down to your cars with hangovers."

They all made it back out in less than ten minutes. Red-eyed, unshaven, uncombed, the men straggled back to the truck, pulling on clothing as they came. The women came in a group, laughing and talking among themselves. They'd all taken time to put on lipstick.

"Each cop here grab a bag off that table to take home," said Goulek, pointing to a table nearby. "Each one's got some crabs and shrimp inside. I know you don't think you'll ever eat again, but maybe you all can use them as a peace offering. There's a couple of gallons of beer left in the keg. Leave it for the cleanup man. If any of you men need an alibi about where you've been all night, have your wife call me at work tonight. We all been together all night, playing football and cards and having a couple of little drinks," he said, chuckling.

"Just good, clean, all-American fun. I'll ask each and every man and woman here to keep quiet about you girls being at the party. Some do-gooder might get us all fired to protect the public from immoral cops. It's been a pleasure having you ladies and I'm sure you'll be included in our next party. Drive home carefully."

The girls all crowded around Sergeant Goulek and covered his face with kisses and hugged him.

"Aw, shit, girls," he growled. "What did you go and do that for? Now I got to wash this lipstick off my homely old mug or my wife will cut my balls off when I go to sleep today."

He rushed into the men's dressing room, his face flaming with embarrassment. A few minutes later, he emerged grinning sheepishly. His thinning hair was wet and plastered to his skull. Getting into the truck, he kicked the engine over. The truck rattled and bumped down the rutted road to the parking lot at the bottom of the hill. The men and women waved and shouted goodbyes. They tore off of the parking lot to the blacktop road in their cars. The long changeover party in the Spring of 1954 was over.

23

"FRITZ! FRITZ! WHAT THE HELL ARE YOU THINKING about? I've been talking to you for fifteen minutes, and you haven't heard a thing I've said."

The police car was parked on the lot at the Towson station. Sean McGee turned the engine off and waved his hand in front of Carpenter's eyes.

"Ah, I see you're back to the world of the living. What were you thinking about? Pink-tipped titties? You were away somewhere in Never-Never Land."

"I was thinking about my first few months here. A lot happened in a short time."

"It always does in police work. We pack more living into a year than the average ass-hole does in a lifetime. Come on, it's time to knock off. I'll buy you a drink at Ruark's."

"Not tonight. I'm taking Mary out for crabs and beer."

"Fritz, you wouldn't say anything about the priest?"

"No, I won't say anything."

"Come on, then, roll call is just beginning."

Sergeant Goulek beat the top of the dais with his clipboard. The shouting and laughter stopped between the facing shifts.

"That's better. I don't know whether police are getting more rowdy these days or I'm getting older and grouchy. Why do I have to beat the hell out of this old fucking dais and scream 'til I'm blue in the face to get your attention?"

Two detectives paused by the open hallway door. They were escorting a handcuffed prisoner wearing a bloody bandage around his neck. The oldest detective waved at Goulek. He grinned and waved back. "Still using excessive force, eh, Clint?" The detective grinned, thumbed his nose and walked on.

Two accident investigation officers ran past the open door at top speed. Their car was parked, against orders, on the post office parking lot, visible through the windows behind Sergeant Goulek. They jumped into the car and tore off the lot with siren screaming and emergency lights flashing. Sergeant Goulek cupped his hand behind his ear and smiled.

"Three business places got broke into last night and the foot man didn't find them. They got into Bill's Electric, Marie's Fashion Shop, and the Ivy League Shop."

"Oh, shit!" Officer McBride said. He was an inexperienced recruit, tall, thin and baby-faced. He feared the wrath of Sergeant Harper for missing the break-ins on his post. Sergeant Goulek glared at McBride and glanced at his notes.

"Now all of you people know these places are side by side in the five hundred block of York Road. They got a load of electric appliances from Bill's, a large amount of men's and women's clothing from the other two places. They got petty cash from all three place amounting to about one hundred and fifty dollars. A delegation of merchants were in to see the Captain demanding more protection on the street. We had two men on the street on three to eleven and the Captain asks that you put two men out until we arrest these bastards. In all three places they got in by prying the back door open with a three-quarter inch jimmy. They must have a truck, because they couldn't have hauled that much stuff away in a car."

Sergeant Goulek paused, cleared his throat and put aside the clipboard. His hand was shaking as he loosened his necktie and continued.

"Officer Joe Marino, of Central Traffic, was eating a sandwich in the kitchen of Pinkie's Seafood House tonight at seven. Hearing somebody yell 'Holdup!' he pushed the kitchen door open a crack. Two white males in their early twenties were holding Pinkie and the counterman at pistol point. They forced Pinkie to open the till and took three hundred and fifty dollars in cash. Joe went out the back door and ran around front just as the two bums hit the sidewalk. In the exchange of gunfire, he shot and killed one man and wounded the other. A third bastard in the getaway car shot Joe in the jaw with a thirty-eight and knocked him down. Joe emptied his gun at the car as it sped away and managed to shoot the right-front tire out."

"Marino's got real balls," said Sergeant Harper.

Sergeant Goulek nodded and continued. "The wheelman only went a block south and abandoned his car. The place was swarming with cops in a couple of minutes. Lieutenant Mark Shannahan, of the Detective Bureau, flushed the bastard out of a dumpster and exchange shots with him. Shannahan knocked the bastard down with a shot in his shoulder and took a shot in the ankle. The wheelman holed up in some asshole's garage one hundred feet away. He left a nice trail of blood right up to the door. Officer Jim Morningstar's K-9 dog, Rip, crashed through the window after him."

The men cheered like children at a circus. Sergeant Goulek pounded on the dais with his clipboard. There were tears brimming in his eyes.

"Hold it fellows. I ain't finished yet. There were three

shots from inside the garage and a lot of growling and barking from Rip. Morningstar kicked the door down and found old Rip working on the bum's throat. The dog had his paw shot off, but didn't let go of the bastard's throat. Morningstar pulled his dog off and carried him out into daylight and found a bullet hole low in Rip's chest. The dog died in Jim's arms on the way to the vet's."

A man on the oncoming shift wiped his eyes with a handkerchief and blew his nose. Trotta cursed under his breath and kicked the water cooler. Sergeant Goulek took a deep breath and continued, his voice breaking with emotion.

"I'm pleased to say that the son-of-a-bitch in the garage bled to death on the way to Union Memorial. Rip chewed his throat out for him. Shit, just last week I was feeding that old dog donuts from Elmer's Place. He was Jim's best friend for sure. Jim raised him up, right in the house with his kids. I used to watch his boys when they were just babies riding old Rip like a pony. He never even growled at those little roughnecks when they hurt him. They were going to retire Rip next month. He was the oldest dog in K-9 and one hell of a fine, loyal, and courageous animal. A cop couldn't ask for a better partner."

"Officer Joe Marino is being treated for a broken jaw down at Union Memorial. He'll be off for a while and he'll eat a lot of soup, but Doc Wolf says he'll be fine in about six to eight weeks. That's all the bad news, boys. Take care of yourselves. I'm going out tonight and try to get a load on."

The following night, Carpenter's shift changed to eleven-to-seven in the morning. After listening to roll call, he was assigned with McBride to the street, with orders to concentrate on the center of the business district, where the burglaries had taken place. Carpenter walked to the business district with McBride.

Tossing his nightstick on its strap, McBride looked at Carpenter out of the corner of his eyes.

"Did you miss finding any B and E's when you were regular footman?" asked McBride.

"No, I was lucky. There were times that I overslept and only checked part of the post out. They could have got in a dozen places on me on those nights. I chased a couple burglars away from the back of the bowling alley one night. They were prying on that old metal door with a B and O pry bar when they saw me walk into the alley from a block away. I chased one of them about ten blocks to Dixie Drive and was gaining on him when I fell into a swimming pool. The last I saw of him, he was jumping picket fences like a high-hurdle runner."

"Fell in a swimming pool? I bet that was a blast in the ass." McBride laughed and kicked a rusty tin can into the gutter. The noise of the can echoed around the street. "Did the rest of the men kid you about it?"

"Well, Sean McGee presented me with a pair of water wings at roll call the night after. Abe gave me a snorkel mask the following night and Sal Trotta gave me a clothespin to put on my nose to keep the water out the third night. They sent me tickets to the swimming meet at Towson State a month later. I guess they feel like they milked it of all the humor or they'd still be giving me the works."

They passed a couple necking in the dark doorway of a dry goods store. The girl saw them, shoved the man away, and adjusted her blouse.

"Where are you going to spot yourself, Fritz?"

"Remember the spot I showed you in the four hundred block where you can get up on the roof?"

"Yeah, I still grab some sleep up there in warm weather. It's really a great spot. You've got a private place to relax up there, but you overlook three blocks in the heart of the business section. If I need help, I'll blast a couple of times on my whistle."

"I'll do the same, Mac. I'm going to get some chow to go at the O.K. Bar. I'll be up on the roof in about a half hour. Why don't you come and eat there too?"

"No," said McBride, lighting a cigarette. "I'm going to hand check every fucking door in Towson tonight, before I even drink a coffee. Did you see the way Snake looked at me at roll call? I thought he was going to chew my ass to pieces. He never even raised his voice. He scares the hell out of me. Everybody says he's a mean son-of-a-bitch. I'll take their word for it. I don't want him on my ass."

"Snake's not so bad, Mac. If you ever need help, he's the man who will be there first."

"Yeah, breaking fingers and smashing balls. Great."

They paused at the front door of the O.K. Bar and stepped back to let a tipsy hustler and her John out. She took her customer's arm and staggered up York Road, swinging a large handbag by its strap. Carpenter smiled and turned to McBride.

"When you're in a narrow corner, Snake looks good to you. You'd take help from the devil when your ass is on the line. Don't pay any attention to stories you hear about him. Someday he might be the only thing between the seat of your pants and a buzzsaw."

Carpenter pushed the front door open. The thick cigarette smoke and heavy air blasted his face as he stepped inside. Sam Rider was working at an adding machine by the cashier's counter. He walked to within five feet of Sam and stood there. Sam didn't look up. Carpenter cleared his throat. Sam looked up from his work and his face broke into a grin.

"Fritz, you old bastard! Where in the hell have you been? You get put in a car and forget your old friends. Don't you like to eat anymore? Can't you stop in and have a fucking drink once in a while? Come on, let's go into the dining room. I'll bring us some good sipping booze."

The blond bartenders were just as beautiful as ever. They smiled their showgirl smiles at him as he passed the bar on the way to the private dining room. Sam Rider stopped at the end of the bar and whispered to one of them. She handed him a fresh bottle of Chivas Regal and two large glasses of ice. They sat down at Carpenter's old table in the deserted back room. Sam Rider poured the Scotch and lit a cigarette.

"You kind of lost touch since you got put in the car," said Sam Rider, frowning. "What's the matter, don't you like my fucking crabcakes anymore?"

"Nobody makes them like you, Sam. They're what I'm here for."

"Yeah, I know. Coming up, kid. I'll throw some fine, thin Smithfield slices on a platter with them. Leave it to me."

"Sam, I've only got a few minutes. I'm to going to stake out for those burglars that visited last night. Can you make it to go?"

"Sure, why not," Sam said. "But you got to have another fucking drink with me."

He walked to the kitchen door, gave Carpenter's order to the cook, and returned to the table. Sam poured two large Scotches over the ice and slid one across the table to Carpenter.

"Here's to you, Fritz. I hope you catch those bastards tonight."

They drank the cold mellow Scotch. Sam poured another for himself and raised a quizzical eyebrow to Carpenter.

"No thanks, Sam. I want to keep a clear head tonight. It's going to be rough staying awake in one spot. When you don't keep moving around on this shift, your body goes to sleep on you a little at a time."

Charlie walked in with a large bag and put it on the table. Smiling at Carpenter, he shook his hand.

"You betch good clab cake pratter. Me fixem."

"Thanks, Charlie. I appreciate it."

Carpenter stood and picked up the bag. Sam shook his hand and patted him on the back.

"There's a quart Thermos of hot coffee in there, Fritz. You can return it if you think about it. I keep a half dozen or so around the kitchen for the football bus trips in the winter."

"I'll return it for sure, Sam. Thanks."

It was awkward climbing the pole with the bag in his hand, but he made it to the top and stepped onto the roof. Opening the Thermos, he sat on a fire wall and sipped the scalding brew. When he finished, he put the Thermos back in the bag and put his lunch against a chimney, out of the way. Walking to the edge of the flat roof, he sat down near the corner, where he had an unobstructed view north and south on York Road for six blocks. He could see the front of every business place on Pennsylvania Avenue, east and west, to where business establishments gave way to residential structures. There was a lot of traffic on the road. All the bars boomed with Saturday drinkers. The night people were out.

Buster Thorn walked out of Ruark's Bar and strolled to the corner of York and Pennsylvania. He was still limping slightly from his encounter with Carpenter in the alley a year ago. His face was hard and crafty in the glare of a match, as he stopped to light a cigarette not fifty feet from Carpenter's perch. A man came out of Ruark's and walked directly to Thorn. He removed his wallet from his hip pocket and handed several bills to the burly weight lifter. Thorn turned away, put his fingers to his lips, and whistled. A black '54 Mercury convertible with the top down pulled away from the curb a block away and swung into the traffic. The car eased to the curb beside Thorn and his companion. A dark-haired girl in a strapless evening gown was behind the wheel. Thorn leaned over the open car and said something to the girl and opened the car door. The man got in with the girl and Thorn slammed the door of the car as he said something to his customer.

The car eased into the traffic and disappeared over the hill northbound on York Road. Thorn walked back to Ruark's and went inside.

Carpenter moved to the rear of the roof to check his field of view in the alley. There seemed to be fewer night lights in the alley than usual, but the moon was full and the sky was clear. Nothing could escape his attention if he was awake. A derelict staggered into the alley from Chesapeake Avenue and weaved his way toward Carpenter. Stopping occasionally, he gulped from a pint bottle of wine in a brown paper bag. He stopped about twenty-five feet away from Carpenter's spot, drained the bottle, and dropped it into an open trash can. Something caught the drunk's eye in the overflowing can. He dipped into the can and brought out a half-eaten submarine sandwich. Looking furtively up and down the alley, he wolfed the sandwich down. He wiped his fingers on the seat of his pants and took a cigarette butt from behind his ear. Lighting six matches before the butt caught fire, he inhaled the smoke and exhaled through his nose. An old cinderblock provided a place for the man to sit and enjoy his after-dinner smoke. Carpenter took his hat off and quickly unbuttoned his shirt. He held his shirt backward over his head like a shroud, leaned over the edge of the building enough for the wino to see him and began to moan under his shirt.

"Oooooooh, Ahaaaaaaa, Oooooooh, Ahaaaaaaaa, Oooooooh, Ahaaa."

The drunk screamed in terror and ran from the alley in record time, looking back over his shoulder at the white figure on the roof. His footsteps could be heard fading into the distance as he ran east on Pennsylvania, toward the black section.

When he controlled his laughter Carpenter put his shirt and hat back on. He walked to the front of the building on the rough slag roof. Two men were cursing each other on the sidewalk in front of Elmer's Place. The argument progressed to a shoving match. McBride came charging out of Elmer's Place and tossed a half-eaten hamburger into the gutter. He grabbed both men by the arm and pulled them apart. One man started to shake a finger in the young cop's face. McBride raised his nightstick and threatened the man. Carpenter could hear the rise and fall of angry voices. The men backed away from McBride. He walked close to them and said something. The men shook hands and thanked McBride. They walked away together toward Carpenter. McBride went back inside Elmer's. The men passed by Carpenter's spot, unaware of his surveillance.

"You son-of-a-bitch," said the fat one, shaking his fist. "I paid you that ten dollars."

"Who are you calling a son-of-a-bitch, you son-of-a-bitch? I'm going to take ten dollars' worth of meat off your ugly face," said the lean one, with hands on hips.

"You'll shit, too, if you eat regular. Come on, you bastard, put your fucking hands up. I'll stomp your ass. I don't have to take your shit."

"Come into the alley here. I don't want that cop saving your ass again."

They walked into the alley, out of Carpenter's sight. Feet scraped on gravel and broken glass. Garbage cans crashed and overturned. Thuds and cries of pain and anger filled the soft summer air. The noise continued for perhaps two minutes, then all was quiet. Carpenter didn't move from his spot. He lit a Camel and watched the alley entrance. A few minutes later both men walked slowly from the alley together. Their clothing was torn and bloody. The fat man had a cut over his eye. The blood ran unnoticed down his face and stained his torn white shirt scarlet. The lean man was dabbing at a split bottom lip with a bloody handkerchief. They got into a new Ford pickup together and drove away.

A red Irish setter bitch ran west on Pennsylvania Avenue from the old residential area adjacent to the business district. She was followed by a male beagle with romance on his mind. He overtook the tall bitch and smelled her private parts. She pulled her tail between her legs and nibbled at his side coyly. The little beagle was exhilarated. He put his front legs around her hips and attempted to breed her, but he was much too short. She lost interest in his fumbling efforts, shook him off, and they ran into the alley together.

Carpenter walked to the back of the building and looked over the edge. The setter bitch was eating a turkey carcass from an overturned garbage can, completely ignoring the little beagle's frantic effort to reach her. The beagle decided to change tactics. He dropped his front feet to the ground and bit the bitch on the back leg. She yipped in pain and spun around, dropping the turkey carcass. Beating the little dog to the ground, she held him on his back with her front legs, growling ferociously. Delighted at the attention, he lay there, wagged his tail rapidly and bared his throat in total submission. The setter released him and returned to her turkey carcass.

The little beagle sat and watched her eat her fill. She was licking her greasy paws when he tried again. He was standing on tiptoe, determined to reach the unreachable treasure when the setter bent her legs and squatted down in the alley. The beagle was in her instantly and was very quick in his lovemaking. She seemed to be rather bored with the whole thing. Attempting to stand, she locked him to her with nature's involuntary contraction of her vagina. The little beagle screamed in fright and pain. They both strained to be free of their coupling, but to no avail. The male was twisted into an impossible position with his front feet on the ground and his loins locked to the larger female. She eventually released him from her exquisite trap. They trotted down the alley together as though nothing had happened between them.

McBride walked south on York Road trying up the front doors of businesses on the west side of the road. He walked to the southern limits of his post, crossed the road, and tried the doors on the east side of the road as he walked north. Turning east on Pennsylvania Avenue, he walked to the alley. He turned south in the alley to try the rear doors. As he passed under his friend's position on the roof, he looked up and waved.

"Everything tight?" said Carpenter, looking over the edge.

"Yeah. All I've got left is the back of the stores from here to Chesapeake and I'm finished. See any suspicious trucks?"

"No. It's busy out here tonight. I don't think they'd consider breaking in 'til after two-thirty or three. Too many people moving around."

"Did you see those two ass-holes getting ready to square off in front of Elmer's?" asked McBride.

"Yeah. They walked into the alley, right about where you're standing, and beat lumps all over each other. You know them?"

"The Singleton brothers. Clyde and Ross. Moonshiners from up around Parkton. Rough boys. They fight each other when nobody else is around to fight. I was talking to Darlene, the barmaid at Ruark's a while ago. They were in there for two hours trying to start some shit. Ruark finally came in to check the till and threatened to call the cops, so they left. They avoid police like the plague."

"I've heard of them," said Carpenter, sitting down on the roof's edge. "They're well-known around the county. They make pretty good corn whiskey, from all reports. State alcohol tax agents arrested the young one, Ross, about five years ago. He was only a kid then, maybe eighteen or nineteen. The agent had the desk sergeant docket him and told him the bail was thirty-five hundred dollars and asked him who he wanted to call to make bond for him. The kid pulled a roll out of his pocket, peeled thirty-five one-hundred-dollar bills off and tossed it up on the counter like it was peanuts. He got Monjer for a lawyer and got off with a five-hundred-dollar fine."

"We're in the wrong business, Fritz," said McBride. He unzipped his fly and took a leak against an overturned garbage can.

"Yeah, I guess so. I should be home in bed with my pregnant wife, not farting around playing cops and robbers. You get to walk around Towson all night trying to find unlocked doors and I'm sitting up here on a lonely rooftop at midnight watching dogs hump in the alley."

"It's going to be a long night," said McBride, zipping his fly.

"Yeah. I'm going to lay down now and catch a little snooze. Make some noise if you need me."

"Aren't you afraid of sleeping right through the night?"

"No. I'm a light sleeper. I can tell myself to wake up at any given time and do it, within five or ten minutes."

"No shit? How did you learn to do that?"

"I don't know. I've been like that ever since I can remember. See you later, Mac."

Carpenter found some old lumber on the roof and leaned four two-by-fours against a firewall for a bed. He laid back on the boards and willed himself to wake up at 3:30. The sky was filled with stars and a mockingbird was singing cheerfully several blocks to the east. Closing his eyes, he slept. He woke up at three o'clock. His right foot was asleep and the lower part of his back ached. Needles of fire poked into his foot as he limped around the slag roof. He leaned backward and felt the bones pop in his spine.

Rumbling noises came from his empty stomach as he opened the Thermos. The coffee was still scalding hot. Steam rose into the damp night air as he poured it into the tin cup. With his fingers he ate the cold crabcakes and the sour pickle slices wrapped in Smithfield ham. As he crushed the paper bag to discard it, he felt something hard in the bottom. A minature of Chivas Regal rolled out onto his hand when he tilted the bag. He put the whiskey in his pocket, and went to the front edge of the roof to sit down.

Only an occasional tractor trailer rumbled through Towson. Two papermen were loading Sunday papers into their trucks from the sidewalk at York and Chesapeake. He walked to the rear of the roof and looked north and south in the alley. A pair of rats were fighting over the spilled garbage. Returning to the front of the building, he poured himself another cup of coffee. Time dragged slowly by. He sat there for a long time, lulled by the isolation of his post.

A blue delivery van went north on York Road and turned west on Joppa. He was surprised to see the same van head north again on York Road ten minutes later, traveling slower. The truck slowed to a crawl as it cruised along the deserted street. The driver pulled into the gas station at York and Pennsylvania Avenue, close to the building. The passenger got out, looked around the station, and put some coins in the Coke machine. A bottle dropped into the delivery slot with a bang. Opening the bottle, he took a long drink. He walked back to the van and handed the bottle through the window to his friend. The driver said something Carpenter couldn't hear, and both men laughed. The Coke buyer returned to the machine and pulled a heavy screwdriver from his pocket. He popped open the door of the machine and pulled the coin box out. He went over to the van, opened the door, and got in. Carpenter wrote the tag number down as they pulled out on York Road, headed north, and turned right on Joppa.

Five minutes later, the van turned onto Pennsylvania Avenue, east of York Road. They had circled around through the quiet old residential section. Heading straight for Carpenter's vantage point, they turned into the alley where the Singleton brothers had fought a few hours before.

The sound of splintering wood broke the quiet of the night as Carpenter made his way to the rear of the building. Directly below him, the men were working a five-foot-long, heavy crowbar on the thick wooden door of the bookstore. The door crashed open from the irresistible force of the pry bar. One man walked inside, while the other waited, glancing up and down the alley. The van was nearby, close to the building with its lights out and the motor running. The inside man walked out and laughed.

"I told you that wasn't the place, it's next door. That's a fucking bookstore."

He tossed a heavy book into the front of the van and went to the delivery door of the shoestore next door. They pried the door open in seconds. The lookout remained in the alley. The inside man took a large box from his van and carried it inside the store. He returned in a few minutes with the box loaded with shoes. The lookout opened the side door of the van and dumped the box of shoes into the back of the truck. He carried the box to his accomplice and remained outside. Carpenter ran to his makeshift lumber bed and picked up a two-by-four about sixteen feet long, and returned in time to see the lookout dump another load of shoes into the van. He positioned himself directly over the door and waited with the two-by-four in his hands. The lookout carried the box back to his friend inside and handed the empty carton through the open door.

"That's enough, Nippy. Come on, let's get out of here."

"Bullshit, I'll tell you what's enough. Just keep your eyes open for that hick cop."

The lookout glanced nervously up and down the alley. Carpenter gave the inside man a half minute to get away from the door. He leaned directly over the man and slowly lowered the two by four until it was a foot above his head. Aiming carefully, he raised the two-by-four three feet and brought the lumber down squarely on top of the man's head. The jolt of the blow surged through the wood to the palms of Carpenter hands. The lookout dropped without a sound and sprawled on the concrete, face down. Carpenter remained poised with the lumber ready to strike again. He didn't have long to wait. Nippy came through the door and looked at his reclining partner.

"Hey, what's going on? Get up from there, you crazy bastard. This is no time to fuck around."

Kneeling by his partner, he grabbed him by the hair and stared at the blood on his hand a full five seconds. He jumped to his feet, his head swinging back and forth like a tennis-match spectator, searching for the hidden assailant.

"Up here, ass-hole."

Nippy tilted his head back in time to see the two-by-four slam into his forehead. He fell backward over his partner's body, out cold. Carpenter pulled the two-by-four back and laid it on the slag roof. Blowing a series of short blasts on his whistle, he heard an answering blast from McBride. He could hear McBride running on the sidewalk in front of the building. Blowing a few more shrill blasts, he heard McBride turn onto Pennsylvania Avenue. He was sitting with his legs dangling over the edge of the roof when McBride came running into the alley, gun in one hand, flashlight in the other. He slid to a stop and walked slowly to the van. Shining his light into the rear window, he whistled. Aiming his gun at the men on the ground, he glanced up at Carpenter.

"What happened to these guys? I didn't hear shots and I was only a block away."

"They had an attack of migraine."

"What?"

"I gave them a piece of lumber to the pumpkin."

"Son-of-a-bitch! Look at them bleed."

"Watch them close, I'll be down in a second."

Carpenter's hands were shaking as he broke the seal on his miniature of whiskey. The Scotch chased the butterflies from his stomach. Walking to the edge of the building, he climbed down the pole. He ran to the rear of the building and turned the corner. McBride was standing five feet from the prone men, .38 in hand. Carpenter ran up to the group and drew his Colt.

"I'll watch them. Search them good, Mac."

McBride holstered his .38 and ran his hands over the man lying on top. Reaching into a front pocket, he pulled out a .32 automatic. He sprung the clip and pulled the slide back. The load in the chamber flipped out and landed on a garbage can lid. He turned the man over, not so gently now, and searched the back of him. Dragging him like a sack of meal to the side, McBride searched the other downed burglar. He found a loaded .22 revolver stuck in his belt with the hammer back.

"Look at this, Fritz. He could have shot his balls off. The fucking hammer's back."

Easing the hammer forward, he swung open the

cylinder and shook out eight full rounds.

"I'm ashamed of myself, Fritz."

"What are you talking about?"

"I was standing here feeling sorry for the way you split them open with that board. I'm so fucking mad now from finding those guns that I could waste these bastards right here."

"Fuck them. Here's my cuffs," said Carpenter, tossing them to McBride. "Cuff both of them behind their backs."

Both men were on their knees, trying to stand. Carpenter walked over to them and shoved them in the chest with his foot, one at a time, forcing them over backward.

"Over on your stomach, you motherfuckers! Try to get up and I'll blow your fucking brains all over this alley. Got the cuffs on good and tight, Mac?"

"I think so."

"Tighten them up until they bite 'em." McBride bent over them and tightened the cuffs until they pinched flesh. "That's it. Walk over to the fire department and call the Sergeant. Oh yeah, you better get the ambulance crew to take our friends to Union Memorial."

McBride ran up the alley to Pennsylvania Avenue and turned the corner. Carpenter walked to the van and opened the front door. The heavy leatherbound Bible was lying open on the passenger's seat where Nippy had tossed it. He picked up the book and dropped the Colt into his holster. He walked to Nippy's side and knelt by the prone burglar. His flashlight's glow on the expensive paper reflected into Nippy's eyes. Carpenter read from the Bible to the bleeding man, Psalm 140:

> Deliver me, O Lord, from evil men, preserve me from violent men, who plan evil things in their heart,

and stir up wars continually. They make their tongue sharp as a serpent's; under their lips is the poison of vipers. Selah.

"What the hell's that supposed to mean?" Nippy groaned and blinked blood from his eyes.

Carpenter closed the Bible and lit a Camel with his Zippo.

"It's from the Bible you took from the bookstore. It was open to that page. What do you think it means?"

"It means I got unlucky. We picked the wrong place at the wrong time."

"What did you take the Bible for?"

"Who knew it was a Bible?" snarled Nippy. Blood flowed freely from the gash in his forehead. "I grabbed a thick book to sit on. The seat is broken down on the driver's side. We got the wrong store. I figured as long as I was there, grab something. My God, you split my head open. Do something for me."

"The ambulance is on the way."

"What did you hit me with?"

"I think it was a piece of Georgia pine."

"I'm bleeding to death," moaned Nippy, looking at his bloody shirt.

"Go ahead and bleed. You'll either live or die. I don't give a shit one way or the other."

"That's a fine way for a cop to talk. You bastard," he hissed, spitting a mouthful of saliva into Carpenter's face. "You dirty bastard. We didn't do you any harm."

"You didn't get a chance to, Nippy," said Carpenter, wiping his face with his handkerchief.

A police car pulled into the alley and stopped. Sergeant Harper and McBride got out and walked over to the prone men.

"Ah, you made believers of them," said Harper. "Good work, Fritz. What did you use, your stick?"

"A two-by-four from up on the roof."

"Well, I'll be damned. Who are they?"

"I don't know."

Sergeant Harper turned them over roughly.

"Nippy Puccinni and Joe Burattzo. They been searched? They always go armed."

"Yeah, McBride found two loaded guns on them."

"They're heist men. What are you doing sneaking around stealing out of back doors?" he asked pleasantly. They looked away from him. "I had this pair of bastards five years ago for armed robbery of the movie over in Parkville. They got eight years apiece. Been out long, Nippy?" he asked quietly.

The pair ignored him. He squatted down beside Nippy.

"You heard me. How long you been out?"

"Fuck you, cop."

Sergeant Harper drew his .38 and jammed it into the sneering mouth, splitting Nippy's thick lips. He rammed the muzzle down the man's throat. Nippy gagged violently. Harper pulled the gun out of his mouth and drew the hammer back. The click of the hammer was like thunder in the alley. Nippy's water let go. The urine stained his light summer slacks dark.

"Don't bother answering then," Harper said, laughing coldly. "You got your rights, you fucking scum. I should have wasted you five years ago. There's no fucking reason why I can't do it now."

"Two months! Two months! I been out two months! Don't shoot, my God, don't shoot! Please! I'll cooperate."

"Did you get in those stores last night?"

"Yeah, yes sir," he said, shaking his head. "We did."

"Where's all the shit you stole?" said Harper, caressing Nippy's cheek with his gun barrel.

"In my garage. It's all there. We were going to hold it all together and fence it in one bunch."

"That right, Joe?" He turned and jabbed Joe in the

ear lightly with the gun's muzzle. "I don't hear nothing from you, you sneaky bastard."

"That's right, yes sir. Don't shoot us, for God's sake."

"What else you been into together, Joe?"

"We got four stores over Parkville three nights ago."

"How many?"

"Four, no five. Five. We got five."

"You take merchandise there, too?"

"Yes sir. Cash too. All the stuff's in the garage."

"How about the cash?"

"Gone. It's gone."

"Where?"

"We been shooting up."

"Junkies? Both of you?"

"Yes sir."

"Where'd you pick that habit up?"

"The Pen. They sell horse down there like it's going to go out of style."

"You hooked?" Harper asked, holstering his .38.

"No. Ah, no, I don't think so. I can quit when I want to."

"How big's your habit?"

"Three dime bags a day, apiece."

"You poor bastards, you're both hooked."

The ambulance rolled into the alley, its red lights flashing. Sergeant Harper leaned over both men and spoke quietly.

"Listen to me, both of you. You'll make bail today or tomorrow after the detectives get done with you. When you get out on the street, I want you to remember one thing. Stay out of Towson."

"Oh, yes sir," said Joe, his jaw quivering. "We live in Parkville. We won't come near here. You can depend on it."

"Good. If I catch you in Towson on the street anywhere after dark, I'm going to shoot you, kill you, waste you. Then I'm going to pick your dead asses up and throw you through a store window and say I caught you breaking in again. *Sabê?*"

"Oh, my God. Yes sir, Snake," blurted Nippy.

"What did you call me, ass-hole?"

"Sergeant Harper! Sergeant Harper!"

"Good. Just for a second there I thought you said something disrespectful."

Sergeant Harper stood and turned to Carpenter and McBride.

"Both of you guys go to Union Memorial with them. Stay right with them every minute. If they admit them, I'll have detectives down to relieve you within an hour. Give me the guns, McBride. I'll turn them in at the property room before I go home."

Sergeant Harper took the automatic from McBride and put it into his pants pocket. Cocking the .22 revolver, he walked over to Nippy. He deliberately put the muzzle to the man's forehead and pulled the trigger. Click! Nippy was shaking like jelly.

"I just wanted to make sure it wasn't loaded, Nippy. Get them in the ambulance, Fritz."

It was time to go home when they got back to the station. The sky promised rain, and a fresh breeze blew in from the Chesapeake Bay. The air smelled of brackish water and marsh grass.

24

THE OLD DESK SERGEANT RAPPED FOR ATTENTION ON the dais with his shoe.

The windows behind him were half covered with wet sleet. Trucks parked on the post office parking lot next door wore white shrouds of snow. The frigid wind bore down hard from Pennsylvania and howled around the eaves of the building. The night sky was leaden and promised more snow.

"Shut up, heroes. I got the gout so fucking bad my toe's going to fall off. If I wasn't so crippled up I'd whip a few of your asses. Show a little respect for us sick old folks. Quiet! Ah, that's better. Please talk to me in easy, modulated tones, do nothing to disturb me and shield me from upsetting information. For God's sake, agree with everything I say and don't step on my toe. I'm in mortal pain and I know if I go to that old grouch, Doc Wolf, he's going to put me on a fucking diet and take me off booze again. Ah, a man has but few pleasures when he gets old. You young studs better enjoy yourselves while you can. All you got to look forward to when you get fifty-five or so is a limber dick and gout and a bad stomach and getting up to pee twice a night. I don't know why I don't take my fucking pension."

A radiator behind the old desk sergeant began clanking rhythmically. The footman on the offgoing shift sneezed and blew his nose in a red bandanna. His reefer was plastered with melting snow. The old desk sergeant shivered and continued.

"Here it is December again. I could be down in Key West drinking a frozen daiquiri and eating a big bowl of conch chowder, resting my tired old bones in the hot sunshine, watching those cute little Cuban broads wiggle their asses, friendly like. Instead, here I am cooped up in a stinking old station house with a bunch of rowdy young cops. It's so cold out there now, the winos come in here begging me to lock them up. Eighteen fucking degrees with a wind chill index taking it down to two below. You men want to watch it out there tonight. That wind's coming down out of Pennsylvania, cold enough to freeze the balls off a Headquarters lieutenant. If you got to get out in the wind, wrap your muffler around your ears, even if some Headquarters cop does get all bent out of shape for your flagrant disregard of uniform regulations.

"Fuck them," the old sergeant growled, shooting his index finger in the air obscenely. "It's better to get your ass chewed out a couple days later than go down to Union Memorial getting your ears treated for frostbite. We got between four and six inches of snow so far, depending on what part of the county you're in. Cockeysville police claim they had nine inches at ten o'clock tonight, but you can't believe those desk men up there. They were probably standing on their heads looking at the ruler and the six looked like a nine. They've been known to take a drink or two. We only had a little bit of crime today. The three-to-eleven shift has been working accidents ever since they came to work. The cold kept thieves off the street, but we had a couple of prowler reports around midnight in Ruxton.

You all know the Ruxton rapist has laid low since the rape-homicides of the Goldbergs sometime ago, and he don't usually operate that early, but you never know about freaks like him. Stay warm, men. I'll see you all tomorrow."

Sergeant Harper stepped to the dais and cleared his throat.

"McGee's off sick again tonight with the flu. He's running a temperature of one hundred and two and shitting like a goose. You work with Abe again, Fritz."

"Right."

"Go to your posts promptly and park your cars after you check out your business places. No use getting involved with some ass-hole in a fender bender. You all know how most ass-holes drive in heavy snow. Like they ain't never seen it before. Okay. Hit the bricks."

Carpenter and Abe Jacobson pulled on heavy overshoes and walked out on the lot to their car. Fine sleet stung the left side of their faces as the wind whipped out of the north.

"You look the outside over for damage, Fritz, and I'll check the back seat for souvenirs for Sean."

Carpenter checked the cruiser over and found it damage-free. When he opened the door, Abe handed him a nightstick. He had the back seat loose from the floor and was leaning over shining his flashlight under it looking for contraband.

"Good God, look at this, Fritz."

Abe held up a World War I bayonet. His hand was shaking when he passed the blade to Carpenter. He snapped the back seat into place and got out of the car.

"Give me the stick and pig sticker, Fritz. I'll keep them in my locker for Sean. I'll be back in a second."

He carried the weapons into the station house as Carpenter started the engine and drove over to the side door to pick him up.

The rat-tat-tap of a broken chain striking the fender

started immediately. Carpenter cursed and stopped the car. He removed his gloves and took the box of repair links from the glove compartment. Checking the right-rear tire with his flashlight, he found the broken link immediately. He lay down on the packed snow and tried to bring the ends together to insert the repair link, but couldn't reach the inside end of the broken crosspiece.

Abe was leaning over, watching him. "Hold it, Fritz. I'll pull forward about a foot."

Abe eased the car forward a few inches. Carpenter ran his hand over the ice-packed tire and found the elusive cross link.

"Hold it there."

Abe stopped the car immediately. Carpenter fumbled the repair link onto both loose ends, his fingers numb with cold. A blast of hot air from the heater greeted him when he opened the door. He got a wipe rag from the glove compartment and dried his freezing hands.

"Who used this bomb on the last shift, Abe?"

"Smith and Crowley. I just checked the roster."

"If I had them here now, I'd beat shit lumps on their stupid heads."

"I'd help, Fritz," said Abe, pulling off the lot.

The tires crunched over packed snow. Abe braked to let a snow plow pass him. They drove toward their post through light traffic. Sleet battered the windshield and bounced off. Glittering snow and sleet covered the yards of houses they passed in the darkness. Abe wiped the windshield with the back of his hand and shoved his hat back on his head.

"That nightstick was on the back seat where Smith left it. The bayonet was slipped under the seat, caught in the springs. Hair went up on the back of my neck when I spotted it. That's the second stick that Smith left in the car in six months. McGee's collection grows in spurts. Sometimes he draws a blank on his search for a week or so, then bingo! Last week, Saturday I think it was, he found three expensive new women's watches stuck under the seat, still in their boxes. I took one for my wife and he gave one to his latest broad. He put the extra one in his collection."

"Somebody put a booster in the back seat without searching him," said Carpenter, turning down the collar of his reefer.

"Right. Chances are it was a woman. Some of the men are afraid to search broads for fear of being accused of molesting them. Fuck it. I always search. So far nobody's turned me in except a broad named Silverstein that we got a call on for boosting crabmeat at the A and P. Can you imagine, a Jewish broad turning in a nice Jewish boy like me? She raised so much hell at the station house that Lieutenant Hollis actually stopped typing one of those bullshit reports and came into the Desk Sergeant's office where we were booking her. She kept screaming that I felt her tits and was trying to screw her."

"Did you?"

"Did I screw her?" asked Abe, slowing down behind a county roads truck scattering salt. "Hell, no. I did run my hand over her boobs to see if she had any, ah, contraband hidden in her bra. Beautiful tits. Big and firm. I admitted that I touched her tits to the Lieutenant. That self-righteous prick wanted to suspend me. He called the Captain up at his house. The only thing the Captain wanted to know was if she had been searched good. Hollis tried to bullshit him into believing that she couldn't have anything else on her. She had the crabmeat hidden in a special inside pocket of her coat, like boosters have. The Captain told Hollis he wanted her searched thoroughly before she was put in the woman's cell. I thought Hollis was going to blow his mind with indignation. That cunt had him believing the crabmeat was the first thing she ever took and she had a hungry old mother to feed."

They were passing through a business section on their post. Abe spotlighted the front windows of the darkened stores. The light reflected back into their eyes as they crawled along at slow speed. Abe lit a cigarette and laughed.

"Well, anyway, we got the matron from up Cockeysville, Tessie Upjohn. Old Tessie's about seventy years old and has been a matron for thirty years. She took the Silverstein bitch into the Captain's office for privacy for her search. The cunt refused to let Tessie search her. Tessie didn't argue with her. She opened the door and called the Lieutenant in and told him. The Lieutenant tried to mealy-mouth the Jew bitch into letting Tessie search her. That was some tough broad. She shoved Hollis up against the wall and knocked a picture of the Captain's bowling team on the floor. She called Hollis every curse word in the book and used a couple of Yiddish combinations that even I couldn't figure out."

"Hey, great. I wish I could have seen the look on his face," Carpenter said, turning down the radio volume.

"Hollis ran out of the room, white as a ghost. He told Sergeant Goulek to make sure that the girl was searched and that he had to go to Parkville on important business. Goulek just smiled and told me and McGee to come into the room. The broad was sitting on a chair in the corner, smoking a cigarette like an indignant queen when we walked in. Goulek walked over to her and smiled pleasantly at her. She told him to fuck off and shoved him. He clipped her on the chin so fast you couldn't believe it. Goulek grabbed her before she hit the floor."

Abe drove slowly down an alley, spotlighting the rear doors and windows of a new car agency. He spotted a broken window and hit the brakes. Dropping the beam of the spotlight to the ground, he looked for tracks in the snow and found none. He started forward again.

"Must be an old break, Fritz. I'll leave a note for the dayshift to have that ass-hole repair it. Where was I, pal?"

"Goulek clipped the booster."

"Oh yeah," said Abe, taking a drag on his cigarette. "Old Tessie Upjohn laughed and shoved some ammonia under her nose. The girl came right out of it, and Goulek leaned over close to her and told her to behave or he was going to pull her clothes off and search her, then throw her in the cell with a group of prisoners who hadn't been with a woman for five years. I never saw a woman peel her clothes off so fast. She had a half pound of sliced ham in her bra and a pack of filet mignon in her panties. The matron made an internal examination of her snatch after we left the room and found a dime bag of horse up there in a rubber."

"What a revolting development," Carpenter said.

"Revolting," said Abe, holding his nose. "You should have smelled that broad. So help me, she had cobwebs on her pussy. Hollis called the station a few minutes later and found out about the search. He was back in the station in five minutes and called the Captain back to tell him how he had tricked the girl into submitting to the search and what was found on her. He told the Captain he was going to take statements from the bitch about her complaint against me and submit a thorough report on me for the Captain's disposition. The Captain chewed his ass out. You could hear him cursing over the phone from six feet away. Hollis let him finish and apologized for calling him. He hung up and told me he was going to give me the benefit of the doubt this time, but to be careful in the future. He went into his office and typed a ten-page, single-spaced report on the matter, and made me read and initial each page. He kept apologizing and telling me it was made to protect him in case anything backfired. He left the report on the Captain's desk. When old Cap got in his office the next morning and saw the report, he blew up. He called Hollis in from his home and ripped his ass-hole out for him. Cap tore up the report, threw it all over the floor, and ordered Hollis to stop making reports to him."

Abe stopped for a bicycle that blocked the alley. Carpenter got out and moved the bicycle to the side. Snow mixed with sleet powdered his uniform. He got back in and blew on his cold hands.

"That must have been a blast in the ass to Hollis," said Carpenter, turning up the heater. "He can't take separation from his typewriter."

"You don't know how it hurts him, Fritz. He was off for his nerves for six weeks. He's back to making reports to protect himself again, but he keeps them in his personal file, all five copies. He never sends them to the Captain anymore, but seems to be happy, though. He washes all the cars in the district, empties all the trashcans, checks the trunks of the cars at each station once a week, and threatens the men if anything is missing. Hollis really has a nose for trouble. If something goes wrong in Parkville that could force him to make a decision, he jumps in his car and heads for Towson. If we got something here, he runs to Cockeysville. Whenever the desk sergeants want to get rid of him now, they get him into a conversation about police work and ask his advice on any matter. He gets a wild look in his eye, heads for the door and stays out of sight for the rest of the day."

"We must have the world's champion ass-holes for lieutenants in this command," said Carpenter, yawning.

"No, not really. It's like that all over the county. Every lieutenant and most of the captains operate scared. Cover your ass, run from what's happening, never answer any questions, put it on paper for the higher-ups to decide. That's the rule of the day, not the exception."

The blare of the radio broke into their conversation.

"Car twenty-one, York and Chesapeake, an abandoned car blocking the streetcar tracks."

"Car twenty-one, ten-four," said Carpenter, into the mike.

"Car twenty-one, ten-twenty-two that last call. Go to Clem's Bar at Loch Raven and Aberdeen Road. A customer threatening suicide."

"Ten-four, Headquarters," said Carpenter, turning on the emergency lights and siren.

They were three blocks from Clem's Bar. They made it through the heavy snow to Clem's in one minute. Abe took the front entrance and Carpenter went in the side door.

There was mass confusion in the tavern. The barmaid and tavern owner were talking to a young woman, sitting with her face in her hands, at a table in the rear of the bar. Two men were shouting through the closed men's room door.

The owner took Carpenter by the arm and pulled him to the side. Abe followed them to a quiet corner.

"Jesus, I'm glad to see you men. There's a young guy locked in the men's room with a straight razor. He says he's going to slash his wrists."

"What happened?" asked Abe, eyeing the men at the restroom door.

"He had an argument with his wife. She's sitting at the table talking to my barmaid."

The man's wife was a plain-looking woman of about twenty-six. She kept biting her lips and holding her hands to the side of her face.

"Take it easy, sis," growled Abe, patting her shoulder. "What's he upset about?"

"We had an argument over where we were going to

eat our Christmas dinner. He wants to eat at home and my parents invited us to their place. He's been under a lot of strain lately, and has been working too hard."

"What does he do?"

"He's a dentist. For God's sake, do something," she said banging her fist on the table. "Don't just stand there asking me questions. He's got a razor. He says he's going to kill himself."

"Easy, lady. What's his name?"

"Roger."

"Come on, Fritz. Let's talk him out."

The men at the door of the restroom were pleading with the dentist to open the door. Abe called the tavern owner over.

"What's it like inside the men's room?"

"Just a toilet and sink. A small room, about five feet square."

"How about the door?"

"What do you mean?"

"What kind of lock?"

"Just a little hook on the inside. The door opens out. You could pull the hook loose with a little force."

"Any window or any other way we can get in?"

"No."

They walked to the restroom door. A long-haired man in his early twenties had his ear to the door. He was talking to the dentist softly through the crack between the door and frame.

"Come on, Roger. Pass the razor out to me. Your wife's all upset."

"Fuck her."

"She's crying, man. She's really uptight over this."

"She should be. The bitch."

"Don't talk like that, pal. She loves you."

"Bullshit. She loves money."

"How about unlocking the door and talking to me?"

"No! Get away. I don't want to live. Can't you

understand?"

"Do you have kids?"

"Sure."

"How many?"

"What the fuck does that have to do with it, you son-of-a-bitch? Get the fuck away from the door. It's already done anyway."

"What did you say?"

"It's done. It's done."

Abe shoved the men away from the door just as Carpenter jerked it open. The door flew back on its hinges and struck the wall. They rushed into the tiny bathroom. The dentist was sitting on the toilet with blood pouring from his left wrist in a puddle on the floor. He was sawing at his throat with the straight razor. Abe grabbed the razor hand with both of his huge paws and bent the wrist back. The razor clattered to the floor. Carpenter kicked the razor out into the bar and turned to help subdue the man. He was spraying the room with his blood as he struggled with them. Abe's glasses were painted dark red. The dentist's blood soaked Abe's face and neck. Carpenter stepped into the slippery blood and fell heavily on his back. The struggling pair fell on top of him. Carpenter wrapped his arms around the man's bloody neck and held him.

"I got him, Abe," shouted Carpenter, snatching back on the bloody throat.

Abe kneeled on the man's chest, blinded by blood. Feeling for the dentist's chin with his left hand, he measured the distance. He brought his right fist back and punched the dentist hard on the point of his chin. He went limp. Carpenter shoved the unconscious man off. The dentist was bleeding bright arterial blood in spurts from his neck and wrist. Carpenter pulled the man's belt off, tightened it around the limp upper arm and twisted the ends with his nightstick. The blood slowed from a flood to a trickle. Abe was washing blood from his eyes and glasses at the sink.

"Are you okay, Abe?"

"Yeah. I was blind for a few seconds."

They knelt by the stricken man. Blood was pouring from the lacerated throat in a spray. Carpenter tried to stop it with his fingers. The blood continued to pour. The bar was pandemonium. Women were screaming and men were trying to crowd into the tiny restroom.

"Get back," said Carpenter. "Get back. We've got to get this man to the hospital."

The door was filled with faces, hypnotized by the spurting blood.

Carpenter lurched at them with bloody hands and grabbed the nearest man by the sport coat lapels with his red hands. The man bowled over those in back of him in his mad rush to escape. Abe was on his knees in the gore surrounding the dentist. His fingers stopped the blood for several seconds. The blood started again.

"Son-of-a-bitch. My fingers keep slipping off. It's one of his jugular veins. Give me your handkerchief."

Abe held the handkerchief on the vein and pushed in with his fingers.

"I can't find it," he said, probing in the bloody gash. "He's still bleeding. We're going to lose him. Oh, God, help me. I got it! Jesus Christ. I got it! It's stopped, Fritz. Son-of-a-bitch. This ass-hole's got a chance. How's his wrist?"

"It's looking good. Just dripping. Can you hold on to his vein?"

"I think so. But we're going to have to move fast. He's lost a lot of blood. Get some of these curious bastards to help us carry him out to the car. We can't wait for a fucking ambulance."

Carpenter stepped into the bar. The crowd shrank away from him. He was covered with blood.

"I need two or three men to help carry him out to the

car."

No one responded.

"Come on. He's going to bleed to death on the shithouse floor unless somebody helps us."

The bartender vaulted the bar and walked to his side.

"I'll go. I was a medic in Korea. I ain't afraid of a little blood."

Five other men jumped forward.

"O.K. You, you, and you can help us take him to the car. Don't drop him or jar him around. If Abe looses his grip on that vein, he's going to die. Follow me."

They crowded into the small room, slipping and sliding around on blood. One of the volunteers took a look and stepped to the toilet, heaving his guts out. The sour smell of vomit combined with pine disinfectant.

"That's okay," said Carpenter. "Three of us can lift him. Abe, can you support his head and hold on to the vein at the same time?"

"Yeah, but you guys have got to do all the rest. Slide your hands under his back, side by side. Show them, Fritz."

"Here, you stoop here," said Carpenter. "Come on, Red, you get down here. Okay. Slide your hands under, but don't lift up. That's it. Now get your back braced. He's not big, but he's dead weight. When I say go, everybody stand up easy and lift. Don't fuck up and slip on this floor. Okay? Ready, set, go. That's it. That's it. Good. You okay, Abe?"

"Okay."

"Through the door, slow," said Carpenter. "Slow, you fucking jerk! That's it. Get out of our way, you people. Easy now. Open the door. Hold it open, for Christ's sake."

They went out into the freezing wind. The snowflakes melted on their sweaty faces. They crunched through six inches of snow to their double-parked car. The crowd followed close behind them.

"Somebody open the door. Can we get you in the back seat, Abe?"

"Yeah. Just don't slip. It's over for him if you drop him."

Slowly, a little at a time, they eased the man into the back seat with Abe. At last it was over. The dentist was sprawled on his back, with his head and shoulders on Abe's lap. The bartender started to get in front with Carpenter.

"No need to, Mac. Thanks for your help. We can take him from here."

Carpenter drove through the driving sleet and snow as fast as he dared, passing stalled cars and fender bender accidents everywhere.

"How's he doing, Abe?" asked Carpenter, pulling onto the shoulder of the road to get around two cars mashed together. The drivers were fistfighting in the center of the road, slipping and sliding in the slush.

"He's still got a pulse. He's blowing bloody bubbles out of his mouth. My fingers are hurting from holding on. It pains all the way up my arm."

"Don't let go. We got only another mile."

Carpenter picked up the transmitter from the dashboard clip.

"Car twenty-one's enroute to Union Memorial."

"Ten-four, twenty-one."

"Call the hospital and advise we have a man with a slashed throat and wrist in the back seat. We need help getting him out. Estimate we should be there in two or three minutes."

"Ten-four, twenty-one. What's your ten-twenty?"

"Approaching the stadium on Thirty-third Street."

"Ten-four. Will advise. KGA three four O."

"Is he still with us, Abe?"

"Yeah. He's got a pulse and is breathing O.K."

"Son-of-a-bitch," said Carpenter, steering around a

stalled motorist who was trying to wave him down. "Hang on, pal. We're almost there."

"Turn the dome light on so I can see. Hurry!"

"What's wrong?"

The yellow light filled the car. Abe's face was a bloody apparition in the rear view mirror.

"I thought I felt more blood. He's okay if my fingers hold out."

They slid to a stop at the emergency entrance. Two orderlies and an intern rushed a stretcher on wheels out into the snow. The intern got in, took one look at the dentist and whistled.

"Can you hold on to the bleeder for a minute?"

"Yeah. Don't fuck around, Doc. My fingers are numb. I don't know if I got him right or not."

"Just 'til we can get him inside. James, you and Art get in back with me. We don't want him handled roughly. O.K. Everybody put palms up under him and lift. Good. Out the door, Art. Feel with your feet. Be careful. Careful. Now you, James. Now me. Good. Easy. Hold him, officer. Now you. Watch his head. Good. On the stretcher."

They rolled him up the ramp and inside. They pushed the stretcher down the hall to the emergency room. Abe was still holding the bloody vein.

The emergency room doctor took his pulse and blood pressure. A nurse plunged a blood needle into his arm and started a transfusion.

"O.K., Officer, you can let go now."

The doctor was applying a clamp to the vein as they walked from the room. They were washing the blood from their hands in the men's room when the orderly found them.

"Phone call for Jacobson or Carpenter."

Carpenter took the call at the nurses' station in the corridor.

"Carpenter."

"Goulek here. Is he still living?"

"Yes."

"An ambulance is on the way there with a six-year-old boy who nearly froze to death in a snowdrift. His mother found him and called the ambulance."

"Where do we come in?"

"The ambulance driver called into the fire station. The kid's beat bad around the face. He's supposed to be cut up pretty bad. Put the heat on his mother. She's riding in with the ambulance."

"Ten-four."

"This is a Cockeysville case, but you handle it all the way. All their cars are tied up on personal injury accidents."

"Right."

"Why don't you grab a sandwich and coffee while you wait for the ambulance? It's going to be a long fucking night."

"Good idea, Sarge."

"Stay warm, kid. See you later."

"So long."

Abe was standing by Carpenter's elbow.

"What's up, Fritz?"

"That was Goulek. Cockeysville ambulance's bringing a half-frozen six-year-old boy here. He's been beat up. All the Cockeysville cars are tied up."

"Well, that's ain't so bad. It beats standing out in that snow, freezing your balls off working a fender bender. Come on, there's a hamburger joint across the street. We can eat while we wait for the ambulance."

They walked into the sandwich shop. Warm air and the smell of frying onions washed their faces as they sat down at the counter. A noisy drunk sat at the end of the counter and a sleepy intern sipped coffee in a booth near the steamy window. The drunk was complaining about his coffee.

"It smells like shit. I ain't gonna drink it. Take it

away. Get me another."

The waitress took the coffee and poured it into the sink and gave him a fresh cup. The drunk smelled the coffee and made a face. He deliberately poured the entire cup over the counter.

"Now, clean this up, you fat cunt."

The waitress walked up to the man and shook her head.

"That's it, mister. Get out of here or I'll have those officers lock you up."

The drunk turned and looked at them. He sneered and lit a cigarette.

"Well, Little Boy Blue, blow your fucking horn. They ain't city cops. They can't arrest me. They don't have any jurisdiction here."

The waitress walked down the counter and stopped by Abe.

"I called Northern, but their cars are all tied up on accidents. They said they'd come, but it might be a long time. He's a bad actor. I'm afraid of him."

Abe looked at the bowl of fruit on a shelf behind the counter. He smacked his lips.

"He's right. We don't have the right to arrest him here. Is that real fruit?"

"Sure it's real. You like fruit?"

"I'm kinda queer for it."

"Get rid of that bastard and I'll feed you guys all you can eat and give you that bowl of fruit for dessert."

"It's a deal. Wait here, Fritz. I'll take care of this asshole."

Abe walked down to the end of the counter and stood close to the drunk. He leaned over and said something into the man's ear. The drunk's eyes widened. He stood up and walked to the door. He hesitated at the door and turned. Abe put his hand on his holster. The drunk rushed out into the driving snow, hailed a passing cab, and got in. The cab drove

329

away. Abe returned to his seat.

"Ah, hand me a couple bananas and an apple, dear. I'll eat them while you're fixing our hamburgers. Put the rest of the fruit in a bag. I'll take it with me."

"Hey, that was magic," gushed the waitress. "How did you get that bum to leave?"

"Friendly persuasion."

"No shit, Officer? Say, you're great. How do you men want your hamburgers?"

"Medium, with everything. Fries on the side. Coffee black for my partner, blond and sweet for me. O.K., Fritz?"

"Fine."

The waitress drew two fresh cups of steaming brew and slid them over the counter to them. She went to the grill and slapped their hamburgers on to cook.

"What did you say to him, Abe?" asked Carpenter, blowing on the steaming brew.

Abe laughed and peeled a banana. "I told him that the waitress was my fiancée. I suggested that he either apologize or leave, or I was going to kill him and tell the city cops that he was trying to rob the place."

"Suppose he would have apologized. She might not have given you the fruit."

"I'd have thought of something."

Abe slurped his coffee and made a comic face.

"That drunk was wrong, Fritz."

"How's that?"

"The coffee doesn't smell like shit. It tastes like piss."

They sat eating hamburgers and talking to the fat waitress until the Cockeysville ambulance pulled up to the emergency entrance of the hospital.

"We have to go, my dear," said Abe, pinching her cheek. "It's for the best. I'm afraid we made hogs of ourselves over your delicious hamburgers. Besides, I think I'm falling in love with you."

"Oh, you big, handsome, bald-headed bullshitter.

It's been nice passing the time with you. Wait a second. I'll get a bag for your fruit."

They walked across the street to the hospital. The snow was mixed with sleet and the wind was increasing from the north. It took fifteen minutes for the doctor to examine the boy. When he finished, he came out into the hall and lit a cigarette.

"How is he, Doc?" asked Abe.

"Frostbite. His toes may have to be amputated and maybe the fingers of his right hand. His front teeth are knocked out. Both the little guy's eyes are black. He has a laceration over his right ear and a couple of broken ribs. He's conscious, but won't talk, because he scared to death. I've got to have some x-rays before I know for sure, but I think his skull is fractured. I don't want you to talk to him today."

"Can we have pictures of him taken later today?" asked Abe.

"Sure."

"Thanks. Come on, Fritz. Let's talk to the mother."

"Officer?"

"Yeah, Doc?" asked Abe.

"Work up a good case. This kid's been beat on before. He has old fractures of his arm that never healed right and probably never were set. Put the son-of-a-bitch responsible behind bars."

"We're going to try. What's the kid's name, Doc?"

"Benjamin Tyler. They live on a dairy farm somewhere up on the Manor."

They found the child's mother sitting on a bench at the end of the hall, smoking a cigarette and looking out the window at the snow falling in the courtyard.

"Mrs. Tyler, this is Officer Carpenter. My name is Jacobson. We're County police. We want to talk to you about Ben."

The woman didn't look up at them. She continued to stare out the window.

"He's all right. The nurse just told me. He may lose some fingers and toes. He fell in a snow bank. What have police got to do with it?"

"The boy's been beat up. His teeth are knocked out. He's got a fractured skull. His arms have been injured in the past."

She looked up into Abe's eyes. Her eyes were pools of anguish. She began to tremble all over. Tears spilled from her eyes and her jaw began to quiver. She covered her eyes with her arm and a strangled sob tore from her throat. Breaking down completely, she put her face on her knees. Great wailing screams came from the pitiful woman. Abe bent over, took the cigarette from her fingers, and patted her on the shoulder.

"That's okay, ma'am. It's over now. Cry. Get it all out of you. You'll feel better. Let it go, honey. Get her something from the doctor, Fritz."

She was still sobbing brokenly when Carpenter returned with a nurse. The nurse handed her two capsules and a paper cup of water. She managed to swallow them, and the nurse left them alone with her. She cried for a long time with Abe's great, hairy paw patting her on the back as though she were a child. She sat up, sniffed, removed a man's red bandanna from her purse and blew her nose.

"It started two years ago. My husband used to beat him with his belt for crying. Elmer's nerves are bad and he's got a terrible temper. It's been getting worse. I think he broke Ben's arms last summer for spilling his pipe tobacco. Elmer would never let me take Ben to the doctor. He hates him. He says he's not his father and accuses me of all kinds of mean things. We work on a dairy farm for the Hoffmasters. Lately, he's been sticking the cows in the legs with a pitchfork when he thinks they aren't listening to him."

"That common son-of-a-bitch," Carpenter mumbled, under his breath.

Abe gave him a warning look and shook his head slightly. Mrs. Tyler didn't notice. She took a big breath and rubbed her face with her hands. "Tonight he sent Ben out in the barn to get his pipe and gloves in the storm. He wouldn't let him put his boots and coat on. Ben was really scared 'cause Elmer was screaming and yelling at him. He didn't come back for a few minutes and Elmer went after him. Elmer came back in the house about fifteen minutes later and said he was making Ben stay out in the barn for a couple of hours to punish him. I didn't worry at first because it's warm in the barn with all those Holstein cows. After an hour went by, Elmer fell asleep watching television. I was taking a glass of milk and a sandwich out to the barn for Ben, and I tripped over him and fell. He was covered with snow. I knew Elmer beat him when I saw the blood on his mouth. I picked him up and ran to the farmowner's house, a half mile away. I was afraid to take him near his father. Mrs. Hoffmaster wiped his face off with a towel, and her husband called an ambulance from Cockeysville. I'm sorry I didn't call you sooner. I can't stand it anymore. What will happen now?"

"Will you sign a statement about what you just told us?" asked Abe, wiping his glasses.

"Yes! Yes! Will you lock that common bastard up?" she said through clenched teeth.

"With pleasure. Will you come along with us, Mrs. Tyler? We'll drop you off at Headquarters so a juvenile officer can take a statement from you."

"Yes. No. I want to be with Ben."

"Okay. We'll have one of them come to you. Do you have any more children?"

"No. Just Ben."

"Exactly where do you live?"

"Old York Road. Sweet Grass Farm. The owner's house sits close to the road. Our house is down in the hollow past the dairy barn. You can't miss it. Follow the driveway all the way back."

Old York Road was deserted. The prosperous farmers in the area were home in bed. The landscape was painted white with eight inches of fresh snow. They didn't pass or meet any cars after they cleared Cockeysville. The farms looked alike under the blanket of snow. Each place was separated by hedgerows of bare osage orange and green cedar. They passed the driveway before Abe spotted the sign.

"Hold it, pal. Back up. I think this is it."

He got out of the car and brushed the snow away with his hand from the rustic wood sign at the driveway entrance.

"Sweet Grass Farm. Welcome. Apples for sale." He got back in the car and licked the snow from his fingers.

"Stop at the main house, Fritz. The boss will need to know we're taking his hired hand to the slammer."

Carpenter pulled the car around to the rear of the old house. There was a light on in the kitchen. A man of perhaps seventy met them at the kitchen door when they knocked. He was dressed in riding pants, rough boots, and an old, heavy, gray sweater. He had the raw, red complexion of a Maryland winter horseman.

"Come in, gentlemen, for God's sake. It's freezing out there. My name's Hoffmaster," he said, shaking Abe's hand.

He turned to an ancient black man cooking at a wood stove.

"Cook some more breakfast, please, Robert. We have two guests."

"No, thank you, sir," said Abe, glancing at the stove. "We don't have time. We're here about Elmer Tyler."

"What happened? It's his son, I suppose."

"The boy's going to be okay." said Abe, inhaling fragrant odors of cooking. "We're here to arrest Elmer for beating the boy."

"My God. Are you sure he did?"

"Yes, his wife told us all about it," said Abe. "He's been beating hell out of the boy for a couple of years now."

"My God! How bad is the lad hurt?"

"A fractured skull, teeth knocked out, black eyes, he may lose some fingers and toes from frostbite. He's got possible broken ribs," said Abe. He watched the cook break brown eggs into the pan.

"How can a man treat his own child like that? My Lord, he must be sick," said Mr. Hoffmaster, shaking his head. "Poor little fellow. He's always around the stable when I take care of my horses. He's a tiny fellow, but he sits a horse like an old hand. I let him ride Seven-Up in the ring. She's a fifteen-year-old mare. A great, huge, gentle horse, but a jumper, by God, a jumper. I won the Maryland Hunt Cup on her eight years ago. What will become of the boy?"

"It's up to the court, sir," said Abe, shrugging. "A foster home maybe. It's pretty certain they'll take him away from his parents."

"It's hard to believe that about Elmer," said Mr. Hoffmaster, chewing his top lip. "He's an excellent herdsman, though a bit quick-tempered. I saw him kick a frisky cow in the mouth a year ago, reprimanded him severely, and forbade him to go near my horses."

"Have you had any trouble with your herd lately?" asked Carpenter.

"How did you know? I had the vet here last month to treat four of them for what appeared to be festered puncture marks on their brisket and legs. We thought they injured themselves on a nail protruding from the fence someplace."

"He's been sticking them with a pitchfork, according to his wife." said Carpenter.

"Why that, that—that bastard," said Mr. Hoffmaster, shaking his fist. "I've got a good mind to take a bullwhip to his mean back."

"We'll take care of him," said Abe, watching the cook turn sausage over in a frying pan.

"Well, you must stay for breakfast. Robert has it almost ready. Surely you enjoy fresh eggs, homemade biscuits, fresh-made country sage sausage, and hot coffee with real cream. Come, gentlemen, eat with me. It's five forty-five. We may as well let Elmer finish milking the cows on his last day. He should be finished in a half hour. If you take him now, I'll have to finish. I'm afraid of cows. Can't reason with the beasts. It's my wife's herd. I'm a retired Navy captain."

"That sausage does smell delicious," said Abe, grinning. "What say, Fritz? A half hour more won't matter. We're going to be late anyway."

"I'm with you. I can always eat sausage and eggs."

"Ah, good. I'm grateful for your consideration. I don't relish milking cows, although we do have modern milking equipment. My brother-in-law and I can manage until we hire somebody to take Elmer's place. Sit down, men. Breakfast will be ready in a few minutes. I'm going to make a small pitcher of bloody marys. Do you prefer gin or vodka?"

"Either way," said Abe, taking his hat off.

"Same here," said Carpenter, sitting down at the oak table.

"Vodka it will be, then. Please excuse me while I mix our drinks. The liquor's in the library."

The old black man set the table for three, with mugs of strong fresh coffee steaming fragrance into their nostrils. Mr. Hoffmaster poured the drinks as his servant served the meal.

"That's an excellent bloody mary, sir," Carpenter said.

"Yes, isn't it? The secret is a couple of ounces of fresh clam juice added to the tomato juice, with a dash of

Tabasco, and vodka. Here, have some of Robert's beaten biscuits, an old Annapolis recipe."

It was a breakfast to remember. They sat and stuffed themselves with eggs and fresh sausage, washed down with Bloody Marys. The captain talked of his early days in the Navy, serving on the China station in a gunboat. Abe glanced at his watch.

"Can I offer you more sausage? Another Bloody Mary, perhaps."

"No, sir, another bite and I'll founder myself. We've got to be going. Thanks for the breakfast," Abe said, wiping his mouth with a napkin.

"By God, I enjoyed it. Stop in to see me when you're out this way. Do you like apples?"

"Love them," Abe said, standing.

"Then be sure to stop in next fall. I have a young orchard I planted the year I retired. They are bearing nicely now. I sold five hundred bushels this fall. I have some old varieties like Northern Spy, for my own use, that I'd like to share with you. Also Red Delicious, Rome, and Grime's Golden."

"We will definitely be up to see you, Captain. I could live off apples." said Abe.

"Well, by God, I'll give you some right now, my boy. Back your car up to the cellar way on the side of the house." He drained his glass and grinned. "I've got a basement full of choice apples."

25

THE TRUNK WAS WEIGHTED DOWN WITH TWO BUSHELS of apples when they pulled away from the old brick house. They continued down the lane, passed the dairy barn, and stopped by the tenant house, a large stone structure that probably dated back to colonial times. Carpenter turned the car around and switched off the lights. The snow had stopped while they were eating breakfast, but the wind continued to howl down from Pennsylvania. A thermometer nailed to an apple tree nearby read five degrees above zero. They watched the sunrise turn the snow diamond-bright.

"It's six forty-five, Abe. He should have finished by now."

"Give him a few more minutes. If he doesn't show by seven, we'll go in the barn after him."

The barn door slid back on its track as Abe said the words. The man stepped out into the raw wind, his lower face covered with a wool muffler. He was dressed for the cold, in an Army overcoat and heavy boots. An old slouch hat was pulled down over his eyes. Bending forward to shield his face from the bite of the wind, he broke through the crust of snow. He walked straight toward them, completely unaware of their presence, and stopped short, ten feet from them. His head jerked up and his eyes were wide in amazement. The hat blew from his head and his long greasy hair whipped in the wind. Carpenter and Abe opened their doors and got out. They walked to the man and stopped within arm's length of him.

"What do you want?"

"We want you, Tyler. You're under arrest. Get in the car," Carpenter said.

"What? Wait." Tyler raised his hands, palms toward them. "What's this about?"

"You know what it's about." Carpenter took him by the arm. "We just left the hospital. We talked to your wife. Get the fuck in the car."

"Wait. I want to talk to you. That kid's no good. He don't listen. A father's got a right to whop his kid." Jerking his arm free from Carpenter, he stepped back and slipped to one knee in the snow. He stood, breathing rapidly, and looked back over his shoulder at the barn. Thick mucus was pouring from his nose. He was spraying saliva as he talked rapidly. The frigid wind whipped his words away.

"What did you beat him for?" Abe asked.

"Discipline. He needed discipline. I sent that kid to the barn for my gloves and pipe. He forgot my gloves. He needed a lesson. I didn't hurt him. He did it himself when he fell. He hit his head on a block of mineral salt when he fell. Oh, I might have belted him once or twice. A father's got a right."

"Cuff this maggot, Fritz. I'm afraid I'll puke if I touch him."

"No! No! Wait! Goddamn it, listen."

Tyler put his hand against Carpenter's chest and shoved. Carpenter's feet slipped from under him and he fell flat on his back. Abe's straight left caught Tyler on his snotty nose, straightening him up. The blood flew, staining Tyler's olive-drab coat red. Abe hit him again, deliberately, solidly in the mouth. His lips split. Tyler swung a wild right at Abe. He rolled under it as Tyler's fist grazed the top of his head, knocking his hat into the snow. Abe lost his footing and slipped to one knee. Carpenter was back on his feet in a red rage. Tyler turned to him and swung a roundhouse left at his head, and missed. Carpenter chopped him once, twice, three times over the eyes with short, solid rights. Tyler bellowed in rage, the blood pouring into his eyes. Carpenter was ready to finish it with another punch, when Abe grabbed his wrist from behind.

"Hold it, Fritz! Don't hit that son-of-a-bitch any more. Let me hit him."

Abe pushed Carpenter to the side and smashed Tyler in the chin with his elbow. Tyler flopped on his side in the snow. His face was a bloody mess. He was still conscious. Abe kneeled down beside Tyler and shoved his face into the snow. Tyler flapped his arms and legs feebly. Carpenter pulled his partner off by the collar of his reefer.

"That's enough, Abe. We'll kill him."

"I just wanted this motherfucker to know what his little boy felt like."

Abe's chest heaved from exertion, and tears poured down his cheeks. He jerked Tyler over on his back, grabbed a hand full of snow, and roughly washed the bloody gore and snot from Tyler's face.

"Can you hear me, ass-hole?" Abe snarled, twisting the coat tight around Tyler's throat.

Tyler just lay there like a dumb animal. Abe slapped him on both sides of his face.

"You better listen up, ass-hole, or I'll slap your ass from here to Cockeysville. Can you hear me?"

"Yeah! Yeah!"

"Okay. Listen to me, you common motherfucker. You're going to jail for a while. A bunch of ass-hole shrinks will jerk you off with a whole lot of bullshit treatment. When they say they've cured you and turn you loose, remember one thing. Don't ever lay a hand on your kid again. Don't hurt your wife. Be a nice guy. You got me?"

Abe was sitting on Tyler's chest jabbing him in the chin with his thumbnail. "If you ain't a nice guy, I'm going to hear about it and come to see you in the middle of the night with a fucking baseball bat. I'll beat you to death a little bit at a time, ass-hole. You hear me?"

"Yes! Yes! Jesus Christ. Yes."

Abe stood and kicked him in the stomach, hard. Tyler pulled his knees to his chest and gagged.

"That was for stabbing those cows with a pitchfork, you rotten cocksucker. Come on, Fritz. Help me load this garbage up. It's time to go home."

It was ten A.M. when they finished the required paperwork for the juvenile authorities. The desk sergeant's radio was turned up loud. There was a lot of conversation between cars in the Ruxton area about a prowler. The desk sergeant laughed and turned the radio down.

"Don't go back to Towson too soon, boys; they'll recruit you to chase that prowler around Ruxton. They been chasing him around the neighborhood since five A.M., but lost him and haven't spotted him for more than an hour."

"Fuck the prowler," said Abe, yawning. "I'm going home to bed."

They walked out of the Cockeysville station and got into the car. The snow growled under the wheels of the car as they pulled out onto York Road and drove south toward Towson. Abe shifted to high gear and took his hat off. He lit a cigarette and slowed to avoid two dogs romping through the snow in the southbound lane.

"Tired, Fritz?"

"No. Not a bit."

"Neither am I. I feel good, like I just came to work. Every now and then you get a chance to lock up a real bastard. It's like a fringe benefit. It always makes things seem worthwhile. You know what I mean."

"Yeah. I'm glad he fought us, Abe. I got a lot of pleasure out of punching him. Damn. This job does things to you."

"How so?"

"It brutalizes you. On the way up to get him, I was hoping he'd give me a reason to kill him." Carpenter tossed a couple of Tums in his mouth and crunched them. Two boys were throwing snowballs at passing cars. They saw the police car and ran between parked cars, dropping their snowballs to the ground. Abe tapped the siren and laughed as the boys ran hard and dove over a privet hedge.

"You think too much, Fritz. I'm the one that blew my mind. If you hadn't pulled me off him, I'd have smothered him in the snow. I never could stand anybody that abuses kids or animals. Did you get a close look at his eyes? You could see the evil and meanness pouring out."

"I saw his eyes. I did my best to close them."

"Ah, Fritz, my lad, let's not think any more of morbid things. Think of all the apples we have to eat. I'm going up to see the old Captain as much as I can."

A milk truck passed them, spraying their windshield with slush. The truck's rear fender was being beat to pieces by a broken chain. The rat-tat-tat of metal beating metal drowned out the chatter of the police radio. Abe shook his head in disgust and took a drag on his cigarette.

"Any man with an orchard is a friend of mine. What kind of old-time apples did he say he grew?" asked Abe.

"Northern Spy, Spitzenburg, American Pippin, Tincup, Black Twig, Somerset of Maine, Vandervere,

Tompkin King, Twenty Ounce, and Grindstone."

"With a memory like that, you should be a soft-clothes cop."

"Bullshit. I worked at a tree nursery for four years when I went to high school. The owner specialized in old and scarce fruit trees. All the names the captain mentioned were just like old friends to me."

They were passing the Timonium fairgrounds. The cow sheds looked like igloos as they squatted in the drifting snow. Exercise boys cantered frisky thoroughbreds on the race track. Air puffed from horses' nostrils in steamy vapor and vanished in the wind.

"How's the fruit on the old-type trees?" asked Abe, as he slowed to admire a Palomino mare prancing daintily in the slush.

"Really good. Superior in flavor to the modern trees in some cases, but not what the American public is used to eating. Some of the old varieties are practically insect-free."

"I wonder how they fell from grace."

"People today eat what's in the supermarkets. The flavor and quality of the produce in stores can't compare to old garden varieties. They sell stuff that looks good and ships well. The big business people don't give a damn how it tastes. Americans who never really had fresh, old-fashioned, home-grown fruit and vegetables will never know what they're missing. They're conditioned to eat the stuff the stores offer."

"Here we are, Fritz the farmer, back at York and Ridgeleigh. Good old Towsontown. I better let them know we're home." He pressed the button on the mike. "Car twenty-one, ten-eight."

"Ten-four, car twenty-one. Report to the lieutenant in charge of the search at Ruxton and Joppa. Possible rape suspect."

"Ten-four, headquarters," said Abe, replacing the mike. "Son-of-a-bitch. I wonder if they know we've been working since eleven o'clock last night."

Abe drove toward Ruxton and Joppa. They passed several police cars heading the other way. A young lieutenant got out of his car when they arrived and walked across the street to talk to them. Mud covered his uniform and his face was haggard. Blinking bloodshot eyes, he lit a cigarette, and spit into the slush beside the car.

"We chased a suspect on those rape-murders around on foot for hours, but lost him every time we thought we had him boxed up. The lawns are too big and all these woods here and there helped him. I secured the rest of the men. Fuck it. We can get him next time. Thanks for the help. I'm going home to bed." He turned and sloshed his way through the slush to his car, got in and drove away.

Abe laughed and pulled away. "Bed sounds good to me, pal. Fuck the rapist." He turned right on Bellona and picked up speed. "There's a shortcut along here in this new development. If we can find it, we can beat that lieutenant back to the station." He slowed and looked at the contractor's sign on the corner. "Apple Valley, a restricted development, for those who appreciate quality."

"I think this is it. Another development for the mighty rich," said Abe, scratching his bald head.

They drove around a curve in the road. Half-finished ranch-type houses were set far apart on a cul-de-sac. The road was deserted, except for a car spinning its wheels in the snow at the end of the road in the turn around.

"Shit, a dead-end street," said Abe, stopping behind the car.

A young man dressed in black, wearing a clerical collar, stepped out and grinned at them. His car was stuck deep in drifted snow.

"Up to the axle yet," Abe said, rubbing his eyes and

cursing under his breath. "Too deep for us to shove him out. Call a tow truck for him, Fritz. I'll make sympathetic sounds to the good father and we'll be on our way in a second."

Abe got out as Carpenter called in the tag number and location of the stalled car. The priest and Abe were talking in front of the police car. He grinned at something Abe said, reached under his coat, and pulled out a long barreled handgun. He shot Abe twice in the chest and spun to face Carpenter. His shots shattered the windshield, spraying Carpenter's face with glass splinters. Carpenter hit the door handle, and dove out onto the street. A shot snapped by his ear as he scrambled on hands and knees to the rear of the car. More shots howled off the trunk lid, tearing his hat from his head. Blinded by blood from glass cuts to his forehead, Carpenter pulled his Colt from his holster and reached over the top of the trunk, holding the .38 in both hands. He emptied his gun in the priest's direction.

A cry of pain, then silence. Carpenter heard the priest's cylinder flick open to reload. He grabbed a handful of snow and scrubbed the blood from his eyes and stood, in a crouch. With blurred vision, he saw the priest duck around the side of the car, hand to his head. Carpenter was trying to fumble rounds from his gunbelt into his .38 when he heard a single shot from in front of the car. His hands shook so badly that he dropped all the bullets into the snow, except one. With one round in his .38, he waited, shaking with shock and fear.

He heard groaning from in front of the car and dropped flat on his stomach. He could see the priest sprawled across Abe's legs, holding his chest with both hands, moaning and crying for help.

Carpenter stood and ran to the front of the car. The priest's gun was stuck in the snow, barrel down.

Carpenter kicked the gun away and bent over Abe. Blood poured from Abe's mouth when he tried to speak. He coughed and spit globs of gore in the snow. He was fighting for each breath. Carpenter had to lean close to hear him.

"Fritz—"

"Yeah, Abe."

"I get him?"

"Yeah, you did, Abe," Carpenter said, taking Abe's .38 from slack fingers. He jerked the moaning priest from Abe's legs and tossed him roughly into the snowdrift in back of the stalled car.

The radio was squawking in the background. "Headquarters, car 21, be advised that described vehicle is a stolen car, taken from St. John's church on Bellona Avenue in the last half hour. Father McShay, the owner, says that the back seat is full of clothing he was taking to the cleaners."

Carpenter ran to the car window, grabbed the mike, and tried to control his voice. "21-Headquarters, I'm on a dead-end street in a construction project, Apple Valley, off Bellona. I got an officer shot. Send an ambulance right away."

"Ten-nine-twenty-one. Did you say an officer shot?"

"Ten-four. Hurry up, for Christ's sake. Send an ambulance."

He dropped the mike on the seat and snatched the keys from the ignition. With shaking hands, he fumbled the key into the trunk lock, raised the lid and moved Abe's apples around to get to the first aid kit and a blanket. He scrambled to the front of the car. Abe's breathing was ragged as Carpenter lifted his shoulders and propped him in a sitting position against the car. He unbuttoned Abe's reefer and cut his sweater, shirt, and undershirt open with his pocket-knife. Blood poured from the wounds and matted in the jungle of hair on Abe's chest. Carpenter pressed two four-inch compresses over the wounds. Abe looked at him and tried to say something. His chin dropped forward to his chest. He shuddered, sighed, and sagged against Carpenter's shoulder.

Carpenter probed in the bloody stubble at the base of Abe's jawbone and felt no pulse. He sat in the snow, sobbing, holding Abe in his arms.

The wounded gunman was crying for help from the front of the car. Carpenter eased Abe over on his back and covered his face and body with the blanket. He went to Abe's killer and turned him over. The killer grabbed Carpenter's arm and held on. Blood was dripping from a mangled ear. One of Carpenter's blind shots had chopped away his ear lobe.

"Help me, please!"

Carpenter jerked free and pulled the man's bloody shirt up. Air was hissing from a hole in his chest. Carpenter packed gauze into the wound and the hissing stopped.

The gunman grinned at Carpenter and nodded. "Thanks."

"Fuck you," said Carpenter. "We thought you were a priest." He noticed a small chamois skin bag around the gunman's neck on a leather thong. He jerked the thong free and loosened the drawstring on the bag. Six brown raisinlike objects rolled into his palm. They were covered with salt. The hair stood up on the back of his neck when he realized they were dried nipples. He dropped them back in the bag and jammed it into his reefer pocket.

The man was watching him with eyes wide with fear. Carpenter pulled his Colt and pointed it at the man's head. As he took up the slack on the trigger, the man started to convulse. His heels drummed rhythmically on the snow and his eyes rolled back in his head. Carpenter eased the hammer down on his revolver and walked back to the trunk of the car. He tossed the first aid kit in between the apple baskets.

The ambulance's siren wailed as it pulled into the cul-de-sac. Carpenter watched them leap from the Cadillac and race to Abe. They knelt beside him and felt for a pulse, held a mirror to his mouth, and listened for a heart beat.

They stood up and ran to the rapist, where he lay sprawled in the bloody snow.

"Your partner's dead, Officer," said the old attendant, turning to Carpenter. "This guy's barely breathing. You okay?"

"Yeah, I'm okay. I don't want Abe to lay there in the snow for two hours waiting for the coroner. Will you take him with you?"

"Sure. Don't you want to ride in with us? You should get checked over."

"No, thanks. I just need a few minutes by myself."

Carpenter watched, with tears pouring down his cheeks, as they loaded Abe and the Ruxton rapist into the ambulance. It pulled away, siren screaming and red lights flashing.

The growl of police sirens were coming closer from every direction. He lifted the apple baskets from the trunk, carried them to the side of the police car and put one basket on top of the other on the bloody snow, where Abe died.

Carpenter leaned in the door of the police car, picked up Abe's hat from the seat and buffed the visor with the sleeve of his reefer. He put the hat on the top basket of apples, got in the police car, and drove away.

STARLOG photo guidebook

All Books in This Special Series
- Quality high-gloss paper,
- Big 8¼"x11" page format.
- Rare photos and valuable reference data.
- A must for every science fiction library!
- Available at Waldenbooks, B. Dalton Booksellers and other fine bookstores. Or order directly, using the coupon below.

SPACE ART $8.95
($13 for deluxe)
196 pages, full color

SCIENCE FICTION WEAPONS
$3.95
34 pages, full color

SPACESHIPS $2.95
34 pages, over 100 photos

Latest Releases

TV EPISODE GUIDES
Science Fiction, Adventure and Superheroes $7.95, 96 pages
A complete listing of 12 fabulous science fiction adventure or superhero series. Each chapter includes (a) complete plot synopses (b) cast and crew lists (c) dozens of rare photos, many in FULL COLOR.

TOYS & MODELS
$3.95, 34 Pages
A photo-filled guide to the fantastic world of toys and games. There's everything from Buck Rogers rocket skates to a mini Robby the Robot! Full-color photos showcase collections spanning four generations.

SPACESHIPS (new enlarged edition)
$7.95, 96 pages
The most popular book in the series has been expanded to three times the pages and updated with dozens of new photos from every movie and TV show that features spaceships-the dream machines! Many in full color.

HEROES $3.95, 34 pages
From Flash Gordon to Luke Skywalker, here is a thrilling photo scrapbook of the most shining heroes in science-fiction movies, TV and literature. Biographies of the men and women who inspire us and bring triumphant cheers from audiences.

FANTASTIC WORLDS $7.95
96 pages, over 200 photos

SPECIAL EFFECTS, VOL. I
$6.95, 96 pages, full color

SPECIAL EFFECTS, VOL. II
$7.95, 96 pages

VILLAINS $3.95
34 pages, full color

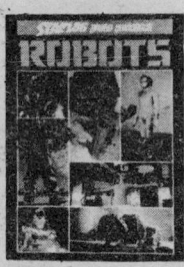

ROBOTS $7.95
96 pages, full color

ALIENS $7.95
96 pages, over 200 photos

Send to: STARLOG GUIDEBOOKS DEPT. FA3 475 Park Avenue South New York, NY 10016

Name _____

Address _____

City _____

State _____ Zip _____

Add postage to your order:

HEROES $3.95	FANTASTIC WORLDS	SPACE ART
VILLAINS $3.95	. . . . $7.95	Regular Edition $8.95
SPACESHIPS I $2.95	ROBOTS $7.95	Deluxe Edition $13.00
WEAPONS $3.95	Prices for all of the above:	___Regular Edition
TOYS & MODELS $3.95	___3rd Class $1.75	___Deluxe Edition
Prices for all of the above:	___1st Class $1.55	___U.S. Book rates
___3rd Class . . . . $1.00 ea.	___Foreign Air $2.50	. . . . $2.00 ea.
___1st Class . . . . $1.25 ea.	**SPECIAL EFFECTS . . $6.95**	___U.S. Priority . $2.57 reg.
___Foreign Air . . $2.25 ea.	___3rd Class $1.50	. . . . $3.30 deluxe
SPACESHIPS	___1st Class $2.00	___Foreign Air . . $7.00 reg.
(new enlarged) . . $7.95	___Foreign Air $5.50	. . . . $8.50 deluxe
SPECIAL EFFECTS VOL. II		
. . . . $7.95	total enclosed: $_____	
TV EPISODE GUIDE BOOK	NYS residents add sales tax	
. . . . $7.95	Please allow 4 to 6 weeks for delivery of 3rd Class mail:	
ALIENS $7.95	First Class delivery usually takes 2 to 3 weeks.	

ONLY U.S. Australia and New Zealand funds accepted.
Dealers: Inquire for wholesale rates on Photo Guidebooks.
NOTE: Don't want to cut coupon? Write order on separate piece of paper.

ORION'S SHROUD
By William Peyton Cooke

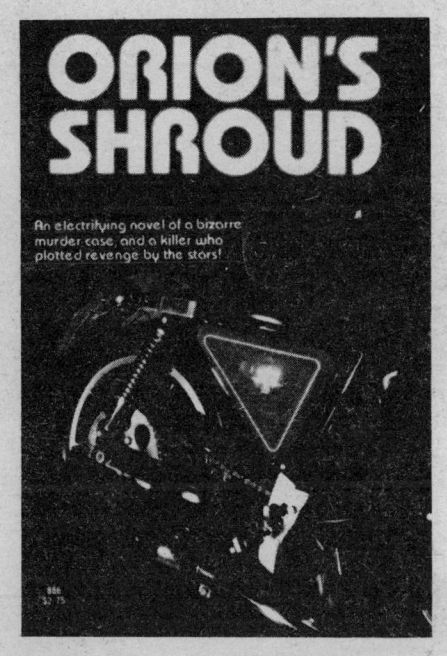

PRICE: $2.75
LB886

CATEGORY: Suspense

It was a long-awaited reunion and hell-raising occasion for the motorcycle gang known as the Devil's Dozen. They were cutting loose on a dark back road when they forced a car to plunge into a lake, killing young Dianne. But mild-mannered Walter saw it happen. He loved Dianne from afar, and now vowed violent revenge. Bodies of the gang began turning up, and to each was pinned a diagram of the constellation Orion. Each circle was filled in as the victims died. And there was one circle left for Walter...

SEND TO: LEISURE BOOKS
P.O. Box 511, Murry Hill Station
New York, N.Y. 10156

Please send me the following titles:

Quantity	Book Number	Price
_____	_____	_____
_____	_____	_____
_____	_____	_____
_____	_____	_____

In the event we are out of stock on any of your selections, please list alternate titles below.

_____	_____	_____
_____	_____	_____
_____	_____	_____
_____	_____	_____

Postage/Handling _____

I enclose..... _____

FOR U.S. ORDERS, add 75¢ for the first book and 25¢ for each additional book to cover cost of postage and handling. Buy five or more copies and we will pay for shipping. Sorry, no C.O.D.'s.

FOR ORDERS SENT OUTSIDE THE U.S.A., add $1.00 for the first book and 50¢ for each additional book. PAY BY foreign draft or money order drawn on a U.S. bank, payable in U.S. ($) dollars.

☐ Please send me a free catalog.

NAME _____
(Please print)

ADDRESS _____

CITY _____ STATE _____ ZIP _____

Allow Four Weeks for Delivery